I0594059
PROTECTIVE
INSTINCT

PROTECTIVE INSTINCT

EBONY OLSON

EBANDMUSE
PUBLICATIONS

EBANDMUSE
PUBLICATIONS

Published 2021 by

Eb&Muse Publications, Sydney, Australia

http://ebonyolson.com/

A NOTE ON READING THIS BOOK.

This book features Auslan sign language for communication. To me, sign language is the equivalent of talking, just in a different language. I didn't want to misrepresent or demean the language by not having it punctuated as speech, but it became clear from early readers that not differentiating the sign language from spoken speech was confusing for readers. Therefore, I have put sign language dialogue in italics, and spoken as per the standard. I.e., in the sentence below, the italics translate the sign language for you, and then at the end, Mitch talks.

Holding his first three fingers up with ring and pinkie tucked, Mitch spread them open and touched them under his eyes and out with a raised brow. *"Ever been here?"* When I shook my head. It made him smile. "Me neither."

Mitch uses a lot of SimCom (Simultaneous Communication) - where someone verbalizes what they are signing. In these instances, I have left the punctuation of speech as per standard.

There are also moments of flashbacks which include speech. In these, the differentiation is first the paragraph is inset further and the italicized speech is punctuated with only single quotation marks. E.g.

'Stop, we can't kill her,' one of my torturers shoved the one who had been holding me under back.

Hopefully, this will help make it clear for you between spoken and signed speech, and flashback scenes.

Xoxo

Eb

PROLOGUE

The streets were dark and wet as I ran. There was so much at stake, and I'd been delayed. Part of me wondered if those constant interruptions, the repeated obstacles to getting out of the compound today, had been organized.

He'd left earlier than planned, and it wasn't like him to go off program. Not that I should have known the plan, but I knew him, and he never digressed, so something must have happened to cause it. Now, I was sprinting through the streets of Turkey to make it in time.

Finding the building I'd heard mentioned, I stopped. The lights were on inside, but there didn't seem to be any sound. Perhaps, I wasn't too late. Trying the door, I found it unlocked, so I carefully pushed it open.

Closing the door, I stood in the foyer, listening for anything that would tell me where my target was. Voices and a thump drew my eyes up. Moving up the stairs quietly but quickly, the suppressed bang of a silenced gun began, and I used it to cover any noise I would make to move quicker.

Stepping into the room, my target stood tall with his back to me. Unholstering my gun, I aimed as his arm swung towards me. I fired. My weapon wasn't silenced, the noise loud in the silent house. My target dropped his gun and turned to face me, his eyes wide and assessing while his right arm fell limply from my gunshot to the right shoulder.

"Lyza? What are you doing here?"

Watching his mouth, I couldn't answer, not without using both hands. Instead, I aimed my gun at his heart, my eyes glassy as I tilted my head in question.

"It had to be done, Lyza. He would have ruined everything, and I would have lost you. We are never given a choice, and I've had enough." He stepped towards me. "I'm giving you a choice now. Join me."

Looking deep into his eyes, I knew it wasn't really a choice. Follow one or follow the other. Either way, I was still following someone else's orders. When I shook my head once, he lifted his left arm and fired. Pulling my trigger, I shifted to try and save myself a moment before his bullet caught me in the right arm.

Bleeding in his upper left shoulder, he attacked still. Hand to hand, he had always been better. He was older and more practiced than someone nearly eight years his junior. While I fought with everything in me, he fought harder, so it came as no shock when he pinned me.

"Last chance, Lyza. Come with me?"

Slipping the small blade from up my sleeve free, I stabbed it into his side. With a ferocious yell, he rolled away, slamming his fist into the side of my head as he did. My vision danced as my body moved the opposite way. Trying to get up, my head couldn't focus to keep my limbs under me.

A boot slammed into my ribs, sending me careening across the floor, landing hard, but luckily, on a gun. Ensuring the safety was off, I rolled again and fired as he came towards me. Falling back, he stumbled away. Gritting his teeth, he disappeared through the door.

Something touched my shoulder. Jolting up to my knees, I turned to aim the gun. Eyes that might have been green, but were a darker, more muted green than natural, blinked at me. Placing the weapon aside at the sight of the injured man, I looked over his injuries.

Searching the room to find a medical kit, I checked for any other survivors. At a Glance, all bar one was dead. Retrieving the Medipak from one of the dead soldiers, I came back, holding my broken ribs as I moved. I pulled the pack apart, locating the items I needed, and poured a clotting agent into the injured man's wounds.

"Angel?" He touched my face.

The comparison made me smirk. "Not likely, but you'll live to die another day." My throat ached with the unusual use, but the likelihood this man understood sign language, let alone was conscious enough to read it, was unlikely. Touching his face just as he fell into unconsciousness, I hoped my efforts could save at least one person tonight. Standing, I picked up my gun, ready to leave, very aware I needed to get out of here.

"Drop it!"

Closing my eyes as the room filled with American soldiers, I cursed with my free hand. This was not going to end well. My gun clattered to the floor.

1

CANDIDATES

The buzzer blared, and the sound of the main door unlocking filled the cells. Lifting my eyes only, I scanned the glass wall of my cell. Those in cells across the corridor moved forward to press against the glass to see what was happening.

While there was no clock or sunlight to judge time, I was used to the sense of time between activities. Depriving the prisoners of time was a torture tactic, one not protected by the Geneva convention. Our biology was based around perceived time, and without it, we could become very unwell or mad. Our detainer's preference was death.

Try as they might, the staff maintained schedules and noted time, so having a keen sense of observation allowed one to judge the gaps in activity as time. This activity was not scheduled, so something was different. No matter what it was, it wouldn't be for me. I was long forgotten. Still, I opened my journal and noted the disturbance before I returned my attention to my book.

Brennan, one of the senior ranks here, was the first to make sound and indicate what might be occurring. "Candidate number one."

"Name?" A deep masculine voice inquired.

"Lily Vale. She's an ex-marine—three counts of homicide. The murder of her boyfriend got her sent to Hilltop. The murder of a male guard there and one of the fellow cellmates landed her here in supermax. The cellmate was an undercover fed who turned."

"File?"

While papers were rifled, I returned my focus to my book—the scenery's description capturing my longing to see the blue sky and walk on natural grass again. Five years had passed since I'd caught even a glimpse of the outside world. My daily exercise allowance provided for running around the internal gymnasium while the others lifted weights or did Zumba. Outside was a thing of the past and would stay that way.

"No. Next?"

"Candidate two, Rebecca Smith." Brennan started to list off her offenses against country and humanity.

"No. I need feminine; she could pass for one of your men."

"Candidate three..." Brennan continued to describe another prisoner. The man asked for her file then declined her.

"Well, that's all I have that fits your profile requirements."

A shadow passed over my cell floor as they strolled up to my end of the line. "What about this one? She looks to fit the physical requirements. Name and crime?"

"Prisoner double zero, two-one-three, or Jane Doe, or no one damn well knows her name. Her crime? Well, a SEAL team was sent in to extract an intelligence agent. She allegedly murdered the agent and took out the entire SEAL team. She might have gotten away, but she was injured. The backup team captured her.

"We don't know who she is, where she came from, or for who she worked. We don't even know what language she speaks because she hasn't said a word since she was captured. Of course, since then, we have come to suspect she is deaf, so it's possible she doesn't speak any language. All we know is that she is extremely deadly, but yes, nice to look at."

"Deaf?"

"She uses sign language to communicate. It was missed during capture and interrogation because her hands were always handcuffed. She couldn't communicate."

"Has she communicated anything of value?"

The question made Brennan chuckle. "After how hard they interrogated her, she's lucky to still be alive. If it was worth enduring what she already has, she's not going to give it up for free now. This one is smart."

"File?"

Lifting my eyes to watch Brennan hand a relatively thin file to the deep voice owner, I assessed the stranger. His large hands took the folder, his charcoal brows rising, nearly joining with the short-cropped hair of the same color. He wore jeans and a button-down shirt hugging a fit body, black boots on his feet, and an expensive diving watch on his wrist.

He didn't look like any official I'd seen, but if Brennan was taking orders from him, he must have held some rank. His eyes skimmed the notes, and I got the impression he was memorizing my file as he read. "She came straight here with no medical treatment?"

"She's considered a terrorist. She wasn't even tried. After she was captured, the second SEAL team interrogated her, but when she wouldn't talk to even give her name, they just threw her in this hole to rot. We provided medical treatment on-site for her injuries."

"Not before further interrogation. She didn't break?"

"No. She was quite happy to die or live, either way. They tried multiple interpreters, but she never blinked in understanding. She didn't start using sign language till after her first year, and only because a guard used it with her first."

"Her behavior here?"

"Exemplary. Never been problematic unless we've asked her to do something she hasn't understood. The guards who don't know sign language have got to the point now that if it is something new, they get another prisoner to do it first then indicate she needs to do it."

"She's reading, so she's not illiterate. Shouldn't that tell us her language?"

"Not sure she can actually read them. Some of us guards have a soft spot for her and give her books and such."

"Why?"

"Because she's well-behaved and courteous, and she saved a guard's life. It's in her file. Another prisoner snapped and attacked her guard during exercise. Doe was willing to stand back and let it happen till the other prisoner went for the kill. Doe appeared out of nowhere, took down the other prisoner in one hit, then walked away again."

The newcomer turned a page and frowned. "What is your impression of her?"

"I use the anacronym BAD for her kind. Beautiful and deadly. Having said that, Doe's never harmed anyone unnecessarily." Brennan indicated the other cells. "I'm around psychopaths, sociopaths, and cold-blooded killers daily. But with this one, part of me wonders if the SEALS got it wrong. She just doesn't seem the sort. My theory is she got injured trying to protect the asset, just like she protected my guard."

The man in the jeans closed my file, crossed his arms, and watched me through the glass. "Protective instinct?" Meeting his moss-colored eyes, I observed the way he appraised me. "Open it up."

Grabbing Jean's shoulder, Brennan glowered at him. "You don't want this one. She's already been through hell and got the scars to prove it."

Shrugging free of Brennan's grip, Jeans stepped forward to the cell door. "Open it!" He passed the file back to Brennan.

Grumbling, Brennan shoved the file away and gestured to the camera. The door into the antechamber opened. While Jeans stepped in, I closed the book I was reading and jotted the note in my diary about this man before slipping it beneath my pillow.

The external door to the antechamber closed, the internal door slid open. Sliding off my bed to stand, I kept my back to the bunk. The man stepped into my cell and the interior door closed. He was a head taller than me, and his body easily twice as broad.

We stood appraising each other silently. The way he moved was graceful, precise, controlled. He was deadly. Casually he collected the book from the bed, read the title, then observed the books on my desk. The book he held was written in French; on the desk were books in English, German, and Russian.

"If you can read English, you understand it," he decided, placing the book on the desk with the others. "By the languages, I'd say you are European, and most of those countries teach English throughout school now. Does your voice work?"

Eyeing him, I failed to answer. Lifting his hands, he started signing. "I understand why you stayed silent initially, but there is no need to stay silent now. This is the deepest hole you can be thrown into; you can't sink any further down."

Remaining quiet, I lifted a brow. Forehead creasing, he rubbed his lips together before his features smoothed over. He was very attractive. "I'm looking for a female—one who has nothing to lose and everything to gain and who fits a certain profile. Effectively, a beautiful woman who has no hesitation in killing when required. Are you that woman?"

Unflinching, my eyes focused on his plump lips.

"You will get out of here, live in luxury, and attend lavish parties." He moved around my cell once more. "Your job will be to keep me safe while pretending to be my wife."

My pale eyes jumped to his. My mother had the same ghostly eyes, but we were very different people.

"No, I don't expect you to act the part in private. You will be the perfect accessory at any event and conduct yourself flawlessly. For this, you will be given deportment lessons."

Unable to prevent the smirk, I averted my gaze, but he saw it, studied it.

"You will act as my bodyguard and give your life to protect mine if necessary." Closing the distance, he stopped in front of me. "I know the temptation to let others kill me and run off might occur to you, but I assure you, there will be measures in place to ensure that doesn't happen."

He leaned in to whisper in my ear. "I just need to know you can actually talk, and I'll have you out of here inside of an hour."

Turning my head to meet his eyes, I saw the movement out of the corner of my eye and realized he had my diary open and reading it. Twisting quickly, I snapped it out of his hands and thrust my elbow back to catch him in the face. He dodged at the last minute, and my elbow glanced off his cheek. Something sharp and tingly pressed against my kidney, and I froze.

"Good, we've established you can fight, and you know when you are bested." Stepping back, he quickly hid his weapon and gave me space. He started signing while he talked again. "Strip off. I want to be sure what I'm buying looks good in a swimsuit."

Considering him, I thought about telling him to go jump, but it's nothing he couldn't go back to the control booth and watch on video.

I was due for a shower anyway. Walking to the corner where the bathroom was housed, I pressed the button which withdrew the toilet into the wall and started the shower. The glass wall instantly frosted, providing me with a modicum of privacy. It was strange that the government didn't feel my going to the toilet required privacy but using the shower did.

The prison uniform was a pair of white scrubs. Pulling the top over my head, I kept my back to him as I dropped my pants to the floor before removing my underpants. Moving into the heated water, I started washing, avoiding getting my chestnut hair wet.

"Turn around."

Ignoring him, I rinsed the shower gel off. The body wash was the only beauty product prisoners were provided. Embedded with moisturizers, it smelled like tea tree and lavender, so I always enjoyed this one luxury.

Not hesitating to come closer, he waited until the water ran clear, then tapped me on the shoulder. When I peered over my shoulder, he twirled his finger, so I turned to face him.

He appraised me clinically. "Physically in good condition, just the scar from your capture, which is easily explained away by a car crash," he discussed without signing.

Rubbing his thumb over my tattoo of the sword crossed by an arrow on my hip, his pupils constricted to pinpoint focus. "It's small, but a one-piece swimsuit might be the safer option for hiding this." Slipping his hand down to the scar on the right side of my lower abdomen, he stroked his thumb across it. "Appendectomy?"

Barely reacting to his touch externally, I needed to resist pressing my thighs closed. It had been years since I was touched by a man other than the doctor. He leaned closer. "You can nod yes or no."

Ignoring his question, I placed my finger on the glass splashback, fogged by the steam of the hot water. Drawing letters in the fog while he stared into my eyes, then I lowered to kneeling with my back to that wall and looked up at him.

Frowning down at me, his eyes went over my head to the wall and widened slightly. Stepping out of the shower, he fidgeted with his pants as if I tried something. "I told you, that wouldn't be needed."

Smiling, I used my forearm to erase the message. Taking my time, I rose up, mischief shining in my eyes. Brennan watched from outside with a frown. Chuckling without sound, I wrapped the towel around my body, then waited, watching Jeans as he rubbed the stubble of his chin.

A minute ticked by, then two, then Jeans signaled to the camera as he moved to the interior door. After he stepped out, the door shut. Moving to the glass wall of the cell, I breathed, so the glass fogged. Drawing a lollypop in the fog, I winked at Brennan.

Chuckling, he shook his head. "No sweets, Pretty Girl."

Pouting, I batted my lashes. Brennan was a sucker for a good pout and always gave me sweets for good behavior. Nothing sexual. Brennan was a stand-up moral man, one of the very few I met. He made sure his staff here upheld those same ethics, which annoyed my horny neighbors to no end. Out of the corner of my eye, Jeans regarded my interaction with Brennan as he passed through the antechamber.

Remaining at the glass, I watched Jeans move out to meet Brennan. "She's no good to me if she can't hold a polite conversation." Glancing at me, thoughts still flitted in his eyes. "She would be perfect otherwise." Turning on his heel in a military-like manner, he walked away. Waiting, I watched as the corridor emptied. When the door sealed, the catcalls began.

"Man, he was a honey!"

"Pretty Girl got naked with him," Mikaela, across the way, informed the others. "Got on her knees in the shower for him."

"Pretty Girl is naughty after all."

"Was he a mouthful, Pretty Girl?"

Ignoring the other prisoners, I returned to dressing. I'd been playing the deaf card for years now and thanked my mother ever since for making me learn sign language along with every other language she could. Collecting my notebook from the bunk, I wrote down the encounter. I never wrote in English, despite it being my native tongue. I needed to stay anonymous.

Sitting on my bunk, I remembered those moss green eyes as he read my message.

'I am Death.'

2

SELECTION

"Double zero two one three." The gymnasium guard stepped in front of me as I completed another lap and held up her palm before signing. "You're wanted in the infirmary."

Frowning at her, I was sure it hadn't been twelve months. Taking my hesitation as not understanding, the guard loaded a picture of a hospital on her phone. Nodding, I took the scrubs that she offered - I typically ran in my underwear. Dressed, I walked towards the door that allowed direct access to the infirmary; the guard followed.

A medical team was waiting with a bunch of various trays lined up. Stopping just inside the door, the guard gave the med staff a sympathetic look. The prison doctor tried to perform a pap smear on me a few years ago. He was still uneasy after I shoved the speculum up his ass. Unfortunately for him, he hadn't added the lube yet.

Three extra medical professionals were waiting this time. It made me uneasy like they planned to harvest my organs. The look on my face must have portrayed my thoughts because the prison doctor immediately back stepped. "I don't want to be involved in this."

"Chicken," the prison nurse muttered.

Another male doctor stepped forward. "Then get out." They all watched the prison doctor leave. "I'm here to do a full workup. These two nurses are my team. You have my assurance none of them will hurt you, but we will need to draw blood for testing, and we will be performing scans. Will you comply?"

Raising a brow, I looked to the prison nurse for further explanation. She'd learned sign language to ensure she could always explain to me what she was doing and now signed for the new doctor.

"It is a full health check, nothing more. We are checking for disease or malnutrition in your blood and organ health with the scans. When they first captured you, the doctor here diagnosed you with a condition. We want to see where it is at since you show no signs of deterioration."

Waiting for the nurse to finish signing, I considered them, then gave a single nod and laid down on the bed. I had been through all this kind of thing before. The staff made themselves busy. "You'll need to remove your top." One of the new nurses directed.

When I just stared at her, the prison nurse huffed and physically mimed lifting her top. "She's deaf or doesn't speak English, so you need to show her what you want."

Complying with the request, I laid back.

Waiting until the prison nurse turned away, the new nurse gave me skeptical eyes and lowered her voice to a murmur. "Funny, my boss says you understand English perfectly well and can read lips. But I'm sure there is some benefit to them not knowing that."

Unreactive, I watched her wrap the tourniquet around my arm while the other female set up the ultrasound on the other side. "I'm going to scan your thyroid first, then heart, lungs, liver, stomach, and reproductive organs. Anything I should know about?"

Ignoring her, I laid back and let them take several tubes of blood and perform their scans. When they were finished taking the blood, the vials couriered out immediately. Eyes narrow and taking in the name of the private lab on the esky, I observed everything. The scans took longer, the doctor watching each scan come up on a secondary screen and writing notes as he did.

When the sonographer finished, she packed up the machine. "You can return to your cell now."

Pulling my top on, I climbed off the bed. Opening the door, the guard followed me back to the cell, escorting me as far as the outer door to the antechamber. As I stepped inside, I swung my head back towards the exterior door and signed a query.

"I don't know, Honey. If you think that wasn't normal, you are right."

Bowing my head in thanks for the confirmation, I walked to the internal door and stepped into my cell. At the bunk, I wrote the incident down.

It took two more days until the routine changed again. I was reading peacefully when the main door opened out of schedule. Like last time, the other prisoners rushed to their glass walls to get a look, and then the catcalling began again. "Pretty girl made an impression. Give me a go, Baby. I can suck dick too."

Placing my book aside, I slid from the bunk as Jeans stepped in front of the glass wall. Today, he wore chinos with a long sleeve polo shirt that clung to his muscular upper body. Meeting my eyes, he smiled and lifted his hands to sign while he spoke. "Can we talk?"

Raising a brow, I queried the question; it's not like I could walk away. Smirking, Jeans made a gesture to the cameras. Striding through the antechamber, he held a manilla folder in his hand, as thin as the government one on me. As he stepped into the cell, his eyes glanced over me. "Did you know that they record every birthmark at birth?"

That was a paper-based record. With millions of people in the world, one tiny birthmark wasn't going to identify you.

"A few years ago, all the European countries digitized their birth records going back fifty years, that included birthmark registration. So, let's say I want to identify a woman. She appears early to mid-twenties but has spent five years buried from the world, so I need to give a decade's wide birth. She had her appendix removed..."

My body tensed.

"...the scar tissue feels relatively old, so it would be reasonable to assume it happened as a child. A genetic marker test indicates European heritage, but mainly English, so we're going to narrow our search to the United Kingdom and British colonies.

"Your hair is natural. Eye color, height, skin tone, is all a piece of the puzzle." He moved a step closer. "The government tried to use facial recognition to identify you and failed. That leads me to believe you never received adult credentials that required photo identification. No license, no student card, no employment within the general public, and no military career."

Scrutinizing each other silently for several moments, he looked down at the folder in his hand. "That would lead me to believe something happened to this woman before she was old enough to do any of those things." Tapping the folder against his leg, he tilted his head as he observed me. "So, I ran a search for girls who went missing ten to fifteen years ago, of Anglo descent, who had their appendix removed and born with birthmarks on the back of their left leg."

My heart pounding in my chest as he lifted the folder, opened it and handed it to me. My mouth filled with spit as my mother's passport photos and my teenage self looked out at me. Lyzebel Jones printed on the paperwork which recorded my birth and disappearance.

"Meet my person of interest. Twenty-six years old. Born in England and raised in Australia, she went missing during a holiday with her mother in France twelve years ago. Her mother massacred; it was a real blood bath. The fourteen-year-old daughter was taken and never found. The authorities believe they were the victims of a human trafficking ring. The daughter was beautiful and believed to be a virgin, so she could have raised a special price."

Closing the folder, I took deep breaths, trying to calm my erratic heartbeat.

"Then I looked into the parents. The father was never listed. There was absolutely nothing on the mother either. Nothing. So, I contacted a friend at MI6." His eyes intensified on me. "You know what he told me, don't you?"

Lowering to sit on the desk's chair slowly, controlled, my eyes staying locked with his.

"The mother was a suspected member of a mercenary group called the Sword and Arrow. Elite soldiers, exceptional assassin's and the only way to recognize one is the brand they all wear - a tattoo of a sword crossed by an arrow on the hip."

Jeans squatted to be eye level. "Your mother betrayed them to save you. Your father was one of them, and when she found out she was pregnant, she hid you from them." Reaching out, he stroked my hip, his thumb pressing over the tattoo. "They killed your mother, didn't they? They took you, trained you, and then used you however they wanted. But I don't understand why they left you in this hole. Do you?" Studying my eyes, his narrowed at whatever he saw.

He stood up suddenly. "You've been released into my custody. You're the best I could find to fit my needs, and if you are half as deadly as everyone fears, you are perfect for me."

Taking the folder back, Jeans grabbed my diary from under the pillow and hid it inside so quickly and smoothly, I barely caught it. Turning his back on me, he signaled for the door to open. "We're leaving."

Stepping into the antechamber, Jeans turned to look at me. "You come with me now, or you will be dead before nightfall."

My instincts to live always commanded me, so I had no doubt he was honest. Standing up, I followed him into the chamber. The door closed behind us as we moved to the main entrance. It opened, and Jeans led me out of the primary cell deck just like they would for anything else, except he wasn't a guard.

"Pretty Girl scored herself a night of fun," one of the others teased. That set off the catcalls until the main door locked behind them.

Walking to the infirmary, none of the guards paid any attention, which was unnerving. As if they were told not to notice me, or this man, or anything else that was going on.

In the infirmary, Jeans escorted me into a curtained-off area where the medical team from two days earlier stood waiting by the bed of a woman who looked the spitting image of me. That stopped me in my tracks. The fact none of the prison staff were present was also noted.

"Sit down, hurry up." Using my arm to drag me into the chair, Jeans didn't harm me, so I didn't fight him. "This woman will take your place in that cell."

Staring at the woman, I noted her eyes were calm, accepting. Amazed, I sat observing it all as the doctor and nurse went about taking my blood and transferring it directly to the other woman. Moving away to use his phone quietly, Jeans kept an eye on things as he tended to whatever he did.

"We are going to take the maximum amount, so you might feel weak and lethargic afterward." Shifting my left arm out to the side, the doctor anchored it in place. My eyes narrowed in on the needle in the doctor's hand before lifting to his lips. "I'm going to give you a local. Then I am going to inject you with a birth control implant that will last a few years."

My head swung around to glare at Jeans. Placing his phone on mute, he stepped closer, using his hands to talk only. *"We don't know what is going to happen over the next few months. I want you protected from either of us having to do a good job of pretending we are married or if you have a bit of fun when I'm not looking. Do you object? I don't think you want to end up back here with a belly full of regret."*

Pressing my lips together, I laid back, letting the doctor do what he needed. Jeans went back to his phone call. The doctor had just finished bandaging my arm when Jeans swung back around, tucking his phone away. "Finish it up; we need to leave now."

"But there are still several minutes of transfusion left to go."

"It will have to do. Finish up now. Get a guard to escort our transfer to her prison. Have everything packed up and be gone in five minutes."

The nurse and doctor rushed about disconnecting the feed, patching me up first. Helping me up, Jeans stabilized me when the world became a little unsteady. Getting my feet under me, I did my best to keep up with Jeans walking me to a back door in the infirmary.

Pushing through the door, we arrived in an ambulance bay, in which a car was waiting. Helping me into the back seat of the black SUV, Jeans pulled out his phone. "Once we are gone, erase the footage back to before we approached the gate." Hanging up, Jeans turned his attention to me, signing. "Get in the cargo hold and cover yourself with the blanket." Shutting the door, Jeans walked back inside.

Doing as directed, I climbed in the back and waited. Minutes later, car doors opened, and the car engine started. Once they were moving, the doctor spoke. "It will work."

"Let's hope so."

"I am good at what I do, Fairchild. It will work."

The car stopped. "Sir, have you finished here today?"

"I was never here, Corporal," Jeans or Fairchild answered.

"Very good, Sir."

The car started moving again, and the silence stretched out. Closing my eyes, I listened as the road passed below. The SUV was reasonably new; at least, it still held that fresh car smell. As the miles wore on, I allowed the rocking to drag me away.

3

RANCH

MOVEMENT WOKE ME. MY EYES FLASHED OPEN TO SEE THE MALE BESIDE me roll out of bed. His upper body was muscled and sprinkled with scars. His boxer shorts covered the start of a long scar on his thigh. His charcoal hair was mussed, and he rubbed his palm through it as he grabbed a fresh pair of boxers from the dresser and walked into the adjoining bathroom. As he turned to shut the bathroom door, his moss-colored eyes passed over me. Our eyes met as the door closed.

Rolling onto my back, I stared at the ceiling. The car dropped off the medical team an hour after leaving the prison, then drove on to Albuquerque and the ranch where we stayed overnight. I'd ascertained this was Fairchild's home or at least one of them by the furnishings and complete wardrobe. To ensure we get to know each other's habits, Fairchild decided to share the bed from here on out like a real husband and wife. We were to study each other as if we were applying for a green card.

Not phased about sharing a bed with this man, I'd slept in my underwear rather than getting tangled in my prison scrubs. Frankly, I would have slept naked, but I didn't want him to see that as an invitation. While I was well overdue for some time between the sheets, I needed to know what the game was first.

What I was suspicious about was that he trusted me to be alone with him. There was nothing to stop me from running now that I was out, nothing but him. He didn't seem too concerned with me slitting his throat while he slept. That made me more afraid. His walking and observation style told me he was trained, and he had bested me once already and quite quickly. Still, he was in the shower. What was the chance he could stop me now? No, there had to be more, something I missed.

Getting out of bed, I collected his discarded shirt from the floor and pulled it on before moving out to the kitchen. After the very light supper we ate when we arrived last night, I was starving. Searching the cupboards, I took down a box of cereal from an overhead cabinet and opened the fridge for the milk. There was a bottle of pills with no label. Considering them a moment, they looked like paracetamol, but then who the hell knows what was out these days. Maybe they were Viagra or something for paranoia. That was the problem; I knew nothing about the guy. Returning the meds to the shelf, I grabbed the milk.

When Fairchild walked into the kitchen, I was halfway into my bowl of breakfast. Dressed in jeans and a button-down again, he took the cereal from the bench and poured himself a bowl. When he opened the fridge to get the milk, he took out the pills and put them in front of me. "Take one every morning." Picking up the milk, he started pouring. Ignoring the drugs, I kept eating. He was going to have to explain why I would poison myself with something unknown.

Screwing the lid on the milk, Fairchild poured me a glass of water, placing it beside me. I kept on eating. With a huff, he pulled out his phone, opened the screen, and pressed something. My left arm went numb. Staring at my useless limb, horrified, I gritted my teeth as it started to ache like a foot I'd been sitting on for too long.

"If I have to ask again, you will be on the floor fitting in ten seconds."

Glaring at him, I got up to walk away from the table. A sharp cold burn rushed from my little pinkie up my neck - similar to when you get a brain freeze - then everything went blank. Opening my eyes, I was sprawled on the floor. My entire body ached as if I laid on ice. Blinking to clear my vision, I held back the urge to puke. Sitting in a chair eating his breakfast, Fairchild watched me. Rolling to my side, I stood up, my muscles not really willing to hold me, but I pushed through it.

Collecting the bottle of pills, Fairchild gave them a little shake before holding them out to me. Gritting my teeth, I backed away. "You don't want to defy me, Lyzebel." His voice echoed in my head, reverberating around and being replaced with one from a man I feared worse. A frightened and beaten teenager stood defiant in my memory. As I took another step back, Fairchild huffed and tapped his phone. The rush of cold was harsher this time. It took me to my knees hard, and then the lights went out.

This time when I came too, I was sure Fairchild buried me in the snow-covered ground, thinking I'd died. My body could barely move; I was so stiff and sore. Dragging myself up to my knees, I sat back on my feet. 'Don't ask why, just do,' the deep baritone of my father scolded in my head. Swaying slightly as muscle recruitment failed and reengaged constantly, I groggily peered at Fairchild.

"You don't give in, Lyzebel. The questioning you endured told me that. It meant I had to find an inventive way to control you."

Glaring up at him, I wasn't impressed, but it confirmed my suspicion earlier that he was being way too relaxed in leaving me unsupervised.

Squatting before me, Fairchild traced the path of a tear down my cheek with the pad of his thumb. "So, here's the thing. One of those injections the doctor gave you was a nano transmitter. It has connected itself to your central nervous system and responds to my commands."

He waggled the phone at me. "I was guaranteed that what it delivers is much worse than pain. For a person who needs to be in control, it is worse still." Putting his phone away, Fairchild held one of the pills between his fingers. "Another of the injections was a toxin. This is the anti-toxin, and as long as you take one every morning, you will remain fit and healthy." He waited for several breaths, his eyes filling with curiosity. "Did you know you were dying when you were captured?"

Closing my eyes, I bowed my head. Getting away to see a doctor in my previous life was complicated. We were always meant to use their medical team, but there were issues my father wouldn't let me seek medical treatment for at home. So, I'd found a doctor down the mountain. He'd initially thought of Multiple Sclerosis, but further testing revealed a genetic diagnosis in origin while similar in symptoms.

"Is that why they sacrificed you and let you rot slowly in that hole? The doctor who examined you believes it's a miracle you've lasted as long as you have. He believes, by the state you were in coming to the prison, you should have been dead in a year, but you're still here."

Tilting his hand side to side, Fairchild continued. "Maybe it was your controlled lifestyle of the prison, perhaps it was getting away from where you were before here; either way, you've escaped the clutches of death several times. Are you willing to risk dying over something as useless as refusing to take a pill?"

Raising my hands, I struggled against my body's weakness to sign. "How do I know the pill isn't the toxin?"

Fairchild turned the pill in his fingers. "This drug has cost my company a lot of money to procure, and I am willing to spend it for this to go perfectly. I need you strong and healthy to do your part, but I need to ensure you don't try and escape either. Do you understand what I am telling you, Lyzebel?"

When he offered me the pill again, I opened my mouth and let him put it on my tongue. Since I didn't try and lift my hands again, he placed the water glass to my lips. Obeying, I swallowed. Once it was done, he stepped away from me, ensuring I could watch his hands as he signed.

"I don't want to hurt you, Lyzebel. God knows the hell you went through after your mother was killed, but I need you to do as I tell you. Quite often, I'm not going to explain myself to you. You will just need to play along or obey orders. The work I do, we will most likely be surveilled heavily. One misstep, we are both dead, and while that might appeal to you, I like my life."

Curling my toes under to press up through the ball of my feet to stand, I staggered a little. Catching me, Fairchild helped me straighten up. Once he was sure I was stable, he released me and turned away, returning to his cereal. Sitting down, he pointed to me, wiped his right hand down his right side, then swiped his hands in front of his body three times as if he were brushing crumbs off his shirt. "You need clothes. Have a shower, then I'll take you to meet Sherrie. She's going to teach you deportment and dress you. I need you to be the perfect trophy wife."

Placing my right index finger in the palm of my left hand, I spelled L. Then continued to spell Y, Z, and A before wiping my hand away. I hated anyone using my full name.

Without waiting, I did as told. Making the water hot to near scalding to ease the ache in my body. There was a pastel cotton dress waiting on the bed for me, and Mitch was dressed in a suit when I came out. Appealing as he was in casual wear, now he was downright irresistible.

After a helicopter flight to Los Angeles, Fairchild jumped in a waiting car and drove us to an upmarket building. Entering via the back door, we were shown upstairs to a split-level loft studio. The mezzanine looked to be a fashion store, while the main floor was set out with dining tables, an elegant lounge room, and even a ballroom.

"Well, if it isn't Mitch Fairchild." The middle-aged woman coming into the room greeted Mitch with a kiss on each cheek. "It has been a long time since we have needed to meet. You look good. Business doing well?"

"Sherrie. I'd like you to meet Lyza, my wife. I need her polished, and I needed it yesterday."

When Sherrie turned her aged eyes on me, I realized I'd misjudged her age by a decade or two. She looked good for her age. Appraising me, top to toe, and front to back, she stepped around me. "Polish the outside first, then we will see the clarity of our little gem. James!"

A mousy man came out from a side room, a notepad already in hand. "I'll start with the clothes. James, book her for hair and nails, and she'll need makeup and a visit to the spa." Sherrie turned her attention to Fairchild. "That will be today. Dinner tonight will tell me what else we need to polish."

Nodding his head, Fairchild stared at an email on his phone. "She is all yours. You should know, Lyza is deaf, so if she seems confused, use gestures. I will sit in the corner and conduct business if you don't mind?"

"Use the office."

"Thank you." Glancing at me long enough to fire me a warning look, Fairchild headed to Sherrie's office.

Indicating I follow her, Sherrie totted upstairs. When we got to the top, she turned to face me, speaking clearly, so I could read her lips. Interestingly, she wasn't one of those who yell and elongate their words to communicate with the unhearing, indicating she probably had experience.

"I'm going to ask you to select three items of clothing from the racks." Sherrie held three fingers. "An outfit for a luncheon, an outfit for home, and a formal gown. You will also need shoes to complement each outfit. I'll wait on the sofa." Gesturing behind her, Sherrie moved away.

Browsing the racks labeled for my sizing, I selected the casual clothes first—a pair of tailored pants, a boat neck top, and a pair of ballet flats. For the luncheon, I chose a tea dress and three-inch heels. The formal gown was a v cut halter dress in rich burgundy, backless with a sleek but not a tight-fitting skirt. Choosing a pair of stilettos, I placed them down.

Perched on the settee drinking tea, Sherrie nodded at my choices. "Good, not so much work to do. Now, let us find you some underwear and get you out of that dress. It doesn't work for you."

After changing into the tailored pants and top, Sherrie asked me to join her for tea. Taking the cup she offered me, I added a little honey instead of sugar and took a sip before placing it back in the saucer and holding it. I couldn't stand tea. Smiling politely, I nodded at random intervals while she discussed various hairstyles she thought might suit me and the color palette of clothes to match my skin tone.

Eventually, her assistant joined us to announce it was time for the spa. Following Sherrie downstairs, I moved to where Mitch was waiting. "We'll see you when we get back, Sherrie, and we can catch up over dinner." Opening the door, Fairchild escorted me to the spa, twenty minutes down the road. Stopping us short of the door, Fairchild lifted both hands loose fists in front of him, thumbs pointing up, and shuffled the up and down alternatingly while he spoke. "Obviously, I can't go in with you. Behave, Lyza."

Walking in by myself, the beauticians hurried me off to a room where I was waxed, buffed, and massaged. To finish it off, I received a mani-pedi while they applied a facial. After five years in prison, there wasn't much in the way of nails for them to treat. Not that I chewed my nails, but the rules were to keep them neat and short. The beauticians wanted to put acrylics on, but I refused, so they made what I had work.

Fairchild looked me over when I walked out, then took me to the next stop, a hair salon. There, the hairdresser informed me Sherrie had called and suggested leaving the length of my hair as much as possible, adding highlights and layers around the face.

By the time they were finished, you would never have known I just escaped jail. Fairchild's pupils dilated slightly when I walked towards him to leave the salon. Regaining control of his expression, he paid the bill and returned us to Sherrie's loft.

"Go and change for dinner, please, Lyza," Sherrie requested on arrival. "We are going to an upper-class establishment."

Climbing the stairs, I selected a figure-flattering knee-length dress with a cowl neckline. Changing into heels, I hung my clothes from earlier and passed them to James, who stood off to the side, his eyes glimmering in the dark as he watched me.

As we returned downstairs, Fairchild's eyes widened, pupils dilating as he looked me over, but he schooled to neutrality quickly. When his eyes went over my head to James, who was following me down the stairs, those moss-green eyes turned dangerous.

Opening the door, Fairchild glared at James, enough that James took a step back. "Don't look at my wife like that again."

By the look on James' face, I swear he wet himself. Turning us towards the elevator, Fairchild escorted me out to the waiting car.

4

POISED

"You two couldn't fool a blind man about being married." Setting her knife and fork down, Sherrie indicated she finished her meal. "You haven't kissed, touched, or made lovey-dovey eyes at each other all day. Look around you, Mitch. Watch the other couples, pick the ones in love, those having affairs, those on their first dates. Recognize how they interact and learn from them."

"Maybe we are behaving ourselves in your company."

Blowing air out the side of her mouth, Sherrie picked up her wine. "Unlikely. Have you even touched her? Kissed?"

Glancing over the table at me, Mitch shook his head slightly. Sherrie nodded as if expecting it. "You know better than this, Mitch. Your entire business is built around camouflage. This situation is no different from when you have bodyguards disguised as friends or assistants, just at a personal level. You're a good businessman, and you were a fantastic soldier, but I've been consulting for a great deal longer. Every time I've ever seen a cover like this fail, it's because the agents didn't practice being comfortable with being intimate. If you end up spending the night as the guest of one of your clients, you need to be comfortable being naked with each other and touching each other. Do that tonight."

While Sherrie sipped her wine, Mitch observed me, searching for a sign of hesitation. When I just continued eating without reaction, Mitch chuckled quietly into his drink.

Folding her napkin, Sherrie drank what was left of her wine. "Lyza is an accomplished lady. She knows how to dress, how to eat, and how to feign interest in a conversation she can't even hear, let alone care less about. She was an excellent choice as a cover wife. You don't need me. Someone has already taught Lyza all she needs. Give her the means, and she will fool even the most observant of your clientele." Sherrie stood. "I've made some appointments at boutiques for your shopping tomorrow. I've emailed the list to you and the appointment times. You might want to go shopping for rings before leaving town again."

Pushing my chair back, I stood and farewelled Sherrie with a kiss on both cheeks. "Though, it wouldn't hurt to actually marry this one; she's perfect for you. She'll never share your secrets, and she will distract with the mere hint of a smile." Turning her own aged smile my way, Sherri enunciated her words for lip reading. "It was lovely meeting you, Lyza. Take care of Mitch out there."

Nodding, I watched her say goodbye to Mitch before taking my seat. Sitting back in his chair, Mitch looked around the restaurant. Taking a breath, he sat forward, placing his hand on the table. With a polite smile, I took the offer and put my hand in his, looking into his eyes until he started to talk, then I dropped my gaze to his lips. It was second nature to me after all these years.

"Tomorrow we will go shopping for more clothes." Mitch's thumb rubbed over my naked ring finger. "We'll need wedding rings too."

When I didn't complain, Mitch signaled the waiter for the bill. "Let's go back to the hotel and do our homework, Lyza." Taking my hand as we walked out of the restaurant, Mitch kept hold of it in the car on the way to the hotel between gear shifts. "It doesn't bother you?" He asked after a few minutes.

Shifting my focus from his lips to our joined hands, I shook my head.

Mitch exhaled. "I can't remember when I last held someone's hand."

Lifting my hands as if I meant to sign a Y, I tapped my right index five times to the area between my spread thumb and index on the left.

"Five years? Were you in love with him?"

Tucking my ring and little fingers, I closed my index and middle on my thumb like a duck bill. *"No."*

"Have you ever been in love?"

Repeating the gesture, I wasn't affected. It was hard to love someone you were forced to marry and given no option otherwise. Even if you liked each other and grew to care for each other, it may never become love.

"Neither have I. I just never found that one who made me miss them when I was gone."

Considering Mitch's ease at torturing me this morning, and his propensity to get injured himself, if his scars were anything to go by, that was probably a blessing in disguise for women worldwide. Studying him, I noticed a red light behind his headrest and reacted. Grabbing his head, I pulled it to me and low.

"What the...?"

The smash of the back window and zing of the bullet passing through the headrest and out the front windscreen was loud. Wise as he was, Mitch stayed low but tense. Grabbing the wheel, I drove us off the road towards a pole. "Brakes." My throat burning to talk.

Cooperating, Mitch jammed his foot on the brake pedal. We stopped just shy of hitting the post, but with the sudden deceleration, the car jolted. To the car behind us, it would look as though we crashed.

Opening the glove box, Mitch grabbed his gun out. Releasing my belt and his, I tracked the attacking car as it pulled up behind us. When Mitch went to sit up, I held him down, face in my breasts as if I was nursing my dead husband's head. Busying myself, I ensured we were free from ensnarement, knowing we would need to move quickly.

Looking up at me, Mitch smiled. "You can talk."

Ignoring him, I held up two fingers before Mitch's face then split them as I moved them back to my body to indicate they were coming to either side of the car. Flipping my hand, I held up five fingers and started counting down their steps to our doors. When my last finger closed in a fist, my car door opened.

Throwing Mitch back to his side of the car, I turned, blocking the gun from pointing to my head. It fired, and the bullet went through the windscreen. Holding the assailant's wrist away, I snaked my hand behind his neck, grabbed and rammed his face into the side of the car at the exact moment my foot kicked into the side of his knee.

With a grunt, the attacker went down to the pavement. Grabbing his gun, I used it to brain the guy, so he was indeed down, then jumped out of the car. Mitch had taken out his guy, and the assailant's car burned rubber as it quickly drove away. Stepping clear of our car, I took aim and fired. The car tires squealed, the wheel turned, and the car hit the curb at a high enough speed to flip the car. We watched as it smashed into parked cars along the street.

Eyes wide, Mitch turned his gaze to me. Grumbling, he jumped back in the car and started it. "Get in; we need to get out of here."

Striding back to the car, I looked at the guy on the pavement and shot three rounds. Two to the heart, one to the head. Sliding into the car gracefully, I buckled up and closed the door.

After reversing away from the pole, Mitch hit the accelerator, but not enough to burn rubber and leave treads, and then we turned off the main road and made a convoluted path through the city.

"You just killed two men without hesitation and caused a major scene."

Leaving my thumb out to the side, I held my fist out in front of me, creating emphasis as if I was thumping an air table. That's what I was trained to do. Did he expect me to stand there and plead for my life? That's not what he broke me out of prison to do. He bought and paid for my skills; that's what he was going to get.

"They could have been policemen."

Reaching behind his head, I stuck my finger through the back of the headrest, poking him in the head. Police didn't use laser sights.

Mitch sighed. "Thank you for saving my life, but next time, can we do it covertly?"

Sitting straight, I ignored the request. There was no way to avoid that mess unless we let the other man escape. That could put us in even more chaos. Lifting my hands, I explained rationally. *"He saw me take out someone. If your enemy is to see me as a weakness and not a threat, no one can know my capability."*

Huffing, Mitch didn't argue with my assessment, just turned his glare from my hands to the street. We took a few more turns in quiet. Turning the wheel sharply into a parking garage, Mitch drove to the top level, just below the roof, and parked. "We have to get rid of this car. Lucky it was a work car and not mine."

I didn't care. Opening the glove box, I wiped down my side of the car with one of the disinfectant wipes he had in there. Handing the wipes to Mitch, he wiped down his area. After Mitch collected his stuff from inside, we abandoned the car, making our way to the fire stairs.

Once we hit the street, Mitch pulled out his phone. "Stacey, we were attacked. I've had to dump the car." He gave the address of the parking garage and location. "I need a new car, and can you call Sherrie and warn her we won't be coming back tomorrow. Quite possibly, that's where they found us today."

Hanging up the phone, we made our way back to the hotel he had booked us into. We were in the room before anything more was said. When Mitch's phone rang, he picked it up and listened. "Damn, they must have put a tracer on the email. Can you go into my account and find out which one?"

Making my way to the bedroom, I went to the bathroom. Starting the shower, I put my hair up while I waited for the water to heat. I was just taking off the last of my clothes when Mitch walked in and settled himself against the counter. "They killed James. We're not sure what he told them. Sherrie assures Stacey that James knew nothing more than you were the new wife of someone important and needed deportment, so we think our cover is still intact."

Watching his hands as he signed, I continued to wash.

Standing straight, Mitch started to disrobe. "Tomorrow, we will do as originally planned, rings and clothes. We won't be going back to my ranch; we will just leave straight from here."

The shower door opened and closed, then Mitch turned on the water for the second showerhead. His eyes appraised me as he started washing. At that moment, I understood why showering was private, but not toileting at the prison. It wasn't to give the prisoners modesty, but to prevent male guards from getting off watching us touch ourselves. It took Mitch reacting to me for me to get it.

Finished with cleaning my body, I stepped towards him. Mitch didn't hesitate to cuff my neck in his palm and crush his mouth to mine. Taking his thick length in my hand, I stroked him. Cursing, Mitch pulled back out of reach, meeting my eyes with combined wariness and desire.

"A wife would know what her husband enjoyed. The sounds he made during intercourse, his favorite position in bed - for sleeping and sex, or if he snores. You should know the same about me." Lowering my hands, I waited to see what he wanted to do.

With a nod, Mitch wrapped my hand around his solid rod, then showed me precisely the grip and speed he liked. He stood there, head hanging as I touched him, breathing heavy. When I tentatively ran my free hand up the side of his neck, my thumb across his lips, Mitch licked and sucked my thumb.

Pressing my back against the wall, Mitch found the heat of my core and started stroking me. We watched each other, noting reactions to particular ways of touching, studying one another through lust glazed and hooded eyes as we learned about each other. When Mitch pulsed, I pressed down on his head and then quickly released by flicking my thumb off.

Cursing as a geyser squirted forth, Mitch panted heavily on my shoulder, then lifted his eyes to my face. Jamming two fingers inside me, Mitch stroked me roughly, his thumb circling my clit teasingly. Biting my lip, I moaned for him, hanging my head back against the wall.

Five years since I'd been touched this way. Five years since I'd kissed a man. Five very long years of no physical contact or sexual release. When I climaxed, lights burst behind my closed eyelids, and I cried out five years of frustration until my legs were left trembling with the effort of staying standing.

Grabbing Mitch's head, I captured his mouth to mine, my tongue seeking his for something more. I didn't know what, but Mitch responded. He kissed me just as heatedly, slowing the passion after a minute until we stood millimeters apart, our breath fusing in the confined space.

Clearing his throat, Mitch stepped back, turning his back to finish his shower. Cleaning up quickly, I stepped out, grabbing the towel to dry off. Our homework was done. It was time to get some sleep and learn how Mitch liked to snuggle.

Climbing into bed, Mitch raised the sheet enough to see me beneath it. "We need to get you some pajamas." When I shook my head, Mitch was quiet for a moment. "Would you be comfortable if I slept naked?"

Yawning, I grabbed at my mouth as if I was pulling something off the lower part of my face, then opened my hand to drop it. I didn't care how Mitch slept, as long as he let me sleep.

Accepting my answer, Mitch switched out the light, and got into bed. Waiting for a second longer, Mitch then squirmed around, removing his boxer shorts. Once he settled, I closed my eyes and let the exhaustion of the day take me.

Waking in the very early morning, I found myself on the edge of the mattress, Mitch close behind me, his body spread across the bed. Rolling to face him, I tickled him. Flinching in his sleep, Mitch retreated back to his side. Chuckling, I went back to sleep.

Mitch answering his phone as he left the room, woke me up at sunrise.

Watching his sexy naked rear walk away, I sighed. It was a delightful sight to behold in the morning. To make the most of it, I rubbed my fingers over my swollen clit and practiced some self-love. Not something I'd done in prison with the cameras watching. Playing wife to a gorgeous specimen like Mitch would leave me frustrated quickly, so I needed to deal with that.

Walking in just as my back arched in the finale, Mitch froze, his eyes widened and pupils dilating. "Ah, *I was going to order room service for breakfast if you're hungry?"* He signed, slightly bewildered.

Flopping onto the bed, I nodded. I was famished.

5

———————

IN FLIGHT

Boarding the private jet felt familiar, even down to it being a job. People were waiting on the plane as we boarded. The female was the first to greet us, handing Mitch a sheet of paper. Signing as he talked, Mitch made sure he faced me. "Lyza, this is Stacey. My personal assistant." Taking the report Stacey held out for him, Mitch sat at a table and read the document.

"Nice to meet you, Mrs. Fairchild." Turning her back, Stacey took the seat at the table with Mitch, effectively leaving me to find somewhere else to sit.

With a smirk, I moved to the couch near where two men were standing. They looked like bodyguards; except they weren't wearing the standard black suit. The jeans and white shirts reminded me more of Texas rangers, but the poise was military. The look they gave me was hostile mixed with lust.

"I'm Fred," the tall, blue-eyed one introduced, holding out his hand. His skin was that latte color that spoke of mixed heritage. He could have been good-looking except for the crooked nose caused by a break that wasn't fixed properly. Being polite, I shook his hand. "I'll be in charge of your security, Mrs. Fairchild." He indicated the man next to him. "This is Mark."

Taking my seat, I buckled in while Fred took the lounge seat across from me. Observing Mark, I could swear his background was Native American, but he seemed to not quite fit that either. Something exotic lurked in his genes but was too shy to come right out and announce itself. His anger issues weren't as subtle.

"Do you understand your part in this?" Mark took the seat to my left. "You're the handbag. Pretty to look at, doesn't talk, doesn't have an opinion. We can't go into many places with him, but they will let the wife through the door. You're there to watch his back and make sure nothing happens to him. You screw up, we'll fuck you over so bad-"

"If I screw up, I'll be dead," Signing with annoyance, I finished by holding both my index and middle fingers pointed up, then dropped them down to face forward, much like an umpire when a goal is scored in rugby. This frustrated Mark by interrupting his 'I man; you woman' lecture and in not using words. *"I know my part. You can stop thumping your chest and go back to swinging through trees."*

Fred and Mark stared. Sitting back, I watched as we taxied out the window. "Why is she signing?" Fred asked when he finally picked his jaw up off the floor.

"She's deaf, apparently. It turns out the reason she never answered her interrogators was because she couldn't use her hands to talk." Mitch looked across at me, and I bowed my head slightly to thank him for not telling them I could speak if I wanted. His eyes flicked to Fred and Mark. "Can you two cope?"

Mark went pale as he cursed while Fred's throat swallowed hard. "Yeah, I think I remember some of the International Sign that we learned."

Since Fred was the one to cop to knowing international sign, I raised my hands to talk to him. *"Where are we going?"*

"Rome," Fred SimComed -signed and talked simultaneously-haphazardly. "Have you been there?"

Flashes of rolling around a bed, grey eyes admiring my panting mouth, eyes that shined with danger and lust. Tracing the scars on a well-defined chest with my tongue, of my first formal event, my first job. Exhaling hard, I tapped my right index to the joint of my left thumb and index three times.

Considering me, Fred didn't ask for more, even though his eyes shined with curiosity. Snapping his fingers at Stacey, Fred pointed to the document she gave Mitch. Stacey handed it to him before she continued planning something with Mitch.

Handing it to me, Fred then tried to sign as he spoke. "This is your itinerary for the week. Memorize it because it doesn't leave this plane."

Part of me wanted to put him out of his misery and let him know I read lips, but it impressed me that he was trying, which was more than my father ever did. Accepting the paper, I read it through once and handed it back to him.

"He said memorize it!" When I raised a brow, Mark grabbed the paper. "Thursday two in the afternoon?"

Holding my index and middle finger as if they were cutlery, I lifted them up and down to my mouth twice for lunch.

Smirking, Fred took the paper, ripping it to shreds. "She's got it."

We took off. Midway into the flight, Mitch went to the bathroom. When he came back, he took the seat beside me. "Try and smile; you're out of American air space."

"How did we meet? How did you propose? Where did we marry and honeymoon? How many people attended the wedding? What about family?"

Watching my hands, Mitch raised a brow, then looked at Fred and smiled. "Okay. We need to keep it as real as possible. Less likely to trip ourselves in a lie."

"What is your story?"

Eyeing my hands, Mitch glanced at my face as he eased back in the chair and started SimComming. "I don't have one. My former military service is there for all to see. I'm using my real name, and I'm the owner of a private security company. These three are exactly as I've introduced them. The only fraudulent entity in this is you."

Narrowing my eyes, I wondered what he was involved in that he needed me. *"I was in an unhealthy relationship with a colleague of yours. You helped get me out. I felt indebted to you. You wanted a wife who owed you her life."*

Scoffing, Mitch started sizing me up again. "Not very romantic."

"Exactly."

Mitch smiled. "Which excuses our lack of lovey-dovey affection and is honest about this being a marriage of convenience. You married me for a good life and to be treated well. I married for the sake of having a beautiful woman on my arm and in my bed at night."

Seemingly lost with my signing, Fred lifted a brow as Mitch explained what I'd suggested. "That's actually rather smart."

Nodding, Mitch sat forward, his brain in planning mode. "We married two weeks ago, a small civil service in Texas. We had two close friends as witnesses. This is our honeymoon. That will cover any awkwardness between us. My family is dead, so are yours. I want four kids."

"You best get yourself a mistress."

Chuckling at the scowl on my face, Fred lifted a brow. "Not clucky?"

Closing my index and middle finger on my thumb, I glared at him. *"No."*

Mitch considered me. "Because of what you went through?"

"Stop imagining what you don't know. Trust me, you wouldn't even come close."

"You could tell us."

"I could eat glass shards too." Crossing my arms over my chest, I refused to converse any longer.

Snickering, Mitch raised a shoulder in a shrug. "Okay, imagination it is."

Not bothering trying to sign, Mark sat forward, glaring at Mitch. "I'd like to know whether she was forced to kill those soldiers or whether she is a cold-blooded killer."

Shoulders tense, Mitch shook his head. "We've all killed when ordered to, Mark. Forgiveness is divine."

Grumbling under his breath, Mark scratched at his forearm, the sleeve of his jacket lifting enough for me to see the beginnings of a tattoo. Darkness eroded my vision, my breath gasping in my ears, water dripping off me as I was thrown back in the chair after being held underwater for the longest time yet.

> *'Stop, we can't kill her,' one of my torturers shoved the one who had been holding me under back.*
> *'Fucking bitch doesn't deserve to live. My brother was in that platoon.'*
> *'You agreed to put your personal feelings aside.'*
> *'I thought she'd talk, that we'd get her boss. I'm not letting her walk away from what she's done.' He scratched at his forearm, the tattoo of the Budweiser- the navy SEAL trident on full display.*
> *'She'll talk, but either way, she'll never be free again.'*

Recognizing my torturer, I didn't react, just like I never responded to their threats at the time. Not the ones of death, rape, or disfigurement. None of it. They'd beaten me, drowned me, electrocuted me, left me naked in a freezing cold cell with not even a bucket to shit in, and starved me. I didn't give in, I didn't speak, I didn't die, and in the end, the most they could do was deny me medical attention and lock me away with no trial as a terrorist.

The second spoke the truth. Even now, I was at Mitch's mercy, a shield he could wear that no one was expecting. It was no different from my life before. Except, maybe, for me, this was a suicide mission. If I tried to escape, I'd die in the worst way. If I stayed and did as they asked, protected Mitch, then I would die while he lived. The one thing I was sure of, is they wouldn't lift a finger to save me.

Licking my lips, I met Mitch's eyes. "What happens when this is over? If I do everything you ask and live? What will you do with me when you don't need me?"

Hesitating, Fred rubbed his thumb across the pads of his fingers together, then flicked his thumb out to the side. "We'll find another use for you." When I met his eyes, he held his gaze steady with mine, not blinking, not looking away. He'd been taught to keep eye contact when bending the truth.

Placing his right fist over his left, fingers together, both thumbs out, Mitch rolled his wrists until the left fist was on top. "You've adapted to everything that life has thrown at you, Lyza. You'll adapt to this."

Maybe I had always been accepting of whatever life threw at me because I knew what was inevitable. It was the one thing I'd never feared, yet remained ever so elusive. Death. The threat that had always hung over me, that I'd always welcomed and never been gifted. I wasn't making a choice to live when I agreed to come with Mitch; I was choosing to die right.

"Mr. Fairchild," the steward approached. "The captain advises we are getting ready to land."

Buckling our belts, Mitch tapped my chin to bring my eyes to him. "When we land, the car should be waiting in the hanger. We'll head straight to the hotel, change, and then to the event. Stacey, I want you to set up comms while we get ready."

"I'll need your wedding rings."

"At the hotel." Mitch assessed me and signed without talking. *"Wear the emerald dress tonight; I want you to stand out."*

Nodding, I played with the platinum set of rings on my finger. The diamond on the engagement ring wasn't small; it also wasn't gaudy. It was kind of perfect and exactly what I would have picked for myself. Mitch chose the set and got a ring for him, which matched.

Shifting in his seat, Mitch tasted his lips, his eyes focused where I played with the rings. Stopping my fidgeting, I tucked my hands in my lap, and Mitch went back to giving direction for tonight.

Landing smoothly, the plane taxied to the aircraft hangar. The black SUV was waiting when we arrived. As we climbed in, Stacey squeezed herself in the back seat first to sit beside Mitch. Not fazed, I slid in beside her. It didn't matter if she was jealous or protective because I didn't care.

Checking into a ritzy hotel, we were shown to our suite personally by the concierge. It was on a floor with six other rooms, a lounge room, and a library. Mitch had booked out the floor, so our keys opened the hall door at the elevator entrance, and we entered the hallway to the first six rooms.

Fred and Mark took the first two rooms on either side of the corridor. Stacey claimed the next one back. Waiting in the lounge that separated the suite's rooms, I waited to be told which room was mine.

Thanking the concierge, Mitch met my eyes, then walked ahead to the suite and held the door waiting for me. Following him into the room, I placed my handbag on the lounge.

After putting his bag in the wardrobe, Mitch came back to me and held out his hand. "I need your rings." Slipping them off, I placed them in his palm. "The porters will be up with our luggage in a moment. You should shower and freshen up."

As I walked towards the bathroom, I pulled my top off. Mitch's eyes dropped to my chest as I walked by him. Pupils dilating, Mitch tensed, then he walked down the hall to Stacey's room. Stepping into the shower, I used the hotel products to wash. Wrapping the towel around me as I stepped out, I dried my hair with a hairdryer.

Mitch undressed, joining me in the bathroom, then stepped under the water, his mind focused elsewhere.

When Fred escorted the bellboy into the bedroom with our luggage, I put the dryer aside and went out to retrieve my makeup and underwear. The bellboy gawked, and Fred's eyes tracked me with interest, especially when I crouched down to open my suitcase.

Removing what I needed, I returned to the bathroom. Fred stood waiting as the bellboy left, then he waited a little longer. Dropping my towel, I hung it up, then collected my underwear and pulled it into place. Opening the toiletries roll, I started pinning up my hair.

Finishing in his shower, Mitch stood beside me, watching me using the mirror before he turned and saw Fred standing there. "Something you need, Fred?"

"She has no shame."

My hand dropped to the counter as the door opened to that cold cement room.

One of my interrogators stepped inside and stepped right into the waste I'd left for them.
'Damn girl, do you have no shame?'
A room with nothing. Not even a bucket. Having to go somewhere, it gave me a tiny spark of pleasure to watch them step in my...

"She spent five years with no privacy, Fred. Men watching her is nothing new." Walking out to the room, Mitch disappeared with his luggage into the wardrobe.

Dropping his head in annoyance, Fred then lifted his eyes to watch me once more, meeting mine in the mirror as I applied my lipstick. Stretching out my leg, I used my foot to shut the door.

6

____

FIRST DANCE

"Can I get you a drink?"

Using his hand in my lower back, Mitch guided me through the room. The question was out of politeness. Mitch already taking a glass of champagne from one of the trays to hand to me before requesting scotch for himself. Taking the flute, I lifted it to my lips as I looked over the room, letting the liquid brush my lips and removed it. Not only was it bad form to drink on the job, but I'd also been in prison for five years, so just the smell alone would probably intoxicate me.

We left Fred and Mark at the door, greeting other bodyguards they seemed to know. Other guests of the party looked Mitch and me over. Looks of interest, jealousy, and desire of varying degrees. Some of the women seemed surprised by Mitch having a woman with him and very unhappy.

As Mitch was delivered his drink, one of the women garnering the most attention from other men in the room broke free of her admirers to say hello. "Mitch, you're back." Her Italian accent was thick and seductive as she pawed Mitch's collar. "You should have called."

"Angelica, my wife, Lyza. Have you seen Julian?" The ease of his dismissal of the woman's indication they were lovers suggested she meant nothing for him, but my introduction as his wife left her flabbergasted. Considering the woman was the center of attention for the men, it was a good sign that Mitch brought his A-game to the bedroom. Beautiful women rarely bothered with a bad repeat performance.

"Ah, yes, he's out by the pool," she gestured vaguely, her eyes blinking rapidly. "Wife?"

Smiling down at me, Mitch moved me closer to him. "Yes. We married two weeks ago." His lips touched the point of my bare shoulder. "Isn't she lovely?"

Seemingly relieved by the time frame, Angelica swallowed and gave a polite smile. "She's beautiful, yes. Congratulations to you both."

"Thank you. Excuse us." Taking my hand, Mitch led me through the crowd towards the outdoor area and pool. Following along without issue, I played the accessory of his wife. Smiling, nodding my head, sipping champagne, and grinning when the others laughed, always a second later, as if I took my cues from them of when to react. There was a knack for acting deaf or mute, one I'd spent twelve years perfecting.

Another man joined us after an hour, greeting the host Julian. "Andre, this is Mr. Fairchild, owner of the security company I was telling you about," Julian introduced. "Andre was asking about my protective detail."

"And who is the beauty?" Andre queried, offering me his hand.

"My wife, Lyza."

Like everyone else tonight who knew Mitch, Andre blinked rapidly. He hadn't expected that answer, which meant he'd looked into Mitch before meeting him. "You are a lucky man to have secured the affections of one so exquisite." Andre brushed his lips over my knuckles, then released my hand. "How long have you been married?"

"It is brand new. This is our honeymoon."

"Ah, I would earn your unhappiness if I tried to steal your husband away to discuss business then, Lyza?"

"Lyza won't mind, would you, Dear?" His signing ended with him hitting his hip twice with the side of his hand, splayed and palm up. This was business, which is why we were here.

The men's eyebrows rising and mouths gaping a little as they looked to Mitch for an explanation.

"My wife is deaf. Beautiful, graceful, and unable to nag me even if she wanted to."

Smirking, Julian looked me over again, the way one does an artwork. "What a catch. Where on earth did you find her?"

"A former colleague had her. He locked her up like a prisoner and mistreated her. Since I helped her escape, I have given her everything she desires."

Appraising me like a glass of fine wine, Andre tilted his head. "And now she is yours."

"She feels indebted to me. My efforts gained me a beautiful wife who can tell no secrets. She only makes noise when it counts." He winked at Julian. Reaching for my hand, Mitch gestured at the garden to Andre. "Shall we have an informal chat about your interest?"

Leading the way into a lonely part of the garden. Andre gestured to the table and chairs by a fountain and fishpond.

While Andre took a seat, Mitch turned to me. Putting his middle and index finger beneath his right eye, as he pulled them away, Mitch spread the fingers to point at me. Holding up his left index finger, he circled the right around it before interlocking his two pointer fingers and dragging them down to the right before holding up his left palm and moving the right towards it. "Why don't you admire the fish and gardens, Lyza." Kissing my mouth in a way that made my toes curl, Mitch took his seat.

Pressing my lips together, I enjoyed the aged-oak taste of his scotch-coated lips. With a quiet smile, I made my way a few meters away to the pond. Walking along the garden bed admiring the plants, smelling the flowers, and ignoring the conversation while they talked, I decided getting myself off in the shower when we got back was a must-do.

Keeping my eyes peeled, I noticed the two men who followed us out into the garden and tried to act casual as they came closer. Noting their locations, I made my way back to Mitch, disguising cuffing my ear as an ear rub as I moved back to the pond to watch the fish.

Standing, Andre shook Mitch's hand. "I think I have stolen enough of your time for tonight, Mr. Fairchild. Your wife is starting to look bored."

"Truthfully, I think she was bored the moment we arrived. She's not really a people person."

"Understandably. Lyza observes the world in a way different from those who talk and listen. Her world is all about sights and smells and the sense of touch. I dare say this escape into the garden was more pleasurable than anything else at this party." Coming forward, Andre took my hand, brushing my knuckles with his lips again. "Till next we meet, Beautiful Lyza."

Focusing on his lips, I batted my lashes a little for him and withdrew my hand. With a wink, Andre walked off into the garden. Moving to my side, Mitch observed the men hovering. Taking me in his arms, Mitch set our frame to dance. Music was playing in the house, but it wasn't precisely waltz music. Still, Mitch started moving us to the beat around the small clearing.

"Stacey, look into our potential new client," Mitch murmured as we danced. "Fred, we have two tails ourselves. We'll need to cut them off when we leave. We'll be out in ten minutes." Smiling at me, Mitch pulled me closer, growing blurry in his nearness. Closing my eyes, I turned my face up to his. Mitch kissed me tentatively and then more probing. Much like our bodies swayed to the beat, I moved my mouth with his.

Mitch pulled back enough, so I could read his lips. "Come along, Mrs. Fairchild. What I have planned for tonight is not for public consumption." Pitching his tease loud enough to be heard by our watchers, but for it to still appear to be an intimate conversation.

Escorting me back to the house, Mitch farewelled the host, thanking him for having us and ensuring they would meet at another party towards the end of the week. Holding my hand as Mitch meandered us through the crowd, I kept my eyes peeled for anyone trying to get close.

We made it to the front door without issue, Fred and Mark stepping in behind us as soon as we were outside. The valet opened the door for the car. I waited for Mitch to slide in first, Fred and Mark taking the front seats. We eased around the circular driveway before we turned away from the house. Our tails stood on the front steps, getting delayed by some of the other bodyguards waiting. I didn't doubt for a second Fred and Mark made that happen.

Lifting my shoulders in question, I held my open hand up, palm towards me, and wiggled my fingers. Just how many of those bodyguards were on his payroll intrigued me.

Watching my hands, Mitch looked back out the window as he slid his right index finger quickly down the side of his left pointer. *Most of them. Julian has provided me a lot of clientele.*" Taking my hand in his for the ride back to the hotel, Mitch took his phone out and put it to his ear. "Stacey, did you get images of our tails?"

While Mitch listened to whatever the reply was, I turned my eyes to the window and tracked the drive back to the hotel. According to our itinerary, we would stay another day in Rome; Mitch having some meetings in the morning followed by a dinner with a client tomorrow evening. The day after tomorrow, we would head to Switzerland for another two days, and England after that.

None of the countries were new to me. I'd seen all of them, and most of what there was, including what tourists wouldn't. After all, I'd spent four years living in France and three years traveling and working in Europe after that.

Mitch held my hand walking inside at the hotel, but once we were in the suite, he let my hand go and distanced himself. *"I need to debrief with my team. Have a shower and get some sleep."*

"I'd rather go for a run." Mitch glared at me. *"I can use the treadmill in the gym downstairs."* I preferred to run outside, but you are better off using the hotel gym in strange cities.

Taking a step closer, Mitch's eyes glinted with danger. *"You step outside the hotel, and you'll wish you just went to bed."*

Watching his hands, I glowered at him, then went to our room to change and wash my face clean. After changing into my workout gear, I headed down to the gym. It was empty this time of night. Standing on the treadmill, I started it up and caught up on the last few days of missed routine.

Not one to focus on time or distance, I set my pace and ran. At the prison, I ran until the guard told me it was time to stop. We would get two hours of exercise time a day there, and I ran until it was up. Everything else, push-ups, hanging sit-ups, katas, could be done in my cell. Running was my time to zone out or put pieces of the puzzle together.

Upstairs were the two SEALs who had tortured me after my capture. They knew who I was. They hated me but allowed their boss to bring me along. Did they recommend me as a disposable body? Was it payback? I already knew once the job was done, they would more than likely kill me if given a choice. I would make them work for that, and I definitely wasn't going to let them torture me again.

Then there was Mitch. People came after him the first day and again tonight. If my hunch was correct, he had an enemy, and they were keen to give him a formal introduction to Saint Peter, complete with a personal escort to the pearly gates.

One of the hotel staff came in to start cleaning. Seeing me on the treadmill, they came over and dropped a bottle of cold water in the cupholder. Slowing to a walk, I cracked the seal and saluted them with the bottle before drinking. Drinking just a tiny amount, I cranked it up and went back to running.

"Lyza." Appearing beside me, Mitch pressed the cooldown button. *"You've been running for nearly three hours."*

Smiling, I drank some more water and finished the cooldown before following Mitch upstairs. Fred and Mark were at the door to the gym, looking concerned as we passed.

Lifting his hand as if he was caressing his cheek with the back of his fingers, Mitch uncurled them out in front until it looked like he was holding a plate and lifted his shoulders. *"Do you always run that long?"*

Splaying my right hand, I chopped halfway up my left arm, then in front of my thumb, hitting the knuckle of my left pointer. Index finger to my chin, I moved it away to point at Mitch, then formed a circle with my right thumb and pointer, the remaining fingers fanning out, and moved it from my chest forward and to the side. Until someone told me to stop, or my legs collapsed beneath me, I ran. That's how I was trained for endurance.

Taking another mouthful of water, I was careful not to scull water after exercise. My stomach would revolt and make me sick. Small mouthfuls every five breaths were a reasonable replenishment rate.

Escorting me into the bedroom, Mitch shut the door then followed me into the shower, where he stood watching me. "You did well tonight."

Rolling my eyes, I was annoyed by surprise in his voice. Did he think assassins just skulked around in the shadows? The best of us can get close to their targets in plain sight and have no one even suspect them. Finishing my shower, I dried and climbed into bed. Joining me shortly after, Mitch watched me for several minutes, then rolled onto his back with a deep exhale. "Goodnight, Lyza."

7

NEUTRAL TERRITORY

A BROAD-BRIMMED HAT PLONKED DOWN ON MY HEAD. "YOU'RE GETTING burnt," Mitch grumbled, taking the seat opposite me on the balcony while I ate breakfast. The place we stayed in Lucerne looked over the lake, and I enjoyed watching the swans glide across the water.

Dropping my cutlery, I treated my face as if it were the face of a clock, pointed to twelve in the middle of my forehead and ticked back three times to my cheek, then uncurled my fist starting with my thumb until all five fingers were out, my palm facing me.

"And you've been underground for five years with no sun. That pale skin of yours will burn quickly," Mitch signed back.

Rolling my eyes, I continued eating. The waiter placed a coffee in front of Mitch and walked away. Glancing over the spread in front of me, Mitch helped himself to what I put aside. Our first morning in Italy, I'd ordered one of everything that sounded good on the menu. I'd nibbled a little bit of everything and then finished what I enjoyed most.

Mitch caught on to me trying to reacquaint myself with everyday food after many years, so he waited to see what I went with and

55

helped himself to the rest. We'd been doing the same at each meal since. Mitch ordered his drink; I ordered the food. Three days in, it was routine.

Finishing his coffee, Mitch met my eyes and started talking by treating his fingers as eating utensils. *"I have a lunch meeting today. You won't be needed. Fred will stay with you and will take you shopping or anything else you would like to do."*

Studying him, I set my cutlery down. *"You'll be safe?"*

"Are you anxious about my safety?"

Left pointer to my right wrist, I swung my fist out to face him. *"No. I just don't want your phone falling into the wrong hands."*

Eyes tightening, Mitch assessed me, his lips thinning. *"Don't worry about it."*

We returned to eating quietly. Drinking a glass of grapefruit juice, Mitch watched me finish eating, already having polished off the rest himself. *"I'm going to ask you a question,"* Mitch's hand gestures portraying the same intensity as his eyes. *"You don't have to answer it straight away, but I'd like you to consider answering me honestly."*

With a frown, I gripped my grapefruit juice a little tighter.

"Why were you there?" After watching me for a moment, Mitch folded his napkin and stood. *"I'll see you late this afternoon."*

Observing Mitch walking away, I was torn. Over the question and the generally fantastic view of his gorgeous backside, tapered waist, and broad shoulders. God, I was horny as hell. And like that, his question sank in. He wasn't asking why I was in prison; Mitch referred to the massacre where the SEALs caught me.

The smell of blood and innards breached my senses as I was momentarily swept back to that building in Turkey.

Grey eyes surprised by my presence and accusatory as I pointed my gun at him.

'How did you know where to find me?'

I kept moving, putting myself where I needed to be.

'Answer me!' Grey eyes raged as he moved towards me. 'Damn it, Lyza!'

Finishing my juice, I stood and walked down towards the lake to clear the memory. Fred moved in beside me when I stopped by the lakefront. He didn't face me to talk, so I kept my eyes on the water and pretended not to hear him.

"I don't know why he sought you out of all people. Whether it was revenge or a way of getting to the people above you. Either way, for what happened to you, us not knowing you could not communicate, I'm sorry. I remember you trying to use your hands to tell us something when we first found you."

Stepping back from the railing, I started wandering along the edge of the water. My eyes burned in anger. No consideration I was innocent, not that I was, but no one even considered it. Fred also apologized, believing I couldn't hear him. That made his apology selfish.

Taking a deep breath, I observed my surroundings. It was such a lovely place; the warm weather and the beautiful surroundings were such a change after cement and glass. I almost felt free.

Later, I would have to thank Mitch for the hat. He was correct about me burning in this heat after so many years inside. Taking a deep breath, I smiled as I continued to take in the pleasure of my surroundings. It took me longer than it should have to catch sight of the two men slowly getting closer—the same two men who tried to eavesdrop at Julian's party in Rome.

Changing direction, I headed away from the incoming threat.

"Where are you going?" Adjusting to follow, Fred grabbed my shoulder and turned me to face him when I failed to answer him or even acknowledge he spoke. Haphazardly, Fred signed the question.

It was poorly done, so I tilted my head and shrugged, brows drawing down.

Taking out his phone, Fred typed it in a message before handing the phone to me.

Typing out the response, I kept the threat in my peripheral vision.

The two men from the party are trying to get close to us. I'm moving us into a large public population to slow them down and prevent them from trying anything brash.

Truthfully, I could have taken them, but I needed to appear defenseless to whoever may be watching.

Reading the message, Fred nodded. Turning away, I started walking again. Since the pause allowed the men to get closer, I picked up my pace a little to reach the playground. Here, many mothers watched their children play, and conveniently, two-foot patrols having a gander. Taking a seat near some mothers, I watched the children play, fascinated by their interactions.

If my life was like I was currently pretending to be, I might want some of my own, but the tattoo on my hip reminded me why I didn't want children, and that prevented me from ever becoming clucky.

"Which one is yours?" The woman beside me enquired with a smile in her native tongue. When I didn't even acknowledge her, the smile withered.

Placing his hand on my shoulder to draw my attention, Fred pointed to the woman and replied in German. "I apologize; she is deaf. She doesn't have any children. She is newly married to my boss, and they aren't ready to have children yet. She's just here satisfying her clucky nature."

Resisting giving Fred a dirty look, I smiled as I watched the kids play tips and push each other on the swings.

It took a few minutes before the police wandered over to Fred. "Excuse me. Can you explain being here?"

Fred explained again that I was indulging my cluckiness and that he was my security detail.

"How many men are with you?"

"Just myself."

"So, the two hovering outside the playground are not with you?"

Feigning confusion, Fred looked around, eyes focusing when he spotted the two men. "No, they are not." Putting his hand on my shoulder, Fred lifted his hands to SimCom. "I should get you back to the hotel and safe."

Pouting like a teenager that corresponded 'really?' When Fred nodded, I stood up in a huff, waving goodbye to the woman beside me. Fred ushered me away while the police confronted the two men, effectively preventing them from following while they asked for identification and their reasoning for lurking around the playground.

Once we were clear, Fred called Mitch. "We are on our way back to the hotel now. I'll keep her in until you get back."

It didn't bother me. After five years locked up in a fishbowl, I at least could watch television or admire the view from the hotel room.

When Mitch came in the bedroom door later that afternoon, I turned the television off. Shutting the door behind him, Mitch took a moment to assess me. With his face severe and body tense, ready for a fight, I stood as he approached me. It was better to be standing than letting a man have a height over you if things were going to go bad. Although when sitting, I'd be set up for the all-important dick punch.

"Do you know those men following you?"

Watching his hands, I shook my head.

"Why are they coming after you and not me, Lyza?"

Giving Mitch a shrug for an answer, I went to turn away. When Mitch grabbed my arm, I countered, blocked, and threw him off me. Mitch instantly changed his approach. Stepping back, I dodged his grab before stepping in to attack. Backing Mitch up to the door, I enjoyed the adrenaline rush. Pent up and frustrated, a physical outlet like fighting was a perfect counter to sex. Mitch blocked and counterattacked but couldn't get the upper hand on me.

When I moved in to finish it, Mitch countered an attack he shouldn't even know, let alone be able to prevent. Stepping back out of reach, I blinked at him. Mitch used the moment to take my legs out from under me in a way I'd only seen used once before.

Blinking up at Mitch, I studied him as he stood over me, adjusting his clothing.

Without bothering to use his hands, Mitch started talking. "Five years ago, I nearly died. The person who tried to kill me used martial arts I'd never seen before. I have a partially photographic memory. When I eventually healed, before I started my business, I searched for the person who could teach me how to fight like that. I spent two years studying in Nepal to master this fighting skill so that if I ever met someone that good again, I could defend myself." His eyes flickered to me. "You're good, Lyza, but you are five years out of practice. Don't try and fight me again."

Caught between anger and admiration, I swallowed the lump in my throat. When Mitch offered me his hand, I observed the blood splatter on his shirt cuff and traced my finger around it.

Tilting his head, Mitch considered my finger and the blood before he grabbed my wrist and hauled me up. "My lunch didn't go as planned." Then he started signing again. *"Are you sure you don't know those men?"*

Nodding assurance, I stepped back, scrutinizing Mitch.

Slipping his jacket off, Mitch sighed. *"They came after you, not me. So, either my enemy sees you as my weakness, or our ploy to have you declared deceased failed."*

Surprised by my non-existence - above and beyond my disappearance off the face of the earth - I cocked a brow.

"The woman we replaced you with at the jail was only given a short time to live; she had an inoperable brain tumor. We paid for the plastic surgery. As predicted, the air conditioning system to your cell suffered a breakdown that evening, cutting off the oxygen supply. You and the prisoners whose cells were also fed from the same system were found suffocated the next morning."

With a furrowed brow, I sat down.

Collapsing into the seat next to me, Mitch hung his head back and looked at the ceiling. "I've made enemies by being good and by trying to protect people. All my men must be trained in at least three different forms of hand-to-hand combat. I introduced advanced fighting skills to the SEAL training program, and I have the only contract ever granted to a civilian for my men to protect and extract intelligence officers. I never foresaw someone coming after me because of it."

Turning side on to face him, I assessed his profile. Touching my index finger below my eye, I moved it straight out into a thumbs up and shook my hand twice. *"Has anyone else seen you fight like that?"*

Observing my hands, Mitch frowned and caught my hands in his. "I know you can talk, Lyza. Use your words."

Watching his lips, I frowned and took my hands back. Standing up to face him, I kept signing, furrowing my forehead to show my concern for his safety. *"If they know you can fight like that and that you are teaching others, that alone will have you targeted."*

Standing with a huff, Mitch stepped towards me. I backed up. *"No. I haven't used that style of fighting on anyone else or taught it. I've never met anyone else who knew that form of martial arts at the advanced level. Not until you."*

Studying his eyes, I noted his dilated pupils, the way his tongue tasted his lips, and I backed up another step. *"Don't look at me like that."*

"Like what?"

Grabbing the air between us, I turned my wrist to take it and throw it away and then pretended to slide a ring on my wedding finger. *"You are worked up, but I am not your real wife."*

Eyes on my rings, Mitch took my hand in his and ran his thumb over the platinum setting. "How unfortunate." His lips barely moved, so I couldn't read them, not using his hands. Lifting his eyes to mine, Mitch released my hand. Wiping his hand in front of his mouth with the fingers spread, then touched a loose fist to his right temple and had his hand explode away from his head. *"Sorry, I forgot."*

Walking off to the bathroom, Mitch removed his shirt as he did, then he shut the bathroom door. A moment later, the shower started. Sitting down on the lounge, I considered the bathroom door. Mitch was making an effort to learn the Australian sign language rather than American; I just couldn't fathom why.

8

———————

FAMILIARITY

"Sorry, Mitch." Flinging the door open, Stacey marched in, apologizing. I could have forgiven the interruption; after all, I couldn't react to the noise she made. Turning the lights on, however, I could respond to that. Opening my eyes, I glared at the woman.

Sitting up in bed, Mitch didn't bother about the sheet dropping down, pooling low enough on his waist that his nakedness was overly evident. "What is it, Stacey?"

"Ah, urgent call." Moving to his side of the bed, Stacey openly gawked at Mitch. When her eyes jumped to me and realized I was also naked, the rage she internalized was only dampened by the lack of steam coming out of her ears.

"Thanks, Stacey." Taking the phone from her, Mitch didn't even notice her skimpy shorts and crop top. An oversight that only further infuriated her.

"Are you fucking her?"

Peering at the clock, I rolled to the other side to prevent anyone from seeing me smirk.

"What business is it of yours?"

"She's an employee. I thought you had a code?"

Oh, that sting of his rejection of her had cut deep.

"Lyza's not an employee; she's never signed a contract with me, and I don't pay her. She's my wife."

"That's even worse. The nano was to heal her and force compliance, not submission."

"Compliance and submission are one and the same, Stacey. But before you tread this precarious slope further, I haven't forced Lyza to do anything untoward. Still, what occurs between my wife and me is none of your business. Now, go back to bed. I think you need the rest."

Huffing, Stacey stomped out. Sliding out of bed, Mitch pulled his boxers on before stepping outside to take the phone call. Wide awake now, I used the bathroom. When I returned to the bedroom, Mitch still stood on the balcony, the phone no longer to his ear. Collecting my robe, I tied it closed as I stepped out beside him. Mitch was looking over the lake unhappily. Leaning on the railing, I watched the dark shifting of the lake waters.

Turning to assess me, Mitch leaned his face to my ear as if to kiss. "We might be being watched. You should go back to bed. I'm stressed, and you look beautiful in the moonlight." His nose traced my jaw to my chin, luring my interest, daring me to acknowledge his words and his confession.

Meeting his eyes, I stared into them for a minute or more. Slowly, the sides of my mouth lifted, the curiosity in his eyes shining brighter than the full moon in the sky.

Mitch's lips twitched. My smile bloomed as I shifted, pushing him back from the edge of the railing so that I stood before him. Running my hands up his arms, I watched Mitch's pupils dilate further from the stimulus. At his shoulders, I applied pressure, and Mitch submitted, going to his knees before me. His hands smoothed up my legs. The feel of his rough hands against my hair-free legs was divine. I'd missed hair removal for five years. In fact, I was so enamored with feeling my own bare legs that it was nearly indecent for me to touch them in public.

Opening my robe, I bared the front of my body to his hungry eyes and hands. Eyes devouring me, Mitch grazed his hands across my skin, mapping the contours of his desire. Lifting a leg, I hooked it over his shoulder, bringing his face to where I wanted it.

Grinning up at me for the briefest moment, Mitch dived below deck and submerged in a five-year pent-up feast. Gripping the rail behind me, I held tight as his tongue licked through my folds, delving into the melting pot of lust mercilessly. Hanging my head back, I stared up at the moon, indulging two pleasures simultaneously.

Gripping my ass, Mitch lifted my other leg over his shoulder, so my weight rested equally in his hands, and mine gripped the rail, holding on for dear life. As he played Mr. Squiggle over my clit, moving his tongue in ways that made my eyes refuse to stay open, I gasped. Lavishing me with pleasure, Mitch drank and sucked how his attentions affected me, driving me beyond my own restraint until I opened my mouth and came. My elbows buckled, and I all but fell on his face. Catching me, Mitch took most of my weight and saw his hard work through to completion.

Legs shaking, I bit my lip as Mitch eased me back to standing, then stepped close to me. Taking my face in his hands, he lowered his mouth. Movement caught my eye over his shoulder. Pulling back, I tapped his shoulder and pointed inside. Mitch turned to see Fred watching us, his displeasure at what he witnessed clear for us to see.

"What are you doing there, Fred?" Mitch turned to face him while I closed my robe over.

"I heard her cry out. Thought maybe someone had broken in and was murdering you."

"That sounded nothing like a woman being murdered, and you know it."

"You can't get involved with her."

"She's my wife."

"Not legally. She's a murderer, and the only reason she's fucking you is to get the device and escape."

"Actually, I think she's fucking me because she's horny." Laughing when Fred looked at him doubtfully, Mitch turned to me as he put his hand to his throat as if choking and pulled it away sharply. "You don't have to believe me. Ask her."

Smirking, I created a clawed hand facing myself and dragged diagonally from high over my right shoulder to my mouth twice. A choke hand to my throat and flowed it down to my sternum as I moved towards them.

Peering at the gesture, Fred tilted his head.

Mitch was laughing. "She said she is extremely horny."

Gracefully sashaying towards Fred, I glided my fingers featherlike over his coffee-colored forearm and winked. Fred's pupils dilated.

"Now, now. Lyza is *my* fake wife. You need to get a handjob; you go get your own." Using his hands on my shoulders, Mitch navigated me back to the bed. "Night, Fred."

Hesitating, Fred then left, closing the door loudly.

Turning me to face him at the bed, Mitch stared into my eyes, waiting. Untying my robe, I let it fall to the ground. Licking his lips, Mitch brought them towards mine. A hair's breadth between our lips, I sat down, surprising Mitch, who barely pulled up. Slipping into bed, I ignored the standing request in his pants and covered myself with the sheet.

Looking to the ceiling with a groan, Mitch cursed. "You used me." When I didn't reply, Mitch turned off the light and climbed in behind me.

When I was just on the verge of sleep, the bed started rocking slightly. Frowning, I rolled over. The moonlight shining through the open balcony doors gave mood lighting to a beautiful midnight show. Mitch's face focused on mine, his hand tugging his desire, large and hard, and making me clench at the idea of mounting him.

As the show reached its climax, spurt after spurt of applause squirted across his defined torso. This time, when Mitch moved in for the kiss, I didn't pull away. His nose circled mine twice, lips brushing mine. "Goodnight, Lyza." Getting up, Mitch went to the bathroom to clean up.

Closing my eyes, I dreamed of what I truly desired and woke moaning, on the verge of orgasm. Surprised and somewhat embarrassed, I opened my eyes. Mitch met my eyes, a knowing smile on his lips, then he rolled away and returned to sleep.

Reaching out, I traced the scars across his back. Stirring, Mitch rolled to face me. His eyes met mine, the smile gone from both of our faces now. Tracing the sternum line down to his abdomen, I fingered the more prominent scar across his left side, dragged my thumb firmly across it, then covered it with my hand, and applied pressure.

"You're playing with fire, Lyza."

My eyes flicked up to see the inferno in his eyes: anger and pain. Lowering my head slowly, wary of his anger getting the best of him, I licked that scar. It was the biggest, the one that would have been fatal if not treated in time. Mitch's breath rushed out of him in a painful moan. Threading his fingers into my hair, Mitch pulled my face from him. Lifting my head up, he crushed his mouth to mine as he rolled us to be above me.

Mitch kissed me furious and deep, his body reacting to all the heat pouring out of him into me. Dawn was raising its weary head outside the window when Mitch pinned my wrists above my head and brought the kissing to an end.

His anger was palpable in his racing pulse, his haggard breath, and the throbbing hardness of his body pressing mine to the bed. "Don't ever touch me like that again, Lyza. We can use each other to get off, we can fuck, but we can't forget you're not my real wife. I don't want your tenderness or your pity. I don't want you for that." The scowl on his face matched the venom in his tone, searing his hate into me. Rolling from me, Mitch gathered up his workout gear and marched from the room.

For the first time in years, my insecurities threatened to choke the air from my lungs. Sitting with my knees pulled to my chest, I hugged my legs tight. Shutting down the areas of my mind that were hurt by Mitch's loathing, I focused on what I needed to do. First, I needed to find out how many devices Mitch had to control my compliance, and then I needed to destroy them all and escape.

Falling back on the bed, I rolled to watch the sunrise. In the predawn, those grey eyes leered at me from somewhere beyond the horizon. He would have been the only one to know, and there is no way, now that I was easily accessible, that he wasn't coming for me. Like the bullet he put through me, I could feel it. My hands traced the scar of the injury that caught me. Had I never stopped to save that one soul, I could have spared my own.

Now, I was stuck standing in the bottom of an hourglass, the sands of time pouring over me, slowly compressing me until I was helpless, and my own body would smother me. Banging against the glass wasn't going to save me, but if I didn't find a way out soon, my past would hunt me down and consume me.

9

———

LUST

GRABBING MY ELBOW, MITCH STARTED LEADING ME TO THE DOOR. HIS face was stern, and while I wanted to ask what was happening, his jaw grinding told me now was not the time to ask. Since I'd been getting ready for bed when he abducted me, I was in my dressing gown, nothing else.

Fred was already at the door, watching outside in the hall. As soon as we stepped out, he started following us. "You couldn't let her dress first?"

"No."

"Mark is in the car. Stacey will pack up your stuff."

Mitch didn't say a word. Taking the fire stairs, we left via the staff entrance where Mark waited by the car. Opening the door for me to slide in, he handed Mitch the car keys. "Are you sure you want to make this trip alone with her?"

"If we leave now, we will be fine. We'll see you back in Rome."

Mark closed my door while Mitch slid into the driver's seat and started the engine. He threw the car in gear, and we were heading out of town a moment later. Adjusting my robe to ensure I was covered, I looked to Mitch for an explanation. I didn't get one.

Sitting back in my seat, I stared out into the moving darkness of night. We headed north out of Lucerne, then turned south towards Geneva. When we stopped for the petrol an hour later, I confronted Mitch. *"Where are we going? What happened?"*

Glaring at my gestures, Mitch pointed to me, then flowed his index and middle fingers with both hands, and the two digits spread like he was giving me directions to turn left. *"I'll drive through the night. You should rest."* Slamming the car door shut, Mitch stalked off.

After he'd filled the tank, he slid back into the car with a jumbo coffee, bottle of water, and a bag of skittles. With a huff, I curled up in the passenger seat and watched Mitch drive.

Four hours into the drive, his phone rang. "Report, Fred?"

"We are heading to the airport. As suspected, we have a tail. They were waiting for us in the garage when we came down to leave, but when neither of you was with us, they backed away and are following from a respectable distance."

"Okay, play ping pong with your flights. Fly to England tonight, spend a day there, then head to Paris, and we'll see you in Rome in three days."

"Your bags are with an express courier on the way to France. You probably shouldn't show up at a hotel with a naked woman."

"It's France; they'll just think she's wearing a new fashion. Have Stacey send me my reservation and coordinates to the hotel."

"Will do." Fred hung up, and the radio filled the car.

Touching my thumb and index together and other fingers loose, I lifted them to the side of my mouth as one would indicate drinking a cup of tea, then flicked my wrist so the back of my hand was facing him. Leaning forward, I raised my brow to show it was a question. France hadn't been on the itinerary.

Turning his face so I could read his lips, Mitch finally answered. "A surprise invitation to meet with a client. He's attending a party and asked me to meet him. It will also be a chance to meet with Andre again. I want his contract."

My eyes narrowed on Mitch's eyes while I studied his rigid posture. Something happened, but he wasn't filling me in on 'the what.' Mitch kept his eyes on the road. "Stop worrying about the why. Your job is to keep me alive. I'm not going to tell you any more than that. Stop using your head and just use your body to protect my life."

Putting my fist under my chin, I rested my elbow on the back of my left hand, ala Rodin's The Thinker. *"Thinking can save you too."*

Winding his index finger in front of his lips, Mitch purposefully set his hands on the wheel. "Use your words, Lyza. I'm driving."

Grinding my teeth, I took a breath. He was right. He needed to watch the road. *"A weapon is only as good as the mind wielding it,"* I whispered, cringing on the strain in my throat.

Resisting smiling, Mitch's lips twitched. "Finally!"

Rolling my eyes, I crossed my arms in annoyance and stared out at the disintegrating night. We said no more, and Mitch focused on the drive. Drifting off sometime after passing through Geneva, I woke with the predawn ushering us through the mountains.

"Where are we?"

Glancing at my hands, Mitch raised a brow as his eyes flitted to my mouth, then turned to the road ahead. With a huff, I turned my eyes forward again.

"Why don't you talk if you can?"

Since he hadn't signed it, I pretended not to hear.

Mitch waited for three breaths. "You speak too well to be completely deaf, or you weren't born deaf."

The car covered distance, the radio playing French music. Gazing out the window, I refused to acknowledge he was talking.

Removing a hand from the wheel, Mitch tapped my shoulder to get my attention. Shaping his hand in a loose gun, he wiped it off his chest. *"Why were you there?"*

Observing his gestures, I pressed my lips together on the emotion. Hooking my finger, I dragged it down the side of my face, then splayed my hand in front of my ribs. Hovering it above my upturned left palm, I then scooped it up to my arm until my fingertips touched my ribs on the other side. *"I was trying to save someone."*

"Did you?"

Holding my left arm diagonally across my body, index finger pointing up, I put my right wrist to the left, with the right index finger pointing down, and slid it down my left arm to the elbow as my shoulders slumped forward. The weight of failure burdensome.

"You failed? Is that why they left you there?"

Slouching into the bucket seat of the car, I pulled my knees up to my chest and wrapped myself up in a ball. What was the old saying about camping? If something happens, stay at the campsite. No one can rescue you if you're not where you should be.

"You saved someone, Lyza. You saved yourself."

Closing my eyes, I bowed my head to rest on the window. I abandoned my duty and failed him. Had I saved myself? No, not likely. Five years in a fishbowl, and now I was a bodyguard for a man who could cause me intense pain and vulnerability with the press of a button. No, I wasn't saved, not yet.

The sun was up, and my stomach grumbling by the time we approached Nice. Opening the screen on his phone, Mitch activated the navigation to find the hotel.

Holding his first three fingers up with ring and pinkie tucked, Mitch spread them open and touched them under his eyes and out with a raised brow. *"Ever been here?"* When I shook my head. It made him smile. "Me neither."

We pulled into an upmarket hotel where the valet opened the door as soon as the car stopped. Raising a brow when I stepped out of the car barefoot and in a long silk robe, the valet appreciated my exposed thigh as he offered me his hand to the curb before shutting the door.

"We have luggage coming via courier," Mitch informed the valet in fluent French as he handed over the keys.

"Oui, Monsieur, je vais l'envoyer directement dans votre chambre."

Taking my hand in his, Mitch walked us to the concierge's desk to check-in. No standing in line like any regular customer. Of course, Mitch wasn't behaving like any other customer with his room choice or showing up with a naked woman on his arm.

"We'll need breakfast sent straight up to our room. I've driven all night, I'm hungry, and I have a business meeting in three hours."

The concierge bowed his head as he handed Mitch a set of keycards and led the way to the elevators. "Of course, Mr. Fairchild."

Our suite was on the top floor, which included a furnished terrace with panoramic sea views of the Bay of Angels. Ignoring everything else, I went to stand on the balcony enjoying looking out over the Côte d'Azur with its turquoise waters that merged to sapphire blue.

Stepping in beside me, Mitch sighed. "It's beautiful."

Turning to face him, I smiled. I wasn't about to disagree, but I couldn't acknowledge I heard him, either. Dark circles encased those muted green eyes of his. Reaching out, I traced one of those dark circles with my thumb. Closing his eyes, Mitch groaned.

Stepping closer, I maneuvered my body between his and the railing. Setting my other hand to his second eye, I gently massaged the dark circles. With his eyes closed, Mitch allowed me to tend his tired eyes. Placing my thumbs over his lids, I applied a slight pressure while my index and middle fingers massaged his temples.

Exhaling, Mitch dropped his head slightly to lean his forehead on mine. Moving my fingers from his eyes, I slid them through his hair to massage his scalp. We stood there, him resting against me while I tended to his exhaustion. Just breathing, relaxing, recovering from the long night.

Ten minutes later, I started to worry Mitch had fallen asleep standing up. Then his hand tugged and released the tie on my robe. The silk fell open, exposing my body to him. When Mitch touched my naked skin, trailing his knuckles lightly up and down my waist on each side, I drew a sharp breath.

Dragging my fingers down the front of his shirt, I lifted it, Mitch raising his arms for me to bare his chest to the bright summer sun. Dropping his shirt to the terrace, I trailed my fingers over his upper body. He was gorgeous. Putting him in the same room as any female would be asking for trouble. Having him in your bed naked when you were randier than a rabbit was god damn torture.

His face lowered until his nose brushed mine. Something with wings tried to take flight in my stomach. The anticipation of just his mouth coming down on mine, whether he kissed me hard or delicate, I didn't care. I wanted him to kiss me, to take me inside to that king-sized bed, and have his way with me. Gods, if he did me here on the terrace with the sun beating down on my moonlight skin, I wouldn't care.

His lips brushed mine, once, twice. My stomach twisted, knowing the third would be it. Making the third pass, Mitch sighed and dropped his face off to the side. My stomach plummeted as he pulled away.

"I want you, Lyza. But for all the wrong reasons. I won't do that to myself. I'm going to shower." Stepping away, Mitch walked inside to the bathroom.

Picking up his shirt, I marched after him. He was as pent up as I was, and I wanted, needed something to happen between us. Despite our situation, there was no denying the chemistry between us. Striding into the bathroom as Mitch turned the shower on, I stopped and glared at him.

Turning back to undress, Mitch stopped and raised a brow at my presence. The eyebrow fell as he wiped his splayed fingers across his mouth in apology.

Shaking my head, I grabbed his neck, kissing him intently. Mitch didn't even resist. His hands swept inside my robe to hold my bare back and press me tight against him. Slipping my arms from the gown, I dropped it to the floor, rubbing my naked body against his bare torso.

Mitch groaned as my fingers released his belt and fly, and I shoved his jeans from his hips. His kisses firmed, tongue more intent in his search of my mouth as I took his rigidness in hand and stroked him. Kissing him once more, I dropped to my knees.

"Fuck!" Gripping my hair as I licked his precum from his tip, Mitch cursed a few more times. "Lyza, you don't need to…"

As I took him in my mouth, his voice cut off on a beautiful groan. Fingers gripping my hair, Mitch stopped resisting, stopped trying to tell me this wasn't needed, stopped denying that he wanted this as much as I did.

Chapter never taught me to connect physical intimacy and love like most women. Instead, sex was explained as a primal need that all humans experienced, like hunger and thirst. Yes, it was a way of propagating the species, but it was born of primal urges.

My sex education taught me to feed my own needs and use men's desires to my benefit. That didn't always mean having sex with them, but just casual flirting to lure them away from a crowd, out into a quiet garden without witnesses. When I was sixteen, I was led into a bedroom and introduced to my partner, Noel. Not just for training, but for everything.

Noel was undeniably good-looking; he was also one of their best. That's why we were matched. That day was spent training in foreplay and sex. From that night on, I sparred with Noel, ate with Noel, and slept with Noel. We were what they called a breeding pair. We worked together for most jobs once I was made active. It was expected we would breed, provide the organization with the next generation of soldiers.

Mitch's grip tightened in my hair, pulling my mouth away. Meeting his eyes, I read his desire and stood up. Kissing me heatedly, Mitch wrapped his arms around me, holding me tight to him. I loved how strong his arms felt as they encompassed me. When Mitch kissed down my neck, I smiled and turned in his arms, moving my hair out of his way so his lips could nip and suck at my throat.

Placing my hands on the bathroom sink, I leaned forward enough to reach between my legs and guide Mitch home. Moaning as his head slipped in, Mitch gripped my hips hard. "Lyza," he breathed my name, eyes watching me in the mirror, "you truly want this?"

Opening my mouth, I spoke. "Yes."

Closing his eyes, Mitch pushed inside me. We both moaned now. Absolute relief from his penetration swept through me. Finally, it was happening. "Fuck me?"

Growling, Mitch obliged me. Gripping my hips, he pounded me hard. As my skin became slick with sweat, Mitch leaned over me and placed one hand on the mirror for leverage, while his other encircled me to cover my mound and rub my clit furiously. Clinging to the sink, I moaned and gasped as my need built to bursting in me.

Taking his hand away to use it to stabilize himself, Mitch grimaced as he stretched me with that loaded weapon. "Damn it, Lyza, it's too good."

Cursing at how large he was, I pinched my nipple and called his name loudly as I came. Losing his rhythm, Mitch pulled the trigger and exploded, praising my existence.

Collapsing on my back, Mitch kissed across my shoulder as he gasped for breath. Grinning like a Cheshire Cat, I turned my head, catching the reflection of a man loosening his collar as he left our breakfast on the dining table, and hurriedly left the room. Biting my lip on a laugh, I closed my eyes and got my breathing under control.

10

CLIENTELE

"Lyza, how lovely to see you again."

Staring out to sea, I ignored the man standing behind my shoulder until he touched the curve of my back. Turning, I stepped out of his hold and lifted my eyes to see Andre smiling at me. "Hello, Lyza. Where is your husband?"

Watching his lips, I frowned a little unsure, then gestured to his phone. Accents could make lip-reading difficult, so I always feigned difficulty with new people. He wasn't to know I was multilingual. I dare say he assumed I was American like Mitch.

Smiling, Andre took out his phone and removed the lock using his thumbprint. He opened the messages and typed his question before showing me. Reading it, I pointed to the door Mitch went through with the man he was meeting an hour ago. Andre continued smiling as he typed again.

"He should know better than to leave a beautiful woman like you unattended." Andre typed the query if I'd like a drink.

Shaking my head, I waved my hand in a polite decline before turning back to the view outside the lounge windows. The party was mainly out on the terrace by the pool, but Mitch met his client inside and came to this room to talk privately on arrival, so I'd waited here.

"So, beautiful. I wonder if you would scream for me." Moving my hair back from my shoulder to expose my neck to him, Andre stepped closer.

Slapping his hand away, I stepped back. Waggling my index finger at him, I glared, pointing to my wedding bands as I created space between us.

Stalking closer, Andre smiled. "Are you scared your husband will get jealous? Don't worry, Lyza, he told me your marriage was of convenience, not love."

Watching his lips closely, I ensured I caught every word. Gesturing pointedly to the rings again, I shook my head.

Smirking, Andre stopped his approach. "Your husband very much wants my business, Lyza, but he isn't the only one. Your beauty could go a long way to securing my contract."

Placing flat hands palms up in front of my rib cage, I juggled my hands up and down to indicate that statement was doubtful, my eyes lifting and rolling to the right to show I didn't believe him. Tucking my index and middle finger away, I pointed my ring and little finger to my sincere eyes with my thumb sticking up. I finished by tapping my middle finger of my open hand to my chin twice, then waved my hand in a no again, giving him a look of sympathy.

Watching my gestures, Andre laughed. "I like you, Lyza. You have attitude enough for it to be endearing, but not too much to be annoying. I just wish I could understand what you are saying."

"She said you're pretty, but not her type."

Andre turned to see Mitch and his client watching our interaction, then glanced at me with a mischievous smile. "We can build on pretty." With a wink, Andre walked to Mitch to greet him properly. "Are you enjoying Níce, Mr. Fairchild?"

"I've only been here four hours, but so far," Mitch's eyes came to me in a very sexual manner, "it's been very pleasurable."

"Most wives would be annoyed about having their honeymoon constantly interrupted by their husband's business."

Holding out his hand to me, Mitch signed and spoke for Andre's benefit as I walked to him obediently. "Are you annoyed by coming to these glamorous parties?"

"Yes, I'd prefer to be fucking."

Eyes widening in surprise, Mitch started laughing. *"It's called recovery time."*

Despite Mitch not voicing his answer, Andre's brow rose. "You should enjoy the sex while you can get it. Give it a year, and you'll barely get it."

Smiling sweetly at Andre, I lifted a brow. *"He has a big dick and is really good with his mouth. I'll have it as much as I can, while I can."*

Andre looked to Mitch questioningly. Blushing profusely, Mitch rolled back his shoulders and shook his head with a smile. "Excuse, Lyza, Andre. She's in a naughty mood today." He looked me over. "She obviously didn't get a good sleep last night and needs an early night."

Smiling mischievously, I winked at Mitch. *"I'll go get a drink while you talk."* Giving Mitch a chaste but wanton kiss on the lips, my head swam with giddiness as I walked out to the terrace to provide them with privacy.

"You said your marriage wasn't of love."

"It's not. That isn't to say there isn't mutual lust. She's beautiful. I won't deny I wanted her the moment I saw her, but it took a little bit longer for me to see my desire reflected in her eyes."

"I think she's falling in love with you."

"That only works to my benefit if she does. Have you considered our discussion further?"

Stepping out into the public gathering, I couldn't continue to eavesdrop. The business was boring anyway. I'd heard the initial discussion. Security teams weren't interesting to me unless I needed to avoid them.

Locating a waiter carrying drinks, I picked the glass of juice to drink while I waited. My eyes scanned the crowd casually, looking for familiar faces or persons who could be a threat. There were men and women everywhere, talking and laughing, all of them dressed to fit in, even the ones in bathing suits enjoying a splash in the pool.

A man stood talking across the pool to some guests, his eyes scanning the crowd continuously. While I didn't recognize his face, I knew that watchful gaze. His eyes passed over me casually, then darted back to lock on me. His entire posture changed as he stopped talking, eyes raking me head to toe. Turning my gaze away before we made eye contact, I continued to survey the rest of the party so he didn't think I'd be interested. He had enough candy hanging off his every word in their skimpy outfits.

A woman swimming through the pool stood up to climb out. Curiosity tickled my spine with how familiar she looked. Dropping my gaze to a tattoo on her left hip, I frowned, then looked back up to her face to see her eyes searching the crowd like mine.

Our eyes connected. Hesitating, she looked across the party towards a huddle of guests then back to me. Glancing back over my shoulder to ensure Mitch wasn't in view, I turned to watch the door as Wenda moved towards me. *"What are you doing here? I heard you died?"*

Considering her hands as she signed, I pursed my lips. Marking off my hand as if ticking an item on a list, I indicated to Wenda, pointed to my temple, and then put my arm across my waist and waved it away. *"I did. I thought you got out?"*

"I did. When I failed the last test, I left, but then Noel found me and offered me a job."

My heart stopped. My hands trembled as I lifted them to talk again. *"You work for Noel?"*

Nodding with way too much enthusiasm to be comfortable, Wenda bit her lip, fear flashing in her eyes. *"Breok works for him too."* She looked around carefully. *"You need to go. Noel is here, and if he sees you..."*

"Will you tell them?"

Watching my hands, Wenda considered me. *"No, but if he sees you, I won't lie."*

Nodding my head, I pivoted on my heel, heading inside. Wenda and I were as close as you could get to friends at Chapter. She'd failed her last test and been discarded; her tattoo was unfinished. Just the sword, without the precision of the arrow. Breok also failed, so if they were both working for Noel, I could assume he had recruited most of the former failed recruits.

Andre was just walking out as I stepped inside. With a smile, he bobbed his head as we passed. Mitch stood frowning out the window. Touching his shoulder to get his attention, I swiped my hand down my ribs, then placed my hands against each other facing opposite ways, and flicked the left away.

Mitch frowned harder. *"Why?"*

"People I trained with."

Face clearing, Mitch took my hand and made our way through the house to the front door. As Mitch drove us back to the hotel, his brain was in overdrive. *"Did they see you?"*

I knocked on the air.

"Will they come after you?"

Holding my left hand bladed with the thumb sticking up, I moved my right hand down the side of my index finger until the thumb barred its way. *"Depends."*

"On?"

Replaying my conversation with Wenda in my head, I cringed, knowing she would tell Noel I lived with absolute certainty. I knocked the air again.

Cursing, Mitch shifted gear. *"We get our things, and then we head for Monaco. We can stay there the next two nights, then head to Rome and meet with the others."*

Anywhere was better than here near Noel.

Forty-five minutes later, we arrived at the resort in La Rousee. Mitch hadn't booked ahead, but since the concierge knew him well, he instantly found us the best room available. It wasn't the penthouse, but since no one knew we were there, we didn't have to stay in the best to flaunt Mitch's prestige. The spa suite was more than enough.

After ordering room service for dinner, we showered separately. When I came out to the room, Mitch looked me over. "You're a little sunburnt, I'll call downstairs for some aloe for you." Holding up a finger to wait, I dashed to the bathroom and came back out with a bottle. Taking the bottle, Mitch lifted a brow as he stood up. "Where did you get this?"

I drew a cross on my chest to represent the Swiss flag with a two-inch gap between thumb and index finger.

Moving behind me on the lounge, Mitch reached around me and released my robe to shift it from my shoulders, and gently brushed my hair out of the road. When the cooling gel touched my hot skin, I jolted a little. Mitch rubbed the gel across my shoulders gently, massaging as he did. "Today was the first time I've seen you worried. Don't, they won't get you back, Lyza. I won't let them have you."

A stone lodged in my throat, making it hard to swallow. Standing up, I covered myself. Facing Mitch, I pressed the tips of my fingers to the top of my right breast with my wrist high, then I let my wrist drop.

Rising, Mitch met my eyes, but then I dropped them to his hands while he signed. *I'm exhausted too. Let's have that early night that I promised.*

In the bedroom, I disrobed as I climbed into bed. Switching off the light before slipping in behind me, Mitch touched my upper arm. "Lyza?"

His query was of concern, but I didn't want him worried for me. Truthfully, I knew Noel wouldn't kill me. If he wanted me dead, he would have killed me five years ago, but neither of us had taken a fatal hit. Rolling to face Mitch, I moved above him.

"Lyza, if you just want to be held-"

Placing my finger to his lips, I lowered my face, then licked and bit my way down his torso until I found his growing interest. It hardened with a jolt as I wrapped my mouth around him.

"Okay, no talking, no comforting. You don't like to be pitied either. Got it."

When I raised my finger to his lips to shush him again, Mitch took the hint, and the only words he spoke for the next hour were prayers to god and my name in a sated song.

The next day, I taught Mitch the beauty of silence. We spent the entire day in each other's company, without a word spoken. The peace was only broken during the lustful sessions where physical exploration induced holy praise and each other's names.

As I slipped into the car the day after, adjusting my seating over the beautifully abused areas of my body, Mitch turned a radiant smile to me. Starting the engine, Mitch took a deep breath and deflated. *"The others can't know."*

"Does it matter?"

"It shouldn't, but it will."

Quirking a brow, I worried he was ending one of the only benefits to this situation. Splaying my first two fingers, I drew them across in front of me, then slashed back on an angle with my hand bladed as I lifted my shoulders in question.

Choking on a laugh, Mitch shook his head. *"Gods, no! I seriously want so much more. I'm just saying we need to be quiet when they are around."*

With a wicked grin, I relaxed. *"I can be quiet. Can you?"*

Mitch heaved a sigh. *"I'll try."*

Watching his hands, I smiled. Placing them on the wheel, Mitch put the car in gear. Sitting back in the bucket seat, I couldn't stop grinning watching him drive. Meeting my smile with his own an hour later, Mitch shook his pointer finger in the air in question.

Lowering my eyes to the bulge in his pants, I lifted a brow. Pointing to him, I twinkled my fingers in a circle by my temple and pointed to my chest.

Glancing at my hands, Mitch quickly looked back to the road. "I can't help it. That dress is very flattering on you."

Adjusting myself in the seat, I lowered his fly. Sucking in a breath as I dropped my head, Mitch cursed. "Oh, god! As if driving in Italy isn't dangerous enough."

11

___

UNEXPECTED INVITATIONS

A HAND SHOVED A PIECE OF PAPER IN MY LINE OF SIGHT. GLANCING UP from my book, I eyed Stacey staring down at me. Despite the stern look and the hatred all over her face, the quick lick of her lips and dilated pupils told me she was scared of me. Casually, I picked up the paper and read it.

'He's just using you. He's never going to love you.'

Lifting a single brow, I put my hand out for her pen. Hesitating stepping closer, Stacey passed me her pen.

'He's hot as hell and fucks like a demon on crack. He can use me until I'm dead. I don't care. Love doesn't come into it.'

Handing the page back to her, I watched Mitch swagger into the room. When Stacey read my reply, her brows bunched, nose scrunched, and her eyes glazed. The woman was probably bipolar with all those mixed emotions.

"What's that?"

Squeaking in surprise, Stacey folded the paper to try and hide it. "Nothing."

Lifting a brow, Mitch snapped his arm and snatched the note from her hand. While Mitch took steps away as he read it, I watched Stacey stare at her hands, wondering where the paper went. Lifting his eyes, Mitch glared at Stacey, the veins of his neck pulsing. "I told you this is none of your business."

Face heating, Stacey licked her lips. "I was just warning her."

"This is petty, is what it is, Stacey. What if what you said was untrue, and you went and told her this shit?"

Pausing, Stacey's mouth fell open. "Is it?"

Since no one was signing, I went back to reading or at least pretending to.

"It's none of your business. What happens with Lyza and I is between us, no one else."

"You can't develop feelings for her and put her in harm's way. Jesus, I heard Mark and Fred talking. I know what she did, what they did to her. She's biding her time, and you know it."

"Keep your voice down! Anyone could be listening. She's not a threat to us."

"Why, because she's fucking you? Wake up!"

"She saved me."

"You gave her no choice."

"No, Stacey, five years ago, Lyza saved me."

"What are you talking about?" Fred interrupted from the door, Mark standing beside him.

Sighing, Mitch turned his back to me. "In Turkey, Lyza didn't do it. She turned up after the attack to try and stop the assassin. She knew him. I think they were lovers. She could have saved herself, but she saved me instead."

The silence was deafening as Fred stepped forward. "You're only telling us this now? We tortured her for days, and she was innocent? She spent five years in a hole, and you only bothered to tell someone now?"

Huffing, Mitch shoved his hands in his pockets. "She's far from innocent. I told them when I woke up. It was days after the attack that I regained consciousness. That shit already happened, and her hole dug. Lyza could have sued the shit out of them for what was done to her, especially when they realized she was deaf. When I told them the truth, they told me to shut up, not to tell anyone else, and to let it go."

Swiping his hand through his hair, Mark shook his head. "Fucking hell. They buried her knowing she didn't do it."

"Which is why no one ever knew they captured her. The brass argued she knew the killer and protected him." Mitch shook his head. "I've spent years finding her." Shifting uncomfortably, Mitch glanced over his shoulder towards me. Keeping my eyes soft and on the book, I turned the page. Not that I'd read a thing for three pages.

Stepping toward Mitch, Stacey gritted her teeth. "So, you give her restricted freedom and benefit yourself at the same time. She saved your life, and you're using her."

"It was her choice, Stacey."

Striding further into the room, Mark held up his hand. "Wait, you're screwing her? Neither of us can touch her, but you can fuck her?"

"She is my wife!"

Getting ready to call bullshit, Mark stepped forward, but Fred grabbed his shoulder and hauled him back a step. "Did you know she was on the cleanout list before you went in?"

"I did. I have a friend who knew I was looking for her. When her file came up, he told me where to find her and gave me unrestricted access to say goodbye."

Crossing his arms, Fred lifted a brow. "Does your friend know she's free?"

"No one other than my team knows she lives or her name."

"What about the one who saw her in Níce?" Stacey asked.

Scrubbing his hand through his hair, Mitch cringed. "Well, yes. Her ex-associates are a factor."

Nodding his head, Fred angled his body when I glanced up at him to prevent me from reading his lips. "If they are running in the same circles, that could be an issue. They may want her back."

"I'm sure they will."

"I'm not keen for them to get their hands on her again since she was already scared up before we got to her. What are your plans for her once your current issue is dealt with?"

Kicking the floor with his toe, Mitch bowed his head. "She deserves her freedom. I have the resources to provide her with a comfortable life."

"At home?" Mark questioned with surprise.

"Maybe. I offer safety and a good life. She's an excellent covert bodyguard. She could train other female ex-military and help expand my service."

"Do you plan to whore those women too?" Stacey snarked.

"It will be Lyza's choice to stay."

The others all stared at Mitch for a moment; Fred's mouth dropped open. "You intend to keep her as your wife?"

"We have good chemistry."

The doorbell rang. Everyone turned to look at me. Reading my book, I pretended none of them existed and that I was entirely oblivious to everything Mitch just revealed. Truthfully, I'd never found it so hard to keep my face neutral than in the last few minutes. Huffing, Mark strode the hall. "I'll get the door."

Brushing his hand across my knee, Mitch waited until I looked up. Raising a brow at me, Mitch looked to the bedroom door. Closing the book, I took his offered hand and let him lead me into the bedroom. Closing the door, he walked to the balcony door and looked out on the view for a moment. Caressing my hands up his back, I placed my chin on his shoulder and admired the view from behind him. We'd found ease in each other's company that allowed for this minimal affection in private.

Taking a deep breath, Mitch turned to face me, tucked his thumb in his fist, then flicked it out. "After this is over, I want you to know you have the option to stay on with me. I've never had this sort of chemistry with anyone before. I can put you on the payroll as my bodyguard, and you can, for the most part, wear pretty clothes and look the part. This lifestyle, it's only a few weeks at a time. Normally, I'm at the office or my ranch with the occasional schmooze with clients. You don't have to give me your answer yet. Just consider it an option."

Circling his index finger by his temple as he finished talking, Mitch met my eyes with a clear focus. He looked confident, casual in the way he held himself, but his eyes were tight. Lifting my hand to my face, I kept my index in front of my nose, with my thumb hanging free facing him, then turned it to meet me as I moved it away and pointed to the wedding rings before pointing to him.

Taking a breath, Mitch tilted his head. "I didn't ask you too. But to be clear, do you mean ever?"

Pressing my lips together, I knocked the air, repeated the gesture, and added to it. Holding my right hand in the pistol grip, I held up my left palm, touched my right hand to the top of the fingers, and then dropped it to the bottom of my palm.

"Not legally? *Is this because you don't exist?*" Stepping closer as he signed, Mitch forgot to talk like he did only days ago.

"To the world, I disappeared. To your country, I was Jane Doe, a number, and that person is dead. If Lyzebel Jones suddenly turns up..." Holding my hands out to the side, I shrugged. *"A lot of questions would be asked."*

Bowing his head, Mitch licked his lips. *"I could obtain a new identity for you."*

Lifting my hand, I dropped them up and down as if miming playing the piano with my middle finger down and other fingers forward. *"Not yet. I might die, saving your life."*

When Mitch smirked, I gifted him a sad smile. Standing there appraising each other, we weighed everything that was just said and possibly, what was unsaid. *"So, I fuck like a demon on crack?"* Mitch shifted forward casually, his eyes already undressing me. The guy was hornier than me, and that's saying something. *"I'm guessing that's a good thing?"*

Grinning wickedly, I pointed to him with my middle finger higher than the index, then twisted my hand to the side, so the index was on top, then pointed to me. It was definitely good for me. Lifting on tippy-toe, our lips brushed just before there was a knock at the door.

"You two decent?"

Gripping my shoulders, Mitch winked as he set me back flat on my feet. "Yes." He signed what he planned to do to me tonight. By the time Fred was beside us, I was grinning like a Cheshire.

"That was the concierge. You have an invitation to the opera with Julian."

Taking the lovely piece of stationery, Mitch sighed. His eyes came to me. *"Looks like we are going out tonight."* Forgetting to speak and sign again, Mitch left Fred unsure what he said. Pouting, I stuck out my hip and crossed my arms, which made Mitch laugh. *"It's an opera. Must be a blessing to be deaf."*

"It is also harder to protect you in such a large gathering with numerous options for a sniper." Watching my hands, Mitch frowned. *"Lucky for you, I like a challenge."* Winking, I walked into the wardrobe to find something to wear.

"Did she say something about a shooter?"

"That this would be a good opportunity for one, yes. I better get changed."

"Mitch," Fred lowered his voice. "We've been friends since grade school, and I know you've never found a girl that just fits with you with the way your childhood fucked you over. Lyza may have been through her own pile of shit, but she ain't…"

"I need you and the team to get your head around the idea that my sex life is none of your business. Right now, Lyza is showing me how much we need to add to our training. She seems to be the only person here who understands that a good cover is in place all the time. I know how you all feel about this, but Lyza is part of the team, at least until the threat has passed." A moment of silence fell between them. "I know what we are doing, Fred. Neither of us is emotionally invested beyond the job, so keep your ideas to yourselves and start acting like she is my wife twenty-four-seven. If you don't believe it, no one else will."

Striding into the wardrobe, Mitch considered the dress I was holding. Screwing up his face, Mitch took it from me and threw it aside before grabbing a long, subtle dress that highlighted my curves. He held it up for me. *"This."*

"It barely covers my breasts."

"It will stop me falling asleep if I'm anticipating afterward."

"Because of the boner you'll have?"

Smirking, Mitch hung the dress up and used his free arm to pull me tight to him. "Let's have a shower."

Wet, Mitch's hands slipping over me as he screwed me nice and slow in the shower was unbelievable. My knee hooked over his hip, shoulders leaning back on the tiles while he controlled his every move, was driving me out of my mind. By the time we finished, I had to rush doing my makeup and hair to leave on time.

"Mitch, I thought tonight would be a good time to discuss that business you asked me to look into," Julian greeted him. "Lyza, stunning," he enunciated to ensure I could read his lips. When I blushed for his benefit, Julian seemed happy.

We took our seats in the box at a high level. When I moved to the place in front of Mitch, he and Julian took the back seats. "It doesn't bother her going to an opera she can't hear?"

Touching my shoulder, Mitch signed the question. Taking off my shoes, I pointed to the floor, put both my hands flat in front of me, and shook them side to side at the wrist.

"She can feel the vibrations through the floor." Moving closer, Mitch kissed me on the lips before taking his seat with Julian. At the banister, I stayed standing as I scanned around the theatre.

"As you suspected, Andre is negotiating with another firm. He's having a trial week with them currently. They are more costly than you, but the best. Supposedly, their security can be virtually undetectable in a crowd. That's what Andre wants; invisible security."

"If he already knows he is going with them, why did he bother talking to me?"

Applause broke out for the conductor. "Inside information is my guess. You're the biggest rival for that company. The owner was asking Andre to suss you out and see what you offer. That is how he scored the trial week."

My eyes spied a man slipping into a booth further around the theatre. He wasn't interested in the stage at all, but what was at his feet. When I turned, Mitch's attention came straight to me.

Hooking my index finger, I wiped the back of it in front of my cheek twice to indicate I needed the bathroom as I stepped out of the curtain. Just outside, Fred and Mark were chatting with Julian's security. Waggling my fingers at Fred, I waited for him to hand me his phone. 'Go stand in front of the boss and talk.'

Handing him the phone, I started jogging around the corridor. "Go with her; I'll tell the boss," Mark countered as I left.

Following me, Fred stayed a reasonable distance behind, letting my ruse of needing the bathroom and him being the bodyguard playout. Reaching the curtain for the place I'd seen the man, I stopped. Peeking inside, I could see him busy with what he was doing. Stepping in quietly, I remained in the shadow, ensuring he was alone.

Quietly, I stepped in behind him just as the female singer took the stage and started singing. The man let out a sigh and began jerking his arm in time with her singing. With my brows in my hairline, I looked over his shoulder.

Disgusted, I backed out of the booth. Some fans were sick. Turning to relay this to Fred, I found him kneeling on the ground, gun to his head. One of the two who tried to nab me in Switzerland twitching his finger near the trigger as he smiled over my head.

12

DESTROYING CLOTHES

PIVOTING, I SWUNG MY ARM BACK AND CAUGHT THE WRIST OF THE MAN behind me. His eyes widened just before my palm struck his nose, and I felt it give. Spinning into his body, I kept his arm under my control and pointing at his buddy. Firing as an impulse to his injury, he shot his partner in the shoulder.

Springing to his feet, Fred took down his assailant. Pirouetting under my guy's arm, I took it with me, and his shoulder popped audibly. The gun fell to the ground as I kicked the back of both knees in quick succession. Grabbing his head as he went down, I jerked my arms to the side and rear.

The crack was audible, and the give was evident in my hands. As his body went limp, he sagged to the ground. Fred was sparring with his assailant. Shaking my head, I picked up the discarded gun, took two steps forward, and pointed it at the man as I clicked off the safety. They both froze instantly.

Pointing to the ladies' bathroom, I indicated he walk ahead. Spying the dead body on the ground, Fred blinked at it, then at me. Looking around, he dragged the corpse behind us into the bathroom and deposited him in the last stall. Coming back out, Fred glared at me as he signed angrily. *"You killed him?"*

With a shrug, I knocked the air.

Shaking his head, Fred turned his attention to the man who now kneeled on the floor. "Why are you after her?"

Glaring at me, the guy snarled. "She was meant to be easy bait. No one said she could fight."

"Bait for what?"

"Wasn't told. Boss just pointed her out that first night in Rome and told us to bring her home."

"Who's the boss?"

"Forget it!"

Raising a brow, I shot his right thigh.

"Fuck! Is she nuts?"

Fred was looking at me, wide-eyed. "Possibly."

Holding up my hand, I slowly started counting down my five fingers as I aimed at his left thigh.

"Get fucked. I'm not telling you…"

Pulling the trigger, I was grateful they were kind enough to provide guns with silencers. Not that it made guns quiet. Silencers muffled the sound, made it harder to locate. Combined with the music going on outside, the shots shouldn't be heard by anyone.

Fred was cursing. The man was crying and swearing. Holding up my hand again, I aimed between his legs as I started dropping one finger at a time. The man spent the count calling me several vulgar terms. The man screamed as the bullet hit an inch below his manhood, tearing a hole in his pants at the close call.

"Fucker! Andre Gonzalez hired us." He continued to curse my birth, my mother, and my father.

Turning my face to Fred, I raised a brow. Turning to leave, Fred nodded. "We've got the name; let's go."

Barely aiming, I double tapped the man. Stopping with his mouth hanging open, Fred stood there, unable to voice his shock.

Cleaning the weapon, I stepped into the cubicle and put it back in the first guy's hand. Stepping out, I went to the mirror, frowning at the blood splatter across my cleavage. Thank god I'd gone with Mitch's suggestion of the black dress, but my makeup wouldn't survive the cleanup. Annoyed, I grabbed some paper towels, wet them, and cleaned myself up, Fred staring at me the entire time.

Once I was presentable, I flushed the paper towel down the toilet and led the way out, returning to Mitch and Julian. Standing outside the box seat, Mitch pretended to be on a phone call. Smiling at him, I stepped back inside, taking my place.

Shuffling forward, I rested my arms and face on the banister, enabling me to feel more of the vibrations. The singer was amazingly talented. Not enough that I would sit here batting off to it, but I guess everyone had their kinks. My eyes drifted back to the man in the far booth, his face caught in agony and bliss. He wasn't looking at the singer, so I dare say it was the opera itself that did it for him.

"I'm sorry, Julian. I have some business I need to deal with. We have to go." Stepping forward, Mitch tapped my shoulder. Lifting a brow as he gestured we were leaving, I slipped my shoes back on and went to stand by him while he said goodbye.

"You will be at the soirée tomorrow?"

"Yes, of course." Taking my hand, Mitch led me out. Fred still looked a little peaky with his wide-eyes and a slight green tinge to his skin. When we got to the car, Mitch went first, I ducked in after him, and Mark closed the door. "What happened?"

Updating them as we drove back to the hotel, Fred left out what I'd done and instead stated that two men made a grab for me, and after questioning, we knew who sent them.

"Status?"

Holding the pointer and middle fingers on both hands up, I dropped them both down to point away from me like an umpire when a goal is scored.

Obviously suspecting as much and that I was the executioner, Mitch nodded. "So, Andre wants you as bait? I guess what we need to know now is why?" The car was silent for several minutes. Leaning forward, Mitch put his hand on Fred's shoulder. "It's an experience, isn't it? Seeing her like that for the first time."

"It just comes out of nowhere. It's so unsuspecting. But it's also a thing of beauty to watch. It's terrifying."

"Absolutely." Giving Fred's shoulder another squeeze, Mitch sat back, appraising me.

Lifting a brow, I used my index and middle fingers on both hands to create a kind of hashtag, then wiped my hand away and lifted my shoulders in question. *"Does this mean no nookie?"*

Watching my hands, Mitch chuckled. Taking my hand, he put it to his groin so I could feel how hard he was for me. Encouraged, I rubbed it, and Mitch reacted by jerking against my hand. Slipping free from my seat belt, I climbed over, lifting my dress to straddle him. With little effort, I released his desire and fed it into my own.

Biting my lip, I moaned at how wonderful he felt inside of me, stretching me open, scratching that itch. Death for me was another man's opera. Keyed up, I was already on edge, and it wasn't going to take much to get me there.

"You know I can see that in the rearview mirror," Mark grumbled.

Mitch kneaded my hips and ass as he thrust up to meet my body with glazed eyes intent on me. "Stop looking in the mirror."

Hungry for him, I slammed my mouth against his as I came, Mitch taking five more deep thrusts to unload.

"Jesus, this is getting out of hand," Mark muttered to Fred in annoyance.

At the hotel, Mitch asked for one of the conference rooms to conduct some business. The concierge showed us to the room and left us to it. Stacey joined us minutes later. "Okay, it's clean. What happened?"

Filling everyone in on everything, Fred still looked a little peaky.

Jaw tense, Mitch started barking orders. "Stacey, look into Andre for me and find out why he would want leverage over me. Look into his connections and this other security company. They know about us, but I don't know about them. Mark, check the room security and find us five different ways to the cars if we need them; prioritize efficiency. I want us to be able to sleep tonight." After Mark and Stacey left to get started, Mitch turned to Fred. "You going to be okay?"

"Yes, it's just," Fred angled his body, so I couldn't read his lips. "She showed no hesitation, didn't even blink. It was like she's scrubbed clean of the moral compass."

"She was taken as a young girl and forced to this way of life, Fred. What did you expect? Pollyanna?" As I wandered around the room, Mitch kept his eyes on me.

"I'm just struggling. It was easy to hate her, see her as the enemy when I thought she wiped out your team. When I found out she was disabled, guilt gnawed at me about how we treated her. I hated that guilt because she deserved it. Then she didn't do it at all. We tortured a deaf girl for days, hurting her, refusing to get her medical treatment for a gunshot wound and broken ribs because she wouldn't talk. The shame is overwhelming. Then tonight, she goes from a graceful beauty to the danger we always thought she was. It's hard to get my head around."

Mitch listened to his friend. "You were doing your job."

"I know, but…"

"You were doing your job. She was doing hers. She could have told you the real killer's name and saved herself. She didn't."

"What are you saying?"

Standing up, Mitch collected my hand. Walking me back to the table, he stood me in front of Fred. Mitch pointed with his left hand, crossing his forearms and banging the wrists together with his right index and middle finger out. "Talk to him."

Watching Mitch's hands, I frowned and shook my head. Stepping behind me to stop me from turning away, Mitch wrapped his arms around me and repeated the gesture, then he pointed to Fred.

Frowning, Fred searched my eyes. Inhaling and exhaling, I steeled myself against everything that could happen at this moment.

Without voicing it this time, Mitch moved to where I could see him make his sharp gestures. *"Relieve his guilt. You know he doesn't deserve this."*

Gritting my teeth, my gestures displayed my annoyance. *"He tortured me. I know what he deserves."*

"Don't make me force this. Do it because it's right."

Our hands flying at each other, Fred blinked rapidly, his eyes showing he'd lost track of our words pretty much the same time Mitch stopped using SimCom.

Leaning forward with my shoulders raised, I circled my right fist with fingers down above my left upturned palm, then slammed the fist into my hand. *"Right? This entire situation is wrong. There has never been anything right about it."*

Eyebrows jumping, Mitch held his arms out to the side in question, then gestured between us. *"What about us?"*

"There is no us. You were very clear about that when I showed you empathy in Switzerland."

Jaw tightening, Mitch pulled out his phone and hit the screen. My left arm went numb. Glaring a thousand painful deaths in Mitch's direction, I took a step back. This was bullshit.

"Tell him the name."

Using just two fingers to give him the international gesture that he could go fuck himself, I gritted my teeth as ice-cold rushed up my throat. As I dropped into the Antarctic hell of the nano torture, Mitch's eyes shut tight in regret.

Coming to on the floor, I was groggy, felt washed out, and ached all over. Angry, I forced myself upright. Touching his fingers to his chin, Mitch jerked his hand forward, the final plea evident in his gesture but also in his sorrowful expression. Meeting Mitch's eyes with pure rebellion, I refused to back down. Swallowing hard, Mitch looked away. The suffocating cold smothered me again.

As I blinked my eyes open this time, Fred avoided my gaze, his feet shifting as he looked like he'd rather be anywhere but here. It felt like sandpaper was stuck under my eyelids. Standing firm, his face devoid of anything but patience, Mitch looked like he had all the time in the world.

Forcing myself to my knees, I struggled through the thrumming ache in my muscles. Lifting my hand as if I was going to sign, I gave Mitch the finger. An iceberg crashed into me, and I sank.

This time, I couldn't focus my eyes, so I didn't even try to get off the floor. I couldn't if I wanted to. My entire body ached beyond reason. Every muscle fiber was frayed, every nerve ending had frostbite, and it hurt just to breathe and blink. It was agony to exist. Swallowing a thousand razor blades, I cleared my throat a bit and forced my tongue to deliver my surrender in a gasp. "Noel."

Exhaling as he deflated into a chair, Fred cursed hard enough to make a grandmother blush.

Studying me, Mitch squatted by me. Pointing to me, Mitch made a fist leaving the thumb out, and tapped it to his temple before pointing off to the side of me to indicate someone else. "You knew him?"

"Yes." Unable to lift my arms to sign, I wheezed the answer as Mitch felt for my pulse. Eyelids fluttering closed, I saw grey eyes sparkling with lust and pleasure as I moved my body over Noel's in my memory. The look of sorrow in his eyes when I pulled that trigger.

Shaking his head, Fred sighed. "If she can speak, why does she always sign?"

"Why did she hold that name back when it could have saved her five years ago?"

"I don't know."

"Exactly." Removing his fingers from my neck, Mitch caressed the side of my face with tenderness. Turning my face away, I refused his kindness, gritting my teeth at the pain.

"Is she okay?"

Lifting me into his arms, Mitch sighed. "She's in a lot of pain. I'll take her up to the room and get her an aspirin."

"She sure can take a punch."

Turning to face Fred with me hanging in his arms, Mitch huffed. "I watched this device demonstrated on men twice her size. Most couldn't even stand the warning level. None of them coped with a full blast even once."

"She just took three hits."

"Makes you wonder what her life was like that she has that kind of pain tolerance, doesn't it?" Moving towards the door, Mitch carried me upstairs.

13

____

ANTAGONISM

HOT RUNNING WATER WAS MY HEAVEN. SITTING ON THE TILED FLOOR with the scalding shower beating down upon me, I didn't even try and move. The release of my seized muscles was gradual as the heat permeated the ice that encased me. Staying in the shower until my body thawed, I sat there staring at nothing, silent tears falling as that night in Turkey played on repeat in my head.

By the time I crawled out of the shower, hours had passed since we left the opera. Stealing one of Mitch's shirts, I put on underwear to sleep in tonight. No matter the chemistry between us, my physical interest in this arrangement just got tortured out of me. Lying down, I let exhaustion claim me. The bedroom door opening woke me; the light stabbing my eyeballs annoyed me. Opening my eyes to see the time, I realized it was morning.

Reaching Mitch's side of the bed, Stacey didn't bother keeping her voice down. "Mitch, I haven't been able to find anything on this other security company. I don't think it's a legalized business." She was just doing her job, but if I was her boss, she'd be dead by now.

Twisting to check the bed behind me, I saw Mitch sitting himself up to listen to Stacey. I must have been exhausted to have missed his coming to bed. Frustrated with being woken up again, I slipped out of bed and went to the bathroom, slamming the door hard enough to rattle the hinges.

My eyes were still sore from the torture, and I could see why in the mirror. One of my blood vessels had bled into my eyeball, stealing all the white and making me look like some kind of supernatural creature. Sadly, bruises and injuries were nothing new to me.

Turning on the taps, I washed my face and then dressed in my running gear. Mitch and Stacey were gone from the bedroom when I came out, so I made my way to the door. Unfortunately, Fred emerged from his bedroom as I passed.

Grabbing my elbow, Fred observed my eyes and flinched. "Where are you going?"

My eyelids shuttered in annoyance. Taking a breath, I forced my eyes to Fred's. Raising a brow, I pointedly looked at his hand on me. Cursing under his breath, Fred thought hard for the best way to ask the question, then settled with lifting his arms and shoulders.

Moving my arms in the way you would while running, I huffed.

"Not alone. Wait." Gesturing to the spot with a stern look, Fred went back into his room. When he emerged, he was dressed for the run as well.

In the gym, we took side by side treadmills. Warming up with me, Fred kept pace, studying me in a way that suggested he was looking for signs of injury or exhaustion. As I picked up speed, so did Fred. After I kept it up for thirty minutes, Fred shook his head. "I'd hate to have seen your training conditions."

Focusing on my run, I tuned him out as best I could, using the gym music as my focus. After an hour, Fred slowed his treadmill to a walk and cooled down. Reaching over, he hit the cool down button on my treadmill, slowing mine down. "There are other ways to work out your anger. Come with me."

Walking off, Fred spoke to a personal trainer, then was shown to a room. Finishing my cool down, I went into the room to find the trainer pulling out some kick pads and gloves. "Thanks." Dismissing the trainer, Fred continued to set up while I stretched out. "When you're ready, Lyza. Show me what you've got."

Raising a brow at Fred holding the pad, I pressed my lips together. Gesturing to him, I then pointed to my eyes, then stuck my thumb at my cheek before drawing my hand from the back of my head forward and over my eyes like I was pulling a veil over my face. He'd seen my skill last night, and I'd seen his. He didn't stand a chance against me.

Frowning at my hands, Fred's mouth pursed. "I'm not good with sign language, you know that. Can you talk to me?"

In response, I threw a flurry of punches and kicks at him until he was against the wall struggling to fight me off. In under thirty seconds, even with the pads to protect him, Fred was standing half in a ball trying to withstand the assault. Throwing a good last punch which made him grunt, I backed away. Pointing to him, I shook my head as I made a C in front of my face and flicked it to face me, then with thumbs out and fingers tucked, moved my hands in front of my chest in circles with the thumbs facing me. Fred wasn't good enough to train with me.

Huffing, Fred stood half bent over, trying to catch his breath. "I was trying to help."

For several long moments, we stood appraising each other. Sighing, I knelt down. Meeting Fred's eyes, I jabbed my thumb at my cheek and drew the veil forward to indicate last night. When Fred frowned, I gestured, holding a gun to the back of my head.

With his brow's scrunched, Fred moved behind me and pretended to hold a gun to my head, mimicking how our assailants kept him hostage last night. Five seconds later, Fred was on the floor with my knee on the nape of his neck, my fingers tapping the back of his head as if I had taken his gun. Having made my point, I released him.

Rolling to stare at me with wide eyes, Fred cursed. "Can you teach me that move?"

Getting back on my knees, I nodded. Going through the move slowly twice, I then swapped with him. Fred tried it three times slowly, and once he had the basics, I stopped playing easy. Flicking the back of his ear with my fingers, Fred cursed. "Ow, what was that for?"

Drawing my right hand up the back of my left in slow motion, I then pointed to Fred and dropped both my arms to point my index fingers forward. He was too slow and would be dead if I was the one holding the gun. To be successful, the first move needed to be faster than a twitch of my finger.

Grumbling, Fred got back on his knees. We practiced again, and again, and again. By the end of the hour, Fred was still too slow, but he was getting better. We called it quits when his phone rang.

"Mitch? Yeah, we're in the gym. Nah, in the boxing room training." Fred laughed at something Mitch said. "Not really. She's just kicking my ass repeatedly. Okay." He hung up. "Mitch wants us back upstairs."

After packing away the training gear, we headed up to the room. Mitch was in the lounge talking to Stacey over her laptop when I walked through. Neither of them acknowledged me, so I kept going to the bedroom to shower and dress first. This time when I emerged, room service had arrived with breakfast for Fred and me. We sat and ate while Stacey filled Mark and Fred in on her night's work.

When it got to the part where Stacey reached a dead end and dragged Mitch from the bed, Mitch took over. "In the last few hours, Stacey and I managed to identify the competition. Andre made a deposit payment to a company called Concealed. We haven't been able to determine the owner's name or anything else about the company."

Looking annoyed, Stacey crossed her arms in front of her chest. "There's no website or web-based information. From what we can tell, business for this company relies purely on word of mouth, or the owner approaches the clientele individually. It would appear, the close covert protection that we offer is their niche market, and they don't like the competition."

Mark sat forward, his frown creasing his forehead. "How does that explain Andre trying to kidnap Lyza?"

Scratching at the scruff on his face from not shaving this morning, Mitch shook his head. "It doesn't. Unless he was asked to provide Lyza in exchange for something that benefitted him."

Huffing, Mark sat back. "He has a major Jones for Lyza. The way he looks at her tells you that. Maybe he wants her for more nefarious purposes. The guy doesn't have a good reputation when it comes to women."

"Maybe we should let him have her and teach him a lesson." All the men stared at Stacey with their mouths hanging open and eyes falling out of their sockets. "What? She would kill him if he tried anything."

"If he drugged her, or worse?" Stacey swallowed the lump of guilt Mitch fed her.

Finished with eating, I stood up, disregarding all that was being said. Striding to the bedroom to collect the book I'd been reading, I ignored the phone when it started ringing beside the bed. Storming into the room, Stacey pushed past me to reach the phone.

"Hello? Mrs. Fairchild?" Stacey's brows furrowed, and my feet paused. "Yes, she's here. Uh, no, she's here beside me, but she can't take the phone. I'm sorry, Mrs. Fairchild is deaf. She wouldn't be able to hear you. Okay, I can do that." With her brows furrowing deeper, Stacey turned to face me. "You want me to tell her what?" Pupils dilating and mouth hanging open, Stacey swallowed and ensured she spoke clearly so I could read her lips. "Does she remember her mother's punishment for bigamy?"

Moving on instinct, Stacey stared wide-eyed at me as I tackled her. A loud bang sounded outside. A bullet zipped by my head as we fell down with a grunt from both of us.

Rolling immediately across the floor, I slammed the shutters shut on the window, then I raced into the lounge room. The others were reacting to the gunshot too. Fred slamming the shutters closed as I dived and took Mitch out of the line of sight. A bullet flying past him as we twisted and fell.

When Mitch went to get up, I blocked him and pinned him. Putting my mouth to his ear, I whispered urgently. "Stay down. It's you he wants." Mitch stared up at me, surprised. Moving Mitch to a safe place with my body between him and the window, I then raced into Fred's room and stayed covered while I peered through the window to find the sniper.

Appearing opposite me, Fred pointed. "The muzzle flash came from that building over there."

Peering across the way, I searched for a glint, but without a sight, I had no chance of finding them.

"We need to leave."

Shaking my head, I pointed both index fingers down.

"You think they want us to leave, to draw us out?"

Nodding, I kept my eyes on his lips.

"Damn it!" Fred moved back into the other room.

Watching the building across the way a little longer, I reached out, opened the shutter on the other side slightly to make it look like someone peering through, then moved the curtain. A bullet ripped through it a moment later.

"Lyza!" Mitch's panic chased me down the hall.

Running followed, and I quickly closed the shutter. Diving to the ground as bullet after bullet fired through the shutter blindly, I hid on the other side of the bed and stayed down.

Sirens sounded outside in the street. The gunfire stopped. Half crawling, half running into the room to reach me, Mitch checked me over. Slapping his pawing hands away, I held my hand up, then made a short open-handed gesture in front of my body.

Watching my hand, Mitch sagged beside me in relief. We sat there, just breathing until the suite doors flew open, and police rushed the hall. At that point, Mitch put his arm around me as if he was comforting me and let the police believe I was in shock.

The police guarded us as they escorted us out of the suite. We went to another room to wait out the 'all clear' to collect our gear, and then we moved to another place. There wasn't that much destruction done, just a few holes in plaster, really. The hotel was more concerned with our safety than the damages.

As soon as we had privacy again, Stacey let loose. "That wasn't about us! That was about her! That phone call was for Lyza. A man called and asked me to give her a message about her mother's bigamy. That's when the gunfire started. As soon as I said it, and she read my lips, they started shooting, and Lyza knew. She moved to knock me over before the first gunshot."

With his brows furrowed, Mitch turned to me. "What were the caller's exact words?"

"To ask Lyza if she has forgotten her mother's punishment for bigamy."

With Mitch's focus on me, I saw the moment it clicked. *"Are you married?"* Glaring at his hands as he asked me that question, I gritted my teeth. "Lyza, are you married to someone other than me?"

Pointing to one side of my chest, I spun my hand to touch the other side, my gestures short and sharp. *"We are not married."*

Taking a deep breath, Mitch nodded. "You're married, though. That's why you told me it could never happen."

Eyes glassy, I knocked the air once.

"Shit!" Sitting down, Mitch hid his head in his hands.

Tilting his head watching Mitch and me, Fred blinked. "I don't get it. Why would Lyza, already being married, bother whoever is trying to kill you? It's not like they would know. When we searched, we couldn't find anything on her."

Exhaling, Mitch lifted his head and met my eyes. The accusation was there in his gaze as I looked away. "He knows she is married because he recognized her. If my gut is right, this isn't about my business anymore, but the fact that I have his wife."

"What?" Mark stood outraged.

Fred sat back as if Mitch slapped him. "Noel? The guy she saved you from. That's her husband, and that's who is gunning for you?"

Eyes growing wide, Stacey opened her laptop. "Maybe this isn't about the business. Perhaps, he recognized you at some point and remembered you. What's his last name?"

Everyone looked at me. Sliding paper and pen in front of me, Mitch gestured I write his name down. With a stern shake of my head, I stood to leave the room. Mitch got in my way to stop me. Blocking his attempt to grab me, I was ready for when he countered. In a blink, I took him down and pinned him with my knee on his throat. Everyone stood in shock.

Glaring at Mitch's bulging eyes, I started signing. *"You trained five years. I trained my entire life. You can't beat me."* Releasing him, I stood up, moving out of reach. I waited until Mitch was sitting up, the annoyance of not even standing a chance with me showing in his eyes. *"Noel is even better than me. We were the best in our generation, that's why we were married. If he finds out, I gave you his name, what he will do to me..."*

Glancing away, Mitch took a breath and stood up. "I need his name, Lyza."

The warning shot went down my arm. Glaring at Mitch, tears welled in my eyes. The numbness was frustrating but not painful. Using my only good arm to speak, I gritted my jaw. *"If you take me down like last night, I will be useless as a bodyguard tonight."*

"I need Noel's full name."

The tension snapped as Stacey called out. "I have it! I did a search for Concealable and the name Noel and Lyza in the Interpol database. Noel D'Avive is the legal owner of the Sword Corporation, of which Concealable is a division. It has Lyzebel D'Avive listed as missing, presumed dead. It also has her listed as his spouse."

14

______

SOIRÉE

When I came out dressed for the evening at Julian's party, Mitch was sitting on the bed. *"Stacey ran the name Lyzebel D'Avive. Other than being married at age eighteen, the rest was generic cover information. British, deaf and mute, educated."*

Watching his hands, I didn't react to what they found. Sitting on the other side of the bed to put my shoes on, I then stood ready to leave. Except, Mitch got in my way when I went to pick up my clutch. *"You said you trained your entire life, not ten years. That would mean your mother trained you from birth. Is that right?"*

Ignoring Mitch, I tried to step past. Mitch got back in my way. *"You see, that doesn't make sense. She escaped for you. Became a traitor to give her child a better life. Why would your mother train you for that lifestyle?"*

Gesturing to Mitch, I touched my hand to my chest and swept it away towards him before I shouldered past him, opening the bedroom door to leave. He could believe that shit if he wanted. It's incredible what people read into things to convince themselves that there is goodness in everyone.

Grasping my elbow, Mitch pulled me back and shut the door. *"Explain it to me."*

Glaring at him, this wasn't the time to be getting into this. Gesturing to my wrist where a watch would sit, I shook my head. *"We will be late. We are safer being early than late."* Dropping my hands, I opened the door again.

Mitch shut it. *"I need to understand what happened to you. How did you end up in this life? Why do you feign being deaf, to the point of denying it even to me when you know, I know you're not?"*

Frustrated, I threw my arms out. *"Why do you think I can hear?"*

"You heard me. Your eyes were on my wound when I called you an angel. You saved my life, and you heard me." Caressing my face tenderly, Mitch moved as if to kiss me.

Stepping back, I gritted my teeth at the sincerity in his eyes. *"Tonight could be problematic. We shouldn't go."*

Observing my hands, Mitch exhaled. *"Julian secures a lot of business for me. We need to go."*

Throwing my clutch on the sofa, my frustration came out in my harsh gestures. *"Noel wants you dead for more than two reasons now. He will make sure it happens."*

"Your mother was killed as punishment, right?"

Bowing my head, I bit my lip and avoided his eyes. Why wouldn't he listen to me? Noel would stop at nothing to get me. The fact he'd already found Mitch and was trying to finish the job he started five years ago just added to it.

Stepping closer, Mitch scooped me into his arms, holding my lower body tight to his, so I had to rely on reading his lips. "Are you scared he will kill you for marrying me?"

Exhaling, I shook my head. God, death would be the best I could hope for if any of Chapter got hold of me.

"Then what?"

"I'm scared he won't kill me. That he will get your device to control me and torture me endlessly."

Watching my hands, Mitch's face fell. "That isn't going to happen, Lyza."

"How can you be sure?"

Mitch hesitated. "You just need to trust me."

"You don't trust me."

"Can you blame me? Jesus, even sex means nothing to you. I've looked into your eyes, and other than a way to get off, I mean nothing to you. Would you trust you?"

No, I wouldn't. Mitch was too smart to fall for that. I knew that before it started, I was just too horny to care. Knowing Noel was close changed everything. Even if Noel hadn't been watching before this, I had no doubt, after this afternoon, that he was close. Caressing my face with his free hand, Mitch gazed into my eyes. "Do you love him?" He asked without signing, so I watched his lips out of habit, then met his eyes.

Did I love Noel? No. I wasn't given a choice in Noel being my partner, but I grew to care for him. When Mitch brushed his mouth across mine, I fought not to chase those soft lips and kiss them for everything I could get from them. Fighting not to respond to the fire his nearness stirred in me, I struggled to withhold my carnal longing for Mitch and how wonderfully he could play my body.

Lips teasing along my jaw, Mitch spoke, his hands busy feeling my body to sign for me. "Does he make you come so hard you forget yourself and call out his name?"

The truth was a clump of cotton wool in my throat since I genuinely couldn't remember sex being as good as it was with Mitch. But it was years between the two, and Noel satisfied me during our time together. Easing back, I watched Mitch's luscious lips.

"If he takes you, will he love you, or will he use you just as they did?"

Closing my eyes, I pushed away from Mitch. He released me. Taking a breath to calm my desire, I lifted my gaze to meet his and pointed to his chest. Touching my index and middle finger to my chin, I pulled it away to have all five fingers spread open in front of me. It was hypocritical of him to make that accusation when Mitch was using me as they did.

Mitch looked away. Waiting for a heartbeat, I clarified things for him. *"Noel was raised like me. He won't let emotion get in his way."*

Mitch's brows furrowed. *"But he does, doesn't he? That's why he didn't kill you five years ago. That's why he didn't shoot you today when he could have. He wasn't your choice, but you were his. I heard him beg you to come with him when you saved me. He loves you."*

"We are not taught to love."

Observing my hands, Mitch considered me. *"Love is instinct, not learned. He turned on the sword and arrow, which means we have a common enemy. How do I contact the sword and arrow?"*

My eyes went wide. *"You don't!"* Moving away from him, I wiped my head, trying to figure out how I ended up smack bang in the center of this mess. *"If you turn him in, you turn me in."*

"They think you're dead."

"We would have to use the channels that were opened for me to contact them. As soon as we did that, they would know I live, and they would come after me."

"They would deal with Noel first."

"Not necessarily."

"Would they kill me?"

The question made me consider Mitch, knowing while the Chamber may not bother with Mitch, my father may have other plans. *"You saved me. As long as you walk away from me, no. If they find out what you know, they will see you as a risk."*

"If you don't tell, I'm safe?"

Knocking the air, I hoped I wasn't lying.

"What do you need?"

"I need us to leave." Opening the door, I stalked out to meet Fred, Mark, and Stacey.

"I have some hair accessories for you," Stacey informed me, indicating the table. Four different fasteners sat waiting. Two were decorative clips; the other two were three-inch-long pins with jewels.

Drawing down the outside of my left arm, I then traced the outline of my splayed fingers until I finished at the thumb and lifted my shoulders.

Staring at my hands, Stacey's mouth popped open.

"Yes," Mitch knocked the air as he stepped to her other side. "Tracking devices and listening. The team will be able to hear whatever you do."

Lifting a brow, I touched my bladed hand to my temple then tapped the same fingertips to the tip of my shoulder. *"Remind me to lose them before going to the toilet."*

Reading my gestures, Mitch grinned.

Picking up the pin that matched my dress best, I inserted it through the French-knot in my hair. Selecting a clip, I added that to the side of my head for decoration.

"They will interfere with each other," Stacey complained.

Holding my index finger up, knuckle facing her, I placed my right hand palm up into my left, then formed an L on my right and put the thumb into my left palm and let the index finger fall forward. It was always better to have more than one device and switch on the backup if the first was lost.

"What the hell is she saying?"

"One is a backup. You lose contact with Lyza, then you switch to the other." Placing his hand into my lower back, Mitch indicated the door. "Let's go."

We arrived at the event twenty minutes later. It wasn't an intimate gathering but more a charity fundraiser. There was a quartet playing in one corner, waiters moved through the crowd carrying trays of drinks and finger foods, and two dancers moved intimately on the small dais. Both dancers were male and made for quite an exciting show.

"Mitch," Julian greeted as we found him in the crowd. "I heard you had some trouble at your hotel this afternoon."

"Yes, it appears someone didn't like us being there."

"Is everyone alright?"

"Yes, though, it gave Lyza quite the fright. She's not happy about being here tonight. She wanted to go home."

Watching me search the crowd, Julian sighed. "She does look unhappy to be here. Being shot at is never fun, so I can't blame her. Still, you can assure her there will be no trouble here tonight."

"Good, or I might be divorced by midnight."

Laughing at Mitch's joke, they switched to talking about business.

Keeping my eyes on the crowd, I saw when Andre arrived and the couple with him. Exhaling, I turned so I could watch them out of the corner of my eye. Touching Mitch's arm to get his attention, I waited for him to face me.

"Excuse me, Julian. What is it?"

Fist to my chest, I waved my hand over my shoulder, then wrapped my right fist in my left hand, shaking it twice. Crossing my fingers, I put them to my chest then moved them outwards before pointing to the floor. Watching Mitch's pupils constrict, I directed him using a discreet finger to indicate my former colleagues.

Eyes glancing over my shoulder, Mitch frowned as he signed. *"I only see Andre talking to other guests."*

"The woman and man he is talking to are his overt security and my former colleagues. They are fails."

Watching my hands, Mitch's brows furrowed. *"Fails?"*

"They didn't pass the final test and were kicked out. Noel must have hired them. The man was good. There is no reason he should have failed."

"You think he failed purposefully?"

"I am starting to believe Noel was recruiting within."

Observing our silent exchange, Julian lifted a brow and cleared his throat. "Everything good, Mitch?"

"Lyza is getting nervous about being here." Wrapping his arm around my waist, Mitch moved me closer to him.

"I suppose that is to be expected." Looking over my shoulder, Julian smiled. "Andre, how good of you to make it."

Mitch turned us to watch Andre move towards us, his eyes intent on Mitch. Smiling, Andre greeted Julian first, then Mitch, before stepping forward to kiss my cheeks. "Lyza, beautiful as ever."

Wenda stayed by Andre's side, but instead of introducing her, he ignored her as he struck up a conversation. Ensuring the men weren't watching her, Wenda caught my eye. Wrapping her hand around her throat, her eyes filled with sympathy as she turned an invisible doorknob. She then paddled her hands before her as if she were floundering.

Forcing my throat to swallow, I looked over my shoulder. Breok was nowhere to be seen. Focusing back on Wenda, I watched as she scooped her hands up to join together in front of her then pointed to her chest. I shook my head slightly. Facial expression drawn in helplessness, she insisted I go with her again.

Gripping my waist tighter, Mitch pulled me closer to him, letting me know he'd seen Wenda signing me this time. Realizing too, Wenda dropped her hands, looking down at her feet in regret.

"Excuse me a moment," Julian stepped away to go deal with something.

"Wendy. Why don't you take Lyza to get a fresh drink and something to eat while Mr. Fairchild and I discuss business?"

Taking a sip of his drink, Mitch didn't relinquish his hold. "Lyza is fine here. It's not like she can overhear anything."

Grinding his teeth, Andre glanced at Wenda and jutted his chin back towards the bar. Waiting for Wenda to walk away, Andre eyed Mitch and the way he was holding me close. "I heard about the attack on you at the hotel today."

"Good news travels fast."

"You've made a significant enemy, it would seem."

"Yes, though, I don't know why." Stepping a little closer so that his height domineered over Andre, Mitch lifted a brow. "I see you've decided to go with another security firm?"

Andre's eyes widened a little. "Why would you think that?"

"Wendy is an overt bodyguard. She hides it well, but you still treated her like one. You didn't acknowledge her or introduce her. One of the things I teach my clients is to treat their bodyguards like their best friends. It ensures the true relationship is hidden better."

Andre looked annoyed. "I will definitely practice that."

"Well, it seems we have no business left to discuss. It was a pleasure meeting you, Andre." Mitch offered his hand, and Andre reluctantly shook it. Taking my hand, Mitch led us to another part of the room, where he started talking with another group of people.

Touching his arm to gain his attention, I waited while Mitch's eyes scanned the room as he casually turned towards me. Hooking my finger, I brushed the back of it against my cheek twice.

Assessing my hands, then my eyes, a frown marred Mitch's handsome features as he nodded, letting me go. Making my way through the crowd, I moved Mitch's phone from my palm into my clutch, having thieved it while he was holding me close earlier. I couldn't chance him making me vulnerable at the wrong moment.

Making my way down the hall looking for the bathroom, I didn't hurry, leaving an opening on purpose. Wenda needed to know why I was with Mitch. Just after I stepped inside the bathroom, Wenda joined me.

Holding her fingers in the devil or rock music symbol, Wenda touched the index finger to her nose before sweeping her hand to touch the outside of her hand to her chest in apology. *"I had to tell them. Noel is here, and he's not leaving without you."*

Biting my lip as Wenda signed and verbalized, I shook my head.

Wenda looked torn. *"I don't want to hurt you. Please, I don't know why you are with Fairchild, why you married him, but you need to leave with me now."*

Pointing to my chest, I made a C with my thumb and index in front of my face, then snapped it back to face my hand the other way. *"I can't, he can hurt me."*

Wenda frowned. *"Fairchild?"* When I nodded, Wenda placed one open palm in the other and opened her arms out to the side in question.

"He saved me but wanted me to stay with him. If I try to leave him, I'll die." Between the nano and the daily tablets to prevent the poison from killing me, I was honest.

The door opened as Breok came into the bathroom. "What's taking so long?" Annoyed, he marched forward to take my elbow. "Let's go, he's waiting."

When I blocked his grab for me, Breok reacted.

"Breok, no, don't..." Wenda's words fell on deaf ears.

Breok tried to grab me, I avoided him and struck out. Unable to stand by doing nothing, Wenda joined in with Breok. My lips turned up as my adrenaline surged. It had been too long since I'd had a proper fight. Frustrated and angry as I was tonight, Breok and Wenda were about to help relieve me. Honestly, it wasn't a fair fight.

15

EXES AND FAMILY

Using the mirror, I tidied myself up. No blood, but my neat French-roll was a mess, and I was going to bruise from the hits I took. Satisfied that I was neat enough to get to the exit without drawing too much attention, I straightened and checked the two unconscious bodies slumped over the toilet. I couldn't kill them. Well, I couldn't kill Wenda. Since Breok was her husband, I didn't want to kill him.

One last check of my reflection and ensuring the torn strap of my dress was tucked away out of sight, I left the bathroom, locking the door before pulling it closed. Making my way back out to the main party, I searched for Mitch, spotting him with Fred by the exit.

With a deep breath in, I scanned the crowd for any dangers. Not seeing any other familiar faces, I started moving through the crowd towards Mitch. Halfway to him, when Mitch found me, his eyes locked onto mine, distracting me.

A man stepping in front of me blocked my view of Mitch. The face was that of the stranger in Níce, the one surrounded by women at the pool. Exhaling in annoyance, I went to step past him, but he put his arm out to the side to prevent it. That made me look at him properly.

"I thought you were dead. I thought they killed you when they caught you."

Scrunching my forehead as I studied this stranger's face in more detail, I found nothing about it was familiar. Meeting his grey eyes, I observed a sense of recognition, hurt, and regret shining back at me. My eyes widened. The face was barely recognizable, but those grey eyes.

Mouthing his name, my eyes itched as my stomach sank into the pits of oblivion. Reaching up, I touched his face, cataloging the alterations. His mouth was wider, nose narrower, forehead broader. He was still handsome but different. Those eyes were the same.

"Hello, Lyzebel." Happy that I recognized him, Noel smiled. Turning his face into my palm, he kissed it before pulling back to look at me. "I knew that woman in the cell wasn't you, though the plastic surgery was good. Still, when I heard the rumor you lived, I was curious enough to risk going. It confirmed for me that you were already dead, and it was a trap. How long have you been free?"

Watching his lips, I swallowed as I pointed to my sternum, shook my head as I waved my hand, then crossed my arms in front of me like I was chained and pulled them down and open to indicate freedom. No matter what it looked like, I was far from free.

Blinking wide eyes up at my husband, I hadn't even begun to comprehend what he revealed when my left arm went dead. Noticing my shoulder drop, Noel frowned as I cringed with the discomfort; my right-hand lifted to cradle my dead arm.

"Lyzebel?"

Biting my lip, I understood Mitch heard and witnessed my encounter with his enemy, and he wasn't taking chances. With his phone in my clutch, that answered my question about there being multiple devices.

Worrying, Noel moved to wrap his arm around me. "Let's get you out of here."

Ice raced up my neck, lancing into my brain, and the world went dark.

"IT'S OKAY. My wife occasionally faints."

Opening my eyes just as Mitch lifted me into his arms, I groaned as he started carrying me away. Fred was clearing a path. Gritting my teeth, I dropped my head to look back at the crowd as we stepped up the two stairs to the exit. Grey eyes in an unfamiliar face watched me being carried away, caught between concern and rage. Closing my eyes, I trembled in Mitch's arms as we made our way out to the car.

"Stacey, pack our gear. We are leaving Rome tonight. Organize the plane, and we will pick you up from out front of the hotel in twenty minutes."

Listening to Mitch give directions to thin air, I struggled to lift my arms to sign. *"I need a hot shower."*

"There's no time."

"You shouldn't have taken me out. I'm useless to you like this. Noel wasn't going to abduct me in front of all those guests."

Capturing my hands, Mitch held them in his. "We heard his people grab you in the bathroom. I wasn't taking the chance." His face was stern as he looked me over. "Where is my phone?"

My eyes dropped to my clutch on the seat between us. Releasing my hands, Mitch opened the purse and took his phone back. *"I needed to make sure you didn't cripple me in the bathroom."*

"You knew they were coming for you?"

"I hoped to persuade them why I couldn't go with them. How many devices are there, and who has them?"

"Only I have access. The rest is not for you to know."

"If Noel gets even one of the devices..."

Gritting his jaw, Mitch glared at me. *"Stop worrying about that and start worrying what happens if I don't get us out of Rome fast enough."*

Pushing through the muscle tension, I sat straight and took a deep breath.

Mitch's phone rang. Pressing the button, he answered it. "Julian? Is he still there? Did he make a move to follow us? How long ago did he make the phone call?" Listening, Mitch looked at his watch. "Thank you." Mitch hung up. "Noel D'Avive didn't even try to follow us. He ordered himself another drink, sat quietly by himself for a few minutes, then made a phone call. He is still at the party."

Heart pounding, my eyes went to Fred, who was driving, my voice weak and wavering. "Turn off this road."

Looking in the rearview at me, Fred frowned. "What?"

"She can talk?" Mark looked astounded.

"This is the direct route back to the hotel. Get off it, now…"

An engine roared then a truck burst out of a side street at high-speed, t-boning our car off the main road and into the opposite side street. The impact sent our vehicle into a roll. We rolled three times; I counted each time I came upright again.

When we stopped, we were upside down. Releasing my seat belt, I dropped to the roof, cringing as broken glass from the windows cut into my bare back. My already aching body screamed from the sharp drop. The side airbags were slowly deflating. "Stacey, get out of the hotel now," I wheezed, knowing she could hear me. "Don't wait. Go to whatever safe house you guys have."

Visually, I checked on the others. Mark and Mitch took the brunt of the impact. Mark was in a bad way. Mitch was unconscious and looked like he'd been in a punch up and lost. Checking his pulse, I exhaled in relief that he was alive and his heartbeat strong. Fred was moaning but not entirely with it.

The sounds of doors opening caught my attention. Grabbing Fred's gun, I slid out of my window, putting me away from the approaching danger. Gritting my teeth on the ache in every muscle and fiber in my body, I moved behind the car. Ducking behind the dumpster that stopped our roll, as the truck doors shut. Checking the rounds, I chambered a bullet and clicked off the safety.

There were three men. Two of them pried the door open to check on Mark. "This one is dead. The other two probably won't last the next few minutes," one announced in French as he checked them all. "The girl is gone, probably taking the opportunity to escape." Standing up, he looked down the road. "You two, go after her. She won't have gotten far. Remember, she's one of us. Use the taser to take her down and bring her back alive. I'll deal with this lot."

The other two took off, running down the road. Waiting until they got to the next intersection, I watched the threat here move around to this side of the car to deal with Fred. Kneeling, he blocked Fred's nose and mouth, planning to suffocate him. They wanted it to look like an accident.

Slipping my shoes off, I snuck across the road. Raising the gun, I brought it down hard to brain him. Ducking at the last second, he turned, barely blocking my next strike. We engaged quickly. When he tried to stand, I shifted my body, throwing a leg over his head and wrapping my thighs around his neck before swinging my body around, taking him off balance and back to the ground.

As he landed on top of me, I had my gun ready. Firing twice, I used his body to silence the gun. Blinking at me with his mouth hanging open, he rolled off me. Gaining my feet, I searched his pockets, finding his phone and keys. Pressing the button on the key fob, I heard a double beep just out on the street. Satisfied I had wheels, I put a bullet in his head.

Running out of time, I released Fred's seatbelt and pulled him from the car. More conscious now, he was able to take his weight as I helped him up. Not questioning me, Fred waited as I crawled over the broken glass and struggled to get Mitch out of the car. The bastard was heavy as all…

Grabbing my underarms as I got my upper body free, Fred helped pull us both free of the vehicle. "What about Mark?"

Since I wasn't facing Fred, I ignored him and slid out from beneath Mitch. "Help me get Mitch to their car."

Grunting as he lifted Mitch's weight, Fred struggled to get him up. Once they were both upright, I took Mitch's other side, and we moved quickly back to the street. Pressing the key fob to locate the car, we dragged Mitch to it, putting him in the back seat.

When I opened the driver's door, Fred stopped me and turned me to face him. "We need to get Mark."

Shaking my head, I dragged my finger across my neck. Making the heavy-metal sign, I touched the tip of my index finger to my nose before moving the outside of my hand to my chest sympathetically in apology.

Deflating, Fred shook his head. "It doesn't matter. We need to take him with us." The phone I grabbed started ringing. Fred groaned, rubbing his head from crown to forehead and over his face. "We don't have time, do we?" Shaking my head, I put my hand on his shoulder in empathy. "My head is messed. Can you drive?"

Really? Mitch tortured me, and I'd crawled out of a car wreck before hauling two men three times my weight out of the car. Did I have to do all the heavy lifting? I guess I trusted myself before them.

Dropping into the driver's seat of the sports sedan, I started the engine. Jumping into the back seat with Mitch, Fred checked his pulse.

"Hospital?" Pulling onto the street, I gunned the accelerator and sped away from the scene.

Shaking his head in the rearview mirror, Fred leaned forward, putting his thumb to his nose with index and middle up on an angle. Fred dropped them down, then he sat back. Following the signs for Germany, I focused on the sharp turns to get us out of here. Finding Mitch's phone, Fred put it to his ear.

"Stacey, where are you? We are heading there too. We are going to need Lennon, his team, and a car." Fred waited and listened. "Got it." Hanging up the phone, Fred input the address she gave him in the Sat Nav. It took us ten minutes to get to the location.

When Fred went inside the dealership, I jumped in the backseat and checked on Mitch. His pulse was still strong, and his breathing steady. Opening his eyelids, I checked his pupils. "You're conscious, aren't you? Barely, but you are with us. I'm guessing a bad concussion."

Gritting my teeth as an aftershock of lightning and ice surged through my body, I inhaled then controlled the exhale to manage the pain. "Don't worry; we'll get you to your team as soon as we can. Then, we need to discuss this Nano shit."

A brand-new SUV pulled up beside us. Fred got out, opened the door for the back seat, then came to this car and opened the door beside Mitch. "Let's get him in the other car."

How they purchased a car this late at night with ten minutes notice was beyond me but damn impressive. Helping Fred move Mitch, I cursed internally with my pain. Groaning, Mitch held his weight a little. Jumping behind the wheel again, I set the seat and mirrors to my liking. After Fred settled in the back with Mitch, I got us moving again.

The phone I stole started ringing again. Tapping me on the shoulder, Fred opened his palm.

Handing him the phone, I met his eyes in the rearview. "They spoke fluent French."

With a nod, Fred answered it. "Oui? Oui, nous l'avons." Hanging up, he threw the phone out the window. "I've bought some time. He told me he'd meet us at the compound."

Not reassured, but I would take his professional experience over my paranoia. The navigation system directed me out of Rome, out of Italy, through Slovenia, and crossing the Alps into Germany. Mitch didn't wake up, but Fred checked his pulse regularly. At every border, Fred phoned Stacey to check her progress and update her on ours.

We had to stop for fuel and bathrooms. Since blood covered the front of me, Fred paid and got us food, then came back to the car and insisted I eat while he checked my back before driving on.

"Your back is cut up, but nothing serious. Most of it has already crusted over." He signed poorly, but I got the gist. "You knew they were going to hit us?"

Signing my response, I gave up when Fred's brows furrowed and just used my voice, cringing on the strain. "I worked with Noel for years. I've seen him pull that move before."

Finishing my food, I got back behind the wheel, a large cup of coffee waiting for me in the cupholder. Three hours later, I pulled into the driveway of a house and parked in front of the door. Two burly men came out to greet us. Ignoring me, they asked Fred for details as they carried Mitch inside.

Sitting in the car, I closed my eyes as my mind replayed what Noel told me. He'd been to the jail and seen the woman Mitch left in my place. When? Before or after she died? Either way, he'd missed me by a matter of hours since she died the same night.

My door opened before Fred bent down to assess me, his eyes angry. "What are you still doing out here?" Interestingly, his signing improved with his temper.

"Taking a moment."

Considering me a moment longer, Fred offered me his hand as his face morphed into sympathy. "Come inside."

With a massive sigh, I stepped out, cringing with the movement. When my legs buckled, Fred caught me and waited until I steadied to escort me inside to a room, so I could clean up. "Stacey is an hour behind us. She will have your clothes. You need to rest. Once the team finishes with Mitch, they'll check us."

"Will he be okay?"

"Lennon is the best Doctor we know in Europe. He will make sure of it."

Confidant Mitch would only hire the best Doctor to keep on retainer, I closed the door of the room. Stripping off, I looked at the bruises blooming over my body, a combination of the fight at the party and the accident. Blood smeared my back, the darker areas highlighting lacerations. Muscle soreness was kicking in, and I finally acknowledged I was injured.

Poking the tender spots carefully, I assured myself it was just a few cuts and mostly soft tissue injury. Stepping into a hot shower to ease my aches, I hissed at the sensation of someone striking matches across the open wounds on my back. Fresh blood circled the drain. Giving up when the water refused to wash clear, I turned off the taps and wrapped a towel around me.

When I entered the bedroom, the nurse Mitch brought to the jail was waiting. "Need anything?"

Tapping my head, I closed my eyes.

"You have a headache?"

Coming closer, she took my face in her hands, feeling around my head, moving it to check my neck. After reviewing my eyes and seeming satisfied I wasn't severely damaged or suffering a concussion, she gave me aspirin.

"You have a mild whiplash. Can I check the rest of you?" Her eyes visually examined some of the bruising on my left arm and shoulder.

Dropping my towel to the floor, I kept drinking the water I'd used to swallow the aspirin.

The nurse blinked twice, her eyes zeroing in on my hip. "Oh, wow, you took a hard hit." Feeling around it, she frowned when I flinched. "I don't think you've broken anything. Let's rest it for now, and I'll recheck it later. Let's deal with your back."

Gathering together some supplies, I stood by the bathroom sink while she removed a few shards of glass with tweezers. Flinching each time, I grumbled curse words in my head as blood started pooling around my ankles, but outwardly, no sound. Using sterile water, the nurse washed my back clean before dabbing each of the cuts with antiseptic cream to help stop it bleeding and heal. When she started to open a plaster to cover the wounds, I grabbed her wrist and shook my head.

"Trust me; these are not the guys you want to give blood samples to. What did you think they took all that blood for last time?" She raised a brow. When I frowned, she exhaled. "It's how they made the Nanos and the toxin to control you. It's all specific to your blood and your genetic makeup. Just like the trigger is connected to his."

My brows bunched as she went to step behind me again. Tightening my grip on her wrist, I held on until she met my eyes.

"Oh, they didn't tell you. If Mitch dies, so do you. But, even if he has a quick death, you will suffer, hit after hit. The continuous activation of the Nano until your heart gives out."

Releasing her wrist, I blinked a few tears free. Stepping behind me, she started covering up the cuts on my back with strips of some transparent film.

"I'm sorry for what you are going through. I was the guinea pig of that device. That Doctor everyone thinks is so wonderful is my husband. He's a brilliant man. He saved Mitch five years ago, that's how they became friends. He saved me too. When my Doctor diagnosed my cancer, he invented the nanodevice to cure me. Your Nanos are curing you of your genetic disorder too, but it makes you a slave to their will."

Her hand pressure increased in her anger. "My husband cheats on me. I caught him one day and tried to leave him. That's when I found out the Nanos inside me had a secondary purpose." Her hands dropped away. "He made sure I can never leave him." She applied the film to the last cut. "Now, I work for him and have helped him do to you what he did to me. I apologize for that. I never expected Mitch to utilize this technology. He always seemed more moral than that, but I guess every man has his breaking point."

The nurse dropped her hands against her thighs with a slap. Facing forward until she started gathering up her supplies, I schooled my emotions. It never failed to surprise me how much people revealed in the presence of someone they believed couldn't hear them. Picking up the towel, I wrapped it around me.

"Okay, I'll let you rest."

Grabbing her arm as she went to walk out, I flicked my eyes to the door.

"He'll be fine. He's already starting to talk."

Letting her go, I waited until the door closed to crash on the bed. It was out of my hands for now. Closing my eyes, I considered all the information thrown at me tonight. It was all pieces of a large and complicated puzzle. Exhaling, I wiped it all away for now. I'd think better after some sleep.

16

OPPORTUNITIES

A FEW HOURS LATER, SOMEONE OPENING MY DOOR WOKE ME. SINCE I didn't want to be awake and feel the hurt of the last twenty-four hours, I pretended I wasn't. The covers lifted as a body slid into bed with me, moving gingerly. Opening my eyes, I could make out Mitch's silhouette in the darkness. Wrapping himself around me, he settled down. "Thank you for saving our lives."

With him holding me, I went back to sleep. Well, until someone started banging on the door. Groaning, Mitch lifted his head as he rolled onto his back. "Come in."

Stacey walked in, switching on the light. This chick and her middle of the night 'light popping' was testing my inner calm. "What are you doing in here? I thought you were in the other room?" Dropping my bag on the floor, she ignored me, her eyes all for Mitch.

Massaging his temples, Mitch glared at her. "If you didn't think I was in here, why were you banging?"

"It's rude to barge into someone's room."

"She's deaf, and when has it ever stopped you before?"

"I was bringing in her stuff and letting her know we are leaving in an hour. The plane is ready. Guess your injuries aren't so severe after all." Storming out of the room, Stacey slammed the door but didn't switch out the light.

Shaking his head, Mitch looked down to see me squinting up at him. When his eyes drifted to my back, he frowned and gently lifted the sheet. "Jesus!" Pointing to me, Mitch shook his hand to the side of his ribs with his fingers spread. *"You got cut up and still pulled me free?"*

Too awkward to sign lying on my stomach as I was, I croaked using my voice. "It's my job to save you."

Sitting up to face him, I cringed on the tightness and stabbing pains radiating through various injuries. Scanning over every bruise, bump and graze, Mitch's eyes widened when they found the shiny black skin of my hip.

Pulling the sheet around my waist, I went back to signing. Shuffling my hands between us to the left with both palms up, I then turned my hands so my thumbs were pointing up and flapped them back and forth between us as I lifted my shoulders. We needed to discuss our arrangement.

Frowning, Mitch made himself comfortable, his eyes wary as they watched my hands.

"I need you to remove the Nano. I won't run. I will stay and protect you, and I won't turn on you."

Patiently waiting for me to finish signing, Mitch firmed his lips. *"You will stay because I have the antidote to that toxin in your system. I dare say you will wait for a decent amount of time, then request I stop that too. And once I do, you'll disappear."*

While he was still signing, I huffed. He was right, but he didn't understand how that would be in his best interest. *"I have nowhere to go. I'm begging you not to make me defenseless. Last night happened because I was too weak even to consider his plan. Had you walked me out of there, I would have known and told you before the car started moving. I couldn't think to save us. The Nanos need to come out. It weakens me in more than strength."*

Stroking my face, Mitch pitched forward, his body tense showing me he was hurting. Pressing his lips to mine, Mitch kissed me slowly. I sat there, taking it, but I didn't fall into it. Pulling away, Mitch got out of bed, taking care of how he moved before he turned to face me. Tucking his ring and pinkie finger of his right hand, he closed the index and middle finger down on his thumb sternly. *"No!"*

Closing my eyes in distress, I turned my face away while he walked out without another word. Waiting for several breaths, I calmed my emotions, then I grabbed my bag and got dressed. The pills I needed to take were in the bag as I repacked it. Picking them up, I looked at the unlabeled bottle. In the bathroom, I opened the bottle of aspirin the nurse had left me. The pills looked similar.

Mitch was willing to weaken me to control me. Let's see if this toxin was just a bluff. Tipping the pills he gave me into the toilet, I flushed them, then I refilled the bottle with the paracetamol and shoved it back in my bag.

Picking up the carry-on, I went out to the lounge room, dumping the bag in the hall. In the kitchen, Fred was fixing himself something to eat. He watched me walk in but didn't say anything. After pouring me a coffee, he sat down to eat his food.

Taking the coffee, I stood by the window looking out, watching the sunrise. In the reflection of the glass, I watched Mitch walk into the room. Observing the backless top I wore, he hesitated, then turned to get his coffee.

Looking between us, Fred nodded hello to Mitch. "How are you feeling?"

"Like I got hit by a truck. You?"

"Much the same. I had a team retrieve Mark's body. It is on its way home. Police are asking questions."

"Have Jacoby deal with it. It's what I pay him to handle."

"He's already on it." Glancing over his shoulder at me, Fred sighed as he turned back to Mitch. "She could have tried to run last night. They would have killed us, and Lyza knew that. She saved me, and then she hauled your ass out of that car, ignoring her pain. Why?"

"Because her instincts are to protect."

"She's more than an ex-lover who turned on him, Mitch. She's his wife, and you've been screwing her. Mark was right. This situation has gotten out of hand."

"Not now. We can talk about this once we are home and in private, but not here. It's not safe." Finishing his coffee, Mitch turned for the door. "Let's go. I want an ocean between Noel D'Avive and me until I'm feeling healthy again."

Tapping my shoulder, Fred waited until I looked at him to gesture to the door. There was something more going on. My involvement in this was more than Mitch making amends for saving his life five years ago. It was more than someone, namely Noel, trying to kill him.

As we drove to the airport, I replayed Noel's words in my head over and over again. He'd come to the jail that night, but did he come to get me or kill me. He said he thought I'd been dead for years, that he expected the jail to be a trap. By whom? Had Mitch known he was coming? And why had both of them taken five very long years to do it?

There was a new bodyguard in the car, one of the guys who met us at the safe house. Mark already replaced, but I didn't doubt for a second he would be remembered honorably when we got home. What happened to me there would be something I was yet to find out.

America is not the place I wanted to be. It didn't hold the most pleasant memories for me. I hoped to return to Mitch's ranch, but that wasn't the case. From the airport, we drove to the city and the office building for Mitch's company in New Mexico.

It wasn't a city high rise but more like an old college that someone renovated into a business. Inside, there were offices on each side of the upper three levels, looking over the building's entry and the central area below. Following Mitch to an elevator on one side, I rode up with him to the top level and out onto the glassed-in corridor.

The void not only looked over the foyer but the ground floor rooms beyond. It allowed anyone from this level to watch what was happening below. There was a gym, an open floor training room, and other spaces that looked set up for various training simulations.

"This building is set up for the intended purpose of training my staff to be the best covert bodyguards they can be," Mitch signed when he stopped in front of a door. *"Why don't you have a look around. I've got some business to deal with."* Stepping through a door into his office, Mitch didn't look back at me for a response. Fred stepped in behind Mitch, with Stacey on their heels. The door shut, leaving me outside with Dustin.

Dustin couldn't sign, and so far, his idea of trying to communicate with me involved tapping me on the shoulder and pointing in a direction. Which he did now, pointing towards a set of stairs. Working hard not to roll my eyes, I moved in the direction he indicated.

One level down, I stepped out onto the walkway and moved along it. Not all the rooms were offices. Some looked to be classrooms. There was one that had a class of soldiers in it. By their uniform, I picked them as air force. Stopping to watch, a man in fatigues sat in a wheelchair at the front of the room giving instruction. One of the soldiers turned his head, saw me, and frowned as he scanned me, my bruises cataloged as his eyes grew angrier. The instructor turned to see what caught his focus and his brows furrowed.

Stopping the class, he wheeled himself to the door and pressed a button for it to slide open. "What's going on here, Dustin?"

"Just showing the boss's wife around while he's in a meeting, Lewis."

"Wife?" Lewis's entire forehead pinched.

"They got married a few weeks ago."

Glaring pointedly at my bruised arm and shoulder, Lewis frowned. "Should I ask what happened to her?"

Appraising me from head to toe, Dustin pressed his lips together, twisting them in a grimace. "They got in a car wreck in Europe. She saved the boss and Fred. Pulled them out of it." Dustin turned back to Lewis. "She's deaf but can read lips."

Rolling closer, Lewis offered his hand. "Nice to meet you, Mrs. Fairchild. I'm Matt Lewis, one of Mitch's instructors here."

Shaking his hand, I stepped back. Waving my index finger, I crossed my fingers and moved it out from my chest towards him, pointed at him before pretending to pinch my temples and pulse my hands forward as I lifted my shoulders.

Lewis looked a bit lost. "Ah, sorry, Mrs. Fairchild, I don't know your language."

Accepting that, I pointed to the classroom and opened my arms out while lifting my shoulders.

"Oh, we do contract work for the military." Noticing the entire class was now watching us, Lewis gestured they get back to work. "I should get back to my job. It was nice meeting you." Lewis wheeled his chair back into the room, letting the door slide close before he started talking.

Tapping my shoulder, Dustin pointed down the hall. Glaring at him, I then shifted that look between his hand and his face. If he rapped me one more time, I would break his finger. Hesitating at my glance,

Dustin took a step back and swept his arm outwards. I walked on. "Jesus, how did I get stuck on deaf psycho babysitting duty."

Rolling my eyes, I huffed. He wasn't the only one annoyed. Looking down at the training room and gym, I turned around and wiggled my fingers at him.

"What is that supposed to mean? I'm not giving you money, honey. If you want food or drink, I'll take you to the kitchen. You can help yourself."

With a huff, I stepped into him quickly and retrieved his phone from his pocket as he jumped back, shocked by my attack. Blinking at me when he saw me waving his phone at him, his brows furrowed. Swiping the screen, I typed the message before handing it to him again.

"Oh, you wanted my phone," Dustin finally caught on, confirming his being brawn rather than brain. "Yeah, the car with your luggage is still here. Did you want something?" When I nodded, Dustin looked equally annoyed and relieved, or maybe he was constipated. "Okay, follow me."

Leading the way to the underground garage and the car, Dustin opened the boot for me. Digging through my luggage to find my workout gear, I changed.

Turning his back to me quickly, Dustin cursed. "Whoa, honey, we have change rooms. You know we have security cameras down here. The guards are probably getting a real eye full right now."

Dustin won the award when it came to overreacting since I still had my knickers covering the essential parts. If the guards were going to get off seeing my breasts, they seriously needed to get out more. Plus, I'd already located the cameras, and the trunk lid was lifted, blocking their view. The camera behind was hindered by Dustin's bulk.

Once I changed, I repacked my bag and slammed the trunk, making it clear for the grumbling babysitter I was good to go. Appraising what I was wearing, Dustin tilted his head in surprise. "You want to use the gym?"

Wiggling my fingers again, I waited for him to hand over his phone without issue this time.

Training room.

Taking the phone back, Dustin stared stumped at the phone for a second. Blinking, he typed back a message.

I'll have to check the timetable.

With a nod, I handed his phone back as we moved to the stairs. After studying the numbers he used to press in the code to get from the garage inside, I trailed behind him to the training room. I was out of practice. I needed to catch up.

17

———————

WIFE LIFE

"Tᴀɪ Cʜɪ?"

Mitch had been in the room for three minutes already, but I ignored his entry, just like I ignored him now. Tai Chi was the only thing I could practice in my prison cell. Now, I'd cycled through all of the health style katas ten times. My skin shimmered with sweat, but I wasn't dripping.

Sitting on the side watching, Dustin answered instead. "She's good. When she does the quick stuff, I lose her movement."

Crossing his arms, Mitch assessed my movements. "It's one of the best martial arts to learn."

Getting up, Dustin came to stand by Mitch. "I thought it was an old person's thing, but when I saw her doing the quick stuff, I could see the karate in it."

Moving through the first few moves in front of Dustin, Mitch accentuated his fluidity. "Every move done slowly encourages strength and suppleness, but they all transfer into fast defense and

142

offensive moves." Repeating those moves quickly, Mitch took Dustin down.

Rolling my eyes, I turned, moving into the next flow.

Helping Dustin back up off the floor, Mitch gave him a pat on the back. "Head home, Dust. I'm going to work out with my wife, then take her home for the night." Toeing off his shoes, Mitch pulled his shirt over his head then stepped in beside me. He flowed into the moves with me, moving in unison, silence, and breath. Finishing the last kata together, I took an automatic two steps away from him. Glancing at Mitch, I lifted a brow. He bowed his head. We both reset and immediately flowed into the fight-style katas.

When we finished, Mitch turned and smiled at me. *"Did you want to spar?"*

Shaking my head, I went to the side of the room to the bathroom.

"We are here alone," Mitch called after me.

Ignoring him, I entered the bathroom to wash my face.

Following me in, Mitch came up behind me and met my eyes in the mirror. *"What's wrong? I thought you would be keen for a fight?"*

Watching his hands, I turned to face him. Pushing my pants to the ground, I pulled the gym top over my head, so I stood there naked. Mitch's eyes raked my body head to toe as I turned slowly to show him all the bruises. When I was facing him again, I pointed to the worst one, the black beacon of pain at my hip. *"This wasn't caused by the car rolling or being hit. I got this fighting the guy who was about to kill you and Fred while you were unconscious."*

Mitch's Adam's apple bobbed as he moved closer. *"You were hurt the most, saving my life."* Grabbing my face, he kissed me hard and fast.

Shoving him away, I glared at him. Blinking through his lust glaze, Mitch stood watching with his mouth half-open. *"I got hurt because I was too weak to control my fall."* Signing aggressively, I advanced slowly towards him. *"I was too weak because you took me out of play, torturing me with your device. We nearly died because of you."* Shoving him in the chest pointedly, I pushed him into the wall. *"Mark is dead because of you."*

Not that I liked Mark. After he tortured me five years back, it was all karma and shit, in my opinion. But I wanted to get it through to Mitch that weakening me would get us all killed. Mouth slowly closing, the lust glaze cleared from Mitch's eyes as he got pissed.

"So, no, I don't want to fight. I've had plenty of fights in the last twenty-four hours. I don't want to fight because I'm in pain." Taking a step back, I glared at Mitch. *"And I don't want to fuck the guy who caused it."*

Taking in my angry gestures, processing them, Mitch closed down his expression. Pointing at me, Mitch made two fists on either side of his body, pumped them, and then lifted them as his thumbs popped out. *"You're pissed; I get it. I'll take you home."* Gazing over my naked body one more time, Mitch glared at the shiny black skin of my hip. "I'll wait outside." Throwing the bathroom door open, Mitch marched out.

Closing my eyes, I took a deep breath. If I had to, I would push every button to get it through to Mitch that the nano was a bad idea. Nothing I'd done deserved that kind of torture, and I sure as hell didn't deserve to have my life tied to his to reassure him that I'd do my job. If he died in that car accident, I'd be suffering a slow torturous death right now if my heart hadn't already given out.

Grabbing my clothes, I dressed. Halfway clothed, I stopped to admire how the black bruising in my hip had bled to purple around the tattoo. Having hated that tattoo from the moment the first needle stabbed the ink into my flawless skin, it was nice not to be able to see it for once. With a heavy sigh, I washed my face and went out to join Mitch.

As soon as I opened the bathroom door, I knew I'd pressed a button. The pounding of a fist into the heavy bag slapped through the training room. Watching Mitch beat the stuffing out of the kick bag, I leaned against the wall for another fifteen minutes before his energy gave out. Stepping back, Mitch glared at the bag, softened his knees, and sprang into a spinning head kick. The chain holding the bag clanked, and the bar supporting it creaked as it bent a little from the force of the impact. Mitch landed perfectly. Shit, if I didn't hate him so much for what he was putting me through, I could bang him here and now.

Stalking over, Mitch snatched up his shirt and pulled it on as he opened the door. "Let's go."

Following Mitch into the hall, I slowed my steps when he stopped by a door and pressed a code to unlock it. Over his shoulder, I could see two guards sitting behind a panel of monitors. Mitch spoke with them quietly as he retrieved a set of keys from a lockbox, then he came back out and shut the door.

Mitch walked us to the car in the garage that collected us from the airport and opened the boot. Taking my bag out, Mitch shouldered his before escorting us to another vehicle. This one was a pick-up — one of those expensive, shiny black trucks. Throwing our bags in the back, Mitch opened the car door for me. As I stepped in, he closed the distance and pressed his body to mine, pinning me against the truck. He was sweaty and still smelled great; Mitch's dirty smell was still all man and spice.

Face to my ear, Mitch kept his voice low, his breath tickling along my neck. "You may hate me for what I did, but I did it to save you. While you were busy looking at your husband's new face, he was uncapping a syringe behind his back. You couldn't see it, I did. I didn't know if it was just going to knock you out or kill you. I didn't give him a chance. I took you out to save you. Your husband killed Mark, not me. Don't ever blame me again."

Marching off, Mitch went around the car to his seat. Standing there, I blinked. How did I process this? If I faced him, I couldn't hide my shock, which means he would know I heard him. It took another blink to know that's why he whispered it to me.

Closing my eyes, I steadied myself and put what he said out of my head as I got in the car, no more annoyed or disarmed than I was before his revelation. Sitting in the car, Mitch watched me for a full minute.

Relaxing back in the seat, I used my fingers like eating utensils and shrugged as I kept signing. *"Are we getting dinner on the way home? Last I remember, your fridge was a bit bare."*

Gritting his teeth at my lack of reaction, Mitch focused his eyes on the steering wheel. Exhaling with force, Mitch bowed his neck, shaking his head a little as he started the engine. He made both hands flat blades and hit the side of his right hand into his left's flat palm. *"Sure."*

When we got back to Mitch's place, I carried the food we picked up at a drive-through, and he lugged in the luggage. When I stood at the table and started unpacking the bag, Mitch pointed to me, made the eating gesture before indicating himself, held his arm forty-five degrees in the air, and used his hand like a showerhead.

Not about to argue, I ate my burger and drank my drink. When Mitch came out, dressed only in track pants, I went to shower. Cleaned up, I put knickers on, put my hair up, and stole one of Mitch's shirts that I could wear to sleep. Crawling into bed, I turned the light off and finally reacted to the information Mitch shared.

Was Noel going to drug me or kill me? Not that the first couldn't lead to the latter after he got me alone. Of course, it could have been neither. He was already planning to hit our transport, or he wouldn't have had that truck ready. Perhaps the syringe contained a tracking device so he could find me later.

Sitting up in bed, my eyes wide open and brain sounding an alert, I threw back the sheets and walked out to Mitch. Sitting on the lounge reading a book, he looked up, confused.

Pointing to Mitch, I moved my hand as if it was a bed beneath my left like a scanner, then pointed to me. Jutting the tips of my right hand into the palm of my left, I let my hand bounce back. *"Now!"*

Standing up, Mitch appraised me with a crease in the top of his nose from his brows pulling together. Tapping the side of his index finger to his left shoulder, Mitch shrugged.

"Noel put his arm around me as I fainted. I couldn't feel anything past the pain you caused, but he likes to use tracking devices to come after his prey when they think they are safe."

Considering me, Mitch picked up his phone and sent a message with one hand while taking my elbow with the other and guiding me into the bedroom. A reply buzzed his cellphone a moment later. Reading the response, Mitch threw the phone on the bed. We stood facing each other. Putting his hand behind his back, Mitch swept his arm out and around, using his other hand to lean me back. Understanding, I fell into his arms, replaying the moment I passed out.

The bottom of Mitch's fist made an impact right near the bruised skin of my hip. Using his other hand, Mitch used his nail to mark the spot, and I slapped his shoulder when it hurt.

"Sorry." Standing us back up, Mitch gestured for me to lie on the bed. While I did, he grabbed a torch and came back to me. Shoving the shirt up around my waist, Mitch yanked my knickers down.

"Hey!"

Smirking, Mitch continued to straddle my knees and start searching the bruised flesh with the torchlight. The bruising stretched the skin so that the needle hole might be visible. While Mitch examined my hip, I studied him. Did I mention he was gorgeous and currently shirtless?

"I don't think my panties needed to come off."

Mitch's eyes flicked up to watch my hands, then went back to the skin. "Your psychotic husband could be on his way here now, and you are worried about me seeing your little patch of a bush?"

Reading his lips, I smirked. *"Most women would be concerned about being found in a bed with a man by their husband."*

Mitch's eyes stopped long enough to watch my hands. "Good point." Putting his finger over a spot, he pressed it. I winced. "He jabbed you here." Placing the torch aside, Mitch continued to press all around the site.

"Fucking ouch!"

Sitting back, Mitch dodged the punch I threw his way and held his hands up in surrender. "I can't feel anything."

Irritated, I touched my pointer to my third eye and pinched it down to close on my thumb in front of me. *"I can!"* The gestures that followed called him several bad names.

Smirking, Mitch collected his phone. Typing out a message, he started stroking my bush with his free hand. "I'll take your mind off it." Shifting himself to spread my thighs apart, Mitch threw the phone aside as he lowered his face.

Tilting my head back, I bit my lip as his tongue swiped me long. No, I wasn't going to stop him; I could use the distraction. Closing my eyes, I enjoyed Mitch's tongue squirming and stroking me out of my pain and worry and drifted on the cloud of lust. It didn't take long for me to tumble into orgasm, and I relaxed back on the bed, somewhat happier than five minutes earlier.

Chuckling as he rose, kissing up my abdomen, Mitch slipped his hand beneath the shirt to find my breast. "I love how you moan my name when you come." My eyes were closed, so I ignored him. When he touched my cheek with tenderness, I slowly opened my eyes to see him. "You look even hotter coming in my shirt."

Smirking, I didn't pull away when Mitch kissed my lips, the tart taste of me on his mouth. Licking and sucking his lips, I moaned. A light flashed down the drive as Mitch started pulling the drawstring of his pants. Stopping his hand, I pushed him away. Snatching up my knickers, I pulled them back on as I got off the bed.

Exhaling in a huff, Mitch waited until I was looking at him to sign. *"You suck at reciprocation. Do you know that?"*

"While this nano is in me, you won't be. Plus, we have visitors."

Forehead creasing as he watched my hands, Mitch looked to the window, then stepped off the bed and checked his phone. *"It's my guys. Stay here."*

Lying back on the bed, I relaxed. Thinking about Mitch answering the door before he calmed himself down made me grin. I was still smiling when Mitch came in with Stacey and two other guys I'd never seen before.

Both men appreciated the view while Stacey scanned my body with a handheld device. "That's your wife?" One murmured to Mitch.

With a Cheshire smile, Mitch crossed his arms. "Yep."

"She got a sister?"

"It's small, but it's here." Looking toward Mitch, Stacey poked me hard in my bruised hip. Grabbing her wrist, I twisted it out, glaring at her. "Ow! Let me the fuck go, bitch!" As Stacey started to swipe the scanner at me, Mitch caught her hand and yanked her away from me.

"Cut that shit out, Stace. She saved our lives."

"No, she saved yours, and she let Mark die."

Face falling, Mitch met her eyes. "Stace, you know that's not true."

Tugging out of his grasp, Stacey pulled up the scan on her computer. "It's small, but it's sending out a signal. They'd have to be close to receive it."

"How close?"

Shrugging, Stacey typed a few things into the computer. "Same city close. They probably just tracked her for the ambush. It shouldn't be an issue here, but if you want it taken out, Miles can grab a scalpel and dig it out."

Brow furrowing, Mitch looked about as impressed as me by that suggestion, but I kept my face schooled as he glanced at me. *"Leave it in or take it out?"*

Considering his gestures, I lifted my eyes to meet his. Both hands bladed and side-on, I drew the right down the left index finger's line to stop against the uplifted thumb. The answer was all going to depend on Mitch's motivation.

"On what?"

Throwing my hands forward as if I was holding something, I then spun my hand as if reeling in a line on a fishing rod. There wasn't a way to sign for using someone as bait, but I had a feeling that's what I'd been from the beginning.

18

___

SECRETS

As Mitch drove towards his company's building, I sat quietly in the passenger seat, watching the passing scenery. Since we got home nearly a week ago, Mitch allowed me to use the facilities to get my training back on track. I used the gym when the training room was booked and the training room when it was free.

There was the same illusion of freedom that I had in Chapter with Mitch. As long as I didn't interfere with Mitch's business, I could wander around the facilities and even go down the street for coffee or food. Hell, Mitch gave me a purse with identification, cash, and a credit card. As long as I was back by the time Mitch finished work for the day, he was happy. So far, we spent the nights doing tai chi together before grabbing dinner and heading home.

Stopping at a set of lights, Mitch glanced my way. "How about we have lunch together today?"

Focusing on the cafe across the road, I swallowed hard, observing the man who sat reading a newspaper at one of the outside tables.

"Lyza?"

A warm hand caressing against my bare thigh sparked my desire. All week, I'd held out on Mitch, standing by my words. He'd been doing everything to tempt me at night—the prick. Turning to acknowledge him, Mitch signed the question again.

Blading my hands, I chopped the right into the palm of my left. Satisfied by the answer, Mitch nodded. The light changed, and as we pulled away, my eyes tracked back to the cafe and the outside table. Now empty.

Inhaling deeply, I exhaled slowly as my eyes scanned the area quickly. The fingers on my left hand started to tingle, pins, and needles spreading through them. Frowning down at my extremity, I wiggled my fingers. As quickly as it came, it was gone. A wave of numbness passing through my hand.

Observing the way that I was stretching my fingers, Mitch cocked his head. *"Everything okay?"*

Holding my hands up as if grabbing someone's shoulders and jostling them, I then turned my right hand to have my palm facing me, fingers splayed, except the middle, which I touched to my upper breast as I slowly dragged it to my collarbone. To the verbally orientated, it was a sensual gesture, but in Auslan, it described the sensation to be odd. I'm sure being tortured repeatedly was causing the strange feeling. There was no point making a thing about it. *"It's gone now."*

Taking my hand in his, Mitch frowned as he massaged the length of my digits. *"You've been taking your pills?"*

Nodding my head, I moved his hand back to my thigh, running my fingers between his casually, enjoying his touch. Scrunching his forehead in my peripheral vision, Mitch stretched his fingers and gripped more of my thigh. Rubbing the pads of my digits in the webbing of his fingers, I slid my hand forward, filling the gap with mine. My hands were only two-thirds the size of his.

Pulling into the company's underground garage, Mitch took his hand back to swipe his card at the gate. Placing my hand over the skin of my thigh he'd abandoned, I frowned at the empty sensation. It reminded me of when I was a child, and I would hurt myself during training. All I wanted was for my mother to hug me. Instead, she would walk off disappointed at my failure.

As Mitch stepped out of the car, leaving me sitting there by myself, the same feeling swept over me. Just a moment of abandonment, then I inhaled, and it was gone. Sliding out of his pickup, I walked beside him to the stairs. Swapping the bag containing our workout clothes to his other shoulder, Mitch took my hand in his. The sun rose in my stomach.

With the training room in use, I spent the morning in the gym. After I ran for three hours and completed a stretching session, I showered and spent ten minutes standing in the doorway of the training room watching Mitch run the training session. When Mitch finally dismissed everyone, he came over to me and gave me a slow kiss and a naughty smile.

Using only his hands to talk, Mitch protected his students from his wanton thoughts. *"If you weren't already showered, I'd offer for you to shower with me."*

Lifting a brow, I put my fingers to my chest and pulled the fingers back as if wiping something off in question, rubbed the back of my left hand three times for the color blue, and then held my hands up as if holding his testicles and jiggling them back and forth.

Watching my hands, Mitch pouted. *"A good wife would take care of me instead of being selfish."*

"A good husband wouldn't hold his wife hostage with a torture device."

Huffing, Mitch dropped his head, then he tilted it in curiosity. Gently, he took hold of my left wrist, examining my hand, how my fingers were trembling ever so slightly. Checking my right hand, his eyes found it steady as always. *"When did the shaking start?"*

Extracting my hand from his grasp to sign, I shrugged. *"It's been happening randomly all morning."*

"Is this normal?"

"No. My hands are steady, normally." Watching my gestures, Mitch scowled as his brow pinched. Stepping back, I slipped out of the doorway. *"It's probably just residual from all the times you zapped me in Rome. I'll wait out in the foyer for you to shower."* Turning my back, I walked away.

Clenching my hand a few times while I walked, I took deep breaths, and the trembling stopped. Sighing with relief, I shook my arm out. Maybe I'd been foolish throwing those pills away. Stacey was in the foyer talking to another staff member when I emerged. She watched me with hostile eyes as I massaged my arm. "You okay?" She didn't look concerned, but her eyes were watching my arm.

Letting my arm go, I nodded.

Taking a deep breath, Stacey met my eyes. "I'm sorry about the other night. I've known Mark a long time, and with all this stress of late, being shot at, and..." Stacey trailed off. She closed her eyes, opened them, and met mine. "Anyway," she exhaled. With a nod, she walked off.

Raising a brow, I watched her leave. Mitch appeared shortly after, and we made our way down the street on foot. Strolling side-by-side, we held hands. It would be easy to get lost in thoughts of romance. Unless, of course, you were slightly paranoid about your husband trying to find you and kill you. Or that the man you are with was willing to put you on a hook and dangle you as bait.

Pain shot down my left arm, and I cringed, gripping my arm as the Nano fired its warning shot. Frowning, I glared at Mitch, and I shook my pointer at him in question.

"I didn't do that."

With my left arm useless for signing, I hissed through my teeth. "You said you are the only one with the device." Moving to the bench nearby, I sat down.

Following, Mitch sat down, taking my left arm and massaging it. "No one else has a device. I'll call Lennon when we get back."

Watching his lips, I sighed. *"This nano will be the death of me."* Standing up, I put my hand in close to my sternum and gave it a quick jerk to let Mitch know my arm felt fine now.

Continuing on to lunch, we enjoyed a lovely meal together. *"Why Albuquerque?"*

Smiling at my hands first, Mitch lifted his eyes to mine to sign his reply. *"The high altitude makes it one of the best places for building stamina while training."*

"You didn't grow up here?"

"No. Nowhere near here. Maybe that's the other reason it appeals."

"You don't like your family?"

Mitch considered my hands. *"Do you like yours?"*

Pressing my hands together as if in prayer, I turned my face away then waved my hand down to signify he could forget it. *"I'm going to go for a walk. I'll meet you back at the office later."*

Rising with me, Mitch took my hand before I could leave. We stood looking at each other for a long moment, then he bowed his head and kissed my lips firmly. Closing my eyes, I accepted the apology. After all, I knew better than anyone that talking about your family could be emotional; that's why I didn't do it.

When Mitch released me, I stepped back, letting his hand slip down to hold my hand before turning and leaving. Squeezing my hand, Mitch kept hold of it until he needed to let it go. As my arm fell limply to my side, something stirred my insides. Glancing over my shoulder, I saw Mitch sitting back down, finishing his drink.

Strolling down the street, biting my lip, I tried to discern these strange feelings I was getting when Mitch touched me.

"Excuse me, Miss, do you have the time?" A European man requested. Usually, I would have kept walking, but he grabbed my arm. Lifting my eyes to his, I glared at his hand on my bicep. "Do you have the time?" He repeated slowly.

Frowning, I looked at my bare wrist and shook my head.

"You are being followed. Go into the shopping center, the second level in the women's department," the man spoke quietly and clearly, so I could read his lips. Letting me go, he walked off.

Shaking off the feel of his grip, I looked behind me, pretending to give the guy a dirty look, but it enabled me to spot Dustin half a block back. Turning forward, I sighed and made my way to the shopping center.

Window shopping on my way to the second level, I took my time to get there. In the women's department, I made my way to the lingerie section. It's the main area most men are not so keen to follow; I don't know why. After browsing a few items, I selected a set in my size.

Appearing opposite me, Wenda made a zero with her thumb and forefinger, moving it out from her chest before hooking her index finger and holding it up while giving it a tremor telling me not to freak out on her. She kept her hands low so as not to alert any watchers we were conversing. *"He just wants to talk to you."*

Holding both hands out as if I was trying to balance plates on them in question, I shrugged my shoulders.

Pointing to the fitting rooms, Wenda walked away.

Taking a deep breath, I moved to the changing area. There was no one waiting to check my items, so I stepped in and checked the first cubicle. Empty. The second and third were the same. Stopping at the doorway of the fourth, I found Noel standing against the mirror. His head lifted, eyes taking me in slowly as they rose. Stepping into the change room, I closed the door before turning back to face him, placing the underwear on the hook to free my hands.

Pointing to my chest, I formed a C in front of my face and twisted it back past my face before putting my palms together, fingertips to the wrist, and twisted them free as I slid them apart. It was apparent what Noel wanted, but I couldn't leave Mitch even if I wanted to.

Tapping the side of his right index finger to his left shoulder, Noel raised a brow.

Indicating Noel, I put my finger below my eye then shook my thumb at him. *"You saw what happened to me in Rome?"*

Noel nodded his head.

"He did that. If I try to leave, he will do that to me."

Noel shifted uncomfortably. "You could have escaped in the accident. He was unconscious," he argued, ensuring his words were clear so I could read them. "Instead, you killed my man."

Gritting my teeth, my anger at his questioning came through in my gestures. *"If Mitch dies, I die. Slow and painfully. I have to protect him to save myself."*

Squinting at me, Noel fidgeted with his phone by his hip. I knew that look. He was deciding whether to go with the plan he made or dump it and walk away.

"Why are you here?"

Watching my hands, Noel raised a brow and spoke his response. He never signed for me if he didn't have to. "You're my wife."

"Do you need a divorce?"

Mouth gaping a little, Noel's brows knitted. "I need my wife."

"It's *been five years. Why now?*"

Glaring at my hands, Noel stepped closer. "I thought you were dead."

"You didn't care if I was. You were leaving no matter what, and you planned to leave me behind then. Why do I matter now?"

Glancing to my eyes, Noel shook his head. "You were so loyal, of course, I couldn't tell you, but I hoped to convince you to follow."

Holding up five fingers, I tapped my index finger to the joint of my left thumb aggressively three times. Five years he'd waited.

Noel stepped forward angrily, but he didn't try to grab me. "I believed you were dead. Just like your boyfriend was meant to be. I killed him for a reason, Lyza. Out of all the people you could have saved that day." Turning, Noel slammed his fist into the wall, his hand pushing through the plaster into the next change room.

Taking steadying breaths, I considered Noel while he extricated his hand from the gyprock and turned away to calm down.

After several deep breaths, Noel faced me with calm, resolute again. "You have a choice as you did then. I either extract you, or you die. Which is your preference?"

He wouldn't meet my eyes. Looking away, I placed my bladed left-hand side on, pressed my right hand against it in a fist, and then swept the right hand away to my right side, opening it to a blade as I did. I didn't fear death, but I wouldn't rush into its arms either.

Touching my chin, Noel lifted my face so he could look into my eyes. "Who do I kill to free you?"

19

INTRUDER

FROM THE TOP-LEVEL WALKWAY, I SPIED MITCH BACK IN THE TRAINING room with new recruits. He hired ex-SEALs or special forces, but they needed further training for what Mitch was hoping to specialize in his business market.

Letting myself into Mitch's office, I opened drawers and looked through his cupboards, trying to find why Mitch was the target five years ago. It didn't make sense. He was a SEAL back then; the hotter target was the asset, so why did Noel go to all that effort for a nobody?

Closing the drawer in frustration, the stationary rattled. There wasn't one shred of paper in Mitch's office; not a memo or a file. Peering around the office looking for anything, but all that was there was a computer. My hacking skills were minimal. We had specialists for that, just like the military. Adding to my lack of talent was that five years had passed since I even touched a computer.

Sitting down at the desk, I moved the mouse and watched the screen come to life. Password protected wasn't a surprise. Glancing around Mitch's office for a clue, I wondered if he was the sort to leave something obvious. There were only two photos. One of Mitch and a dog, but since he didn't own a dog and was in his fatigues, I doubted it was his dog. So I immediately ruled it out as either a trap or a memory of something else that happened that day.

The second photo was of his platoon. The faces were familiar, my memory placing half of them in the room with Mitch dead ten years ago. Fred and Mark were there, along with Ellis, who I met the other day. Frowning, I considered that Ellis hadn't seemed to recognize me, but he must have been one of the ones who captured me.

The door opened as Stacey marched into the office. "What are you doing in here?" She asked clearly as she moved towards the desk to see me looking at the picture. Ignoring her suspicious glare, I pointed to the computer.

"It's password protected. You can't hack it; I set up the encryption."

Figuring that was the case, I shrugged.

Stacey slammed some papers on Mitch's desk, frustrated. "I know you can talk, so just talk."

Lifting a brow, I cleared my throat. "I don't like it." It couldn't hurt to be truthful.

"What? The computer?"

Touching my throat with my index finger, I swirled it away.

"Talking?" Eyebrows lifting to her hairline, Stacey tilted her head. "Why don't you like talking?"

"Hurts," I rasped. "I was strangled. It nearly crushed my larynx. It was months before I could make a sound. Talking has hurt since."

Ignoring the photo frame in my hand, Stacey considered me. "When did you go deaf?"

"Paris."

"When they killed your mother?" Stacey looked confused.

Turning to face away from her, I stared at the photo in my hand. "They didn't kill her for days after my father found her. He tortured her first."

"You? They tortured you too, didn't they?"

Studying Mitch's photograph of his platoon, I ignored the question since I couldn't see it. "I know you hate me. It's okay. I'd hate me too." My left arm went dead. The warning shot took me by surprise, causing me to drop the photo frame and grab at my arm as I cringed.

Mouth falling open, Stacey pulled a cell phone from her pocket, tapping quickly. Stumbling over to the desk chair, I dropped into it. This was worse than usual—a march of ants pincering my nerve sheaths instead of the standard pins and needles.

"Mitch isn't doing this." Stacey stared at her phone like the reply was in a foreign language.

"I know." Dropping to my knees as the intensity grew, I put my head over the empty trash can and regurgitated my lunch. Kneeling beside me, Stacey went to comfort me. "Don't touch me!"

Backing off, Stacey watched me vomit, then she turned and opened Mitch's desk drawer and puked into it. "Sorry, I'm a sympathetic vomiter."

That is what Fred walked in to find. Stacey and I gag tagging. At least I had the decency to use the trash can. By the time Stacey finished, Mitch was going to need a new desk. When the pins and needles faded, I collapsed and enjoyed the comfort of the timber floor.

Kneeling by me, Fred checked my forehead as he put his phone to his ear. "Lyza's burning up. Could she have a virus that's triggering the device?" Listening, Fred frowned. "Sorry, Doc, the boss needs more than a best guess. Mitch is not going to be happy if the nano is malfunctioning and tortures her to death."

Hanging up the phone, Fred wiped the sweat from my brow. Closing my eyes, I tried to calm my body's reaction. Sleep sounded good about now. "Stace, you feeling unwell too? Could it be food poisoning?"

"No, just reacted to Lyza being sick. I'll call the cleaner."

Scooping me off the floor into his arms, Fred started walking with me. "I'll take Lyza down the infirmary and get her checked over. Tell Mitch to meet us there."

Mitch beat us there, probably because it was across the hall from the training room. Waiting long enough for Fred to put me on the bed, Mitch stepped up beside me, placing a hand to my forehead, pulling the eyelid up to check my eyes, then using my chin to try and open my mouth. "Say ah."

Placing my hand to my chest, I lifted it slightly then motioned it up and forward to replicate vomiting. Turning my hand palm down, I wiggled my fingers as I moved it away from my mouth. *"I need mouthwash or Passiona."*

Mitch smirked. *"Passion?"*

"Passi-ona," I spelled it out on my fingers for him. *"It's a passionfruit flavored drink in Australia. It tastes the same on the way down as it does on the way up."*

"Charming." Walking over to a cupboard, Mitch came back with the mouthwash. *"You Aussies have some rather interesting habits."*

Sitting up, I swished the rinse around my mouth before spitting into the plastic cup he handed me, which he then handed off to Fred.

"Say ah!"

Trying to bat Mitch away, I pointed to my chest, then spread my fingers and moved my hand in a short gesture from sternum to lower rib. Whatever it was had passed, and, other than exhausted, I felt fine.

Touching the tips of his fingers to his chin, Mitch moved it towards me. *"Humor me."*

With a huff of frustration, I opened my mouth.

"Fred?" Mitch moved aside for Fred to see.

Wincing at what he saw, Fred shook his head. "I'll call the doc." Pulling out his phone, Fred walked across the room and faced away from me.

Turning around to put the mouthwash away, Mitch kept his voice low while he spoke to Fred. "Get him on the first plane over here."

When Mitch faced me again, I held my hands out and lifted my shoulders.

Shaking his head, Mitch scrunched his nose. Forming a ring with his thumb and index finger, Mitch waved it back and forth.

Nothing important, my ass!

Assessing me, Mitch sighed and turned his back again as Fred finished his call. "Get Moses. He's got the skills to guard her. He can take her home and watch her until I finish tonight."

"You want to assign a newbie to her?"

"Yes. Call it a test run. If he can guard my wife covertly, then I'll trust him in the field. Tell him she's his first assignment." Turning back to me, Mitch caressed my cheek, then took his hand back to sign. *"I'll have someone take you home to rest."*

Frowning, I pointed to my chest, then spread my index and middle fingers and placed them to the palm of my left hand like a person standing there, then lifted and dropped my hand. Mitch caught my hands in his to stop me, but I reefed my hands out of his angrily. *"Stop doing that! That is the equivalent of putting your hand over someone's mouth when they are talking! Would you do that to Stacey?"*

With his brows lifting, Mitch considered my accusation. Shaking his head, he signed an apology. *"I'm sorry. You are right. That is inconsiderate."*

Spreading my fingers, I placed my palm towards my face, then turned it and pressed it towards Mitch. *"It's rude!"*

Watching my hands, Mitch bowed his head conceding. *"You are right. However, you need to rest. I'll have one of my staff take you home."* Mitch turned away before I could argue with him.

Jumping off the bed, I smacked his shoulder. Facing me, Mitch had his brows in his hairline. Whacking the side of my bladed right hand into my flat left palm, I bounced it out, so both my hands were out to the side in question. *"Really? You don't think to turn your back is any worse than covering my mouth?"*

"No. I have always chosen to walk away rather than start a fight."

Fred was watching on, trying to keep up with our hands. Glancing at him, Mitch tilted his head to indicate he should leave. Huffing about missing out, Fred walked out. Capturing my face in his hands, Mitch put his mouth level with my eyes. "You are running a fever, and it is affecting the nano. I need you to rest until you are well again. I don't want to lose you, Lyza."

His eyes seemed sincere, but his reason for needing me may not be. *"It's your own fault for putting a torture device in me."*

Frowning down at my hands between us, Mitch sighed. "It was a necessary evil, Lyza." Moving closer, he circled his nose around mine, making it impossible to read his lips. "If I thought for a minute that I could trust you, Lyza, I would never have used it."

Putting my full-force into my arms, I shoved him away from me so I could sign; plus, I need the space from his tempting lips. *"You tortured me for a name. Don't sweet-talk me after you've shown your bitter side. I know a warhead when I see one."*

"Warhead?"

"It's a lolly. Google it." Storming to the door, I yanked it open.

"What the fuck is a lolly?" Mitch grumbled out loud behind me.

Halfway up the hall, Fred was waiting with a man, probably thirty in age. He was built strong, my height, dark hair, tanned skin, and a five o'clock shadow that could pass as a beard in the right light.

As I approached, his dark eyes locked on me, and I considered that I would have named him Moses too. His eyes had the depth of weighing your soul to them—a preacher with enough experience to spot a sinner a mile out from the church doors on Sunday.

"Lyza, this is Moses. He'll be your bodyguard for the next few weeks," Fred introduced.

Pointing to Moses, I tilted my head at Fred, tapped my head, and then pulled the fingers away as I closed the thumb to fingertips. Leaving an inch gap between my thumb and index, I circled them around my neck to indicate a clerical collar as I lifted my shoulders.

Fred laughed. "No. Moses was never a priest."

"He should have been."

One eyebrow jumping above those judgmental eyes, Moses signed while he spoke. "I'll keep that in mind for my next profession."

Tilting my head, I assessed him. We stood there for a moment, eyeing each other up quietly.

"Um, are you two about to draw pistols?" Fred asked, shifting his stance.

Shaking his head, Moses smirked. "No, just two blades determining the sharpness of another. You said she's the boss's wife?"

Impacting right below my rib cage, Moses's words knocked the wind out of me. Pivoting on my heel, I started walking for the garage door before Fred saw me react. I had no doubt Moses was watching for it.

Catching up to me in the stairs, Moses grabbed my arm. Immediately, I swiveled and dropped two stairs to get out of his reach. Moses held up his hands in a sign of peace. "I'm not here to hurt you, Lyzebel." Dropping his hand slowly, Moses crept his shirt up to expose his left hip as he pushed the waistband of his cargo pants down with his other hand to reveal his sword and arrow branding. He was a full member, not one of Noel's group. Unless he was a traitor like Noel.

Taking another step backward, I was assessing my chances of running.

Retrieving a phone out of his pocket, Moses hit a button. "I have a message for you."

When Moses offered me the phone, I didn't take it. Smirking, Moses pressed another button. A video started playing with a middle-aged man signing a message. My stomach dropped, my heart jumped out of my chest, and my soul raced for the door to escape while it could. The conflicting emotions of the message forced me to sag against the wall. When it finished, I lifted my watering eyes to Moses.

"Your father sent me."

20

WISHING FOR DEATH

"Your father was sure you hadn't gone with Noel, but you just disappeared. Can you tell me what happened?"

Sitting with my hands between my knees on Mitch's couch, I refused to answer any of Moses' questions.

Moses brushed his hand through his hair in frustration. *"I know you aren't with Noel. I found you while hunting him. Noel has been tracking you for over a week. Once your name was mentioned, I informed your father. When we discovered you were posing as Fairchild's wife, I was given permission to infiltrate his company and make contact with you."*

"You gave up Noel to come after me?"

Watching my hands, Moses sighed with relief. It was the first thing I'd said since he showed me the video. *"No. Noel is coming after you too. It's a two for one deal."*

Placing my hands back between my knees, I sat rocking, staring out the window. Why did the idea of going home feel horrifying? It was all I'd ever known. It was a thousand times more appealing than jail or going with Noel. Yet, inside, I felt abject misery.

Studying me, Moses drew his brows together. *"Did you run away? It's okay if you did. If you thought you might be punished for Noel, or perhaps you felt responsible?"* Lifting my eyes, I glared at the insinuation I was in any way responsible for Noel's actions. *"Okay, not that."* Slumping back in his seat, Moses studied me a bit longer. *"You're sick?"*

Pointing to my sternum, I tucked the fingers on both hands, leaving the index and middle fingers tight together pointing up, then dropped both my hands to ninety degrees, swiveling the wrists, so the palms now faced forward. The truth was I'd known I was dying before I left Chapter five years ago to save Noel, and while prison might have held it at bay, it didn't change my life expectancy.

Mouth falling open, Moses stared at me. *"How long?"*

Holding my arms out to the side, I shrugged. Hours, days, months. Did it matter? There were more important things to discuss. *"Noel is here in Albuquerque. He was going to take me today, but I told him it would kill me. My life is connected to Mitch's. If he dies, so do I. It forced Noel to step back."*

Following my gestures, Moses assessed me. *"Well, that at least falls in my mission."* When I tilted my head in question, Moses shrugged before he continued to sign. *"Keeping Mitch Fairchild alive is one of my tasks. Killing Noel is primary, bringing you home, tertiary."*

This information was a new development. Mitch was ranked higher on the priority list than me. Sitting up straight, I eyed Moses. *"Do you know why Noel wants Mitch dead?"*

My left arm went numb. Cringing, the intensity as close to the warning as I was going to get. My eyes flashed up to meet Moses'. He was signing, but my sight was blurry, and all I caught was something about a mother. Cold liquid metal slithered through my shoulder, wrapping around my collarbone as it reached for my neck.

Putting my trembling right hand to my lips as if to shoosh Moses, I pointed my finger forward to the side to indicate Mitch. Making the heavy metal symbol, I struggled to touch the index to my nose before dropping and turning my hand, so the side of my hand tapped my sternum. Mitch needed to know I was sorry. For not listening to his warning, for pushing this, and for bailing out on him.

Cold swept up my neck as darkness encased me.

MY NERVES WERE FRAYED. Blinking my eyes open, tears streamed down my cheeks. Moses was on his phone, panicking. Opening my mouth to talk, I gasped a breath before the cold swept through me again. Liquid nitrogen burned through my brain, making me want to scream in pain, but I couldn't breathe to make a sound.

THE DARKNESS WASN'T PEACEFUL, and it wasn't pain-free. It was distant, like being out of your body, but you could still feel the fire sweeping through your neural pathway. A grapevine of nerves trapping you in the suffocating heat of the inferno as it engulfed everything in its range.

MY EYES FLEW OPEN, I gasped for breath. Cold and wet, I spluttered as someone dunked me in the waters of Antarctica. Taking my face to force me to look at his mouth, Moses studied my eyes. "Lyza, hold on. You're burning up. I need to cool your body down."

Was he insane? I was a fucking iceberg, and he was dumping me in a cold bath. My body was frozen; I couldn't fight to get out, and I couldn't have kept my head above water if Moses wasn't holding it. Gasping for breath, the brain-freeze-of-death raced up my neck again, and the world vanished into a dark cylinder of pain. My body ripping up the nervous system, muscles and ligaments seizing, my heart thudding incredibly fast in the vast emptiness of my chest.

ONE BEATING HEART. That's all I could hear as the pain receded. One lonely heart beating strong and steady. Floating in the darkness with the double thud of its regular rhythm, I wondered if this was death. That drumbeat became my everything as I drifted in the nothingness that held me prisoner. The harder I listened, the less I hurt. The more I relaxed, allowing every synchronized beat to cocoon me further in the darkness, the more the cold ache seeped from my veins. It became my home, my haven, a place my ravaged body and soul could hide and find peace.

BLINKING IN THE DARKNESS, my eyelashes brushed against whatever was pressed against my face. The drum was still beating in my ear. Repeated double strikes on the membrane of my eardrums soothing me. Da-dum, da-dum, da-dum. Exhaling, I leaned closer to the electric blanket wrapped around me. My body still ached, torn up and torched in ice, but the heat was helping.

The blanket moved as lips pressed to the top of my head. "You scared the shit out of me, Lyza," Mitch's voice informed sleepily. "I don't want to lose you. Not because you're bait, and not because you might be the only one who can save me. I need more of you. I crave those moments when our lives aren't ruled by what we are, but when it is just you and me and the world can go fuck itself." Mitch exhaled dynamically. "That's why I need you. I never planned on who you were when I came for what you are."

Managing to fully open my eyelids, I could finally comprehend I was in a bed wrapped in a blanket of Mitch. Inhaling his scent deeply, I filled my lungs with him, his heat drifting through me like radiant sunshine. He warmed my insides like hot chocolate on a winter's day. Closing my eyes, I melted into him. "I am death. You are life."

Holding me a little tighter, Mitch kissed my forehead. "One cannot exist without the other."

The fact he thought I couldn't hear him, that we were potentially having two different conversations, was beside the point. "I am death. That's all I know how to be." A tear streaked down my cheek. Another followed. The gates of my heart opened as a deluge poured forth.

There was no memory of the last time I cried, and I couldn't remember anyone ever holding me, comforting me while I did. Not saying a single word, Mitch hugged me. When I could breathe again, I fell asleep in his arms and dreamed of those two days in Monaco. When it was just us, and everyone else's expectations and plans didn't matter. It was just us and what we wanted.

When I woke, I was alone in bed. Sitting up, my muscles were tight, and not happy about moving. Limping to the bathroom, I washed my face - I looked like shit - and pulled one of Mitch's shirts on with some underpants. My hand was reaching for the door to go searching for coffee when I heard voices. Not wanting to interrupt, I pressed my ear to the door.

"...the device wasn't faulty. The reaction you are describing is the toxin activating. Lyza must have stopped taking the tablets."

"I've watched her take them most mornings. Something else caused this."

"Mitch, none of the other subjects have had this problem. It's unique to her, so the problem must be her." Just how many had this mad man subjected to this torture?

"Could it be a genetic thing, or possibly an environmental thing?"

"Genetic, no. It was made specifically for Lyza, ensuring her body wouldn't reject it. However, that's not to say something else couldn't have caused it. I'll run some blood tests, see if I can determine the cause, and create a new batch for you."

"Forget it. I won't be needing it."

"Are you sure? If she finds out?"

"I'll deal with it then."

There was a moment's silence. "Okay, Mitch. But she'll need a follow-up to ensure the virus is destroyed."

"Of course."

"Can I get the pills?" The fridge door opened and closed. "Mitch, these aren't the antitoxins."

"What do you mean? That's the bottle you gave me."

"Yes, but this is aspirin. Someone has swapped the pills for aspirin. That's what caused the virus to activate."

"Can you tell me how long ago?"

"It's normally fourteen days to get to this point, but accounting for her training regime you've described, I'd say at least seven to ten days allowing for her metabolism."

Cursing, Mitch slammed something shut or on the bench. "Either way, it happened while we were in Europe."

"Were the pills ever away from you?"

"Several times. They got left at the hotel with Stacey while we were out. They got left behind in Lucerne when I needed to move Lyza quickly. Any of the team and several hotel staff could have swapped them, but why would they?"

The doctor sighed. "Maybe a staff member thought they were something more exotic, either way, we know the cause now. Are you sure you don't want a second batch?"

"No, I'll deal with it. Just make sure the virus is out of her system. Let's tell her it was caused by a virus."

"It was," the doctor seemed humored.

"She can keep taking the pills. Aspirin won't hurt her. Let her think she still needs it." The fridge opened and closed again.

"Ah, I see your game. Okay, well, let me check my patient. I'll stay for the week just to ensure she's clear. I just hope the time she had was enough to reverse her illness."

Moving back to the bathroom, I turned on the tap, rewashing my face. If I didn't need the pills anymore, that meant the toxin wasn't an issue. One obstacle down. If the virus was the long-term preventative to my leaving, then the nano's activation range was restricted. Wiping my face dry, I assessed my reflection to see that I still looked like death warmed up.

When I stepped into the bedroom, Mitch was waiting with the doctor. Since Mitch was dressed casually, I hazarded a guess he was skipping work today.

Touching his fingers to his chest, Mitch tucked them in to give me a thumbs-up as he asked how I was feeling.

There was no way to just give a thumbs up after that experience. *"Like I was cryogenically frozen, stored for a hundred years, then thawed."*

Watching my hands, Mitch sighed. *"I'm sorry that happened. We think you have a virus that caused it. The doctor is going to give you something to ensure it doesn't cause any more problems."*

Lifting a brow, I considered Mitch. *"The last time he gave me an injection, he infected me with torture."*

"I promise he will give you nothing more than an antibiotic. He'll even show you the vial first."

Peering at the two men with the distrust they deserved, I let the silence between us fall into that uncomfortable area. Hesitant, I stepped towards the bed and sat down. The doctor approached and stuck a thermometer in my ear. While we waited for the device to get the reading, I glanced at Mitch, held my hands out to the side and moved them in and out, pointed to the doctor, and then drew a cross on my upper left arm where the nurses in the military wore the red cross.

"She went to get some supplies." Mitch looked at his watch. "She should have been back by now." Taking out his phone, Mitch hit a button as he stepped out of the room.

The doctor put the thermometer away and used a stethoscope to check my breathing. After that, he came back holding up an otoscope and tongue depressor. "Say, ah."

Opening my mouth, I stuck my tongue out.

The doctor frowned. "The tongue is still discolored. I'll give you a second hit of antitoxin to ensure it's gone for good." Taking out a vial, he handed it to me, indicating I should roll it in my palms.

Reading the label, I noted the name on the label and rolled it to warm it up.

By the time the doctor was packing up, Mitch was coming back into the room. "That was Stacey. Jenna is missing."

Stopping, the doctor's brows drew down low over his eyes, taking him from handsome to sinister looking. "What do you mean, missing?"

"She never turned up to pick up the supplies. The car she was in is at the hotel, but she's not there."

"She wouldn't just leave, Mitch."

"I know. There were signs of a struggle. We think Jenna was abducted."

21

____

LIFE AND DEATH

Flipping the toasty on the frypan, I waited for it to brown up. Stepping back, I observed Mitch through the glass sliding door, still talking on his phone. Switching off the burner, I plated up the toasty, poured two sodas, and set Mitch's dinner on one side of the table, mine on the other. Walking to the glass door, I rapped my knuckle against it. When Mitch turned to look at me, I pointed the index and middle finger to my mouth as if they were a fork I was about to eat off, moved it away, and did the same with my left hand before doing it with the right again.

Holding up a finger, Mitch indicated he'd be a minute. Sighing, I went back to the table. Sitting with one leg bent up, so my foot was on the chair, I picked up my toasty and started eating. Mitch came in as I was just finishing mine. Setting a hand on the table, another on the back of my chair, Mitch bent down to meet my eyes. Staring into those moss irises, I noted they weren't curious; they were sure as they stared into mine. Without flinching, I sat there with Mitch studying my eyes for over a minute. Holding his stare, I even raised my brow in challenge. Smirking a little, Mitch shook his head as he looked to the floor for a second.

As his head came up, his hand secured my cheek before his lips found mine in a deep, hungry kiss. Guiding me up out of the chair, Mitch pressed my body tight to his. Melding to his form, I threaded my fingers into his hair, gripping the short charcoal strands to bring us as close as possible. When my muscles protested being used, I whimpered but pressed onward. Mouth traveling south, Mitch kissed over my neck and exposed décolletage. Grabbing the top of my singlet, he pulled it down, so there was nothing in his way to my nipple.

A phone buzzed loudly in the breathy silence. Pulling back, eyes glazed and hungry, hair mussed, Mitch checked his phone and swore. Moving my top back into place, Mitch walked out. Closing my eyes in annoyance, I dropped back in my seat. Lost in thought about that kiss, my eyes stared over at the molten cheese seeping out the side of Mitch's toasty. Still hungry, I grabbed it and started eating.

Reappearing with Fred and Moses, Mitch went to the fridge, getting them both a drink before they all joined me at the table. "The security camera showed Jenna getting in the car with another woman." Fred slid a photo across the table to Mitch.

Assessing the woman, Mitch shook his head and put it in front of me. Pointing to me, Mitch brushed his thumb against his temple then held the photo up, his finger tapping on the unknown woman.

Spotting the nurse in the picture, I studied how she was getting in the car calmly, with little coercion, but her eyes were wide with anxiety. A person's eyes and body language could tell you so much. Holding the car door was a woman with African heritage. Exhaling, I nodded as I spelled out the name on my fingers. *"Talia. Very smart, good with computers, but didn't have the stomach for fieldwork."*

Making a fist, Mitch left his right pinkie out and lifted his shoulders as he pounded the fist into his left palm. *"She failed?"*

Shaking my head, I pointed to Mitch, flipped a C in front of my face, and repeated his gesture before forming a ring with my thumb and index, pushing it out, and then scratching my hooked index down the side of my face. *You can only fail if you try.* *"Talia freaked out around guns and knives and couldn't handle violence. She was redeployed."*

Eye twitching, Moses sat back in his chair and folded his arms.

Signing and talking out loud for Fred's benefit, Mitch peered at me. "What does redeploy mean?"

"I couldn't tell you."

"Best guess?"

Keeping my eyes off Moses so I couldn't react to him, I answered honestly. *"I always thought they harnessed other skills, found your strength, and utilized it."*

Watching my hands, Mitch lifted a brow as he raised his eyes to meet mine. "What was Talia's strength?"

"Communication. She was very good at getting people to do what she wanted."

"Coercion? And now she works for Noel."

Frowning to myself, I couldn't fathom how Noel could have recruited Talia, but maybe it happened. Risking looking to Moses for confirmation, I shrugged. Moses stared at the photo, not giving anything away.

Chewing the inside of his cheek, Fred took the photo back. "How did she convince Jenna to go with her? Jenna knows what is at stake."

Mitch scratched his head. "They offered her something worth the risk. We can't really blame her for taking the chance. Lennon is a megalomaniac asshole."

Fred lifted his brow. "He is good at what he does. Why do you think they took Jenna?"

Mitch turned his eyes to me. "I'm not sure. I thought they would have tried for Lennon; hence, the protection we gave him." Raising a brow, Mitch silently questioned me.

Picking up my soda, I took a drink.

"But then, a smart person might have foreseen that and gone for a different avenue." Chuckling to himself, Mitch ran his hand through his hair, swearing under his breath.

Fred and Moses were looking between us. "Did I miss something?" Fred asked. "Do you think Lyza set this up?"

Mitch tilted his head towards Fred, so I couldn't see his mouth, and shrugged. "You don't think it's a hell of a coincidence that Lyza got sick, needing Lennon to be brought here, and the only other person who knows how I was controlling Lyza is suddenly taken?"

Fred looked to me, bewildered. "But she hasn't been in contact with anyone since she got back."

"Who said Lyza planned this? Someone swapped Lyza's pills for aspirin, remember. You and I both know Jenna wanted out of that marriage. Maybe through Lyza, she found the way."

Hiding his face in his hands, Fred cursed. "Jesus, I was tired and hurt, and I left them alone together."

"Jenna has been hurting for a lot longer. I can't blame her for taking the chance." Standing up, Mitch sighed. "Secure Lennon and make sure his facility is secure. We don't want his research falling into the wrong hands."

Pushing away from the table, Fred stood slowly. Watching him, I wondered if he was still hurting from the accident. Mitch barely showed his injury, but the bruises were still there, as were mine. "Come on, Moses. You're with me tonight."

Moses and I exchanged looks. Standing to his full height, Moses didn't appear half as short as I knew he was next to Fred. Not that he was short for a male, he was just smaller than the two in the room.

Taking another drink of my soda, I stood and started cleaning up from dinner while Mitch showed the men out. When he returned, Mitch wrapped his arms around me from behind and put his mouth to my ear. "I understand why you did it, Lyza. I would have done the same, but others can't know. We need them to feel safe around you."

Staring at my hands in the soapy water, I ignored his words. "She won't be hurt, will she?" Mitch turned my face half towards him, so I could see his lips as he stroked my cheek. "Stacey told me it hurts you to talk. I don't want to hurt you anymore. If you don't want to talk, don't. Just know that I know."

Watching his lips, I felt my stomach warm. Moving his hand from my hip, I slid it up to my breast. Leaning in, Mitch pinched my lips with his tenderly. Sucking and biting his way down my throat, Mitch reached beneath my skirt to grab my knickers and peel them down my legs.

Dropping to his knees behind me, Mitch spread my thighs as I rose up on my toes and leaned over the sink. The first glide of his tongue made my toes want to curl, my fingers gripped the porcelain, and I bit my lip as Mitch skipped dinner and went straight for dessert. Licking and sucking my honeyed core, Mitch didn't stop until my body seized, and I breathed his name with reverence.

When Mitch stood, I turned to face him, kissed his mouth slowly, sipping my honey from his lips while my hands worked his belt buckle loose. Lowering to my knees, I unzipped his fly, shoved his pants to the ground, and gave thanks. Mitch gripped my hair, controlling his thrusts and my head, but nothing he did could hold my tongue and lips. I licked and sucked him with everything I had. I wanted the emotions he stirred in me to be transferred to him through my mouth. He needed to know those moments he longed for weren't his alone.

Pulling away quickly, Mitch cursed, grabbing his bulging shaft to control his need. Lifting my face, I smiled up at him, ensuring he saw the way I enjoyed the taste of him on my tongue. Grabbing his shirt, I yanked him down to me and kissed him carefully. Mitch moved beneath me willingly, letting me direct him to lie on the floor. When I straddled his hips and took him within me, Mitch breathed my name like it was the best word in the world.

Taking my time, I enjoyed the feel of him, letting his long thickness occupy every bit of vacancy inside me, allowing him to stroke my lust, creating a slow burn of desire. Every stroke building another climax in me, adding wood to the fire, knowing, in the end, it would be an untamable bonfire.

Half lifting, Mitch pulled my singlet over my head. He spread his legs so he could sit up, and then he captured my nipple between his teeth. Crying out, I threw my head back as my body rocked forward. Mitch licked and sucked and catalyzed my passion. On edge, I used his hair to lift his face and kiss him with everything in me.

Gasping from the kiss, I stared into his striking eyes as I rode him. Smiling, Mitch kept his eyes locked with mine. "Come," he whispered as he gripped my hips.

One word, and I was undone. Throwing my head back, I cried out my fulfillment, body clenching and electricity firing through me. Pumping my body, Mitch followed me into neutral territory. A place where we stopped being our jobs. A state of being where the world couldn't find us, where we could be lovers without consequence.

As I sat wrapped in his arms, both our chests heaving, I knew it couldn't last, but I would steal as many of these moments as I could get. Kissing along his shoulder, my fingers massaged along his back as I put my lips to his ear. "They've found me. They want Noel first, but after he's dealt with, I have to go home." Mitch's arms tensed around me. I swallowed around the sudden lump in my throat. "If you let me go, they won't harm you."

"Lyza..."

"I can't defy them without consequence. You know that."

Bowing his head, Mitch rested it on my shoulder. "Is there nothing I can do?"

Closing my eyes, I squeezed him tighter. Sighing, Mitch lifted us off the floor and carried us to his bathroom. We showered quietly, washing each other clean, kissing, and holding each other beneath the running water.

For the first time since the opera in Rome, I slept naked beside him. Mitch held me in his arms, and we kissed until we fell asleep. In the morning, we kissed the sunrise into the sky, and when light filtered through the window, Mitch covered me like a blanket and made me feel him in places I'd never felt anyone before.

Biting my lip at the emotions his touch induced, I wondered if it was real or a temporary fantasy, a bubble that would be popped the next time our interests clashed. I'd never felt anything but lust during sex before, but this, what I had with Mitch, it was the first time the word intimacy seemed right.

As we lay catching our breath afterward, I wondered again why Noel wanted Mitch dead and why my father guaranteed Mitch wouldn't be harmed if he didn't interfere. What was I missing? Moses knew. As soon as I could get him alone, I would find out.

Wrapping me tighter in his arms, Mitch kissed my forehead. Closing my eyes, I savored this moment, just in case it never happened again. It was a dream that would stay with me for life. I knew it wasn't real. I was Death; Mitch was life. We couldn't coexist.

22

ROMANCE IN VIOLENCE

GRABBING MY LEG LIKE I EXPECTED, I LET MOSES TAKE MY WEIGHT AS I pushed off on my other leg, jumped up, and used my free leg to stamp on his chest just below the sternum, forcing all the air out of his lungs. Releasing my leg, Moses curled over. Twisting to land, I quickly spun back and drove my elbow down next to his shoulder blade. Grunting, Moses reached behind him, grabbed my leg at the knee, and yanked it forward. As I went down, I kicked up with my free leg and hit the crown jewels. Cursing, Moses fell to the ground in pain. Jumping up, I grinned.

Tapping the nail of his left index finger with his right forefinger, Moses glared, accusing me of fighting dirty. With a shrug, I offered him a hand up. Waving me away, Moses rolled onto his back to recover. Walking to the side of the training room, I picked up my towel, wiping away two hours of sparring. Collecting my water bottle, I started drinking as I put my back to the wall and slid down it to rest.

Lifting my head, I observed the walkway outside Mitch's office. They were still trying to locate Jenna. That was a lost cause, especially since they thought Noel took her. Noel asked who he had to kill, so he received Lennon's name. I gave Jenna to the arrow. Moses confirmed this morning that Talia still worked for one of the chapter houses.

Since Moses was with me when the nano malfunctioned, he was there when Mitch produced a hypodermic hidden in his fridge and stabbed me with it. Moses informed me he pocketed the syringe while Mitch fussed over me. That's all he'd revealed.

Sitting up slowly, Moses rubbed his sternum and winced. With a groan, he stood and limped over to get his water bottle, sinking down beside me before he took a long drink. *"It's been a long time since someone kicked my ass,"* Moses signed.

It made me smirk. *"Quite literally in this case."*

Watching my hands, Moses shoved my shoulder playfully. Holding in a chuckle, I smiled while Moses vocalized his humor.

"You two are looking cozy," Fred strolled in with a frown.

"I was just telling her I took it easy on her," Moses teased, signing for my benefit.

Pointing at Moses, I put my hands together in prayer and rocked them back and forth. He wished he could claim that.

Expression full of suspicion, Fred shoved his hands in his pockets. "She wouldn't train with me."

"I've been doing Wing Chun since I was a kid. We are fairly evenly matched."

Rolling my eyes, I repeated my previous gesture about his bullshit, making Moses laugh.

Fred assessed the two of us. "She's the boss's wife."

Moses' smile dropped along with his hands. "Yesterday, it sounded like she was his hostage. What's the story with that implant and toxin shit?"

"She's got a genetic disorder. It's been killing her slowly for years. The implant was treating it. The toxin stopped her body from fighting it."

Frowning, I tilted my head as I read Fred's lips. Looking at Moses, I smacked his leg and held my hands out to the side as I lifted my shoulders. *What did I miss?*

Lost in thought, Moses looked up at Fred, ignoring me. "Is it still killing her?"

"I don't know. We have to wait for the toxin to clear her system to test for it again. Two weeks may not have been enough."

Smacking Moses' leg again, I pursed my lips when he ignored me. As I went to do it a third time, Moses grabbed my forearm and held it, his brow pinching right above his nose. Releasing my arm, Moses stood up and turned his back to Fred, so neither of us could see his face. "If it didn't work, how long does she have?"

"It's hard to say. Five years ago, Lyza was given a year. She went into remission, and the disorder became dormant. She could potentially have years or months."

Pulling his shirt back on, Moses kept his back to everyone. "If it's genetic, will it be inherited by children?"

"She doesn't want any, so it's not a factor."

Freezing, Moses dropped his eyes to me, shock clear on his features. Studying his reaction, ideas burst to life in my head. I was married to Noel, he knew that, but his mission was to kill Noel.

Stepping back around, Moses used SimCom this time. "I'm going to go have a shower." Turning military style, he marched off.

Watching him go, Fred then returned his gaze to me. "He has a crush on you."

Waving the idea away as I stood up, I kept my voice low so only Fred could hear. "He knows I'm married."

"Hasn't stopped men before."

He had a point. "I have two husbands as it is. That's already one too many."

Seeming relieved, Fred relaxed his stance. "How are you feeling?"

"Tired."

"Have a shower, then find a lounge in the rec room to rest."

Nodding my head, I stepped into him and kissed his cheek. "Any news on Jenna?"

Fred shook his head. Grabbing up my stuff, I headed towards the showers, but Fred grabbed my arm. "Ah, maybe wait until Moses has finished," Fred blushed as he said it, remembering the change rooms were unisex.

Smirking, I gave Fred a wink. "You could come and watch. Make sure I behave myself?"

Fred chuckled. "Let's get something to eat."

Rolling my eyes, I walked with Fred out to the rec room, which held a full kitchen and a completely stocked fridge. Fred and I got busy making lunch.

"What are you making?" Fred asked as I wove bacon strips into a mat.

Spreading smashed avocado over it, I covered half the square with warm shredded roast chicken and topped that with cheese. Rolling it like a sushi roll, I then cooked it on the stovetop. Turning it on the pan to make sure the bacon was cooked.

When I turned off the heat, I placed the roll on the plate and cut it up like sushi. I put the plate between Fred and me as I helped myself to a glass of goat's milk while I waited for it to cool. There were five different milk types in this fridge, of which six liters was chocolate-flavored and only one-liter soy. Gee, I wonder if this was a male-dominant workplace?

Ready to sit, I returned to the bench and picked up one of the slices, enjoying all the yummy protein. Trying a piece, Fred looked surprised by how good it was. "This is fantastic."

"What's fantastic?" Walking in with a raised brow, Mitch grabbed a carton of chocolate milk from the fridge. I smirked.

"You're wife's cooking. You have to try this."

Considering the plate, Mitch picked up a slice and took a bite. "Jesus, this is scrumptious. It makes me regret not eating dinner last night. Somewhat." He winked at me. Fred scoffed.

Taking another slice, starving for food, I smacked Mitch's hand when he went to grab another. Waving the men away, I wrapped my spare arm protectively around my plate.

"Seriously, you're not going to share?" Fred pouted.

"If you let me have another slice, I'll take you upstairs and eat you for dessert," Mitch signed, Fred not understanding.

Pausing, I considered the offer. It was a hard choice. Mitch was so much more satisfying, but he wasn't going to ease my hungry tummy. Shaking my head, I kept eating.

"I'm insulted," Mitch huffed.

Keeping my elbows low to block any would-be-quick hands from pinching my lunch, I signed for Mitch. *"Don't be. It was a hard choice. If I was male, I could show you how hard."*

Mitch started laughing. *"Well, thank god you're not."*

Brows pinching, Fred looked between us. "Wait, I missed what she said."

"You should practice your sign language then," Mitch signed without talking.

"Oh, that's how it's going to be." Fred stood up and stepped out of my eye line. "You may want to rethink her bodyguard. He's developing a thing for her."

Blinking, Mitch's humor faded, and he didn't bother signing. "I saw. I'll keep an eye on it." Satisfied, Fred made himself scarce. Circling around the bench, Mitch wrapped his arms around me, put his face next to mine, and kissed my cheek. "It looked like you got a good workout with Moses. He definitely has some fighting skills. Some of those moves I've only seen in one type of martial arts. One that is very rare and requires training overseas."

Picking up another slice of the bacon roll, I shoved it in his mouth. Taking the last part, I started eating.

Biting into his slice, Mitch put it down. Holding his hands out in front, he signed his next question. *"Is Moses a plant?"*

Considering his hands, I pointed to the side, knocked the air in front of me, then turned my hand back toward me and opened it as releasing something, and finished by turning both fists upside down, leaving my little fingers out and knocking them together. *"He's not your enemy."*

"That didn't answer my question. Is he a..."

Grabbing Mitch's hands, I wrapped them back around me as Moses walked into the rec room, freshly showered. "That smells great," he used SimCom. "I could smell it down the hall. I'm starving now."

Tensing, watching the fluidity of Moses' sign language, Mitch squeezed me a little. When I looked up to meet his eyes, he gave a slight nod then kissed my nose. Butterflies stretched their wings in my toes, and I had to wiggle my digits to stop myself from getting giddy.

"It tastes even better." Stepping back, Mitch turned to me as he signed. *"How about you teach us how to make it?"*

Rolling my eyes, I stood up. *"You'll need bacon rashes."*

"I'll get it," Moses replied instantly.

Smiling, Mitch tenderly held my face in his hands, placing the most delicate and swoon-worthy kiss on my lips. Closing my eyes, I let it permeate through my very being. When I opened my eyes, Mitch was smiling down on me like the moon on the earth. A movement to my right caught my eye, and I turned my head to see Moses watching us, his eyes sharp and assessing.

Dropping his gaze as he placed the bacon on the bench, Moses used that moment to slip his mask on, then lifted smiling eyes, mouth, and hands to address us. *"Okay, chef, what's next?"*

Smiling at Mitch, I pointed to the other side of the bench, indicated to myself, and waved my hands in front of me. *"I'm not doing it for you."*

Mitch clicked his fingers. "Damn! I thought I'd got away with it." Dropping another peck on my lips, Mitch joined Moses on the other side.

Standing on the far side, I finished my lunch while instructing them how to weave their bacon. The filling I let them get adventurous with. Mitch chose to add an egg to his; Moses went for a BLT with mayonnaise. Once they had sliced their rolls, I stole a slice of each.

"Hey!"

Holding a hand up to Moses, I left my index and thumb out like an L, turned my arm, and sprung my hand up so the thumb was pointing to my mouth. *"The master must check the apprentice's work."* Watching my serious consideration of their meals, they both laughed. Tucking my thumb, I held my hand splayed and pointing up close to my chest and gave it a little tug down. *"Passable."*

"Is she always like this?" Moses asked Mitch.

Eyes glazing over, Mitch smiled. "Only when she's happy." Our eyes stayed locked for a few moments following.

Moses cleared his throat. *"So, what're the plans for this afternoon?"*

Standing up, I held my hand above and to the side, gesturing a shower. Taking Mitch's wrist, I pulled him with me out of the room. Mitch made sure to bring his plate with him, but I didn't mind. It was empty by the time he undressed and followed me into the shower.

Chuckling as he pulled me close under the water, Mitch met my eyes. "I need to get a do not disturb sign for the bathroom door."

Reading his lips, I kept my voice low, my hand busy stroking his rising passion. "That could be awkward with the men. Make sure you invest in soap on a rope during training."

Laughing, Mitch reached past me and pressed his hand on the liquid body wash dispenser. "Way ahead of you."

23

SEX TOYS AND ORDERS

"You need to stretch your legs," Moses signed when he found me in the rec room again later.

Exhaling in annoyance because I was still recovering from my self-inflicted repeated torture, I stood up and grabbed my handbag. Sticking his head in the security room, Moses reported where we were going, then he walked me out the front door.

"How come I never saw you when we were at the compound?" I signed as we walked.

"Because we weren't in the same chapter house."

Watching his hands, I frowned. *"Where were you based?"*

"I am based here in one of the American Chapters."

"Why were you trained here? I thought the different chapters had different skills?"

Moses looked sidelong at me. *"We do. You're a Scythe. You are told where to go, who to kill. You are sent on a job with that end result in mind. Assassination is your Chapter's specialty. I'm a Hunter. My main priority on a mission is to find the target. Sometimes, that's all I do. I tell the Chamber where to find them, and I go home. Other times, I find and protect. Occasionally, I find and kill."*

I absorbed what he revealed. *"I didn't choose my skill."*

Moses considered my hands. *"I know. Your file actually nominated you to a different Chapter, but your disability made you ineligible, so they left you with your father."*

"He was never going to give me up to another Chapter. That's why he did what he did."

Stopping with his brow pinched, Moses turned to face me with a frown. *"Explain that."*

"I wasn't born deaf. My father did this to me." Not that I thought my father's intentions were to deafen me. He probably would have succeeded had it been, but he definitely intended to silence me. *"My mother told me I was a natural Guardian. She brought me to Paris for the transfer to the Guardian Chapter. I was never meant to see my father, let alone end up with him."*

Brow furrowing, Moses took a step closer. *"What you are suggesting is a massive breach of the rules."*

"So was torturing and killing the Father of the Australian Chapter house. He still killed the man because my mother took up with him."

Observing my hands, his pupils dilated slightly, and his breathing hesitated. He thought long and hard about his answer. And still, he stayed silent.

"My father told me he is the angel of death. That my mother should have known he would punish her for her betrayal eventually."

"I see." Moses conveyed his displeasure with that straightforward response.

We started walking again. "*I wasn't the only one. Noel was recommended for Guardianship too. It's why he did what he did. He wanted the choice.*"

"*Did you choose to go with Noel?*" I shook my head. "*Can you tell me what happened?*"

Turning to face Moses, we stopped walking again. "*I went to stop him. I knew that his move that night was to set a wheel in motion. I didn't know what or why, just that it would change things, and he could never come back from it. I was too late.*"

"*Why didn't you come back?*"

"*I got injured. Noel shot me. I was caught by the Americans, interrogated, and locked in a facility. Mitch rescued me.*"

"*Why?*"

"*Because I saved him that night. I gave him medical assistance to hold him over until help arrived.*"

Blinking several times, Moses took a deep breath. "*Stopping to save him is why you were caught?*"

Hanging my head was my silent confession. In the end, I was Death and I should never have messed with life.

Exhaling hard, Moses waved for me to move with him as he started walking again. "*I've been hunting Noel for years. My entire Chapter has. No one has come close to finding him. We even tried hunting you to find him.*"

"*But you found him this time.*"

Shaking his head, Moses opened his hand and then lifted it as he snatched it closed before pointing to me. "*When Fairchild ran your name, it popped up on my radar. I tracked him to find you, and while chasing you around Europe, I finally got a lead on Noel. He surfaced for you, Lyza. If Noel gets you, I doubt we'll ever find him again.*" Turning a corner, Moses used my arm to turn me too.

Glancing over my shoulder at the store window, I caught sight of our tail. *"Relax, Noel's not going to grab me until he has a way to free me from Mitch. He's already got me alone once."*

Moses didn't look happy but seemed relieved to know I'd stalled Noel. *"He will still kill Fairchild before he goes. We probably shouldn't leave him alone."*

"I told him if he kills Mitch, he kills me. Mitch is safe for as long as Noel wants me alive."

Moses slowed his pace a little. *"Good to know."* Turning another corner, Moses opened a door and stepped us inside. He moved us into a recess in the wall so we couldn't be seen from the door.

The shadow of a man fell across the floor, lifting its arms to block the light and peer into the gloom of the entryway. After a moment, the shadow moved away. Slipping his phone from his pocket, Moses used the camera function to spy around the corner at the door, putting his arm across me to stop me from stepping out. Not that I was going to. I could tell our pursuer was still there. Even though the shadow had withdrawn, the light in the hall was still duller than it used to be.

It took another two minutes of standing there for the light to grow brighter, but I still stayed put. Moses kept watching around the corner with his phone. Thirty seconds later, the entryway became dull again. Another minute, and it cleared. Moses was keeping an eye on his phone while we waited.

The phone started vibrating. Lifting it up, Moses read the text. *"We're clear,"* he signed after putting the phone away. Stacking his flat hands in front of his chest, Moses took the top hand and swept it up to be level with his eyes, indicating we were going upstairs.

From the outside, it looked like your regular access to an above shop office. I'd initially thought it was a lawyer's office. The sign by the steps made it clear what we were about to enter. *"This is a sex shop!"* My cheeks felt warm while I signed my surprise.

Watching my hands and then looking at my face, Moses chuckled. *"They have rooms for hire too."* He winked when my cheeks flamed even hotter. Checking the door one more time, he led the way upstairs.

It wasn't as seedy as I feared. Upstairs was light and bright. The alcove at the top of the stairs housed some high heels shoes for sale. Spotting a pair I liked the look of, I decided to try them before we left.

Going straight to the counter, Moses slipped the cashier a hundred. *"We're not here,"* he informed the busty blonde with heavy makeup behind the counter. She had a fantastic figure, but the boobs were not natural. Her ease with the skimpy outfit and how she appraised Moses with barely any interest suggested I shouldn't be surprised to see her in one of the films on the shelves inside. Of course, she could just be dressing the part.

Gesturing I follow him, Moses went through the entry gate. Taking the shoe I liked to the counter, I held up nine fingers.

"Should have it in the back, I'll take a minute," the cashier informed me.

Gesturing that I would go in and look around, then come back, I checked to make sure she understood. Not sign language, but charades worked too.

"Sure thing, honey." Smiling sincerely, she collected the shoe from the counter.

Walking through the gate, I glanced back, noting all the cameras, and I caught her checking out my backside. When her eyes lifted, she winked at me. I wasn't sure what to think. I'd never been hit on by a female before, even in prison. But then, I was basically in solitary. Catching up with Moses, I found him laughing.

"First time in a sex-positive establishment?"

Bowing my right fist over my left index finger, I gave a shrug. *"I've never needed help."*

Lifting a brow at my signing, Moses smirked. *"Me neither, but civilians are right into this stuff."* Leading the way into a hallway, Moses opened a door. Holding it for me to step in, Moses then closed and locked it. Already in the room was a middle-aged woman with black hair. She sat on the bed, flipping through a dirty magazine.

"Surprisingly, these articles aren't half bad," she began with wide eyes. The woman's facial expression limitation made me wonder if she endured Botox treatments to defend against aging. Rising off the bed, the woman placed the magazine aside as she eyed me up and down. "I'm Emily. Moses' Mother."

They looked nothing alike. For starters, Moses was as white as the Cliffs of Dover, and Emily was as black as a starless sky. She was beautiful in her age, slim, muscles in her arms, and calves well-defined. I knew straight away she wasn't his real mother, but the mother of his Chapter, just like my father was called Father by everyone in our Chapter. Emily was the head huntress.

While I bowed my head in greeting, Emily waited. Once I lifted my eyes to her face again, she started talking. "Moses scored quite the medal for locating you, Lyzebel. Even I went hunting for you years ago and came up empty," Emily huffed. "You are my dead albatross." Observing my lack of reaction, Emily turned her unemotional face to Moses. "Did you get it?"

Stepping forward, Moses gave Emily what looked like a hypodermic syringe in a plastic bag. "Good, we'll reverse engineer it to free Jenna from her husband." Shoving the package in her purse, Emily kept talking, not bothering to ensure I could follow the conversation. "And you are sure the doctor's work is undone on Lyzebel?"

"Positive. I heard the doctor trying to convince Fairchild to let him create another set," Moses reported.

Nodding, Emily turned her face away, so I couldn't see her lips. "Is she still loyal?"

Moses didn't even hesitate. "I believe so. Though..." he shifted to stop me reading his lips too. Moses then informed Emily of everything I'd revealed on the way here, my imprisonment, how I'd been caught, and my disability.

Emily turned to consider me, then looked away again. "Debbie will be grateful to know how Mitchell survived, but that won't change orders."

"You could support her moving chapters."

"She is deaf and mute. Guardianship is out. She proved herself in her father's house. That will be her home for life."

"We could bring her into ours."

Leaning closer to Moses, Emily's voice dropped an octave. "She is not a Hunter."

"As my wife. If we are designated a breeding pair, then we have grounds."

Emily blinked. "She's married, Moses."

"That will be resolved shortly. I've never been designated a wife. You could assign her to me, and the matter is done. Her missions will still come from the Chamber; she just won't be under her father's control."

Shifting her stance, Emily stepped forward and put a caring hand on Moses's shoulder. "I'll see what I can do, but most likely, she will be assigned a new husband from her own house. She is also an adult now, so she has the right to refuse. Her father can't accept advances on her behalf like he did with D'Avive."

"Exactly, and I'm in a place to win her affection. Something needs to be done now, or..." Moses cut off, but Emily encouraged him to continue. "The way she looks at Fairchild, it's not good, Mother."

"She's in love with him?"

"I don't know; she could be faking it, but he looks at her the same way, and I believe he is sincere."

Studying Moses, Emily frowned. "Are you sure the problem isn't you coveting what you cannot have?"

Growing annoyed with the conversation, I tapped Moses on the shoulder and waited until they were both looking at me to start signing. *"If you don't need me, I'm going to go try on those shoes."*

They both watched my hands. Emily frowned. "What did she say?"

"She's bored and wants to go shopping," Moses relayed while signing to me that Emily wanted to talk to me.

Allowing my agitation at being ignored to show in my gestures, I asserted my presence. *"Well, tell her to talk to me already, so I can go."*

Moses put his hand to his chest and rubbed it down, then repeated, telling me to be patient. Taking a deep breath, I glared at them and waited.

Facing me directly, Emily squared her shoulders. "Chamber has issued orders. Moses is to protect yourself and Fairchild."

Pointing to my chest, I lifted my fists and, crossing them in front of me, I turned them as I pushed them forward as if blocking something and indicated to the side.

"She's already protecting Fairchild," Moses translated.

"We thank you for that, but that is not your role here." Emily took on an air of authority. I remember being scared of the Chamber members when they spoke like that, but it didn't seem to affect me the same way anymore.

Stepping forward slowly, eyes flashing my warning, I lifted my shoulders as I touched my chest, then banged my crossed wrists together.

Clearing his throat, Moses took a protective step between his mother and me. "She wants to know what you think her role is?"

Emily blinked but didn't back down. "Your mission is to terminate Noel D'Avive." Emily waited for a reaction. It didn't happen. "You are ordered to kill your husband."

24

DESIRES AND INSTINCTS

"Where have you been?" Mitch asked, sounding annoyed as he walked into his office.

Propping my feet up on his desk, I waved a foot around, admiring the four-inch platform stilettos I was wearing.

"Shoe shopping?" Mitch raised a brow, but there was something off in the way he held himself.

Lifting my hand, I let the silk handcuffs hang from one finger. Mitch's eyes widened. Coming closer, he spotted the unmarked bag by the side of the chair. With a mix of excitement and fear in his eyes, he peeked inside the bag. Pulling out the tube of lube, Mitch read the front of the bottle.

"Vanilla flavored warming lubricant." Clearing his throat, Mitch put the bottle back in the bag before he stood straight and met my smiling eyes. *"Lyza, you are so wet as it is. Why would we need lube?"*

Lifting my hands to sign, I had to stop to think about it. Lifting my shoulder and arms out to the side, I then flashed my hands to the left side. The sign language for what I wanted wasn't something I knew.

Watching my hands, Mitch pressed his backside against his desk and brushed his thumb over my lips. "Then, use words."

Licking my lips, I caught his thumb and sucked it into my mouth. Pupils dilating as I wrapped my tongue around his digit, Mitch groaned as I worked my mouth as if it was another part of his body. Swallowing hard, Mitch pulled his thumb back and pressed my lower lip as his fingers cupped my chin. "I love your voice, Lyza. I want to hear everything you want me to do to you, fall from your lips."

My body trembled with desire. When I stood up, Mitch spread his legs and used my hips to direct me between them. Caressing his chest through his shirt, I ran my nose along his jaw. My breathing was labored, just thinking about what I wanted from him. "Take me home."

Holding me tight against him, Mitch kissed across my shoulder. His lips heated every bit of skin he touched, tendrils reaching from the contact to my nipples and sex.

"You're the only man I've been with other than my husband." Eyes blurring from the inferno of lust igniting in my skin, I licked my lips. "I want to experience things."

Raising his gaze to my eyes, Mitch leaned back so I could see his mouth. "What things?"

Considering him, I lifted the silk handcuffs. "Trust."

Mitch blinked. His eyes searching mine as if there was a double meaning. Suddenly, his facial features closed in anger. "You want me to tie you up and have sex with you to prove you can trust me?"

Swallowing my disappointment that he didn't understand what I was asking, I stepped back. Touching my right fingers above my right breast, I waved them out. Dropping the handcuffs in the bag, I turned towards the door.

Catching my wrist, Mitch turned me back to him. "I don't want to forget it. I want to understand what you want."

Tears filled my eyes as Mitch's brows furrowed. How could I explain what I was feeling? That I was risking so much asking to explore more but terrified it was my last chance to ever experience this.

Hands caressing either side of my face, Mitch peered into my eyes. "Lyza?"

Shifting the skirt of my dress to my hip, I pointed to the tattoo. Brow's dropping low over his eyes, Mitch stroked the scar tissue.

Pointing to my chest, I brought my hands together in front of me, connecting to join the two circles I'd made with my thumbs and index fingers. Releasing the linked rings, I pointed to the side of Mitch as tears streaking down my face. *"I belong to them. You will be the last thing I get to choose for myself. Once Noel is dealt with, I will be taken back, and my freewill will remain here with you."*

Mitch watched my hands, anger in his eyes. His response was already in the tightness around his eyes and the hard clench of his jaw. "Mitch, you can't save me. All you can do is to make it, so I'll never forget this time with you."

Exhaling, Mitch stepped into me and caressed my face. "I love the new shoes, but save them for later. Where I'm going to take you, you'll need your running gear."

Lifting a brow in question, I tilted my head.

"Go get changed. You'll love it."

Intrigued, I headed downstairs to the change room. Mitch came in as I was pulling my sneakers on and proceeded to strip his business suit off. I watched. He watched me watch. When I licked my lips, he smirked and pointed his finger at me. *"No. Save those thoughts for later. This isn't about sex."*

Pouting, I sat back to watch him dress. Once he had his training gear on, he packed his bag. *"We won't be coming back tonight, so bring the shoes."* With a wink, he headed out.

Sporting a cheeky grin, I packed my bag and followed him. Moses was there waiting for Mitch. "Fred asked me to let you know he looked into that thing for you. He said he found some stuff worth investigating, and he will call you later."

"Thanks, Moses. Head home for the night. I'll take care of Lyza for the evening."

Nodding to Mitch, Moses turned that soul-deep gaze on me, looking me over as if I might be bleeding. Pointing the peace sign to his eyes, he then moved it towards me and dropped it down in farewell, telling me he'd see me tomorrow while talking to Mitch.

Stepping past us, Moses kept his eyes intent on me until he walked through the door for the change-room. When the door closed, Mitch lifted a brow in question. *"Did something happen between you two today?"*

"Stuff." With a shrug, I started towards the door.

Frowning at my gesture, Mitch let it go until we were in the car. Before he started the engine, he looked at me, thought about it, and huffed as he signed. *"You told me he wasn't my enemy?"*

"He's not."

"He wants you. That makes him an 'unfriendly.'"

"Nothing will happen between Moses and me. My father won't allow it."

Considering my signing, Mitch studied me before replying. *"That doesn't ease my concern. Not out of jealousy, but for your wellbeing. For your happiness."*

Nodding my head once in acknowledgment, I drummed the dashboard then held my hand in a pistol grip, pointing forward. Right now, I was living in the now. *"Let's go."*

Watching my hands, Mitch snickered. Putting his pickup in gear, Mitch headed out of the car park, and off we went.

MITCH HAD A REALLY NICE ASS. I'd often admired it since we first met, but now, trailing after him as we ran up the hillside, it was distracting me from how hard my body was functioning. The run wasn't challenging, but my lungs were working twice as hard.

Glancing over his shoulder, Mitch smiled when he saw I was still right behind him and picked up the pace. Keeping up with Mitch wasn't overly exertive for me, and the view was worth the extra effort. When we finally reached the top, Mitch stopped to catch his breath, and so did I.

The last time I was bent over, leaning on my knees to suck in the air, was a faint memory of my childhood. Normally, I could run for hours, and this trail wouldn't have taken longer than an hour. But it did feel harder to breathe.

"Albuquerque has a high altitude," Mitch huffed as he signed, but he was handling it. *"Thinner air makes you work harder. It makes you stronger and faster at normal altitude."*

His explanation made sense. Touching the side of my index finger above my brow, I saluted it forward to let him know I got it. Catching my breath, I gazed down at the city and the view beyond. The great Rio Grande flowed through the center of the town. *"That's why they could pounce so quickly. There is probably a chapter house located here."*

Mitch frowned. *"What do you mean?"*

"The chapter houses are always based in places with environments suitable for training strength and endurance. My chapter is based in the alps. There is another in the Canadian Rockies." I indicated the town below. *"This would be the perfect training ground for one of the American chapters."*

Exhaling hard with a curse, Mitch kicked at the ground. He'd set up his business smack bang in the center of a Cross and Arrow training center. Tapping his shoulder, how I had seen people comfort another, I tried to offer sympathy. When Mitch shot me a bizarre look, I took back my hand and returned to signing.

"More than likely, there are others who come here for the training environment, including athletes, with no knowledge of the local chapter." It's not like any of them would have known.

Watching me step away from him to take in the view, Mitch walked up beside me and placed his hand on my shoulder. He gave it a gentle squeeze, which felt nice. *"When you comfort someone. Just a gentle squeeze works best. Unless they are crying, then a hug is better."*

God, he would make me cry in a moment with the way he was looking at me like I was an abused child.

"No one ever comforted you before?" I shook my head slightly. Mitch nodded as if understanding. *"My mum. Comfort wasn't her thing. She was very awkward in dealing with me. The only thing she could do well was discipline. I learned comfort through girlfriends and teachers at school."*

"I was home-schooled. Too many bruises got questions asked."

Shifting his stance, Mitch frowned. *"Mine was just excused as me being a boy. Can you tell me about your childhood?"*

Meeting his eyes, I closed my index and middle finger on my thumb like a duck's bill.

"No, you can't, or no, you don't want to?"

Taking a deep breath, I considered the best way to explain it, then worked out the sign language I'd need. Not every word in the English language had an equal sign. Sometimes you had to swap words out or make signs up. *"I was an experiment. To see if raising soldiers outside the chapter houses worked better. To see if being raised in society made us better at our jobs. Too many were detached from society and wouldn't hesitate to kill innocent bystanders. So, they tried raising a few babies outside."*

"What went wrong?"

"My father was against the experiment. But an order from Chamber is an order."

Face contorting, Mitch shifted again. *"Chamber?"*

"Our leaders. The ones who pick our targets, our charges, our jobs. I don't know who they are, but I would guess they have influence high in the political powerhouses of the world."

Mitch stepped back a little.

"So, my mother went with a member of the English Chapter. He was to set up a new chapter house, and she was to raise me as a citizen of normal society and a soldier of the arrow. My mother fell in love with her protector. When it was time to bring me back, she informed my dad she wasn't going to return. That she was part of the Australian Chapter house now, and she was staying there. The rest, you know."

Mitch considered me. *"Why did she return you?"*

"I was tested. I didn't fit the Australian Chapter house. I was meant to meet a member of the chapter I'd tested for, who would take me to my new home. My father came to me instead. As it turns out, my father hadn't been sticking to the rules, and many of the young soldiers were kept when they should have gone elsewhere."

Looking off in the distance, Mitch seemed unsettled all of a sudden. *"You said you weren't the only baby raised outside?"*

"As far as I know, it's normal to have one leave every few years or so."

"What happens if the kids fail? If they are too soft or caring?"

Watching his hands, I translated the gestures and shrugged. *"I don't know. Different chapters specialize in different things. They would usually identify a house where we belong, I guess."*

"You're an assassin. What were you meant to be?"

"A Guardian. A protector."

"And Moses? What is he?"

Remaining quiet, I met Mitch's eyes without flinching. *"What are you puzzling in that head of yours?"*

Mitch came closer. *"Please. Trust me."*

"A Hunter. He locates people they need to find."

"That's it?"

"Sometimes. Other times he stays and protects until the Guardian is in place. If the target is to be killed and they have a window of opportunity, they take them out."

Mitch fidgeted. *"You called me life. Why did you call me that? Why am I life to your death?"*

My feet took a hesitant step towards him. Touching his face, I followed the contours of his features with an index finger. "I kill. It's what I was taught to do. My natural instinct is to protect, so it overrides what I was taught occasionally," I whispered. The pads of my fingers felt Mitch react to my voice. A slight tremor went through his body as he relaxed a little.

"I have never clung to life or desired it above dying. I don't desire death either," I murmured as my hand caressed over his heart. "You clung to life the night I met you. You desire it. Your morals and instincts are to protect and to give people a chance at living. You created your business out of your desire to live and give your fellow soldiers a chance at life after serving their country. You desire a normal existence with a wife and kids. That is why you are life."

Mitch turned his head to see my face. "I've never seen myself married, Lyza. I can't make relationships last. You are the first woman I could ever see it working with, but there are so many obstacles to that happening."

"You want kids?"

"Yes. I want kids."

Stepping away, I dropped my hands. "I don't."

The sun was starting to sink low. Moving to the track, I started running back to where Mitch parked his truck. When I reached the bottom, I stretched out while I waited for Mitch to catch up. He approached slowly, and I stood to meet him. His eyes were deep and thoughtful as he came so close our chests would touch on my next inhale.

Slowly, Mitch lowered his mouth to mine. He kissed me, slow and controlled. Lips pinched a path to my ear then Mitch nipped the lobe between his teeth. Gasping, I grabbed his biceps as my body automatically fell into his hold as he whispered in my ear.

"I won't be like your father. Choose me. Choose life with me. We can breed or not breed. I don't care. Just find a way to stay with me, Lyza. I desire my life with you."

25

A WIFE, A LOVER, A BROKEN KITCHEN CHAIR

"Are you sure about this?"

Considering Mitch's question, I raised my brow as I signed my response. *"Are you? You've been a little distracted tonight."*

"Of course, I'm distracted. You look stunning. I've been dying to get you home."

Observing each other like opponents in a chess game, we each waited for the other to make a move. Dropping my gaze to where Mitch held the silk restraints, I knew he wasn't entirely honest. Something changed on the mountain top today, but I couldn't pinpoint what.

We'd gone home, showered, dressed, and gone out to dinner. Just so I could wear my new shoes. All through dinner, I'd been replaying our conversation in my head and couldn't figure out what I'd said. Not wanting to miss this chance, I gave Mitch a quick, sure nod.

"Undress. Leave the heels."

Lowering the zip on my dress, I let it fall to the ground. Admiring me in only my skimpy knickers and heels, Mitch caught my wrist as I went to take off my scanties. "Leave them. The barrier will slow me down. And trust me, I need to slow down right now." Taking my wrist behind me, Mitch wrapped it in the silk cuff. Doing the same to the other, he locked them together behind my back. Tremors coursed through my body as my breath rushed out of my chest.

Squeezing both my shoulders tenderly, Mitch waited for my body to ease, then he placed a solitary kiss on the base of my neck. Shivers raced up my spine for an entirely different reason. Pulling a chair away from the dining room table, Mitch shifted me into the spot. "Lay back."

Setting my bum on the table, I lay back. It was uncomfortable with my arms pinned beneath me. Watching me struggle to get settled, Mitch took my arm and sat me back up, moving me onto the chair instead. Shifting my bum to the front of the chair, he spread my legs.

Standing there admiring my body, a small smile tugged at the side of his mouth. "God, you're beautiful, Lyza. The more I've gotten to know you, the more I've grown to admire you, but I desired you, the very moment I stepped into your prison cell with you."

Considering I hadn't seen a mirror, hairdresser, or razor in five years at that point, I can only assume I'd improved vastly after my visit to the spa and salon. Mitch wasn't signing, so I had to watch his lips intently. Especially with only the kitchen light providing illumination.

Opening the bag, Mitch took out the blindfold. My breathing hitched a little. "Are you sure? For others, they would have their hearing. This is going to isolate you in sensation."

Fear was lurking, whispering the torments of my past. Swallowing all that pain, the fear catching in my throat, I met Mitch's eyes and used my voice. "Trust."

Slipping the satin blindfold into place, Mitch fastened it. Instantly, my breathing was restricted, and I needed to force myself to inhale and relax. Not even a minute later, the blindfold loosened and lifted. Squatting in front of me, Mitch used his hands.

"Safeword. People who do this stuff use safewords, right? Give me a safeword. If it starts to get too much, just say that word."

Meeting his eyes, I came up with one instantly. "Lego."

Frowning in confusion, he laughed. "Lego? Okay. That one will work." Still smiling, he placed the blindfold over my eyes.

My breathing hitched. The last time I'd been handcuffed and blindfolded, Mark had been torturing me, and Fred had been questioning me. My breath rushed out suddenly, my chest constricting, refusing to draw air. As the memory played over my body, I whimpered. Squeezing my shoulders, Mitch held there while my mind relived those three days of hell. I'd been trained for interrogation, but no amount of training could stop them from breaking you if you didn't have the will to die rather than live. My father taught me the hard way.

Removing the blindfold, Mitch used his thumb to wipe away my tears. "That's too much."

He was right. Too much darkness lurked, waiting to paralyze me. "I'm sorry. This was a bad idea," I mourned, fidgeting in the restraints.

Squeezing my shoulders in reassurance, Mitch pulled me out of the chair. He turned me and pressed me against the table. His hands weighed my breasts. His thumbs circumnavigating my areolas. Lifting my eyes to Mitch's, I bit my lip as the tension eased out of my body with every circle.

"Trust me. I won't hurt you, Lyza."

Dropping his mouth, Mitch placed a kiss to the point of my shoulder, easing my tension a little. Taking my nipple between his lips, Mitch sucked. Arching my body to give him better access, I loved how his hand instantly moved to support my back. Sighing, I gripped the dining room table with my bound hands behind me.

Mitch rose to kiss me with so much heat and longing that I couldn't breathe. Melting into him, I gave him absolute control. Moaning, Mitch wrapped me in his arms, pressing me tight to the front of his hard body. His clothes didn't stop me from feeling or seeing just how hard he was for me.

Slowly, Mitch stepped back. Unbuttoning his shirt, he removed it, exposing his hard-muscled chest to my hungry eyes. Licking my lips when he unbuckled his belt, my body sizzled at the snicker it made as he yanked it free of the belt loops in one movement.

"Like this?" Double-checking before going any further.

"Like this," I whispered, throat starting to chafe after all the talking this afternoon. Coughing a little, I tried to ease it.

Eyes sliding into kindness, Mitch placed his finger to my lips. "You don't have to if it hurts."

Opening my mouth, I took his finger between my lips. Smiling, Mitch stepped forward, hand grabbing a handful of hair and tilting my head back. His mouth pressed hard to mine, tongue probing until I opened it to him. My body grew ready, and I slumped into him.

Suddenly, Mitch spun me and bent me over the table. A loud smack echoed through the room. The intense heat on my backside from the impact of his hand, making me jump. Still blinking from the surprise when Mitch dropped into a squat, I bit my lip as he pulled the gusset of my scanties aside and gave my heat a hard lick. "Oh my god!"

Mitch chuckled. Using his broad tongue to cover my lips, he tapped the tip of his tongue against my clit hard and fast. I swore. Was that a typical move of guys? Noel had never done it. Moaning, Mitch swiveled his tongue, opening my folds to probe my entrance. Squiggling his tongue back through my folds until the tip pressed against my clit, Mitch tapped out morse code again.

Eyes rolling back in my head, I exploded. My body spasmed under the sudden impact of my orgasm that I hadn't even felt building. It was just right one moment, and stars bursting behind my eyes the next.

Panting against the surface of the table, I caught Mitch standing behind me in my peripheral vision. When he lowered the zip of his pants, I let out an audible groan seeing his hard thick length jump free from its confines.

Tenderly, he removed my scanties. When he stood again, I turned my head a bit more to watch him pick up the bottle of lubricant. Then Mitch assessed my dripping pussy. "You seriously don't need this, but the warming part of this could be interesting," Mitch spoke to my back, so I ignored him.

Squirting some on his finger, he pressed it against my clit. Sucking in a quick breath, I bit my lip at how cold it was. Wasn't it meant to be warm? Chuckling, Mitch slipped the finger back, slowly pressing that digit into me. My body gripped him. "So tight, Lyza."

Massaging that spot inside of me with the pad of his finger, Mitch pressed his thumb hard to my clit. Slowly, those two areas grew warm, and then they were hot. Not burning, but a throbbing heat calling all your blood to play there. As long as it took to draw breath and cry Mitch's name, I was coming again.

When I looked over my shoulder, Mitch's face was stretched in an evil grin. "That good?"

"Try it."

Lifting a brow, Mitch uncurled one of my hands from its tight fist. Squirting a dollop of the cold gel into my hand, he placed his thick appendage into my palm. "Shit, that's cold," he chuckled.

Wrapping my fingers around him, he started moving in my grasp. When the gel warmed, I felt it, but I had no doubt it felt a lot more intense against his sensitive flesh. Mitch stopped suddenly, tremors wracking his body. "Jesus, that's amazing."

Slipping out of my grip, Mitch went to the kitchen. Coming back with a cloth, he wiped my hand clean. "So considerate." My tease was rewarded with another hard smack. Jolting, I laughed this time while Mitch massaged the abused area helping relieve the sting.

Stepping closer, Mitch slid his engorgement through my slick folds and pressed into me fully. My body resisted, but the lubricant allowed him to slip through. My clutch released to his girth, allowing Mitch to shove hard the rest of the way until he hit the dead end. My breath rushed out. Slumping a little against my back, Mitch kissed up my spine before straightening.

Taking my hip in one hand, the cuffs' connection in the other, he nailed me to the table. His body the hammer, driving his spike forcefully and without relent. Gasping, I climbed quickly towards another orgasm in seconds. Mitch had strength and stamina, and he wasn't afraid to use it. Gripping his wrist with my hands, I dug my nails in as he catapulted me to the brink of nirvana, but the rough sex wasn't quite getting me over the edge. Still, it felt fantastic riding that edge while Mitch pounded my body with all his strength. If I could even walk tomorrow, I'd be impressed.

Letting out a primal growl, Mitch pulled out quick and fast, taking several steps back and grabbing his pulsing cock. He stood holding it while he brought his breathing and desire under control, and I took a moment to catch my breath.

Slowly, I turned to face him. Mitch's eyes were glazed over in lustful possession. If he were a target, I could take him out right now, and he would never see it coming. Not that I had ever fucked a mark, and I never planned to, but if I killed my husband, that would undo that plan.

Sitting down on the kitchen chair, Mitch gestured that I come to him. Taking a deep breath, I managed to walk the two meters without cringing - I guess that gel had a purpose after all. Guiding me to straddle his hips, Mitch directed me over his swollen glans, growling as he slid deep into me.

Reaching around and grabbing my bum, Mitch instigated the tempo he wanted. Slow, long rolls of my pelvis, making me close my eyes and bite my lip every time he brushed that deepest most part of me.

Palming my breasts, Mitch lifted one to his mouth, licking and sucking my nipple until my body was racing towards the pinnacle of ultimate pleasure. Stopping my movements, Mitch pulsed deep inside me as he lavished my chest in kisses.

Cautiously, he released his hold and lifted his face to mine. His kiss was deep, slow, and full of more than just the lust blazing through our veins. It tempered my need to climax a little. Suddenly, I was feeling Mitch higher up, in my stomach, butterflies swarming as if they were vampires who smelt blood and just needed to find the source.

Pulling back to meet my eyes, Mitch focused. "Slow."

Nodding, I started moving, taking it nice and slow. Mitch's hands explored my body, his eyes fluttering with every circle of my hips. Groaning, Mitch reached behind me and unlinked the cuffs, freeing my hands to the front. "I need you to touch me. I love having your hands on me, Lyza."

Unable to resist smiling, I ran my hands over his chest, up to his neck, and into his hair. Adjusting myself on his lap for better leverage, I stopped being slow. It felt too good to drag out. Wrapping my arms around Mitch, I rode him hard, using the back of the chair for leverage. Grabbing my hips, Mitch tilted them so he could go deeper, and he fucked me as hard as he could.

I'd never been a screamer, but the noise that came out of my throat as I orgasmed this time was as close as I got to it: cursing, Mitch pulsed hard inside me. A tremendous cracking noise sounded, but I was too caught up in the fantastic sensation of Mitch's body filling mine to even care.

It wasn't until we stilled, holding each other tight, that I wondered what the noise was. We found out as soon as Mitch slumped back against the chair, holding me tight to him. There was a second loud crack, then the chair gave at the same time the legs on the back of the chair collapsed. Falling hard to the floor both of us cursed.

"Shit!" Mitch groaned, looking back at the broken chair. Glancing at each other, we started laughing. For several minutes, we laid in each other's arms laughing until Mitch caught my chin and kissed me until I was desperate for air.

When we calmed down, his eyes were full of happiness as Mitch smiled. "I've never heard you laugh. It's beautiful." When my cheeks burned, Mitch kissed me again. The sound of his front door opening startled him. If this was Stacey, I was going to kill her. Especially if she turned on the lights.

Scurrying to our feet, Mitch yanked on his pants while I grabbed his shirt and quickly buttoned it up as a slim brunette strutted into the living area. She was wearing a revealing dress as she passed through the kitchen for the bedroom. Throwing her bag on the kitchen bench, she was entirely oblivious to us.

Mitch stepped out of the dark. "Kym?"

The brunette stopped with a massive smile on her face. "Hey, baby. I'm back. I expected you to be in bed."

"What are you doing here?"

"I missed you," she purred and ran her hands up his chest.

Mitch was sporting the deliciously boned-out of his brains look, but she seemed to miss it. She did stop smiling when Mitch caught her wrists and removed her hands from him, forcefully, yet without hurting her. "When did you get a key to my place?"

"Oh, I borrowed your spare keys when I stayed over once and forgot to return them. Come on, Mitch. Haven't you missed me?"

Annoyed with the interruption to what had been a great night, I stepped forward, getting her attention. Eyes flaring, she stepped away from Mitch.

Ensuring I could read his lips, Mitch looked over at me. "Kym, this is Lyza. Lyza, this is Kim, my ex."

Kym pouted. "I don't remember saying it was over?"

Blinking, Mitch lifted a brow. "It's been six fucking months, Kym. Six months since you threw a brick at my head, smashed my window, and stormed off. That pretty much ends a relationship in my book. Especially when you start fucking one of my employees and friends."

Kym shifted uncomfortably. "Well, when you put it like that." Her eyes came back to me, scanning me. "Nice shoes." When I smirked, Kym huffed. "Look, can we talk? Maybe ask your floozy to leave, and we can discuss us." She put her hand on his chest again. Well, she tried. Mitch caught it before she could connect. "We were good together, Mitch."

"No, we weren't. It took meeting Lyza to realize how bad my past relationships have been."

"Oh, really? That sounds serious. Are you actually considering something serious with her or something because you wouldn't know the meaning of long-term."

"She's my wife, so yes, I'm thinking long term."

Kym looked horrified. "Wife?"

Tapping Mitch on the shoulder, I ensured I flashed the set of rings on my finger before I started signing. *"Have you got this? I need a shower after the load you dumped in me. If you get what I mean?"*

Mitch burst out laughing. Taking my face in his hands, he kissed me. Knocking the air, Mitch proceeded to sign without speaking. *"Yes, I'll get rid of her. Then expect me to get you dirty again."*

Keen for the next session to start, I smiled, waved to Kym, and grabbed my dress and knickers from the floor before heading to the bedroom.

"I'll have my keys back." Mitch put his hand out.

"Is she deaf?" Mouth hanging open, Kym placed her entire key chain in Mitch's palm.

Disconnecting the keys to his place, Mitch handed her back her keys. "Yes. Let me show you to the door, Kym."

"What happened to your chair?"

26

───────

LENNON

Wrapped in Mitch's arms when I woke in the morning, I smiled to myself and snuggled deeper against his sleeping form. The movement announced my body's soreness from the night's activities. Mitch's hand caressed my squirming hip. "Tender?" He asked, half asleep. When I didn't answer, he slipped his hand between my thighs, causing me to bite my lip on a whimper. "I take that as a yes," Mitch chuckled.

Moaning, I rolled to face him, taking his morning glory in hand. Mitch made an animalistic sound. "Jesus, Lyza." His mouth just landed on mine when his phone started ringing. Mitch rolled away with a frustrated groan and sat up on the side of the bed as he answered. "Morning, Fred." Crawling up behind him, I started kissing over his back. "When?" Checking his watch, Mitch listened to Fred's report. "How bad?" Cursing at the response, Mitch tensed, and he physically shook me off with his shoulder. It was subtle, but I understood subtle. Many other women wouldn't have taken the hint.

Backing away to my side of the bed, I pulled the sheet up around me. That phone call was bad news, and if it had anything to do with me, then I was smart enough to understand this small piece of happiness

218

I'd found may have just disappeared. A new emotion swept through me, one filled with despondency. Mitch peered over his shoulder, not at me, but so he could see me in his peripheral vision before he looked back out the window. "Give me an hour and bring breakfast. Bring a babysitter too." Running his hand through his hair, Mitch gripped the ends a little. "Don't we have anyone else to fucking do it?"

Deciding I didn't want to be naked for the conversation coming, I threw back the sheet and started to get out of bed. Mitch caught my wrist to hold me there. Lifting my eyes, I found his gaze angry and hostile as he gave me a single shake of his head. "He will have to do. Oh, and get Stacey to organize having my locks changed? Kym had cut herself a set to my house and showed up last night. I want to make sure they were the only set." Listening to Fred, Mitch lifted his lips in a smirk. "Yeah, you should probably change your locks too." Hanging up, Mitch put his phone aside.

Trying to wait patiently, I met his stare without flinching, but the look in his eyes wasn't what I aspired to wake up to today. Mitch studied my eyes for a long moment. The longer he did, the more I wanted to get out of the house. Moving back onto the bed properly, Mitch put an arm out, welcoming me into his embrace. Hesitant, but knowing this could go bad quickly if I refused, I slowly lowered myself to rest my cheek on his chest. Not that I relaxed into it. The rigidity of his body told me how affected he'd been by that phone call.

Moving his hands around me, Mitch started to sign. *"The doctor's lab was attacked last night."* When I lifted my hands to respond, Mitch blocked my move with his hold. *"You're just listening right now,"* he signed aggressively. *"The lab was attacked. Nothing was taken, but everything was destroyed. Years of research and samples were removed from the minus eighty freezers to ensure they were destroyed quickly by the fire."*

Watching the quick movements of his hands, I listened to the steady thudding of his heart beneath my cheek.

"Now, I know you were here, and I know you had no idea where the lab was, which means that information came from somewhere else. So, I'm not angry with you about the lab. However, simultaneously, Lennon was extricated. The men guarding him were killed. It's a fucking mess, and I'm damn sure that one is your doing."

Shoving away from him, I went to my knees so I could face him. Pointing to my chest, I sliced my right hand past my left side facing fist, then nicked my index finger against the bottom of my neck. *"I have never killed innocents. Your men would still be alive unless they threatened me somehow by remaining so."*

Mitch caught my hands in his. "You gave your husband Lennon's name, didn't you? He asked who he had to kill to free you. Whose name did you give him?"

Eyes wide, I blinked at Mitch, the moment with Noel in the change room playing in my mind. How did he know the exact words? Slowly, Mitch released one of my hands and grabbed his phone. He opened an app and went to a date, pressing play. Every word Noel spoke to me started playing.

Staring at his phone, astonished, my heart raced in my chest, blood pumping through my ears, causing my breath to shorten. Opening yesterday's date, Mitch pressed play. Emily and Moses discussing my return and Moses asking to have me as his wife.

Frowning, I pointed to my chest, held both hands out in front with fingers open, then flipped them and wiped them away before touching my index finger to my temple and sweeping it forward. My brain wracked, trying to understand how Mitch had those recordings.

"I think we can cut the deaf shit out now, don't you?" Mitch grumbled, throwing the phone aside. "I have to admit, Lyza, you're a hell of an actress. Even though I suspected, you had me doubting the entire time whether I'd been wrong that night."

Mitch inspected my face. The way I was staring at his phone in disbelief. Lifting my left hand, Mitch caressed the set of rings he'd put there on our first day together. "Did you forget these were chipped? Every time you left the building, I listened to what you got up to, Lyza, because I didn't doubt for a second, you were up to no good."

Needing a moment to process what was happening, I glared at Mitch. Just how much had Mitch realized from those conversations? Propping himself up on his elbows, watching me take it in, Mitch lifted a brow. "Right now, what I really want to know, is how much of last night was good acting?"

Without thinking about it, I punched him square in the jaw, reacting to how much that question hurt me. Mitch took the hit, not that he was fast enough to stop me. He did, however, wrap his arms around me and throw me on my back beneath him. Lifting my arm, ready to fight him, Mitch's eyes cleared of hostility. "Don't!" I hesitated at his plea. "Lyza, I don't want to fight you. I want to love you, but I need to know you want me the same way I want you."

A tear slipped from my eye and rolled off the side of my cheek to the pillow. "Mitch," I whispered his name.

"Tell me what you want, Lyza."

More tears flowed. "I just did."

Watching the emotions leak from me, Mitch exhaled in relief. "We'll find a way to be together." His mouth fell across mine hungrily, his body covering mine. Hands pinning mine above my head, he drifted south and kissed across the base of my rib cage. Twisting and turning in his hold, a sob escaped my throat when the emotions I felt became too much to hold.

Crying because my choices never mattered, and I knew after this was over, it wouldn't matter again. As Mitch rose above me and filled my body with his, I knew it didn't matter what I wanted. I was a soldier, and a soldier followed orders, no matter the consequences. But, if it was never going to matter again, it had to matter now.

Taking Mitch's face in my hands, I forced him to meet my eyes. "You were the first person I talked to after my mother was killed and my throat damaged. I woke up deaf, and my hearing took a few days to return, but I feigned being deaf afterward because I didn't want to talk to anyone. It worked in my favor, so I kept it up. You were the first, and you will be the last. My voice belongs only to you. So does my secret."

Eyes wide with surprise, Mitch kissed me, soft, searching, hesitant until he pulled back breathless. "Whatever happens. You are my wife for life."

We kissed heatedly, his body claiming mine just as passionately. For the first time, I understood emotional sex. It crept up on me slowly over the last few days but being with Mitch had stopped being a way to get off and become something more. I wouldn't label it for fear of destroying it, but as Mitch and I held each other afterward, I knew others would mark it with a four-letter word of the heart.

***

AFTER A SHOWER, I came out to the kitchen to find Moses seated at the table, eating breakfast. Opening the package, he slid across the table to me, I found my breakfast. Outside, on the alfresco, Mitch stood talking to Fred. *"Was the doctor you?"*

Watching my hands, Moses pointed to himself, tapped his temple, then pointed to me and then his ring finger.

"The lab?"

Considering my sign, Moses checked to make sure Mitch was still too busy outside with Fred to notice. *"Jenna told us the doctor still had samples of your blood. We needed to make sure that shit ended here."*

Pointing to Moses, I jutted both index fingers to the ground, then spelled out Mitch's name. *"You need to stay with Mitch. If Noel has Lennon, he will know he's free to kill Mitch. You have to keep him safe."*

"I'm assigned to you. How am I going to convince Mitch to let me go with him?"

"Well, he already suspects you are an arrow, so we need something that will force him to leave Fred here with me instead." Thinking about it, I hooked my index finger, putting it against my chin, then moved it to the left as I turned my hand to indicate he should make Mitch jealous.

Assessing me, Moses gave me a quick nod. His eyes went to the other end of the table. *"What happened to the chair?"* Cheeks filling with warmth at the memory, I smirked and shrugged my shoulders. Moses shook his head. "Always the quiet ones," he mumbled under his breath.

Absolutely famished, I started eating. Moses was watching outside. When Mitch turned to watch us inside, Moses moved a seat closer but made his signing so obvious it could be read from mars.

"I was thinking about us."

Frowning, I tapped my index fingers to opposite shoulders then swept them around between us until my hands were open and my shoulders up in question. Was there an us?

"When you are done here, there is a way for you to avoid going back to your father's house. If you get knocked up to another arrow from another chapter, you would be permitted to transfer and marry."

"What if I don't want to marry you?"

Moses sighed. *"You know that's not done. It's the only way I can help you."*

"And help yourself too? You get a child to raise and a wife, something they've denied you so far. Why is that?"

Watching my gestures, Moses sagged in his chair. *"There is an extreme lack of female Hunters. It's rare to meet another arrow from a different chapter. I'd be mad not to take the chance to give us both a future prospect."* Moses flicked his eyes to the window. *"You don't have to say yes now. I just want you to consider it an option."*

The sliding door opened as Mitch came in with Fred. Mitch's eyes were hard and angry as they fell on Moses. *"You're with me today. Fred is going to stay with Lyza. Let's go."* Coming to me, Mitch touched my chin, lifting my face to his so he could place a possessive kiss on my lips. Holding his thumbs-up, Mitch brushed his chest with his fists alternatingly. *"Behave."*

Sweeping my cupped right hand across my left palm, I signed for Mitch to stay safe.

Kissing me again, Mitch left, Moses smiling as he followed him out. Sitting down at the table with me, Fred waited for me to stop looking where Mitch walked out. When I met his eyes, they were soft. "You're in love with him."

"I'm not free to love anyone."

Fred sighed. "' From forth the fatal loins of these two foes, a pair of star-crossed lovers take their life, whose misadventured piteous overthrows, do with their death bury their parents' strife.'"

"Dramatic much?"

"Let's hope it doesn't prove fatal for either of you again. Death brought you to each other twice before. Let's hope it doesn't make a third house call."

Pressing my lips together on my doubt, the doorbell rang. The irony of the timing wasn't lost on Fred either. Standing, he immediately pulled his gun and followed me to the door, which I opened carefully. A body lay slumped on the porch.

Peering over my shoulder, Fred threw open the door. "Lennon, shit." Rushing to his side, Fred checked his pulse.

Scanning the surrounding area, I looked for any sign of Noel, but there was nothing, not even the glint of a sniper scope. He was out there. I could feel his eyes on me even from this distance. On the step beside the tortured body of the doctor was a gift. Picking it up, I opened it.

"He's still breathing. I'll call Mitch and the ambulance," Fred announced, running back inside.

Throwing the lid aside, I lifted a handwritten note from the Glock inside the gift box.

You are free. Prove you're not your mother's daughter.

Tears filled my eyes as I lifted the gun. With a deep breath, I buried my emotions deep down, where Noel would never find them again. Had I known it would be the last time I could tell him, I would have given Mitch one last kiss. Checking the gun, I aimed it at Lennon and shot it twice.

Fred came running out of the house. "What the..." he let the phone drop to his side as I pointed the gun at him. "Lyza, what are you doing?"

"My job," I muttered. Feigning a kick, I slammed the butt of the gun down on the back of Fred's head. He dropped to the porch like a sack of potatoes. Kneeling down to check his pulse, the phone was right by his side.

"Fred?" Mitch called. "What the fuck is happening? Where's Lyza?"

"Turn the car around," Moses demanded. "If your man is down, Noel is there."

Standing, I stepped off the porch and started walking to the road. Noel would be watching and waiting.

27

THE JOB

REACHING THE END OF THE DRIVEWAY, A BLACK SUV CAME DOWN THE road and stopped before me. Wenda got out of the passenger seat with a smile. Putting her hand out for the gun, I handed it over, and she opened the back door. Sliding into the empty back seat, I closed the door while Wenda jumped back in front.

Once both doors shut, Breok pulled back onto the road. A kilometer away, they pulled off onto the shoulder. Noel, dressed in tactical gear and with a sniper rifle in hand, slid in next to me.

Placing the rifle in the boot, Noel tapped Breok on the shoulder to start driving again. Noel turned to me, eyes gray and angry. "The Arrow is all over you," he informed in his native French. "They shouldn't have found you this quick, but they found you nearly the same time I did. In fact, every time I've located you and come for you, they've been on my heels."

Wary of the mistrust in his voice, I pointed to my chest, put my hands' palms up and fingers open in front of me before flipping them and wiping away, then lifting my hands and dropping my index fingers to just touch together before pointing to his side. If Noel thought I contacted the Arrow, he'd have to be nuts.

"Oh, I know you didn't, Lyza. You would have stayed hostage to Fairchild rather than go back to your father." Staring into my eyes, Noel brushed his hand against my cheek. "There is no greater heartbreak than a wife's betrayal."

Pulling a gun, Breok shot Wenda in the head. Jolting in surprise, my wide eyes went to Breok. He was cold and calculating as he put his weapon away and continued the drive. Shocked, I looked back to Noel. "She's been in contact with your father since I found you. I don't have time for traitors."

Still wide-eyed, I stared out the window. Wenda had been my friend, so I couldn't look out the front of the car. All the dead bodies I'd seen in my life, none had affected me like this. Was that a sign I changed during my time in jail, or was it Mitch who caused this?

Keeping my face sober as we drove in silence, I focused on my mission. We pulled up at an airport by a private jet. When Noel's phone rang as we exited the car, he answered it. Approaching the passenger door, one of Noel's men opened it, and catching Wenda's body as it fell out, he heaved it into his arms and walked off. The gun she'd taken from me was left lying by the seat.

Moving quickly, I picked it up and walked around the other side of the car, where Breok talked to Noel. "Hyacinth and Ezekiel are dead," Noel informed Breok.

"Both?"

Noel nodded. "Apparently, my brother has learned to fight better than we anticipated, and the employee with him also fights like one of us."

Brother? I stopped walking.

"Could your mother have trained him after all?"

"Possibly. She could be in trouble if the Chamber found out. He was deemed unfit for training," Noel conversed as if it meant nothing. His eyes lifted to me as I raised the gun and aimed. Noel had time to frown before I fired. The bullet penetrated the back of Breok's skull, and he crumpled.

Immediately, I dropped the gun as Noel and his men took aim at me. Standing still, not bothered by the three guns pointing at me, I signed directly to Noel. *"When my father found me, he gave me my next target. I gather it was something he negotiated with Wenda for her return, but I did the job."*

Blinking at my hands, Noel met my eyes and relaxed a little. "Did he give you any other jobs?"

"To deliver you a message. You've built a good business, and he wants in. You come back to Chapter, and you can run the business from there. Failed recruits get sent to you instead of released."

Chuckling, Noel lowered his gun, and his men followed suit. "I bet Chamber doesn't know about this deal?"

Shrugging, I doubted the Chamber knew a lot of what my father got up to. Noel waved his men back to preparing to leave. One started taking bags out of the boot, and Noel's sniper rifle went with it. "What do you think?" Noel asked me.

"I don't trust him. You know that."

Watching my hands, Noel nodded. Moving towards me casually, he scratched his head with the gun. The safety was on, so that wasn't an issue. "You have every reason to hate him. Why didn't you ever try to kill him?"

"By the time I was good enough, I had you."

This surprised Noel. He stepped closer, considering me. "How long were you with my brother?"

"Who is your brother?"

Noel chuckled when I signed my response. "Well, I guess we don't really look alike, and have different fathers..." Noel shrugged. "But Fairchild and I share a mother. Debbie Fairchild is head of Chamber and Great Grandmother of the Guardian Chapter. Before that, she was Debbie D'Avive and was married to my father, Lazar, until he died a year after I was born."

Sucking in a deep breath, I swallowed the surprise. Lazar had been a Scythe. I had no idea how he ended up with Debbie unless she was one of us and tested out to Guardian.

"With my brother, she raised him civilian, in much the same experiment you were part of. He was deemed too soft to complete full training, and she was ordered to abandon him to the civilian world. That's the story anyway. But then Mitch joined the forces and not only became a SEAL, but he also excelled at it. Chamber took notice. They started talking about how perhaps Debbie raised him right, and they should bring him in, now that he had proved himself via other means."

Snickering, Noel stepped back. "Your father pulled me aside. He told me, if my brother passed the test of entry now, it would change everything. That when you got with child, you would be sent away to raise our child the same way. That you and Mitch, who were meant to be catastrophic failures, were now seen as true successes."

Indicating to Noel, I sliced my throat's base with my index finger then pointed to his side. *"You killed him because of what my father said?"*

"Your father made me a deal. I kill Fairchild. I get to leave, and I could take you with me. As long as any children were sent back to Chapter for training."

"He would never have stuck to that deal," I signed in disbelief.

"Oh, I realize that now, but I was eager to escape back then and took the offer anyway. Then you showed up and ruined the entire fucking thing."

"I didn't know. I just knew if you succeeded, you would cause chaos in the Arrow, and that would give my father control. I couldn't allow that."

"I understand, Lyza."

"I don't understand why you still want your brother dead?"

Noel's eyes filled with hate. "To punish her. She was meant to abandon him, the runt, the useless pup. Instead, she abandoned me to our father's chapter and gave the runt the free will I was never allowed. I want to punish her for abandoning me."

My heart filled with sympathy at the pain in his voice. *"But she was a shit mother to him too. He told me. She was no different from mine."* Dropping my hands, I suddenly realized why Mitch was off-kilter last night. He'd figured it out that his mother was one of us.

Noel considered me. "Do you care for him?"

Knocking the air between us in affirmation, I shrugged. *"That doesn't change where my loyalty belongs."*

"To your husband?"

When I lifted my eyes, I saw his smile hesitate. *"To the Arrow."* Grabbing the gun out of his hand, I stepped on his foot. Shoulder slamming me back into the car, Noel twisted away as I brought my arm up to aim, and he stripped the gun of the barrel.

Thumping my arm down on his elbow crease as he made a grab for me, I spun away from him. Sliding to my knees next to Breok, I yanked his gun out as Noel pulled his secondary. Clicking off the safety, I turned and fired. Catching the bullet in his right thigh, Noel lifted his weapon.

Grabbing Breok, I rolled, his body shielding mine and taking the bullet Noel fired at me. As my gun arm came free to fire, Noel ducked behind the car out of sight.

One of his men ran around, gun in hand. Shooting him in the head, I saw another running around the car. Staying low on the ground, I fired beneath the vehicle and hit his ankle. As he fell, he caught another bullet to his forehead.

Getting up quickly, I used the car as a shield, making sure my legs were hidden by the tire. Needing to find Noel, I lifted a little, and the car window above my head smashed.

Thumb to my chin with index and middle finger shooting up in front of my nose, I yanked it away to close my fist on the left in a curse out of habit.

Laughter broke out somewhere high. "Did you seriously just sign to yourself?"

Ignoring Noel because I couldn't let on that I'd heard him, but I knew now he had me in line of sight. I either surrendered or left here in a body bag. To make it look legit, I tried lifting once more.

The laser light flashed a second before the bullet impacted the car, right in front of my face. I'd had a second to fall back on my ass before it did. Turning my head, I spotted the gun Wenda took from me, still on the ground between me and the car where I dropped it earlier.

With a huff, I lifted my hands, released my grip on the gun in hand, and let it swing over my finger. Dropping it to the ground, I kicked it away.

"Good girl." Noel set the laser light on my chest, and I followed the beam back to his place on the overwalk. He kept the rifle targeted on my heart while the only one of his men left came around and kicked the weapon even further away.

"Careful, she's a fucking ninja. Don't get in my line of sight," Noel warned the man.

Waiting for the lackey to come forward to restrain me, I counted my moves in my head. If the guy was an ex-sword, I knew why. The first thing the idiot did was cross the laser sight.

"Don't!"

Kicking both legs forward, I caught him in the ankles, tripping him off balance. Grabbing his shirt to pull him down on top of me, I grabbed the other gun and aimed over the guy's shoulder. Firing as his body impacted mine and knocked me to the ground. Noel cried out, and his rifle clattered to the floor.

Rolling, I put the gun to the lackey's chest and fired twice. The hanger was suddenly quiet. Only the sounds of Noel trying to suck in a breath echoed now. That, and the tinnitus from all the gunfire.

Peering up, Noel was lying on his back on the overwalk. I collected Noel's rifle and checked the safety before using the strap across my body to carry it on my back. Climbing up, I went to Noel. I'd shot him in the throat, so he was going to bleed out in a matter of minutes anyway.

"Lyza," Noel wheezed.

Clicking off the safety on the handgun, I held it ready.

"Your father... Check the office. A present... to show how much..." he struggled, growing grayer by the second. That's what happens when someone exsanguinates. They don't turn blue or white. They go gray.

Squatting beside him, I caressed his cheek. His eyes softened as my eyes filled with tears, and I signed an explanation. *"I would never have done it had you left Mitch alone."*

Gasping, Noel stared into my eyes, his own glassy. "I know. I saw how you kissed... But I love you."

Tears splashed on my lashes. Noel choked, then his pupils withdrew to pinpoints. His breathing stuttered, and he gave one long, ghostly exhale.

Sitting there for a full minute, my tears fell silently as his pupils remained fixed and nonreactive. Closing my eyes, I squeezed the tears out, then I closed his eyelids. Rising, I did what any sane person would do. Aiming the gun, I put two in his heart and one in his head. No one wants an assassin with a grudge coming back from the dead.

28

REVENGE AND HEARTBREAK

APPROACHING THE CLOSED OFFICE DOOR FOR THE HANGER, I WAS ON high alert. Keeping the gun ready, just in case, I cautiously turned the handle and swung the door open. Feeling for the light switch just inside the door, I switched it on and waited while the fluorescent lighting flickered to full power.

Inside, a man sat in a chair chained to a support post behind him. A big red ribbon wrapped around him. Lifting his head, he blinked rapidly in the sudden light. "Lyzebel," he greeted in British English.

Curling my thumb to touch the tips of my middle and ring finger, leaving my index finger pointing up, I tapped it to my temple. *"Daddy."* I was so tired, and this was the last thing I needed to deal with today.

"I tried to reason with Noel, but he is truly a traitor. I'm so glad you put an end to-," he cut off in a scream as the first bullet shattered his knee, just like he had my mother's lover. "Lyzebel, whatever he told you was a lie. I would never want you dead."

The following bullet shattered his other knee.

"Fuck, Lyzebel!" He glared up at me in anger. "Think about what you are doing."

Blinking as his words sunk in, I tilted my head and assessed my father. He came to Noel and offered him a way back into the Arrow if Noel killed me. I didn't doubt it. He'd told me he'd offer Noel a way home in his video message, so I didn't even have to question the logic that my father wanted me murdered.

"I am the Chapter Father. If you kill me, you will be a target," he preached, his voice in agony.

At that moment, I also understood something else. *"You gave Noel Wenda as your source."*

Watching me sign, he glared at me. "You kill me, and you die."

"Was she? Did she contact you?"

Seeing my annoyance grow in my gestures, my father smirked. "As if Wenda would ever come to me to help you." He opened his mouth to say more, but I lifted the gun and fired. His eyes went wide as he started choking, the bullet shredding his throat and probably lodged in his spine.

"You are one fucked up man," I signed. *"No one deserves your misery."* Putting two in his heart, I fired the final bullet between his eyes. "I have always feared you more than death," I announced verbally.

There was no point going into the room further. I didn't close my father's eyes in respect, and I didn't shed a tear for that asshole. Turning off the light, I shut the door. Wiping my prints off the guns, I dropped them, then found the other guns I'd held and cleaned them as well. Stepping back into the car that brought me here, I plugged in Mitch's address to the GPS and started driving.

PULLING up out the front of Mitch's place, I observed Mitch standing on the porch with a cold beer pressed to a cut on his head, another in his hand. Fred sat on the stair, holding a cold pack to his head, and Moses sat by him drinking his beer. They all watched me emerge from the car and walk towards them.

Stopping on the bottom step, I lifted my splayed hands' palms facing me, then turned and dropped them to be parallel to the ground. The reason Mitch saved me and the mission Chamber gave me was completed.

Mitch closed his eyes, but I wasn't sure if he was relieved or worried. Draining the rest of his beer, Moses stood up. "I need another. Come on, Fred."

Lifting his eyes to me, Fred radiated anger and sadness. His head turned to observe Mitch. "She did it for you. Job or not. She did it for you. Don't let her convince you otherwise." Patting Mitch on the shoulder, Fred went inside.

Stepping forward, Mitch offered me the beer he'd had against his head. "It's still cold."

Hand sitting in the left palm, I spread both hands out to the side then curled my hand to hold the little finger up in front of me, asking Mitch how bad it was here.

"I'd be dead if Moses hadn't been there." Pressing the beer into my hands, Mitch took a seat on the step.

Using the railing to pop off the top, I took the stoop next to him. We sat drinking our beers in silence. It should have been night, but it was lunchtime, and the sun was shining bright. I'd killed my husband and father in broad daylight, and no one gave a flying...

"Was it hard?" Mitch asked.

"The second hardest thing I'll ever do."

Hesitating with the bottle to his lips, Mitch eyed my gestures. Taking the mouthful, he waited until he swallowed. "What's the hardest?"

Dropping my head, I took a moment to feel the regret that was already crushing my chest before meeting his questioning gaze.

"Oh." Taking another mouthful, Mitch checked over his shoulder. "So, I have a brother?"

"Had," I corrected. Meeting my eyes, Mitch glanced back to my hands. *"You listened?"*

"Yeah. Then I deleted it. I don't want anyone ever hearing the last bit."

"You knew I was heading back here?"

"We beat you by fifteen minutes." Mitch considered me. "It's cliche, isn't it? I fell in love with my brother's wife. Him wanting to kill me because he thought our mother loved me more. That we would probably never have met if he hadn't come after me."

"Noel was considered a prince in the Arrow. Your mother is a queen. She rules the Arrow. She doesn't report to Chamber; she runs it."

Tensing, Mitch didn't move for two heartbeats. Then he relaxed and exhaled. "She was still a fucking bitch."

Meeting each other's eyes, we both smirked. A car coming up the drive caught our attention. Closing my eyes in pain, I cursed internally. So soon? Couldn't they have given us another night? Neither Mitch nor I stood for it. We both continued drinking our beers, waiting.

When the car pulled up, the back door opened, and a woman stepped out of the vehicle. She was middle-aged and familiar in the way she looked like my ex-husband.

Playing with the rings on my finger, I put my right hand to my throat and turned my hand like I was turning a doorknob. *"It's a pity you didn't live in Las Vegas. We could have got hitched for real."*

Mitch stifled a chuckle. "Maybe next time."

"Mitchell."

Keeping his eyes locked with mine, Mitch spoke to the woman. "Mother. Are you here for her or me?"

"You know?"

Huffing, Mitch stood up. "Yeah, I figured it out. I'm fine, by the way. Thanks for asking. My brother, not so much." Mitch turned to walk inside.

"Mitchell, I'm sorry." She sounded anything but apologetic.

Releasing a sarcastic laugh, Mitch turned back to face her. "For what? For lying to me my entire life. Or the fact my brother tried to kill me because he hated you too? Or maybe, it's none of that. Maybe you're sorry because you are about to take away from me the only woman I've ever cared about."

Dropping her gaze to me at last, Debbie glared, her pupils a little wider than they should be in this bright sunlight. Jesus! It should be fucking pouring rain for this shit. If it were a movie, it would be night, stars shining, and it would have started raining the moment Debbie stepped out of her chauffeur-driven car like the boss she was. But no. Not in my life. It shines bright as a fucking supernova while my life gets ripped apart.

Taking a deep breath, Mitch dropped his gaze to me. Lifting his hand, Mitch pinched his thumb and pointer together as if picking something out, then he pointed to his chest.

'Choose me. Choose life with me.'

"She can't," Debbie answered on my behalf. "She's not a civilian like you, son. She belongs to the Arrow."

Mitch turned on her angrily. "Your order likes to experiment. So, make us another experiment," he raged, advancing on his mother. "Let us be together. You can have our kids, but let me have-"

Getting in his way and putting my back to Debbie, I shoved Mitch back angrily, shaking my head. Waiting for Mitch to meet my eyes so he could see the fierceness of my intent as I clutched my hand to my chest and then moved it forward as if tossing something to him. There was no way I agreed to those terms. *"Not my kids. They can't have mine."*

Breathing hard, Mitch glared with the rage boiling inside of him. "Not even if it allowed us to be together?"

"I am not a human trafficker. I do not sell lives that aren't mine to give. I will not enslave my children to this life. If I can't give them a choice to pick their future, I won't give them life at all." Mitch didn't back down, but he didn't press the negotiation even though his rage stayed near the edge.

Debbie's phone rang. "Excuse me," she stepped away to answer it.

Taking a step closer to Mitch, I caressed his cheek before waving my hand in as if grabbing something and closing my fist on it. I wanted to stay. I wanted to live out my days with Mitch, even in the capacity of his fake wife and bodyguard. I would choose him over anything except death.

"Why? Why are you so fucking important to them? You are deaf and mute. Why can't they let you go?"

"Because of her bloodline," Moses answered as he stepped out onto the porch, Fred right on his heels. "Her bloodline is one of the oldest in the Arrow. Lyza is a descendant of the founder himself. And if that wasn't enough, she is the best Scythe they have. Her disability didn't detract from her skill. They won't give her up."

Mitch turned his rage toward Moses. "That's why you want her."

"I want her because she's beautiful, intelligent, and the best. I want her because I can give her a better life away from her father. I could have protected her."

"That won't be necessary," Debbie chimed in, returning to the conversation. "Caleb Spencer is dead. It seems Noel D'Avive killed him as a makeup present for his wife."

Ignoring everyone around us, I kept my eyes set on Mitch. I knew going back was never an option, but I needed him to see if it was, that I would never leave.

"It's time to go. Moses, since you blew your cover, you may as well exit now too."

Exhaling, Moses handed his beer to Fred, saying goodbye. When he walked off the porch, Moses squeezed Mitch's shoulder, leaning in to whisper something before he continued past me.

"Lyzebel."

Staring into Mitch's eyes, I couldn't do it. I couldn't leave him. I wouldn't.

"Say goodbye to her, Mitch. She needs to go."

"No," Mitch answered, staring into my eyes, the two of us connected in this time and space, where I would make the choice that I wanted. The side of his mouth twitching, Mitch shook his head slightly. "She's not going with you."

"Jesus!" Grabbing my shoulder and turning me around, Moses signed his appeal. *"You have to say goodbye. She's the head of Chamber. You have to do what you are told."*

Looking past Moses' shoulder, I stepped out from him to face Debbie Fairchild. *"I don't belong at Chapter anymore. I will be loyal, but I will stay here. My home base shouldn't matter. I can work from anywhere in the world. Why can't it be from here?"*

"Because I said so. Get in the car, Lyzebel," Debbie was miffed. Looking between us, Moses stepped back. When I gave a slight shake of my head, Debbie reached around to the back and pulled a gun from beneath her tailored suit jacket. Her driver followed suit, both of them trained on me. "If you stay, it's as a corpse."

Stepping between, Mitch used his body as a barricade and turned to face me. Holding his hand in front of his chest and waved me away. *"Go."* Looking up at his face, I frowned. *"Go,"* Mitch repeated. *"We will find a way, but I can't bring you back from the dead."*

Pivoting on his heel, Mitch glared at his mother. "She'll go with you. You can put the guns away."

Taking a step closer to Mitch, turning my back on his mother, I went up on tippy toes and kissed his cheek. "I'll always remember the kitchen chair," I whispered as I pulled away.

As I turned to go, Mitch caught my arm, his eyes angry. "I'll keep it until you come back and help me break another."

Giving him the faintest of smiles, I wished the Arrow had never found me, but I'd keep Mitch in my dreams and be back with him every night I could be.

"Be cautious while walking in the darkness alone, Lyza. You could lose the light in your soul."

Caressing his cheek, I turned and went to the car. Waiting by the car, Debbie faced her son. "Mitchell, I'm sorry."

Mitch took a deep breath. "If you were, you wouldn't be doing this."

"It is her duty."

"Fuck duty!" Debbie tensed and backed up a step from her son. "If you take her now, don't bother calling or visiting again. If I can't have Lyza, I definitely don't want you in my life. Consider both your sons dead."

Bowing her head, Debbie didn't reply, just sank into the car and slammed the door. Glaring at me with tears in her eyes, Debbie threw mental daggers at me.

Not intimidated by her, I turned and looked out the window, guarding my emotions against her. I couldn't fathom what my life would be like now, but at least my father wouldn't be a part of it anymore. Hooray for small mercies.

29

____

MONOLOGUE

"THE EVIDENCE SUPPORTS HER STORY," THE DOCTOR POINTED TO THE scans. "Her larynx was severely damaged in her teens, and the scarring is consistent with the time she joined her chapter. There is enough scar tissue of the same severity and age to suggest she was tortured either just before or after she arrived at Chapter."

"And the claim she has a genetic disorder?" Debbie questioned the doctor. She'd driven us straight to the airport, but not the same hanger Noel took me to. Moses was left behind after a quick briefing, and I was flown to Norway, home of the Chamber.

After spending an entire day being tested and scanned, I'd gone to bed in a room that could have doubled as a prison cell if it had an outside lock. The second day, I'd been repeatedly questioned about my upbringing, father, disappearance, and relationship with Noel. So far, the only person I hadn't been asked about was Mitch, and I think it was because Debbie already knew the answer.

After thirty hours of questioning and my story remained unchanged except for the addition of extra details, or my refusal to repeat myself, they'd let me sleep. This morning, I'd been given breakfast and

243

escorted to meet Debbie in the infirmary. Sitting on the examination table, I stared at my feet while they swung back and forth. So far, neither had said a word to me.

Flipping to another page in the file he held, the doctor read over some notes. Finding another page, he turned it to study what looked like many dots on the page and another bunch of numbers.

"Confirmed. Though, there is no sign of complications that I would have expected to see by her age," the doctor informed with raised brows.

"Such as?" Debbie pressed.

"Well, it presents much like multiple sclerosis but is even rarer—both caused by the demyelination of nerve cells. Most children born with this don't survive their teenage years, the early twenties at best. For Lyza to still be alive and have a functional body is quite impressive."

"So, the treatment was successful?" Debbie pressed.

The doctor frowned, reading through his notes. "Honestly, I think she'd been treated before two weeks ago." He kept reading. "For the recovery her body has made, the effects started reversing during her imprisonment."

"So, her body just decided to heal?" Debbie asked, peering at the doctor.

Frowning harder, he flicked through some more pages. Eyebrows jumping, he tilted his head as he considered my medical file. "Or she was rebooted."

"I'm sorry?" Debbie frowned.

"The file you managed to procure from her imprisonment suggested that on at least two occasions during her questioning, her heart stopped, and she needed to be resuscitated," the doctor elucidated. "I came across a case in Australia over a decade ago about an MS sufferer who was so declined she was not listed for further medical intervention. She died, and a new nurse who wasn't aware of her situation resuscitated her. The patient came back fully-functioning except for her sight. Remarkably, the disorder has not reemerged."

"So, by dying, it killed the symptoms?" Debbie looked confused.

"Think of it more like this," the doctor closed the file. "The brain is much like a computer. When a computer freezes or is glitchy, what do you do?"

"Turn it off and on again," Debbie shrugged.

"Exactly! But we can't do that with the human brain or the body. Turning it off equals death. But what if that is what this patient needed? What if it was what Lyza needed? A system reboot? And now she's fully-functional again."

Chewing her cheek, Debbie considered the doctor. "The other patient, you said she remained blind? What if Lyza's hearing loss was a symptom of her disorder?"

The doctor gave a one-shoulder shrug. "Possibly, but I performed a hearing test. She remained non-reactive to ninety-five percent of noise. She might hear an explosion or a gunshot in the same room, but not verbal communication."

Turning their eyes my way, they both considered me. Staring at my feet, I wondered what Mitch was doing. It would be night in Albuquerque now.

"So, she is healthy?" Debbie finally asked.

"Very."

"Will her genetic disorder pass to children?"

"Potentially, though none of her ancestors have suffered from this, so maybe it's a recessive gene disorder."

Debbie looked at the scans and pointed to an opaque object in my arm. "Is this a contraceptive?"

"Yes. It's only new."

"Take it out. Then send her to the meeting room."

When Debbie left, the doctor looked me over and sighed. As he approached, I lifted my gaze to his mouth as he explained what he would do.

When I mimed writing, he found a pen and pad for me.

I don't want it out.

The doctor read my note. "I'm sorry. It was an order."

"CAN YOU HEAR ME?" I murmured into the darkness of my bedroom.

After undergoing skills testing at Chamber, they'd questioned me for a full day again, retested my capabilities a second time, and then sent me back to my home chapter. Chamber was amiss with my test results. I was too proficient to qualify for any one instinct, but they all agreed that deaf and dumb couldn't work as a Guardian or a Hunter and sent me home to Scythe a week ago. Two weeks after I'd killed my husband and father.

Running my right fingers across the wedding band set that still adorned my left hand, I sighed. No one had thought to take them from me, or maybe they didn't dare ask. "I'm not sure if you can still hear me on the other side of the world, but I can't stop thinking about you. I don't just mean sex. It's the little things. When I'm training, I wish you were there beside me. When I'm cooking myself dinner or eating breakfast, I miss you sitting across from me. When I run, I imagine running up that mountain with you. When I'm in bed, I miss your body next to mine.

"While I was in prison, I read stories where people fell in love at first sight, and I would get annoyed at how it was bullshit. I never understood falling in love because my life had no place for love. Then you saved me and made me hate you as an enemy, but like you as a friend, and respect you as a colleague. Even though you make me randier than a minx, I never expected to care for you as a lover. I could never have hoped to know love."

My alarm went off beside me. Silencing it, I climbed out of bed, moving to the window as I wrapped my satin robe around me, more because I was naked than cold. The compound wasn't some ugly cement building fortified for war. It was a collection of Swiss-style chalets built apart, surrounded by forests in the mountains between France and Switzerland.

Families lived together, and I'd lived with my father until I was given to Noel, then I'd moved into his place. Scythes didn't have long life expectancies, so they had never needed to extend the village, but the chalets were renovated every ten years to bring the latest technology and creature comforts into our worlds.

Coming home, I'd been given a choice between my father's house or Noel's. I'd chosen Noel's. While I'd been away, it had been renovated. All our stuff was gone, but it was furnished and comfortable, and it didn't smell like my father. Staring out at the still dark view of the mountains out of my bedroom window, I remembered putting a bullet in Noel's head. "I never missed him like this."

Leaving the window with a loud sigh, I went to get ready for the morning tai chi session. As I joined the others by the chain of ponds, our new Father approached me.

"Good morning, Lyza," he greeted. Tapping my right index and middle finger over my left same fingers, I returned his greeting. Scott smiled sadly. "Is it awkward calling someone else Father after all these years?"

Frowning, I shook my head. Scott was about ten years younger than my father was, putting him on the underside of forty. So, I used the term as a sign of respect for his chapter's role rather than relation. Not that I'd ever felt affection for my father.

"I don't want to hold up the practice, but I'll need to see you afterward, so please don't disappear like normal."

Bowing my head, I took my place with the others. They were all wary of me now, not really accepting me back into the community yet. Two children were running around like usual this last week; their mother focused on her training and not paying attention to them. The one teenager, a young male around thirteen, was trying to keep the kids in line but failing miserably.

Giving up on trying to find my inward focus, I walked over and tapped the teen on the shoulder. He turned, his eyes going wide at who was engaging him. Pointing to my eyes, I then indicated the kids, then to him before sweeping my hand toward the seven adults - all except one were male - moving through the tai chi sequences.

"Thank you, Lyza," he smiled and ran over to join the others.

Approaching where the twins were trying to catch the fish in the small channel between ponds, I stepped a leg on each side of the canal. They stopped, watching me warily. No doubt, their mother may have discussed my return to them.

Jumping one-eighty to face the other way, so I had my back to them, I bent over to touch my toes and looked through my legs at them. They watched me, confused. Reaching both hands down into the channel, I quickly splashed them both with water.

The boys' mouths fell open as I stuck my tongue out at them and ran down to the next pond with a foot on each side of the channel. Curious, the boys chuckled and followed. They put their feet on each side of the narrow channel and raced along to join me. When they caught up, I splashed them both again. Laughing, they tried to splash me back. Dashing away to the lowest area of the ponds, I went into a low stance.

As the boys approached, I reached out slowly for them. They dodged; I pivoted and started doing my tai chi, trying to grab them and avoiding their attacks. They thought it was a game, but they mimicked my movements. Without the kids knowing, they were performing introductory tai chi while we played. They laughed and had fun.

When their mother called them, the boys stopped and realized the tai chi class had finished. Scott stood with the mother of the kids watching. The two boys turned back to me and bowed low as if I was a respected sensei, then they dashed off to their mother. She stood, watching them confused. When she turned to Scott, he tilted his head to direct her to her daily training. Everyone trained independently after the group session in the morning. There was a schedule.

As I walked over to meet Scott, he watched me. "That was interesting," he announced as I came close. "Is that how you were trained?" I shook my head. "You can talk to me, Lyza. I understand sign language."

"Then why do you not respect me enough to use it when you talk to me?" I signed in a challenge.

"Your father never did. Nor did Noel."

"No. But they should have."

Studying me, Scott lifted his hands and knocked the air as he started to SimCom. It was always hard for people to stop vocalizing. "You are right. They should have. Why did you play like that with the boys?"

"It gets them interested, keeps them busy, and it makes it fun. It is how I should have been trained. The problem with how we raise our kids is that we forget they are kids. We forget to love them and to let them be kids. Maybe if we did, they would be less likely to kill innocents and suffer narcissism."

Considering my hands, Scott bowed his head before lifting his. "Perhaps, it is something we can try here?"

"You wanted to talk to me?"

"Yes. Have you settled in?"

"Enough for what?" I lifted my shoulders and arms out to the side.

Scott smiled. "Chamber has put you back on active duty. You have a job. You leave tonight. Jonathan will meet you at transport at eighteen hundred. You know the procedure." With no further discussion, he turned and walked away. I wasn't fooled; this was a test. The question was, how hard a test?

Returning to my house, I started the coffee machine at the same time I opened my new Arrow-issued laptop and logged into our intranet. Sure enough, a file was waiting for me to access—an arms dealer in Moscow. Oh yeah, this was a hard one. A live or die one.

Sitting down with my coffee, I started my research. Twelve hours later, I was departing the helicopter that transferred me to the airport. "Bon chance, Lyza," Jonathan farewelled. He made his hand into pistol grip and touched the index pad to the tip of his nose before taking it away. It wasn't a perfect sign, but at least he'd made an effort to learn something.

As I strode inside the heliport to collect my burner phone and kit, I thought about Scott and how accommodating he'd been since my return. Right now, I didn't know if I could trust him, but I'd find out soon enough.

30

LETTERS

03, August,
Mitch,
I'm sending this to you via Fred, just in case they are monitoring your lines of communication. I can't resist contacting you. I tried. Even if you burn this on receipt, I had to do it.
It's weird being home. Without my father demanding better of me and without Noel, it's almost peaceful, but it doesn't feel like home.
I often think of you. I remember running up that mountain behind you and the way you smiled over your shoulder at me. I imagine being back there with you, and with the altitude similarities, the environment encourages such fantasy.
I can't look at my kitchen chairs without thinking of yours. You will never know how much that night meant to me. Or maybe you do. The way you understood when it was too much, without me having to say Lego. That you wouldn't allow me to try and push through it. It was perhaps the first time I was given permission not to move beyond my capability.
I'm in Moscow now. I'm about to board a plane home. I can't write to you when home, but I can use these moments after my work is done before returning home to let you know I think of you.

Say hello to Fred. I hope he has recovered. I tried to be gentle. Keep my shoes safe. I want them back one day.
Lyza.

31, August
Mitch,
I'm tired. This last job took a lot of prep work and wasn't easy. I spent a week posing as a waitress to get close to my target. How do women spend eight hours waiting on others all day, every day? It's a damn hard job. Physically and mentally. Civilians are rude!
Thankfully, the job is done, and I'm waiting for my plane out of Manchester. I think I broke a rib and will have to visit the infirmary when I get home to check it over.
Home is getting easier. I'm helping train twin four-year-old boys, using games to teach them rather than discipline and pain. It's like having a second childhood, and I like it. Each day I miss you, I focus harder on the benefit I can make for these boy's lives. Some days, it's what keeps me going.
I can't believe it's already been six weeks since I last saw you. It feels like it's been years, and it was only yesterday since I woke up with you. I hope that makes sense.
I've had an idea. I always leave for work from Geneva. The helipad terminal has lockers there, which we quite often use to store valuables. I've purchased a permanent one and included the spare key in this letter. You can drop off my shoes the next time you are in Europe for business.
I hope these letters don't anger you. I know you hated me leaving, but I knew the consequences of staying. I couldn't do that to us.
I hope you can forgive me someday.
Lyza.

08, October
Mitch,
Sorry it's been so long. I was in Spain a few weeks ago and meant to drop you a letter, but I couldn't take the time to get one written. I always worked with Noel previously, and I'm finding doing the job by myself harder. No, not harder, more dangerous. Taking down ten men by yourself is far more hazardous than in a tandem.
Anyway, I'm in a taxi heading to the airport again. I've been three days in Abu Dhabi this time. It was my first time here. This job was a bit more relaxed, and I managed to get through it unscathed. Perhaps, I'm getting better at doing this by myself.
My training with the twins continues. They are turning five tomorrow, and I might have moved my job forward a day so I could be back for their birthday. I don't know if your mother did this, but I received my first swimming lesson on my fifth birthday. It wasn't my first time in a pool, they are hard to avoid in Australia, but I'd never been taught to swim.
On my birthday, my mother tossed me into the pool and told me I had to make it to the side and get myself out or drown. I think it was the first time I ever truly hated my mother.
Having overheard the twins would start swimming lessons soon, I started sneaking them down the indoor lap-pool. I took them one by one into the center of the pool, taught them to float and how to get to the side and out. They could do it without assistance when I left, so I'm looking forward to the looks on everyone's faces tomorrow when they manage it calmly.
I'm pulling up at the airport. I miss you.
Lyza

21, October
Mitch,
Will I ever stop missing you? I talk to you whenever I'm alone. I'm not sure if you hear me or if you care. I'm based in London this week. I've

*been notified I'll be heading to Chamber when I leave here today. I
was sure they had been testing me with the assignments they gave me
over the past three months, and it seems I was right. I'm not sure what
will happen. I'll write when I can.*
Lyza

23, October
Mitch,
*I'm flying home. The meeting was to settle Noel's estate. As his legal
wife, I inherited his business, etc. but, it seems you are already aware
of that since your mother brokered the deal selling you the Sword
Corporation Noel created without even asking me.*
I'm not sure how I feel about this. I need time to process it.
Lyza

After landing in Geneva, I caught the taxi to the helipad. I was
tired and emotionally rung. They just divided up my husband's assets,
sold his businesses and properties, and gave me no say in it.

*'Here are the contracts. The money has been deposited into your account.
Sign here to be declared widowed. Thank you for coming.'*

At the locker in the helipad, I dropped the burner phone left for me - I
never got the same one twice, though, I was always given a phone
with a video messaging app preloaded. That way, I could sign any
messages and send them.

Checking down the row of lockers to ensure Jonathan wasn't waiting
for me, I went to my private locker. Not that I expected anything, but
I always checked it. Surprisingly, inside was a shoebox. My shoebox. It
made me smile. Taking it out, I made my way out to wait for Jonathan.

Opening the lid, I found only one of my heels inside, along with a note.

Cinderella,

I hear you. Don't stop. I wake up eager just for that every morning.

The letters are wanted. Don't stop writing them, please.

I'm sorry it's taken so long. I was going to have one of my men drop it off for me, but then I was called to Switzerland on business. So, I get to drop it off personally. I'm on the plane there now. Part of me hopes we might cross paths, but then, how could I resist you if I saw you? Would I be allowed to approach you? If I see you and you are working, I worry that I might blow your cover and get you killed. Even worse, I fear to see another man with you, that they might make you remarry.

I've noticed I've never heard you at work, so I know you take the rings off when on duty, and I guess I should know you well enough to know you would do the same if there was another. I appreciate you saving me from that. Listening to either would be torture. The experience of listening to your divorce mediation process was hard enough to hear.

I don't know if you were told, but the reason I'm on my way to Switzerland is that you are selling The Sword Corporation to me, Concealed included. Moses approached me with the deal. I refused to take the calls from my mother.

There wasn't much of Concealed left. You fired everyone who wasn't on active duty during your divorce discussions with your ex. From what it looks like on paper, Noel actually ran a good company. They protected people for the most part. Not always good people, but mostly. Despite his issues with me, I think my brother might have been very similar to me. He had a good head for business at any rate.

I'm going to spend a week in Rome before heading home after this deal is closed. Julian has some new clients for me to meet. If you can get away, you know where to find me. If you can't, I understand. Another time, perhaps, but

I'm keeping the other shoe hostage until I see you personally. Hence, the Cinderella greeting - I'm not even sure if you will get the reference.

I want to see you, Lyza. I need to hold you, kiss you, and tell you how much I miss you. Find a way to come to me.

Mitch.

Wiping the tears from my face as I folded the letter, I put it back in the shoebox. Going back to my locker, I stowed it away. Hearing the helicopter coming, I sighed and made my way out onto the helipad. The wind was buffeting as I approached the aircraft. Jonathan smiled as I climbed in and shut the door.

Clenching his fists and tucking his boxer arms close to his body, Johnathan grabbed his harness. "Hold on, it's rough up there tonight." Nodding, I strapped myself in. When we landed, I made a beeline for Scott's house and knocked.

Opening the door, Scott's jaw dropped for a second before he lifted his hands to SimCom. "Lyza, I didn't expect to see you until morning. Come in." When Scott stepped back, gesturing that I come in, I stepped into his house for the first time ever. It felt weird being there. The community was close, but our homes were sort of our private space.

"Did everything go okay at Chamber?" Scott queried once he'd closed the door and taken his seat back on the lounge. Closing the laptop he'd been working on, he picked up his drink. Before he put it to his mouth, Scott made the devil's sign with his fingers and tapped the index finger to his nose, then turned his hand to touch the outside of his hand to his chest as he lifted the glass with his other hand. "Sorry, did you want a drink? I have alcohol if you need something strong?"

Shaking my head, I pointed to my chest then formed a circle with my left thumb and index, tapping my right index finger to the bottom quadrant to make a Q, indicting I had a question. *"Is it normal for Chamber to just deal with a deceased member's estate?"*

Watching my hands, Scott tapped his index and middle finger to his left palm. "It is normal for the parents to deal with it instead of the spouse," Scott confirmed. "It's easier for a parent to handle than someone who is intimately connected."

"We aren't taught, love. We are taught sex. Shouldn't a parent be more stricken by their child's death?"

Frowning, Scott chewed the inside of his lip. "We aren't taught love, but, in most cases, husband and wife do come to have a deeper connection than what the parents do."

"I don't believe that."

Tilting his head, Scott considered me. "You don't believe you loved Noel?"

"No, I didn't love him. I cared for him, and it was hard to be told I had to end him, but I did it."

Eye narrowing, Scott shifted uncomfortably. Pointing to me, he put his splayed hand to his stomach and swept it up and away to face the palm up as he lifted his shoulders. "You're upset about this?"

Struggling to gather my thoughts in a way that I could describe, I took a deep breath and shook my head, deciding it wasn't worth pursuing. It was done. As far as the arrow was concerned, I needed to move on. *"Noel and I, we used to take a day or two after jobs were done. Just for us, away from here, to see what else is out there."*

Tapping his temple, Scott knocked his right fist on top of his left twice to confirm he remembered.

"I'd like to do that occasionally. Take a few days away from here for me."

Considering me, Scott shook his head. "Now is not a good time for you to do that." Picking up his drink again, he took a mouthful before putting it back down. Accepting his answer, I stood to leave. "You could stay a little longer," Scott offered. "I don't mind the company."

Pointing my bladed hand to my right chest above my breast, I allowed it to slowly deflate down to indicate I was tired. Though I was more disappointed.

"Lyza," Scott sighed. "We all know what it was like for you. We all saw it. I was also informed of how your disability came about before your return. Chamber knows you don't want to be here. Everyone in this community can see you don't want to be here. They won't accept you being back here until you do."

"It's not here that's the problem," I signed, bored. *"My downtime should be mine to choose how I want to spend it. If that's here or sunbaking naked on a beach in the south of France, it should be my choice. Being forced to stay here just feels like being in prison again. As long as I do my job well, why should it matter where I go between jobs?"*

Frowning, Scott put his hand to his throat as if turning a dial at his voice box. "I'm sorry you feel so restricted here." Licking his lips, he stepped closer. "If you want anything, my door is always open." Accepting the offer, I turned to leave, but Scott touched my shoulder. "Liam turns fourteen in two days. I was hoping you might help with the testing. He likes you. After it's over, he'll need to leave for his new chapter. You can catch a lift to Geneva and go where you need to go from there. Take a phone, and I'll call you if a job comes in while you are gone."

Frowning, I considered Scott. *"What if he tests for Scythe?"*

Smirking, Scott pointed to his left shoulder, circling it around to tap to his right collarbone, held up his splayed index and middle finger, and gave it a little shake before thumbing his temple. "We both know that is not going to happen. He could make an excellent Hunter, though." I nodded with a smile. Liam was a lot like Moses, so I could see him ending up there. Stepping forward, I gave Scott a hug, something the twins had gotten me used to over the last few months. He tensed, then slowly, his hands gripped my waist.

Stepping back, I put my fingertips to my chin before taking them away like I was offering it to him.

"You're welcome," Scott smiled, his eyes happy.

At the door, I turned back to him. Holding my open hand up, I snatched it into a fist, pointed to Scott, cuffed my ear, and spelled out Cinderella as I lifted my shoulders.

Blinking, Scott frowned. "It's a Disney princess."

"Yes, but what's her story?" I pressed.

Holding his arms out to the side, Scott shrugged.

Pursing my lips, I nodded and pushed through his door. I needed to go do some reading, I guess.

31

MISLEADING

"GOOD LUCK, LIAM," SCOTT FAREWELLED THE TEENAGE BOY BEFORE WE headed to the helicopter. "Lyza will see you to the airport and will stay with you to meet your escort to your new chapter." Nodding, Liam headed to the helicopter. Scott's smile dropped when he met my eyes. "I'm sorry. I know I said you could get away for a few days, but you were perfect for the job."

Putting a loose fist to the bottom of my chin, I let the curse fall away as I opened my hand like I was dropping that pile of rubbish on the floor lazily, not even trying to hide my scowl. *"Anyone here could do this job,"* I signed angrily. Throwing my bag over my shoulder, I turned away before Scott could argue.

I'd done as asked and stayed the few days, helping with Liam's testing, only to wake up this morning to find a new job appointed. It was a basic hit. Any of us could have done it. To make matters worse, I overheard one of the others complaining to Scott this morning about how busy I'd been with them barely getting a job a month. Scott told them Chamber wanted me kept occupied for a few months, so this job's timing was entirely suspect.

Joining Liam in the helicopter, I buckled up while Jonathan showed Liam how to strap in. Mitch would hear that I was on the job and know I wasn't coming. Pissed did not begin to explain how angry I was.

Beside me on the flight, Liam was all nerves. It was his first time leaving here, and you could tell he was terrified and excited simultaneously. At the helipad, I collected a new phone, checked my locker, and then took Liam to the airport. I wondered who would receive him, but I knew who it was as soon as I saw him. Moses's smile lit up like a beacon when he saw me.

"Lyza," he signed. *"How fortunate am I to see you. Are you the transfer?"*

Shaking my head, I put a hand on Liam's shoulder, squeezing gently as I stepped him forward. *"This is Liam. He's a good kid. He'll make a fine Hunter."*

"Oh, really?" Moses laughed. *"And your judgment is based on?"*

"He's a younger version of you."

Watching my hands, Moses's grin got bigger. *"Pity the flight leaves soon, or I would have insisted you have dinner with me."*

Pointing to my chest, I sat my right hand in my left palm up, then forming a pistol grip, put my thumb to my left hand, and ticked my index finger forward to indicate I was on the clock. *"What are you doing here?"* I pointed to Moses, then lifted my shoulders as I gestured to the floor.

"I was here for a job. About to board the plane home, and they called to tell me I was bringing in a transfer. I hoped it was you. What's the job?"

"Sitting on an asset until some unfriendly tries for him. Kill them, then go home."

Moses frowned. *"Is the asset Moore?"* Tilting my head, I appraised his hands, him, and then nodded. *"Why don't you just go take out the unfriendly tonight?"*

"I was told we didn't know where or when they would hit."

Now it was Moses's turn to look cynical. "Lyza, I did the hunt. *That's what I was here for. I gave a detailed report of where to find them, how many there were, and that the best way to take them out would be a surprise attack."*

"I seriously need to learn sign language," Liam cooed. "You two have been having an entire conversation in silence. It's cool."

"I'll teach you," Moses promised. "Go sit right there and wait for me," he directed.

Swallowing, Liam took the seat. Pulling out his laptop, Moses fired it up. Opening the file with his report, he gave it to me to read. I could have committed harakiri on a few select individuals. The asset was in Germany, my targets were in Italy. In that instant, I knew that Chamber knew Mitch was still in Europe and deliberately blindsided me to try and stop me from seeing him.

Pointing to Moses, I sliced my bladed hand into my right palm as I lifted my shoulders. *"You are sure this is still current?"*

"I just came from there, so yes," Moses assured.

Grinning, I kissed his cheek. *"Thank you. I have to go."* Farewelling Liam, I raced off. Instead of catching the plane Chamber had booked, I went to the car hire then drove through the night to reach Venice and the location Moses identified.

The street was busy, so I parked the car and went into a coffee shop to enjoy breakfast while I cased the location myself. By mid-morning, one of the targets came across the road to get coffees. Slipping off my rings, I shoved them in my backpack in a place they wouldn't be able to pick up any noise and went back out to my car.

Dumping my bag, I followed as the target went back to his building. Inside the lobby of the apartment building, he headed for the stairs but stopped to watch me. Smiling softly, I started up the stairs with the confidence of someone who knew where they were going. He followed with his eyes on my bum in my skinny jeans the entire way up to the fourth floor. He departed my company to go to his apartment, but I kept on to the next level.

At the apartment above theirs, I knocked. No one answered. Tapping again to be sure, I then picked the lock and let myself in. Moses had detailed the best way to sneak up on the targets perfectly. In the kitchen, I stopped for a sharp knife. One of the first things we learn is to take advantage of what's available to us. Walking around with weapons gets you noticed. Being unarmed stops you from looking like a threat. Especially in a pair of skinny jeans and a low-cut sweater.

At the balcony, I let myself out and shut the door. Gazing over the edge at the drop to the target's railing, I assessed the fall. I'd fallen further. Climbing over the balustrade, I started.

"Bastardo, you think you can treat me like this? I'm not some floozy you can use." With a bit of a scream, I dropped. Catching the next railing down, I took a moment to ensure I had a safe grip. The two men inside noticed the sudden adornment to their balcony.

Glaring up, I made a rude gesture above me. "Fuck you, asshole," I yelled in accented English. Then I climbed over the railing and allowed myself to look devastated.

One of the men came out looking unsure about the crying female on his balcony. "Ah, miss?"

"He used me," I sobbed. "Then, he tried to… He tried to…. Oh god, he tried to kill me." Rising to my feet, I was clinging to the man in front of me. "He pushed me off his balcony. He tried to kill me."

Now, most civilians would be offering to call the police about now. Not criminals, though. No, instead, they smelt a rat, and instantly the other guy was checking out the peephole of his door while this one was trying to look up at the balcony above.

"Did you know the man, Miss?" The one holding me queried. American accents, Southern at that. He made me think of Mitch.

"No, not really. We met a week ago, and he was all charming and sweet. Then he just told me he was done with me and tried to kill me," I started sobbing again. "He's American, but he doesn't talk like you. His accent, it's posher."

The one holding me gestured to his mate, and he unbolted the door and went upstairs to meet their American neighbor. As soon as the door clicked shut, so did my acting. Striking like a viper, my fingers hit his throat to stop him from yelling an alert. His eyes went wide, and my palm struck up into his nose, breaking it and forcing the nose bone up into his brain. He dropped to the ground.

Moving into the apartment, I appraised the weapon collection. Helping myself to one of the garrotes, a pistol with a silencer, and two throwing knives, I tucked the gun and knives away. Really, the weapon selection was rather impressive. Relocating to the apartment door, I listened as big steps ran down the hallway stairs. It opened as the other ran in, ready to tell his friend no one was up there.

Stepping in behind him, I wrapped the garrote twice in quick succession around his throat and tripped him simultaneously. His weight tightened the wire for me as he went down with my resistance. Taking out the sharp knife I stole upstairs, I quickly stabbed it between his cervical vertebrae, wiggling the knife to ensure the spinal cord severed.

He'd suffocate in a matter of moments, but his body was useless to him now anyway. Moving into the first bedroom, I shut the door. A man was singing in the shower. Checking the gun was loaded, I aimed and shot him mid-tenor, following up with another shot to the head— the silencer muffling the noise.

Checking the coast was clear, I made my way into the last bedroom. The woman was still sleeping in the bed. Two shots and she wasn't waking up ever again. Her photo had been in Moses's file but also in mine. She was the daughter of the asset and the ringleader of this merry band of gentlemen. I guess I wasn't the only one with daddy issues.

Checking through the apartment, I placed the cleaned weapons back where they belonged. All the targets Moses identified were present, and their souls were collected. After using the phone to take photos of their faces, identifications, and the plans they'd developed detailing the asset's movements and his intention to attend an opera in Wien in two days, I cleaned up and left the apartment. After the last few missions, this job seemed too easy. As I'd told Scott, any one of the others could have done it.

Across the road was a lovely boutique with some stunning dresses in it. Smiling, I ducked back to the car for my wallet, then went into the store and bought a handful of day dresses, a few pairs of shoes, and a formal gown. The dresses weren't cheap, and the owner was over the moon with my purchases. The balance of my bank account barely blinked at the purchase after my inheritance from my late husband. Blinking away the memories and pain, I forced a smile for the sales assistant and collected my bags.

Back in the car, I started the engine and headed for Rome. Arriving just after dinner time, I located the hotel that Mitch stayed at last time and parked. Stopping at the front desk, I mimed for a pen and pad to query if Mr. Fairchild was in and if they could ring his rooms for me.

The attendant looked at the note. "I'll just check, Señorita."

Moving away, he rang upstairs. A moment later, he came back. "Mr. Fairchild isn't in, but his friend will come down to meet you."

Stacey only took a moment to appear at the elevator foyer. She stalked straight up to me with some serious resting bitch face happening. "I thought you left? Everything happened, and then you were gone, and he was so, so, angry, and Fred was sad, and Moses disappeared too, and now you just show up out of the blue?"

Restraining a smile as I watched her lips, I lifted a shoulder and checked out the lobby in disinterest. If Mitch hadn't told her what went down, I wasn't about to. It's not like we became friends during my time there.

Huffing, Stacey waved me off like I was a peasant. "He's at Julian's soirée." Turning, she went back upstairs. Guess it was time to get my glam on.

32

A LATE DATE

WHEN I EXITED THE TAXI IN MY BACKLESS SILK DRESS, THE GUARDS didn't even question my entry. If this was a job, it would be damn easy. As I entered the foyer, I pulled out my phone and opened the video messaging app to contact my chapter. Most of the others called in, their voices enough to identify them. Performing a selfie, I signed my message.

> *Job complete. All targets acquired. Evidence collected. ETA: Two to three days.*

Knowing it was going to ruffle feathers, I shoved the phone in my purse. A guard standing to the side noticed me when others stopped their conversation to admire. Disengaging from the group, Fred approached with concern, lifting his shoulders as he held his arms out to the side before pointing at me and then the floor. "Lyza, what are you doing here? Are you working?"

Smiling, I shook my head. Putting my finger to my lips, I winked. A slow smile spread over Fred's face. Shaking his head, he pointed through the door. "Try not to break the furniture."

Heat filling my cheeks at the reminder, I stepped to the doorway then stopped to scan the room and find Mitch. He stood talking with a man who I gathered was a client. Happiness flooded my body at just the sight of him. Mitch looked breathtaking in his tux, and several women were trying to catch his eye.

Taking a deep breath, I took the rings out of my purse and slipped them back on my finger. Moving through the crowd, I collected a drink from a waiter's tray and kept tracking Mitch. Instead of approaching him directly, I eased my way to the hallway's opening and made myself comfortable against the wall.

Mitch was focused on his conversation, and I didn't want to interrupt his business, so I waited, watching the crowd shuffle and chat, the fake laughs standing out from the real ones. Those who smiled warmly but then turned and lost the fake smile while they searched for someone else.

Mitch's shoulders dropped in my peripheral vision. Understanding his conversation was wrapping up, I turned my shoulder into the wall to watch him. I'd studied him for a week while we were here last, so I knew his body language fluently. After the client walked off, Mitch took a long drink of his scotch while he glanced over the room.

Moss-colored eyes swept over me once as he did an initial scan before lowering his eyes. Smirking to myself, I waited for him to process all the faces he saw. His brows pinched, and his face quickly lifted to where I stood. Pupils dilating, he didn't move. The tension of his shoulders held the same hesitation I'd seen in Fred. Was I working?

Not wanting our reunion to be public and needing to be alone with him, I gave him a cheeky smile, lifted a brow, and turned, making my way down the hall to the quieter area of Julian's abode. I wanted to kiss and touch him, run my nails down his back as he buried himself in me hard and fast, staking his claim on me. God, I wanted his teeth marks and fingerprints etched in my flesh, so days later, I could touch them and be here with him again.

Intending to continue out the back door and into the pool area, I strode with focus, but Mitch took my hand as he caught me and led me down a side corridor before letting us into a guest bedroom.

Shutting the door, he locked it, then his mouth was hot and wet, tasting of aged oak as he possessed my lips. Closing my eyes as his arms encased me, I lost myself in his kiss. Kissing Mitch was a dream. A good dream. The best kind because he was real. This was finally happening. Giddiness flooded my body.

Pulling back, both of us breathless, Mitch held me tighter. Inhaling deeply, I breathed him into me. My body responded to the familiar scent of his aftershave. My muscles relaxing, heat firing to all my erogenous zones, my scanties growing damp. "Lyza," Mitch panted. "I thought you got sent on a job?"

"I did," I whispered back. "I finished early and came straight here."

Mitch caressed my face with worry. "Will you get in trouble?"

I traced his lips with my fingertip. "They have no grounds."

"Are you sure," Mitch checked as my finger relieved him of his bow tie.

"Most sure thing I've done in three months."

Grinning, Mitch captured my mouth again as his hands explored my body, teasing my nipple through the thin material of the dress. He broke free. "I still have one more potential client to speak to, then I'll take you back to my hotel for this."

Was he really willing to wait? I certainly wasn't. I'd lost the count of deaths I'd handed out these past few months, let alone the four just today, and it had been months since I got off. I needed this now. Lifting a brow at his suggestion, I waited. Smile growing, Mitch turned me fast towards the wall and started lifting my dress. While I pulled the crutch of my knickers aside, Mitch shifted one hand forward to cover my mound, tapping on my clit with proficiency while his other hand freed his longing.

Lifting my leg, I used an arm to catch my knee against the wall. Lining up his aim, Mitch drove into me without restraint. Tears filled my eyes as I cried out; I was that happy to be with him again. Using my hips to bring our pelvises hard against each other, Mitch was forceful enough to drive the air from my lungs.

Already swelling inside me, Mitch was ready to blow. The hard pump his hips inflicted nearly had me there, and I knew his explosion would push me over the edge. Mitch's hand suddenly grabbed my left bicep, his fingertips pressing over the empty space that once housed our protection beneath my flesh. "Fuck!" Mitch panted and pulled out.

"Don't stop," I begged, so close to coming.

"Lyza?"

Turning to face him, I let him see the tears in my eyes. "It doesn't matter. Don't stop. I've changed my mind. I want kids. I want to be the mother of your bastards. I want you, and I don't care how they feel about it."

Tilting his head, Mitch stepped closer and made me meet his eyes; it was so natural for me to watch people's lips now. "You mean that?"

"I've loved training the twins, showing them fun games that lead to the same outcome. I know I can raise our kids differently, so I'm okay with it."

Mitch's eyes softened. Taking my hand, he walked me over to the bed. "The client can wait a little longer. You are more important." Turning me side on, he lowered the zip on my dress and pushed it down until it slipped to the ground. "I want to feel you entirely," Mitch murmured.

Facing him, I assisted in the removal of his clothes. "Okay, but I was close, so let's wait until later for passion and deal with our lust right now."

Laughing, Mitch shoved my knickers over my hips. "Fuck, I love you, Lyza." When he leaned forward to kiss me, I hesitated. Blinking, Mitch considered me, then his eyes widened as he realized what he said out loud, and he pulled back a step. "You know that, right? Yes, we have lust, but there is so much more between us."

"Love?"

Caressing the rings on my fingers, Mitch blushed. "I realized it only a few days after meeting you. By the time we had sex, I was lost to you. You were too; you just took longer to realize it."

Biting my lip, I closed my eyes as I suddenly understood what I'd been feeling all those weeks. "That's why it hurt me so much when you tortured me to get Noel's name."

Head bowing when pain flashed in his eyes, Mitch exhaled hard. "Jesus, that killed me. I knew for sure after that. The guilt I felt, the way it bothered me when you wore clothes to bed that night. I didn't know how to talk to you the next day because I didn't know how to face what I was feeling for you or that I had potentially ruined everything for some bastard's name."

Sighing, I caressed his cheek. "He wasn't a bastard. His parents were married, and he was your brother and my husband."

Mitch pulled me close. "Was your husband, and he was still an asshole." Mitch rubbed his nose across mine. "Can you come home with me?"

Closing my eyes, I shook my head. "I can take a few days here and there, but they won't release me permanently."

"So, this will be random at best?" Mitch deflated a little as he sank down on the bed.

Feeling the same disappointment, I stepped forward onto his lap, straddling his thighs. Automatically hugging my bum with his hands, he pulled me firmly against him. "It's this or nothing, Mitch. I'm sorry."

Lifting his eyes to mine, Mitch massaged his thumb across my cheekbone. "It's insane they don't see the logic in us being together." Kissing my chin, his hardness pulsed against my pubic bone.

Rising up, I gently took him inside me. I started rocking my hips, but it just wasn't scratching the itch. Exhaling roughly, I met his eyes. "Mitch, I killed before coming here. I need more than this."

Catching my chin, Mitch planted a deep kiss on me, his tongue delving inside, tasting me entirely. Without warning, he threw me on the bed, flipping around behind me, and knelt between my thighs. "I'll give you this now, but when we get to the hotel, I'm taking my time," Mitch decreed. "If I'm only getting you occasionally, I'm going to make it last."

Happy to get my way, I bit my lip as he thrust inside. The sharp smacking sound of his hard and fast pumps filled the room, accompanied by our heavy breathing and the creaking of the bed. My fingers gripped and released the comforter as my body quickly rose to its pleasure, working off that excess adrenalin from work this morning.

When Mitch delved deep, I cried out at the combined pleasure and pain. "There?" Mitch asked, thrusting hard at that angle again.

"Yes!"

Obliging me, Mitch found that brink spot over and over until my body seized, and I cried out his name. Growling, he dug his fingers hard into my hips as he kept thrusting. Suddenly, Mitch cursed and pulled out, spilling all over my back. Collapsing on the bed, sated and happy, I sighed as Mitch fell beside me. "I can just wait here while you meet that last client," I offered, exhausted.

"Like this? Hell, no! Some other man may come in and take advantage of my wife."

"We aren't legally married."

Mitch combed my hair out of my face with his fingers. "At this party, in my heart, you are my wife, Lyza. As soon as I can make it legal, I will." Kissing my shoulder, Mitch rolled off the bed and walked into the adjoining bathroom. Coming back with a warm towel, he wiped me clean. "I know you said you changed your mind, but I want to discuss the concept of children a little bit more before we throw caution to the wind."

Exhaling, I rolled to face him as I sat up and kissed him. "Okay." I wasn't upset. He was right. We needed to work out the logistics of our relationship first. How we could tackle the obstacles Chamber could put in our path. Moses told me if I got pregnant to him, they would insist we marry, and I move chapters to be with him. Part of me might have been considering that rule when I offered to bear Mitch's children. Mostly, I was just horny and needed to get off.

Drawing me up to standing, Mitch pecked my nose. "Get dressed before I forget this is Julian's house and take you back to bed." Chuckling, I collected my clothes to start dressing. Mitch did the same. "You want to tell me about those new scars you are sporting?" Mitch asked, all humor washed from his voice.

Running my hand over the still angry scars along the side of my ribs, I grimaced. "Spain. It's why I couldn't write. I had to focus on getting home."

Considering me, Mitch frowned. "That's awfully close to your liver, Lyza."

Breathing evenly, I zipped my dress up. "Just two stab wounds and a bullet grazing by. Nothing life-threatening."

"How often are you getting hurt?"

Fussing with my hair, I didn't meet his eyes. "Don't worry, I can handle it."

"Lyza," Mitch touched my shoulder, eyes expressing his unhappiness. "Don't tell me not to worry. I do. I think you do too."

"Can we talk about it later? I just want to enjoy being with you right now."

Inhaling, Mitch nodded. "Come on, Julian was asking about you earlier. He will be happy to see you. I think he worried you'd left me."

"Never by choice," I breathed, already hating the looming end to this short reunion.

Kissing me lightly, Mitch unlocked the door. His eyes flicked back to the bed. "I'll let Julian know his maid needs to tend his guest room."

"Your bed is going to be worse later."

Mitch laughed, "It better be."

33

———

LOVE

WAKING UP IN MITCH'S ARMS FELT LIKE A GREAT DREAM, MADE EVEN better by that delicious tenderness between my thighs from a rigorous pounding, and the ache in my hips from having my legs spread for an extended period.

God, how many times did I come last night? Mitch definitely made up for the lost time. Rolling over to face Mitch, I smiled at his sleeping form. Tracing the edges of his face, his brows, his delicious lips, I awed at how he was perfect for me in every way. The man I would have chosen if given the option.

Climbing out of bed, I used the bathroom, then grabbed Mitch's button-down and pulled it on as I went to stand at the window. It was chilly and dark still, the sun on the edge of rising, so I didn't go out on the balcony. My body clock was on Chapter time.

"Come back to bed."

So entrenched at ignoring people, I didn't respond; plus, my throat was hurting after all the noise I made last night. Sighing, Mitch threw the comforter back, sitting up in the reflection of the window. Scrubbing his face, he went to the bathroom. When he came back out,

275

he wrapped his arms around me and kissed the junction of my neck and shoulder. Closing my eyes, I enjoyed being there in his arms.

"This is the time you get up every morning. Do you stand at your bedroom window watching the sunrise while you talk to me?"

Smirking at how ingrained the habit had become, I nodded.

"I've been ensuring I'm somewhere quiet every evening so I can hear you talk to me," he admitted. "Every syllable that falls from your lips makes me fall all the more in love with you." He caressed my throat with the palm of his hand, and I stretched my neck up and back for how nice it felt. "You're in pain, aren't you?"

Moaning, I rested my head on his shoulder while Mitch nibbled on my ear lobe for a second. Slowly, his hand brushed down and groped my breast through his shirt. "I love the way you put my shirt on after we've had sex," Mitch breathed. "It's like your subconscious wants to still be wearing me, to be surrounded in my scent. You never pick a clean shirt. It's always the one I just took off."

Twisting the button open in front of my breasts, Mitch slid in his hand. Closing my eyes, I enjoyed Mitch's caress. Slowly, he turned me, pressing my back gently against the door jamb for the balcony. His lips pinched mine with a delicate slowness, allowing us a moment to believe we had all the time in the world.

Kissing down my neck, Mitch ensured the softest of brushes from his lips right over my larynx, then he dropped to his knees. Lifting heavy eyelids, I found Mitch looking up at me with raw need. His hands grazed up the back of my thighs, lifting his shirt to reveal the heat of me. Giving me a wicked smile, he kissed my lower lips, his tongue performing a slow dance that left my legs trembling and nails gripping the wall and his hair. Spiraling into euphoria with barely any sense of reality, I struggled to breathe or hold myself upright. Standing, Mitch carried me back to bed.

When I tried to relieve his need, Mitch redirected my mouth to his and kissed me deeply. Slowly, he pulled away and held me to him. "Later, I'm out of condoms."

Had we seriously fucked that much last night? No wonder I was exhausted. Mitch had made his driver go buy him some while he'd talked to his last client for the evening. Fred barely restrained his laughter when the driver handed him a box labeled 'ribbed for her pleasure.' Frankly, I'd enjoyed the textured ride, so the packaging spoke the truth.

When I was about to remind Mitch that you didn't need protection for head, he kissed me and placed his thumb against my lips. "I've made a decision, and I'm hoping you'll agree." His eyes were determined, so sure in whatever he was thinking. Caressing my face, Mitch brushed his thumb over the rings on my left hand. "Let's make it real."

"WE SHOULD TALK WHILE WE CAN," I panted against Mitch's chest. The man was a machine. It had to be all the training he did. Those long runs in thin air in the Sandia Mountains.

Mitch groaned beneath me. "Sure. You start. I'll catch my breath." When I smacked his chest, Mitch laughed and rolled us, so we were side by side. Keeping me in his arms, he kissed me steadily. Slowly, we both got our breath back. "Where should we start?"

"What happens now?" I asked.

Mitch exhaled. "That's up to you. You could come home with me-"

"They'd hunt me and kill me," I dismissed immediately.

"Or me."

"Debbie has been protecting you all these years. She'll let my bloodline go before she kills her own."

"She ordered my brother killed."

"She hated his father. Never had anything to do with Noel growing up. Apparently, her first husband wasn't her choice, and he was an ass. Your father, I think she loved him. I think she loves you. That's why she gave you the freedom she did."

"No, I just refused to test," Mitch dismissed my theory. "When I was fourteen, she took me to Canada, to the Rockies, and a little lodge that is there. There was like a cult of people living there. I don't know. I just remember them all watching me with interest and me thinking they were a bunch of freaks."

"She took you to Chapter."

"I figured that out on our run, but I didn't know it then. There was an obstacle course, a treasure hunt, some sort of exam, a game sort of like bullrush,"

"What's bullrush?" I frowned.

"You have to run across an open field, and people try to catch you."

"Oh, the evasion and reflexes test."

Tilting his head, Mitch nodded. "Now that I look back on it, yeah, I can see how each of the events was a test. Back then, I was just pissed that mum forced me to go to some back hills carnival when I wanted to be at my friend's birthday party. So, I refused to participate."

Mouth falling open, I sat up. "You what?"

"I refused to participate."

"But you would have got the shit beat out of you." My eyes were bugging out of my head.

"Yeah, I did. And it pissed my mum off so bad. So, I took the beatings and gloated internally at how humiliated she was," Mitch sighed. "I heard one guy telling her I was a complete failure, that I had no respect or discipline, and he was disgraced to be associated with me.

That's when I realized he was my father. I'd never even met the asshole, but after he walked away, my mum was in tears, and I felt bad, so I tried to give her a hug."

Falling silent for a second, Mitch took a deep breath. "She lashed out; told me I'd let her down more than anyone ever could have. She tried to gouge my fucking eyes out, crazy bitch she was. I overpowered her and took her down. She was so surprised, and admittedly, I was shocked as shit. I'd always been scared of her until that point."

"What happened?"

"She realized what I had done, that I failed on purpose. After taking me home, she packed her bag and told me I chose a civilian life, so I could damn well make my own way like one. Then she left." Mitch caressed my spine. "The bitch even put the house up for sale while I was still living in it. The realtor turned up and accused me of being a squatter. So, I moved in with my best friend and his family. When we were eighteen, Jeb and I enlisted, and we went all the way to SEALs together."

"Where is Jeb now?" I asked, wondering if he was still on active duty.

Shifting uncomfortably, Mitch rubbed the scar along his side. "My brother killed him."

Shoulders rolling forward, I deflated beside him, a dense ball of guilt loading my stomach. "Do you still hear from Debbie?"

"She'd call for my birthday, drop in if she was in town. We are civil to each other, but I've refused to talk to her since she took you away." Mitch's hand continued to trace my back as if he was concentrating on keeping his emotions at bay or thinking about something more complicated. "I should have told you before, but we weren't really talking about this stuff," Mitch began. "When I met with your lawyer for the purchase of the Sword Corporation, they made me a secondary offer."

Tensing, I lifted my face to study him.

"They offered for me to retest, to join the Arrow and Sword, and for us to be together," Mitch revealed. My heart stopped in my chest. "I refused." Exhaling in relief, I wrapped him in my arms and squeezed him tight. "You're not angry?" Shaking my head, I started crying against his chest. God, I was anything but angry. I was so relieved it wasn't funny. "Lyza?" Mitch pulled back, concerned as I cried.

"It was a trick. Had you taken the offer, we would never have been allowed together. You would never have tested for Scythe. You would have been sent to a different Chapter and realized too late they screwed you. You would have disappeared, and I'd never know where you went. They could have convinced me you didn't want to know about me anymore, and I wouldn't be able to find you to prove them wrong."

Offering me a kind smile, Mitch kissed the tip of my nose. "I told them, I am life, you are death, by their laws, we can't coexist. That's all the answer I gave them, but by the look on the guy's face, he understood that I knew it was a trick," Mitch shook his head. "Still, I worried they would try to tell you I turned you down, so I wanted you to know."

"They will. I suspect they always knew you would say no but wanted the offer on the record."

"I'm surprised they haven't tried to marry you off already?"

Closing my eyes, I considered how the single men at Chapter appraised me like they would a new shiny gun. "They will. They are just waiting to see if I survive."

"Survive?"

"The jobs they have been sending me on. They aren't giving me all the information. They are sending me into situations that would normally see a team dealing with them. We normally have a one to five ratio. For every five targets, one of us is assigned. In Moscow, I went into a situation with ten hostiles, and in Spain, there were closer to thirty, but not one of the packages identified those odds."

Mitch sat up, considering me. "They're trying to kill you?"

Eyebrows lifting, I huffed. "Yes. But I don't think all of Chamber is aware of the situation. I'm going to test the theory when I get home."

"How?"

"Each Chapter parent is sent a copy of the job file. I want to see what detail he has. Father would notice if the report from the Hunter lacked sufficient material. He's got nearly twenty years more experience than me."

"And if someone is filtering the information out?" Mitch worried.

"I make my father aware of it, you contact Moses for me and get him to make his mother aware of it, and then we let them try and figure it out," I shrugged.

"What makes you think I know how to contact Moses?" Mitch's brows bunched. Smiling, I lifted an eyebrow. Mitch's face relaxed from his fake confusion, and his smile slowly spread. "How did you know?" Eyes sparkling as he pulled me tight against him, I winked and sucked his ear lobe into my mouth as he grew eager for another round. "You're too smart for your own pants, Mrs. Fairchild," Mitch purred.

"I'm not wearing any pants."

Mitch's hand looked for evidence as he rolled me onto my back. "Well, aren't I a lucky man?"

Putting a hand on his chest before anything could start again, I held him at bay. "We got sidetracked."

Lowering his head, Mitch kissed above my heart. "Do we have any choice?"

"No."

"Then we play it by ear and see where life takes us. If we find an opportunity to be together, we jump on it." His eyes and hands went to my abdomen. "When you're ready to try for more, we do it and use their own rules against them."

"This could prove fatal for one or both of us."

Settling himself between my thighs, Mitch made my breath catch as he pushed his way into my core. "They will have to kill me to ever get me to give you up." He was absolutely sincere.

Wrapping my legs around him, I pulled him deeper inside me. "I love you."

"Do you ever work in the states?" When I shook my head, Mitch huffed. "Then, I'm going to need to come to Europe more often. Where should I buy our house?"

"I'll take care of it. After all, I just got paid a ridiculous amount of money for the sale of my ex-husband's estate."

Mitch pulled back a little. "Were you angry?"

"Yes." There was no point hiding my feelings from Mitch. If our half-baked relationship was ever going to work, I needed to always be honest with him.

"At me?"

"No. It was them not giving me a choice again. That's what always gets to me."

Pecking my lips, Mitch rubbed his nose against mine. "Tell me we'll make this work."

"Somehow, I'm going to turn up at your door one day and tell you I'm there to stay," I assured.

"Promise?" Mitch breathed.

"Promise."

34

UNKNOWN KNOWLEDGE

"FATHER WANTS TO SEE YOU," JONATHAN INFORMED ME RIGHT AFTER landing.

Nodding, I climbed down from the helicopter, grabbed my bags, and walked down the path to the village. Scott was standing on his front porch, waiting as I walked towards his place and stopped at the bottom of his steps.

Browsing the bags in my hands, Scott left his thumb up from the fist and knocked it against his bladed left palm, so the mounds touched before touching his temple. "Retail therapy?"

Looking down at the bags, I nodded. Waving me inside, Scott pointed to his chest, his eye, then me, and then made the same sign for shopping, but instead of knocking the hands, he pulled the right fist down away from it. "I want to see what a girl like you buys."

Frowning at the unusual request, I followed him inside and went to his lounge room, happy that his curiosity would give me my opening. Putting the bags down, I turned to face him. "Did you want a drink?" Scott offered.

Shaking my head, I wiped the offer away. Holding my left bladed hand in front of my body as I twisted forty-five degrees, I shuffled my right hand forward from it before tapping my index and middle fingers to the top of my left palm and then the bottom. *"I should file my report."*

"Just one drink," Scott replied, moving to the kitchen.

Glancing at his computer on the coffee table, I lifted a brow and pointed to it before signing. *"I could use your computer to file the report?"*

Stopping, Scott considered. *"I guess that would work."* Moving forward, he lifted the lid of his laptop before logging in. Opening the file for the job, Scott turned the computer towards me. "Juice?"

Touching the bottom of my chin, I dropped my hand and tucked my four fingers down, so I was giving him the thumbs up. Sitting on the sofa, I quickly browsed the file. Like I suspected, I was looking at the full report that Moses showed me. The pictures of targets, locations, etc.

Sitting next to me with a concerned look, Scott placed our drinks down. Touching his thumb to his pinky in front of his chest, he rubbed the thumb across all four fingers as he tucked them down quickly and moved it to the right. Pointing his pinky forward with the closed fist upwards and twisting it to have the closed hand facing down as he lifted his shoulders. *"Is something wrong?"*

Glancing from Scott's hand to the file and back again, I bit my lip. *"This isn't the same package I received."*

Watching my hands, Scott bunched his brows. "Clarify that."

"This has a lot more information than my file." Dropping my hands to the mouse pad, I scrolled through, crossing the screen of all the things missing from mine.

"Go get your laptop," Scott directed. Standing, I gathered my bags. "Come straight back," Scott ordered as I looked back at him before stepping out the door.

Nodding to Scott, I left, walking fast through the cold evening. A few days, and it would start snowing up here. I dumped my bags on the table in my house and went straight to my safe, taking out my laptop and stashing the phone Mitch bought me. It was a burner and was only to be used in an emergency. If I got caught with it up here, the punishment was worse than marrying a civilian.

Taking out a thumb drive, I quickly copied the files to be safe. Then I put that in the safe too. Locking everything up, I raced back to Scott's. He was waiting inside, his glass of scotch already empty.

Sitting down, I opened my files and put my laptop side by side with his. Scanning the most recent first, Scott then reviewed all my past jobs since my return. Every single one of them was missing information. Scott sat back with a huff.

"You made a powerful enemy," Scott finally signed without talking, then went to refill his glass. Taking my spare thumb drive out, I copied my job files on his computer. Then I put it back in my pocket. Once he'd taken another hit of alcohol, he turned to face me.

"Every one of your files is missing or has a doctored Hunter's access file. The data on targets has been adjusted, and you are missing vital information which put your life at risk," Scott went back to using SimCom. He bowed his head and ran a hand through his hair. "No wonder you were getting so badly injured," he muttered to himself. "I'm surprised you survived Moscow, let alone Spain."

Hand in the pistol grip, I brushed my thumb from my right shoulder to breast. *"Why was I sent alone? Aren't you meant to assess the file and decide who will go?"*

Scott hesitated over my question. "I'm an idiot. I trusted them. I'm sorry." When I frowned, not understanding, Scott exhaled hard. "Your dad ran this place hard, but he never trained anyone to take over his role. When the news he was dead came in, I was nominated to take over. I really had no idea what I was doing. Chamber told me they would nominate candidates for jobs for a while until I got a handle on my new role. I've been so busy just learning how to run this place, I didn't even think to double-check the jobs."

Sculling the rest of his scotch, Scott poured a third glass. After considering the amber liquid, he put it down. "Why are they trying to kill you?"

"I don't know?"

Scott shook his head. "Yes, you do. You just don't realize what knowledge you have that is dangerous to them." Coming back to sit beside me, Scott looked at the screens. "Now, I know I can't trust them; I need to learn how to do this."

"Has my father's house been cleaned out yet?"

Watching my hands, Scott nodded. "Sure. The procedure is to do it within days of death."

Palms up, I shook my hands back and forth. *"Where are his files on the Chapter members?"*

"Boxed up and in my study. I haven't gotten around to reviewing everything."

Putting my index finger to the bottom of my left palm, I turned it to Scott. *"Show me."*

Standing, Scott waved for me to follow and led the way to his office. Opening the door, he pointed to the collection of boxes. Lifting the first lid, I started scanning the file names, then looked to Scott and linked my pinky fingers.

Scott lifted lid after lid with me until we found the box with S files. Thumbing through to find the file 'Summary,' I pulled it out. Leafing through until I found a folded chart, I pulled it out, placed the file aside, and unfolded the personnel map on his desk.

Pointing to myself, I banged my right fist on the left then pointed to the chart. *"I made this for my father. It summarizes everyone's skill set, who they work best with, and what sort of jobs they best fit,"* I explained. "He referred to it whenever a job came in and picked his teams using it."

There were additions and erasures, so it was still up to date. Scott looked it over, eyes wide. Frowning, he looked at me. "You know the business side of the Chapter?"

"I spent four years as my father's lackey."

"Could you teach me?" Scott requested. "I want to be a good Father."

"I need to write my report first, then I can teach you."

Observing my hands, Scott sat back on his desk. "How did you know to go to Venice when it wasn't in your package?" Scrutinizing me, he crossed his arms, watching me.

Mimicking aiming a rifle, I explained what happened at the airport. "The Hunter who picked up Liam was an acquaintance. He also wrote the report."

Assessing me, Scott gave a singular nod and sent me back to the lounge. Sitting down, I wrote my account and then closed my laptop. Scott's laptop dinged with my completed report. Opening it, he read it.

"You didn't mention your friend?"

Shaking my head, I waved my hand. *"I'm not giving anyone else a target for their back. Let whoever my enemy is wonder how I knew where to go."*

Scott considered. "Your father used to tell me you were the sharpest weapon here. Do you know why?" I shook my head. "He said you had the skill, the beauty, and the brains, which made you great. But he said if turned the wrong way, you could be a weapon against us too."

Lifting an eyebrow, I pointed to Scott, cut my bladed right hand into the palm of my left, and wobbled it. *"You doubt my loyalty?"*

"Yes, I do," Scott replied honestly. "I don't doubt it because you hate what you do or what we are about. You don't become a skilled assassin by hating it. Look at Jonathan. He hated being born here, being kept here when he tested for Technical Chapter. He's a lousy assassin. That's why he's our pilot. It's something he's good at, and giving him that role is probably the only reason he didn't throw himself from the mountain years ago."

"Then why am I disloyal?" I queried his logic. Not that Scott was wrong. I didn't hate what I did. I hated the lack of freedom.

Lifting my left hand, Scott brushed his thumb over my wedding band. Letting my hand go, he met my eyes while he SimCom'd. "You don't want to be here because your heart is out there somewhere."

Taking my hand back, I played with the rings.

"Those rings aren't the ones Noel put on your finger. You were locked in prison for five years. There is no way you still have your ring," Scott assessed. "You came back with those rings, and you kept wearing them, even after Noel's estate was divided. So, I think those rings are from your lover. Since you couldn't marry while Noel was alive, I don't think they come with a legal union, but I believe in your heart, you are married to whoever put them on your finger." Swallowing, I watched Scott's hands. When he finished, he lifted a brow. "Am I even close?"

Biting my lip, I put my fingers to my chin and wiggled them. *"How much did they tell you about where I've been?"*

"You were incarcerated. You escaped and worked as a bodyguard for some rich guy. Noel saw you at a party and came after you. Chamber found you and used you as bait to get Noel. Your father was killed by Noel before they got there." Scott watched me. "What did they leave out?"

Bowing my head, I shook it at the half-truth. Slowly, I lifted my teary gaze to Scott and raised my hands to clarify. *"They didn't use me as bait. He was my first job when I was brought back in."*

Sitting back, Scott stared at me, jaw falling open. "They made you kill your own husband?"

"And the rich guy wasn't just any guy. It's Debbie Fairchild's son. Noel's brother."

Forehead creasing, Scott sat forward. "The one Noel tried to kill?"

"I saved him from Noel five years ago. He's the one who got me out of prison."

Placing his hands in front of his face in prayer form, Scott breathed into his palms. He took several deep breaths before signing his next question. *"Is he the owner of those rings?"*

When I bowed my head, Scott stood suddenly and moved away from me, jaw tense. Suddenly, he started laughing. "This is fucking unreal. True Romeo and Juliet bullshit. The best of ours with him of all people."

Because he didn't sign it, I couldn't react, but it took effort. Finally, Scott turned around to face me. "Is that who you were with these last couple of days?" Meeting his eyes, I didn't reply.

Scott sighed. "Let me tell you a story. It's a tale that very few people know. Sixteen years ago, one of our Guardians took her civilian-raised son to her chapter for testing. He refused to test. The kid had the living shit beaten out of him, and in the end, he still managed to get up and walk out of there. Do you know what happened next?"

Not liking where this was going, I shook my head.

"What happened next was kind of a unique situation. You see, about twenty years ago, things started to happen, which indicated a new shadow company of some sort formed that had a contrary agenda to ours."

Forming loose upturned fists with the pinky out, I banged the side of my hands together. *"We had an enemy?"*

Scott swayed his hand. "It wasn't often, but occasionally our interests collided, and this shadow company always seemed to be a step ahead. It wasn't until I killed one of our fails on a job that Chamber realized there was something to concern them. It took years to realize what we stumbled upon because we started to see a pattern in our fails. They all went off to the military, all excelled, all ended up in black ops or special forces. A full investigation was launched, and I was on the team."

A full investigation required a member from each chapter to join a task force so they can see all the angles. *"How does that relate to Mitch?"*

Watching me spell it out, Scott raised a brow at the name. "Because we believe he was recruited before testing. We think they found him and recruited him and told him to fail out. They put him through school and directed him into the military, and he climbed the ranks fast. Fairchild was good. Really good." Scott looked impressed.

It made me think of Breok and Wenda. How many had been recruited within? Maybe Noel hadn't done the recruiting. But Mitch? There was no way Mitch was working for some seedy version of the Sword and Arrow. I shook my head in denial.

Scott showed me his palm to request patience. "What we found was Fairchild didn't fail out because he was weak. He failed out because he was strong. He didn't just walk away when his mother abandoned him; he thrived. We believe he did that with help, but we determined that he wasn't part of that company after investigating. We don't know why or how, just that he chose not to join with them either.

"We encouraged Debbie to reach out to her son. He agreed to meet his father and trade what he knew for a price. The kid was pretty smart and saw a way to set his future up. We sent his father to meet with him under cover of a government asset, and Fairchild's team was appointed to transport him to safety. That was the night Noel attacked his brother. The night you disappeared."

Considering what Scott revealed, I frowned. *"You're suggesting Noel worked for this company?"*

"Only a select few people knew about that meeting. He wasn't one of them."

"No. Noel told me why he went that night. My father told him they were recruiting Mitch. He told Noel if Mitch came in, they would consider the civilian raised experiment a success because I was initially considered a failure like Mitch and then proved myself," I argued. *"Dad told Noel if that happened, I would be sent away when I fell pregnant to raise our child outside. Our father manipulated Noel into killing Mitch. It had nothing to do with a shadow company, or Mitch's knowledge of it."*

Watching my hands, Scott frowned, his brows dropping lower over his eyes with every gesture. *"You're sure?"*

"Noel told me when he found me. He revealed he did it because he didn't want them to take me away from him. Our father offered to let him leave with me if he killed Mitch. He confessed he realized afterward my father lied to him too, but it was too late."

Jaw clenched; Scott cradled his head in his hands. "That's why he killed your dad. He knew he'd set him up," he murmured to himself. "Still, your dad wasn't on the task force, so he shouldn't have known about the meeting. There was someone else in on it."

"Chamber doesn't trust me because I went after Noel that night?" I asked. *"Do they worry that I am one of them?"*

Knocking the air in confirmation, Scott studied me. "If you are romantically involved with Mitchell Fairchild, then that lack of trust might be warranted. It might also be the reason someone in Chamber is trying to kill you. They might be worried the pillow talk goes both ways."

"You mean, they are trying to kill me on the off-chance Mitch told me what my father was involved in?"

"Or even just what he was going to tell his father that night. You did reveal you saved his life," Scott watched me with a calculating gaze. "Perhaps, they are wondering when your love affair actually started."

Inhaling with effort, I realized how this may look to Chamber. Even with my version of the story, I'd gone after Noel to stop him, attacked him in my attempt, and Noel shot me. Of all the people in that room, I saved Mitch. A man that was coming to them with information about inside corruption. He'd been raised one of us and failed. Someone they suspected had been recruited by the enemy.

Five years later, I turn up with that same man, and when Debbie comes for me, her son becomes hostile about losing me. Yeah, I could see how it looked. Bad. Really bad if they believed I'd been cheating on Noel with Mitch. Sex for the sake of maintaining a cover or to get off was one thing. An ongoing affair with an outsider was all kinds of no.

Placing both hands flat in front of me, I then raised my right as if giving a pledge. *"I swear, I'd never met Mitch Fairchild until that night. He was the only one still alive when I got there. That's why I saved him."*

Scott watched my hands. "But he is your lover now?"

Unable to deny the current situation, I closed my eyes. *"We became intimately engaged during our time together."*

When I opened my eyes, Scott looked miffed. His anger was jealousy if ever I'd seen it. Realizing he'd been hoping to win my affections, I felt awkward. Scott was kind, but he was a lot older than me.

"Well," Scott considered his laptop. "I think we know why someone wants you dead."

35

TRAINING ASSESSMENT

My flow was interrupted by tugging on my shirt. Pulling up, I peered down at the brown-eyed boy. He would make girls' hearts melt with those puppy dog eyes when he was a man. *"Father is calling for you."* The twins had mastered sign language in a matter of months. Well, enough to communicate that I was wanted.

Glancing towards the adults, I noticed they were finished their practice, and Scott stood on the far side of the ponds waiting. Once he caught my eye, he waved me over. Acknowledging him, I signed for the twins to keep up their flow before I jogged over to the others, who waited patiently.

When I joined the lines, Scott started explaining, signing while he spoke for my benefit.

"Today will be the biannual training assessment. Master Usagi and his team will arrive in the next hour and assess each of you today. At the end of each assessment, they will create your new training plan for the next six months. Lyza, you have been absent and not following a training schedule for some years. Master Usagi has requested to assess you first as he feels you will take the longest. Maria, you will be after Lyza, then Kit, Zane, Neil, Bruce, Stig, the twins will be assessed together, then I will be last. Any questions?"

Maria stepped forward. "Children do not normally get assessed for another two years. Why are the boys being assessed now?"

Scott shifted his eyes to me before addressing Maria. "With the games Lyza has been playing with the boys, they are already more advanced than most children their age. I believe it would be good to start them on a light training regime. It will be interesting to see how much more advanced your boys are with a different approach to their training." Scott noted Maria's hesitation. "You should be proud, Maria. Your children are potentially going to change the future upbringing of all our children."

Looking sideways at me, Maria took the step back.

"Lyza, go get ready. I will come to get you when Master Usagi is ready for you," Scott dismissed. Turning, I started walking back to my cabin.

"The rest of you should know Chamber has decreed Lyza is to take a new husband by New Year. Since she is now an adult, it is her choice. Therefore, if you are interested, please see me and register your interest. I will start assigning you to work together for you to have a chance at building a connection."

Frowning, I walked out of the area behind the hedge and stopped.

"I would advise anyone interested to learn sign language. Lyza takes offense if you aren't willing to make an effort to communicate with her," Scott continued.

"Is that why you are using it now, Father?"

"I started out of respect, but yes, Kit, I am also hoping to gain Lyza's affections and convince her to choose me," Scott admitted.

Grumbles from the others filled the ponds that he may have already been seducing me for months.

"You should also know, while Lyza was held prisoner, she was tortured brutally, even dying twice only to be resuscitated and tortured again. It is believed during this captivity, Lyza was sexually abused."

Murmurs of disapproval echoed around the pond. Barely able to believe this adulteration of the truth, I gaped hidden from view.

"For this reason, I highly suggest you not try to make your interest known to Lyza through the usual physical means," Scott suggested.

"How are we meant to flirt then?"

"I would suggest with your personality, Zane," Maria snarked, "but we all know you don't have one."

"That's enough," Scott ordered. "Expressions of interest are due by the end of the day. I suggest you heed my advice. Dismissed."

Picking up my pace to get back to my house and change, I ate breakfast and considered the coming two months. What happened if I didn't pick a new husband by New Year?

My door opening and closing caught my attention, but I ignored it until Scott stopped in the kitchen entryway. Meeting his eyes, I stood up. Scott led the way back out and to the community hall.

Master Usagi was precisely what you expected. He was a Tibetan monk in appearance and only came to my shoulder in height. His assessors were not all monks. Some of them were arrows who reached a high enough level in training to be taken on as a personal student of the Master.

Maria's husband, Tate, was one of them. Tonight, after training, he would be given leave to spend time with his wife and hopefully produce more progeny. Noel had told me that one of the trainers always sits and studies you, looking for your weakness. If you make it through all the assessment levels, then that person challenges you, and it was typically unusual to beat them. If you do, that is when the Master will consider you for personal training.

Master Usagi stood front and center; his six elite students stood in a line behind him. As I entered the hall, Scott gave my name and reminded them I was deaf and mute, then he took a seat to the side and took up a checklist. The checklist listed the minimum requirements to be a Scythe. I'd passed them at age fourteen; since then, I'd only built on my skill.

Showing respect for the masters, I bowed and then knelt, sitting back on my heels. Master Usagi walked around me in a wide circle studying me. Once he completed a full ring, he addressed his trainers in his language.

"Lyza has never failed basic requirements. Despite her absence, her reported performance since her return would suggest that there is no chance she would fail now, so we will skip to direct combat, levels five to nine." Pointing to two of his trainers, Master Usagi walked over and sat cross-legged on the floor.

The two he pointed at came forward and, without hesitation, launched into an attack. The problem with coordinated training assessments? After a while, you learn the choreography yourself. Staying on my knees, I blocked both attackers and dropped back to slide beneath their strikes and come up behind them.

It took me less than a minute to pass level five. When Master Usagi pointed to a third, he joined in, the dance instantly changing to fit the new performer. For the next hour, I fought without a break, a new attacker joining as I surpassed each level until I was facing off against five attackers.

The thing about our training is that, even though it was full-contact, we had to be careful to defend without serious injury. The trainers still had to work the rest of the day, and the assessed may need to go to work the following day. That meant you had to keep strict control. While you could kick someone's knee, you couldn't cause muscle injury, no broken bones, no dislocations, no concussions.

This was absolute opposition to fighting in the real world, where your aim was to take someone out as quickly and quietly as possible. It was frustrating and required even more mental clarity than a job. You could pay heavily for causing long-term injury to a trainer.

In all my years, I never passed level seven. Today, I made it to nine. There was no doubt my recent missions, which put me in difficult situations with numbers higher than we usually allowed an individual to attempt, contributed to my ability to make nine.

Making it to nine was good enough. I didn't have to win, but I had never given up a fight. Noel used to always make nine. He made it to ten once but was taken out in a matter of seconds of the spotter joining the battle. He didn't want to be a trainer, so he had dropped at nine from then on. I wanted to push the envelope just once.

Throughout the entire session, I fought to defend; I didn't attack. As one, all five of my attackers stopped and took three steps back. Making level nine, I was still standing. I was bruised, battered, and exhausted but still standing. With grace, the sixth trainer, the spotter of weaknesses, rose and turned to Master Usagi. The Master bowed his head, the spotter bowed and stepped into the circle.

Once again, everyone took their stances. That was it. That was my breather. When I inhaled, they came at me. This time, I didn't just offend, I attacked, and I went directly for the spotter. His eyes widened in surprise when I drove forward, blocking others, taking hits, but I went at the spotter, so he couldn't attack my weaknesses because he was too busy defending.

His arm dropped, and I punched him hard in the jaw, staggering him, opening his lip. Touching the bloody mouth, he smiled at me, eyes full of mischief. Instantly, all the rules went out the window. The spotter ducked around behind his colleague and came at me from behind. Spinning to follow him, I defended and held the others back simultaneously. However, the choreography was gone, and this was totally ad-lib.

It took two minutes for the spotter to find his opening, catch me in a headlock I couldn't get out of and for one of his colleagues to wind me. Even then, I had enough strength left to catch that one in the spleen with a kick before I dropped and turned, taking the spotter to the ground with me. With no oxygen, I threw my elbow back into his ribs. When he released his hold, I rolled away and collapsed on the floor, trying to suck in air.

The attack stopped. Bowing towards me, the trainers all returned to a line. The spotter stopped by me and bent down with a hand on my back to check I could recover. When I successfully dragged five breaths in, coughing and spluttering between, the spotter squeezed my shoulder and went to join the others.

Master Usagi used the time to quietly talk to Scott. When I got my breathing back under control enough, I sat back on my ankles and waited. Rising, Master Usagi walked over to his trainers. "What did she do that was unexpected?"

"She held back," the spotter spoke. "She stayed defensive until I stepped in, then she swung into a full attack to prevent me from attacking."

Master Usagi nodded. "She passed after having five years away from training. How?"

The trainers all stood, considering me. Master Usagi pointed at one. "Do you think she received training?"

"No, Master. Her skill, while good, did have obvious weaknesses. That is how we struck her."

The Master nodded. He pointed to another. "Did she fight for her life?"

This one tilted his head to consider me. "No. She does not fear death."

"Then why did she fight so hard?" Master Usagi queried, punctuating the question.

The spotter stepped forward. "Because she can."

The Master smiled. "And what would have happened had you not stopped?" He moved towards the spotter.

"She would have fought until she couldn't," the spotter answered again.

"Why?" He asked the question of the spotter specifically.

The spotter met my eyes. "Because she doesn't know how to give up."

Master Usagi watched the spotter assessing me. He lifted a brow in an unspoken question, and the spotter nodded once. Master Usagi bowed his head. "Rest."

The trainers bowed. Lowering my head to the ground until they walked away, I rose up, my ribs catching with pain as I straightened. Master Usagi folded to his knees and sat back on his ankles before me. We sat there, watching each other for a solid ten minutes. Then we sat for a further twenty.

The Master bowed. I returned the honor, then he stood. "You are strong. But there is always a limit, a line where a good trainer ends and a great warrior cannot return from. I would say you are beyond it, that you walk the field of death already, but I have heard you are achieving great things with the children, so we will wait and see. I am always keen to be proven wrong." He walked over to join his trainers.

Minding the ache in my solar plexus and ribs, I stood. Already, the bruises bloomed along my thighs and arms, back, and probably my face as well. Scott met me at the door and escorted me back to my house.

"Are you okay?" Scott asked.

"Sure," I signed back. Then I dropped on my couch, pulled my throw blanket over me, and closed my eyes. Next training day, I needed to quit at level five.

36

CROSSING LINES

"I miss you," I murmured to the empty room. "God, you don't know how much. I'm pent up as hell. Three jobs in the last three weeks, and I'm not used to denying my need."

On his way back from the infirmary, Neil passed by my house, pouting with his arm in a sling. Unlike Zane and Bruce, Neil had waited until we were on the helicopter home to make his move on me. Jonathan didn't even flinch when I took the hand that Neil slipped between my thighs and twisted it up behind his back before throwing him out of the helicopter. Luckily for Neil, we hadn't taken off yet.

"It's getting hard, Mitch. They are going to press me to choose a new husband. Maybe we shouldn't have made it legal. Maybe we were hoping too much that we could make this work. I should have let you go, like Debbie told me too. Like I knew I should have. I was selfish holding on to you."

Meeting Neil on the path, Scott asked about his shoulder. His eyes came to me at my window, glaring with anger. Stepping away from the window, I walked to my bedroom.

"I've done something I'm going to be in trouble for. I need to get away from these guys long enough to check the locker and see if you've responded. If I don't, I'm going to get in worse trouble, or I'm going to break our marriage vows."

Walking to my closet, I pulled out a backpack. "I'm going to go hiking. It will take me three days to reach the helipad. From there, I can catch a taxi and meet you somewhere, anywhere. Just please come and see me."

Grabbing a few changes of clothes, toiletries, and my wallet, I shoved them in the bag. Next, I grabbed some food and bottles of water. I was still in the kitchen when Scott came in. The downside to feigning deafness, no one bothered knocking. "What the fuck, Lyza?" Scott SimCom'd angrily. "What are the rules? We don't injure our family to the point they cannot work."

Pointing to Scott's side, I pinched my fingers in front of me and shifted them forward as if moving a chess piece. Indicating Scott's side again, I used my right hand to hold up my left hand in a pincer grip, pointed up, and then cuffing my waist I spread my hands out to the sides on an angle to indicate my skirt.

"You broke his collarbone because he felt you up?!" Scott yelled, forgetting to sign. "That's two months he can't work for."

Pointing to Scott, I gestured outside then my chest before pretending to snap a twig in front of me. Grabbing at my sternum with both hands, I clawed back across my ribs.

"Your ribs were four weeks healed, and you passed the physical. A collarbone is different, and you know it," Scott growled. "Do you think you are the only one pent up after a job? The only one who uses sex as an outlet? We were all raised the same way, Lyza. We are all taught sex is a physical need, a natural necessity, and not to get emotional about it. That is why you were married as soon as you were legal, so you didn't become promiscuous. You're single. Nothing is stopping you from taking a lover here at Chapter. I'll turn a blind eye. Just don't get pregnant until you are married."

"I don't want anyone here," I signed angrily.

Scott met my eyes, disappointment flashing in the depths of his. Huffing, Scott stabbed his thumb into his bladed left palm and twinkled his fingers at me before ending with the pointer accusing me and then gesturing to my side with raised shoulders. "Because of him? Do you even comprehend what you are doing? The situation you are putting yourself in. You don't have the option of saying no, Lyza, only who. If you don't pick soon, they'll pick for you. Do you get that you only have two weeks?"

When I didn't answer, Scott took a breath and looked around the room. His eyes fell on the bag I'd packed in a rush. "Are you going to see him?"

Shaking my head, I pointed to my chest, then pretended to grab straps at my shoulder and slid my hands down slightly like a hiker holding their pack before signing the rest. *"I need a time out."*

"How long?" Going hiking to clear our heads was healthy. Many of us did it after a job went bad, or a family member died or left. Hikes were encouraged when our minds weren't where they should be. Anywhere up to a month was permitted, providing we weren't on active duty.

"I'm hiking to Geneva," I informed honestly. *"Then I'm going to have one or two spa days. I'll be back within a week."* Each arrow could only be used once a week at most. Even if another job came up, I'd be back before I could be made active again.

Glancing at my wedding ring, Scott considered me. "Give me a chance, Lyza. I won't treat you wrong. I know I'm older than Noel was, but I still have good stamina, and I can please a woman."

Watching Scott's hands, I felt terrible for him. He was a good-looking man in his mid to late thirties, maybe five years older than Noel. Even through the winter layers, his fit body was evident, but that was part of being a Scythe. Our bodies were always in peak condition as part of our role. Even though he was the Scythe Chapter's Father, Scott still had to maintain his fitness and be ready to go on a job. If it was just sex, if Mitch wasn't holding a part of me that I'd never expected to recognize, then maybe.

Inhaling, I taped my chest, then pointed to my temple before turning and hooking that finger as I held it aloft. *"My decision is not a reflection on you. You are a good Father, and you have made coming back here easier than I thought possible. But it doesn't count because I met him first. I'd give up everything to be with him."*

Assessing my gestures, Scott's gaze flicked to my eyes as he scoffed. "No, you wouldn't. That's a very romantic notion, but I saw your eyes when I revealed who he was. You want to believe he has no connection to the shadow company, but you are wary of him." Observing Scott's hands, I gritted my teeth. Fingering the rings on my finger, I wondered how Mitch would take that.

Stepping towards me, Scott cupped my cheek in his hand and tilted my face to his. "You are a brilliant woman, Lyza, and you have always trusted your instincts," he verbalized, leaving enough space for me to read his lips. "You know someone in Chamber is trying to kill you, and you know Fairchild is linked to it somehow. Don't ruin your chances here for someone who isn't one of us."

His lips brushed mine, soft like a feather. Refusing to close my eyes and fall into the need for my physical outlet from weeks of work, I stared at Scott, and he back at me. Letting the kiss pass, Scott moved his face to the side, then stepping back, he released my face.

Making fists with his hands, Scott crossed them at the wrist, right on top and his right index finger pointing. "Next week, I need everyone here. We will be trialing something new. You gave me an idea a few months back, and I've reached out to another chapter to trial cross-collaboration in training. If it's successful, I'm going to contact a few more chapters and do the same. I think it would be good to learn what the other chapters do and to stop being silos."

Circling my hand, fingers relaxed as if holding something, I kept my index finger a little more open than the rest and thumb out to the side.

"Just, okay?" Scott smirked. Lifting a shoulder, I couldn't find any enthusiasm.

Rolling his eyes, Scott smiled to himself as he stepped out of my way. "It's going to snow, so dress for it. Stay safe. Be back by Monday," he SimCom'd. "You'll miss order day. Is there anything you need?"

Walking over to my fridge, I grabbed my shopping list and handed it to him. Taking it, Scott looked it over. About to leave, he turned back and hugged me. Blinking, I wrapped my hands around him, my annoyance easing in his hold. "Don't get yourself killed in the pursuit of love, Lyza," Scott murmured to my hair, then he released me and left.

Taking a deep breath, I blinked away tears. Grabbing everything I needed together, I headed off. It was already approaching sunset, and I wanted to be well away from here by full dark. As I set off, the twins chased after me, but Maria grabbed them back and explained I was seeking solace.

Hiking for us wasn't like a civilian hike. We didn't hike by sunlight and camp at night. Hiking was initially taught as a means of escape. If a job went south and you needed to get away, but your exit was breached, sometimes you would need to go overland on foot, and you wouldn't have time to stop.

When my dad ran the Scythe Chapter, he would send you to hike if you got injured. Learn to suck it up when your life wasn't in danger because next time, it might be. So, while healthy, this was easy for me. Having done this hike numerous times, I knew exactly how long it took me to reach every village and town below the alps around us.

Walking through the night, I avoided the dangerous drop-offs. The snow falling and my breath fogging made the night mysterious and beautiful. I loved being out here and free of the restrictions of Chapter. Hiking through light snow in the dark had always been my paradise. As the sun started to rise, I stopped and closed my eyes, allowing the first rays of morning light to fill me with warmth. Stopping long enough to drink some water and eat something, I then continued on my descent.

By lunchtime on day three, I reached the helipad. It was snowing, I was tired, but that state of mind is what the hike was about. You became too tired to worry about the little things, and you could see the bigger picture, make plans for your future.

There was a black town car in the parking lot, which was new. Noting it was empty, I continued inside. Passing a casually dressed man on my way inside, I smiled, recognizing Dustin's face from my time in Albuquerque, and felt the butterflies take flight. His eyes slid over me appreciatively, despite my three days of going bush appearance.

Checking my designated Arrow locker first, I made sure there was no urgent message for me to return. Grabbing the phone, I then went to my personal one to find a single bit of stationary. Opening the envelope revealed a folded letter and a chipped key card. The hotel information was inked at the top of the paper, letting me know Mitch was there already.

One night. Room 1306. The car will bring you to me.

Grabbing my shoebox from inside the locker before closing it, I moved into the bathroom to shower and change into fresh clothes. Outside, I found Dustin waiting. By the looks of things, he'd replaced Mark permanently. Frankly, I would have chosen a more competent guard, but Mitch must have had his reasons.

Starting at my heels, Dustin traipsed my bare legs with his eyes until the dress and jacket I wore hid me from view. Shaking his head, he opened the car door. "Boss made a special side trip for you. Stacey was pissed; now I know why," he winked as I lowered myself inside. Then he closed the door.

When we started the drive, Dustin hit dial on his phone, and Fred answered. "What's wrong?"

"The boss put the mission on hold for a fucking booty call; that's what's wrong," Dustin complained.

"Lyza turned up?"

"Yeah. Looks like she hasn't slept in a while. Where the hell has she been?"

"Hiking," Fred answered.

"Bullshit. She had a backpack, not a hiking pack, and I meant where she was for the last six months? She disappeared, turned up in Rome with no notice, and then we left her behind. Now we take an emergency detour for her?"

Fred was quiet for a moment, and I could imagine him chewing his lip. "Dustin, you know everyone the boss brings in has a skill set he needs. All I can tell you is that his wife is no different from the rest of us."

"And I thought her skill revolved around fucking," Dustin scoffed. "Guess that's just a bonus for him."

"Just shut your mouth and drive. You should never have been in Comms to see that," Fred growled. "We are using this time for intelligence gathering, so once she is in the room, come report to me." The call disconnected.

Gritting his teeth, Dustin adjusted the mirror to see me better. "Boss gets to dip his wick, and we have to work through it. Fucking bullshit." After that, he did shut up, and I used the remaining ride to close my eyes and doze.

Thirty minutes later, I was in the hotel elevator and exiting to level thirteen. Following me to the door, Dustin watched while I swiped the card. When I opened the door, Dustin waved goodbye and continued to another door three rooms away. Closing the door, I walked into the room, removing my jacket. It wasn't Mitch's usual penthouse or even a suite. A standard room in a five-star hotel, but still, it was just the bed, a desk, and the bathroom. Throwing my jacket on the table, I considered what Dustin revealed.

Mitch was on a mission and diverted everyone because I begged to see him. I should be relieved, be happy he cared enough to make time for me, but my brain assessed all the reasons Dustin used the word mission. They weren't in Europe meeting clients, so what were they here for?

When the door opened, I turned, expecting to see Mitch. Instead, Fred came in dressed in what could pass for a uniform but was more tactical gear minus the weapons. He smiled when he saw me, eyes appreciating the dress and shoes before he focused on my face. "You look tired," Fred greeted as he typed something into his phone. Putting his finger to his lips, Fred handed me the phone as he spoke. "Boss will be here in a few minutes. Can I order you something to eat?"

Taking the phone, I expected it was to type my order, but on the screen was a question I didn't expect.

Are you working?

Blinking, I shook my head and handed back the phone. "A burger would be good," I verbalized for Fred.

"I can do that," Fred agreed as he handed me back the phone.

Are you coming with us for good?

Again, I shook my head, wondering why he thought that. "Why don't you help yourself to the minibar, and I'll call before bringing the food in," he told me cheekily as he handed me the phone for the last time.

Make a choice. Them or us. Make it soon. He can't keep dropping everything to come to see you, and he's fucking pissed about being here right now. Just so you know.

My mouth dropped open. Covering my mouth before I could say anything, Fred took his phone back. Kissing my forehead, Fred stepped back. "We've missed you, Lyza." Turning on his heel military-style, Fred walked out, leaving me gaping at his back. Mitch didn't want to be here.

37

ROUGH LOVE

WHEN THE DOOR OPENED THIS TIME, I DIDN'T BOTHER TURNING around. The view of the lake outside the window was peaceful, and I worried that looking away from it would steal that momentary peace from me. "Well, that's a breathtaking sight," Mitch remarked from further back in the room. I stayed quiet. "Lyza? You asked me to come. I'm here. Can you at least turn to face me?"

Taking a deep breath, I turned around. The answer I feared stood before me. Mitch, not in his suit or jeans and shirt, but in black military-style boots and pants and a black long-sleeved shirt. Hating what I saw, I closed my eyes and leaned back on the window jam. "You were meant to be life."

Inhaling, Mitch clenched his jaw as he sat down on the bed and started unlacing his boots. "You were raised a certain way, to see things their way. It shouldn't surprise me that you would assume the worst of me."

"Like you did of me when you came for me?" I retorted.

Dropping his first boot to the ground, Mitch started on the next. "As I said before, I knew what you were; I didn't count on who you were. I didn't expect to feel for you. It took one god damn minute in that cell with you, looking into your eyes, seeing the scars on that fucking hot body of yours, and realizing you were so much more than they knew."

Chucking his second boot to the floor, Mitch stood up, pulling his shirt over his head. Throwing it to the side, he started unbuckling his belt, his eyes intent on mine. "You knew what I was too. I saw it in your eyes when I was reading your diary. When I stopped you from taking it back," Mitch dropped his pants, but the darkness in his eyes kept me mesmerized. He stepped towards me. "You knew, and it turned you on to be in a confined space with me. It still does."

"I was sure you were life," I whispered as he stopped directly in front of me.

"I was sure you were protection," Mitch reminded me as he caressed my cheek. "You saw my nature, and you discarded what you glimpsed in that cell. You ignored what they made me, just like I ignored what they made you. But I can't ignore that anymore because that's the reason I don't have you."

My heart trembled in my chest. He was right. "Why now?" I dared to ask.

"Timing," he whispered as he placed a kiss on my temple. "I wasn't going to come. It hurt to hear you beg me, but I was neck-deep in a mission and days away from engagement. Then your boss threatened you and the idea of allowing you to be disappointed in me and you going back there and letting one of them put their hands on you..." Mitch gritted. "I had to take the risk and come. My team is fucking spitting chips, but I didn't want to get home and find myself served with divorce papers because you had a moment of weakness, and I didn't fight to keep you."

"You could have changed, pretended-"

"You would have seen it in my eyes," Mitch stretched his fingers into my hair and took handfuls. Opening my eyes wide to meet his, I bit my lip on a sigh. "We are good fakers, Lyza, but we aren't good actors." He applied pressure, forcing me to my knees. When I looked up at him, Mitch raised a brow. "You're not the only one pent up. So, before I serve up my frustrations on you. Rough, or no?"

It wasn't a choice of rough or gentle. It was to take it or go home. Mitch was angry; with me, our situation, having to walk away from his mission, and cop flak from his team about a poorly timed booty call. God, we were fucking hopeless. How could this ever work? What were we thinking when we committed to each other with a mountain of death between us?

Anger burned inside me. Scott had said I trusted my instincts. I'd known the moment I met Mitch that he was dangerous, and I'd let love derail me. Fred was right; I needed to give Mitch up or find a way out.

Taking his hard cock in hand, I moved it to my lips, licking over his head. Gripping my hair, Mitch pressed between my lips. Running my tongue along the base of him as I took him in, he pushed all the way into the back of my throat, setting off my gag reflex. Mitch pulled back slowly, and I squiggled my tongue along his length.

It was stupid of me to think just because he owned a company and met the clients, he didn't do any other work himself. People like us don't walk away from this life. He'd probably never even stopped serving. Lewis said they do contract work for the military. I'd assumed that meant teaching and training. Now I knew I'd been deluding myself.

Mitch might have been a civil contractor, but that just meant the military could hire him to do what they didn't want to dirty up their hands. Did I really want to know what he did? He'd never asked for details about my work; in fact, he seemed relieved I didn't wear my rings on the job.

My eyes caught sight of my rings, and I wondered if he was recording this. If he would listen to it later and get himself off remembering.

Grabbing the base of his thickness, I sucked his tip hard, flicking my tongue against him.

"Jesus, I've missed you," Mitch groaned.

Smiling, I forced all my worries out of my head for this moment and focused on what I could affect. Because my logical brain had already determined there was not a damn thing I could do about Mitch's lifestyle when we couldn't even be together. What right did I have to be upset by him being black ops for the military when I was a trained assassin? He still loved me, knowing what I was. Shouldn't I feel the same?

Tuning out of my doubts and worries, I focused on the fact he had dropped everything and come to me. That despite our situation, he loved me. That part of his anger today was probably knowing it was always going to be this way. So, I had to make it worth it. I sucked his cock, knowing it could be months before I saw him again. Taking my time, I allowed him to press beyond my comfort zone, aware it would give me a sore throat later.

Moaning his appreciation, Mitch massaged my head, and when my jaw stiffened, he gently rubbed the hinge and surrounding area so I could keep going longer, slowly sucking him to the edge. When I dragged my teeth up his length for extra sensation, Mitch cursed, his entire body shuddering. "Your teeth are sharp."

"You want me to stop?"

"I want to be rough."

Settling back on my ankles, I licked his tip as I looked up at him. "Do you still have those ties?"

Stepping back three steps, Mitch grabbed up his pants and started pulling his belt out of the loops. "Stand up."

Rolling over my toes, I turned my back so Mitch could tie my hands.

"Those shoes," Mitch purred. "And the way that dress shows off your body. If I didn't show, were you going to wear this for your new daddy?" I cringed at the idea. Mitch tied my wrists tight, the fabric of the belt rough and chaffing. "Lie on the bed, head up this end," Mitch directed.

Following his direction, I rolled to my back once I was on the mattress. Taking hold of my shoulders, Mitch pulled me up the bed until my head hung off the end. He rubbed the smooth head of him against my lips, and I licked and kissed him, tasting the salty precum he glossed on like lipstick.

"Safeword?" Mitch questioned.

"Going to be hard to use it, don't you think?"

"I'll hear you."

"Lego."

Nodding, Mitch pushed forward. Opening my mouth, I swallowed him down, the angle of my head giving him direct access to my throat. I gagged, but other than biting, I couldn't block him. As he started throat fucking me, Mitch moaned, cussed, going as deep as he wanted, as fast as he wanted. All I could do was lay there, take it, and try to breathe between pumps.

Tears ran from my eyes, from my gag reflex kicking in, and from the abuse my poor delicate tonsils were receiving. Wrapping his hands around my neck, Mitch squeezed slightly, applying pressure where his engorgement blocked my airways momentarily. He released as he pulled back, allowing a ragged breath before squeezing as he pushed in. The benefit was at least he'd slowed down to torture me like this.

Slipping his hand beneath the neckline, Mitch massaged my breast. The dress was backless, so there wasn't a bra to limit access. His hand came back out and yanked up the hem of the dress to expose my bare sex. "Fuck, Lyza. You certainly come prepared," Mitch growled in appreciation. "Spread your legs."

When I dropped my knees open to the side, Mitch pressed deep, his hand squeezing tight, then he leaned forward and smacked my pussy. I tried to cry out, but my airway was obstructed. The muscles of my throat reacting. Moaning, Mitch rubbed the red heat of his handprint as he withdrew, waiting for me to draw breath, and then he did it again.

Heat rushed to my sex, the sting of his smacks making my clit swell and pulse, his firm palm rubbing in between, bringing me online for my own pleasure. Squirming my bound hands further down beneath me, I curled my back and lifted my knees to my chest as I brought my hands to the front. Mitch had to pull out to make sure I didn't kick him, his eyes wide as if he didn't expect me to be able to escape from being bound like that.

Reaching above my head, I grabbed Mitch's balls as he positioned to thrust again and gripped them as he squeezed my throat the next time. Swearing, Mitch smacked me harder than before, and I cried out as the after rub swept me over the edge to a staggering fall. The clench of my throat was too much. Mitch praised my name like it was holy and spurted so deep I didn't even have to swallow.

For a moment, the room darkened, and I was back in that basement with my torturers asking me who I worked for. With Mark's hands around my throat as he shoved my head into the barrel of water again, and his filthy whispers in my ear about what he'd do to me.

Suddenly, I was free as Mitch pulled back quickly, allowing me to roll over and scramble away a little. "Lego," I gasped, barely audible. "Let go!" I wheezed on a more extended breath.

Eyes a little wide, Mitch hesitated. "Lego is short for let go. That's why it's your safe word. Quicker and easier to get out?"

With a nod, I fell limp on the bed. My mind was back in this room, in a safe place, with someone I considered to be a dependable person. Squatting by the bed, Mitch caressed my hair and face. "I got carried away. I'm sorry."

I didn't know what to say. Yes, I came, but it was so close to how Mark tortured me - minus the cock and pussy slapping - with the constant suffocation. So, my using the safeword wasn't so much about what he'd done, but the psychological torment it induced.

The room phone rang. Kissing my brow, Mitch walked to the desk. His knees looked a little jellied, and part of me liked that I did that to him. "Yes?" Mitch answered. He looked at me. "You still want that burger?"

"Yes. I'm starving," I croaked, my epiglottis bruised and battered, my throat raw. "And hot tea with honey, please."

"Yeah, leave it by the door. Thanks, Fred." Hanging up, Mitch moved back towards me.

"Can you untie my hands, please?"

Mitch smirked. "Maybe later."

38

MORNING AFTER BITTER PILL

SORE IN ALL THE RIGHT PLACES, I WAS LYING IN THE ARMS OF THE MAN I loved. This right here, no matter the location, was my happy place.

Caressing his jaw, I smiled as his eyelids fluttered. "You should be asleep. You must be exhausted," Mitch murmured.

"I can sleep when I'm not with you," I whispered. Anything louder hurt too much after the night of slap and tickle. Mitch was not in a gentle mood, and he'd let me feel him as hard and deep as he could. I gave as good as I took, and his chest bore my nail marks that would make him remember this night for a good week yet.

Opening his eyes slightly, Mitch pulled me tighter against him. "You're stressed? Even after all that venting?"

"How can you tell?"

Mitch touched between my brows. "I've only seen this crease when you are stressing out and thinking hard. Do you want to talk about it?"

"Fred said I need to choose. You or them. One is a death sentence, the other..." I struggled to find the words. "The idea of giving you up hurts too damn much that I can't even consider it."

Rolling to face me more, Mitch tightened his grip. "Good, because it's not an option." He combed my hair back from my face. "Leave them. I can protect you. You tell me when, and I will be there to get you."

"What if you are on a mission like now?" I asked, hands caressing his chest where I marked him.

"I'm here, aren't I?" Mitch lifted both brows making his point.

While I couldn't deny he was, as his eyes drifted to the clock again, I wondered if he really was. Turning to see the clock shining three in the morning, I faced Mitch. "What time do you need to leave?"

"Five," Mitch sighed, pulling me closer. "I wouldn't let you go back now, but I can't take you with me."

Kissing his chin, I snuggled deeper. "It's okay. I need to go back. I have evidence hidden away that I need to get to Moses."

"Why Moses?"

"It affects his chapter."

"You could give it to me, and I can pass it on?"

To this, I lifted a brow. "Drinking buddies, are we?"

"He and Stacey have a thing going. They hooked up while he was working for us. Not that it stopped him chasing after you."

"Jobs end. We go home afterward. With so few females in our chapters, the men take the opportunity where it arises," I sighed. "It's okay for them to be promiscuous, but the women need to be chaste and loyal."

"Good to know. Though, I doubt the chaste part." I bit his chest. Chuckling, Mitch pressed the side of my jaw to force me to release. "Haven't you marked me enough?"

Crawling on top of him, I considered my marks. "Are there others?"

"You know I've never felt for anyone the way I feel for you," Mitch soothed.

"That's not what I meant. Are you having sex with others?" Disturbingly, I couldn't meet his eyes. Fear clenched my gut that he didn't need to be faithful to an absentee wife. It's not like he had any guarantee I was ever coming back.

Clearing my hair from my face, Mitch considered me. "I'm not going to make it easier for you, Lyza. Stop looking for a way out of this mess that involves leaving me. I'm not giving you up without a fight. I would never have let you go the first time, but you promised to come home to me. I'm patient. It's you who is running out of time."

"That doesn't answer my question."

"I'm not going to answer it. You need to trust me like I trust you."

Sitting back, I studied his raked chest, his dreamy-eyed look as he locked on my breasts, and his interest knocked on my inner thigh. "Ready again, already?"

Mitch moved his hands to mold my breasts. "I can't help it when I'm with you. The way you make me feel, I just want to spend every waking minute inside you."

Smirking, I lifted my hips, moving to accommodate his need, and enjoyed the moan that fell from our lips as he filled me. Being tender just turned me on more, my body flooding my core to ease the friction. Taking my time, I rode Mitch, his hands on my hips, assisting but letting me have the control this time. As I grew tight, Mitch dropped his thumb to my pearl and massaged me into a higher state of pleasure.

"Don't stop," he murmured after I came. Urging me to keep riding him and driving me to another orgasm shortly after. Giving me a minute to recover, Mitch encouraged my hips onwards again, taking a bit longer to reach that edge this time.

Biting his lip, Mitch arched a little as he swelled deep against my cervix, making my body jump forward to the brink. "Condom?" Mitch reminded. Meeting his eyes, I shook my head. Mitch's eyes widened, his grip on my hips tightened, holding me still. "Are you sure?"

"I'm game if you are?" I offered, ensuring he had a say in this.

"Fuck, Lyza," Mitch groaned, his eyes suddenly wicked and focused. "I want this."

Smiling, I ran my thumb over his lips as I leaned forward and kissed him, slow and deep. Mitch's grip eased. Pulling back to stare into his eyes, I rocked my body over his. Mitch's eyes were filled with emotion as they stayed locked with mine.

I wasn't stupid; I knew my cycle and understood why I was so randy. My eyes shuttered as the first tremor went through my body, so close to a total fall. Cursing, Mitch arched his spine away from the bed as his entire body tensed, and then he plummeted into ecstasy, stealing me away with him, and I had no doubt sealing our fate.

Lying upon Mitch's chest, I tried to catch my breath. Wrapping his arms around me, he kissed the top of my head. "Two weeks," Mitch murmured, checking the time. We only had an hour left together. "I'll be ready to go home in two weeks, and I expect you to be ready to go with me."

Closing my eyes, suddenly tired, I couldn't find the will to argue. "They'll hunt me down and kill me."

Mitch's hands pressed along my spine, easing the tension out of my body. "I'll make sure they don't."

DREARY LIGHT FILTERED through the window, white flakes of snow falling outside. Waking snuggled alone in the blankets, I lifted my arm and collected the note from the bedside table.

The room is yours for three more days. Take the time. I think you need it. Meet me here on New Year's Eve by one. We'll fly home and start our life together.

I love you.

Putting the note back on the table, I sighed. Two weeks and I would repeat history and leave my chapter without permission to follow my husband. Let's hope it didn't end badly this time.

Curling back into the covers, I went back to sleep. Exhausted as I was, I knew if I even started considering the consequences of my choices, I'd probably never sleep again.

LIFTING my eyes from my book, I found Scott standing in my lounge room. "I heard you were back," Scott signed while he talked. "You look more relaxed." Eyes going to bruising on my wrists, Scott narrowed his focus, and the skin around his mouth tightened. He looked away, then moved and sat at the seat across from me. "What happened?"

Considering him, I put my book aside. *"Have you ever had your power taken from you against your will?"*

Swallowing, Scott looked at the floor. He tucked his ring and little finger and closed his index and middle finger on his thumb pad.

"It sucks. It leaves you feeling less," I gestured. *"I wasn't raped or assaulted other than threatened, but being restrained and blindfolded for days on end, while you are in agony, bleeding, and being beaten and drowned continuously, it steals a part of your soul."* Blinking away the dark memories, I turned my eyes to the window for a moment. *"I can only imagine how much worse it is for a sexual assault victim."*

Exhaling dynamically, Scott deflated. "You don't have to imagine. You know. I saw you the night after your father first gave you to Noel. You sneaked out to the lookout and cried for hours. I kept watch over you, worried you would throw yourself over. But you just sat hugging yourself, drawing yourself as tight in on yourself as you could while you cried." Scott's eyes were glassy. "Your father didn't talk to you and prepare you for it, did he?"

Refusing to meet his eyes, I shook my head. Face hard and angry, Scott cursed under his breath. "Our girls are meant to be counseled before they are married. You can't just send a girl into a room with a man unprepared and expect her to come out of it okay."

Holding up my hand as if his words sat on my palm, I flipped my hand over my shoulder. That was so far in the past, and I'd learned to like sex since then. Noel had been gentle; he never realized I hadn't been told what was happening either.

Pointing my finger forward, I then flipped my hand so it was palm up. Closing my fist, I slapped it on my left open palm, then let my hands drop, lifted my elbows out to the side, and pressed through my shoulders to move my arms forward like a zombie walk. Despite moving on, he was right. It all adds together in the end, and it haunts you.

Scott sighed. "I've heard it's common, for women who can compartmentalize their lives, to seek out situations similar to that of their negative experience and turn them into a positive one. To control the situation or give permission not to control is empowering."

Standing up, Scott moved forward, brushing his fingertips across the bruised flesh of my wrists. "You have always been strong mentally, Lyza. It's what made you such a good fighter physically. Just be sure you don't trust the wrong person to reexperience you or submit to."

Moving to the door, Scott swiped his hand over his face before turning back and meeting my eyes. "Maria is pregnant. She's been made inactive again."

Giving him a nod of my head, I frowned after Scott left. Staring out the window, I watched Scott walk off. My eyes drifted back to my wrists and traced the physical reminder of my night with Mitch. Closing my eyes, I relaxed, wondering where he was, what he was doing?

Just remembering the night with him flooded my body with feel-good hormones, and my muscles relaxed. I'd been overdue for a good mattress session. My hand caressed my throat, already feeling normal again. He'd worshipped my body entirely, but it was my soul that he touched.

Leaving the hotel, I'd felt lighter, more at peace with who I am and my role in this world. Mitch was giving me back more than what Mark took from me. He was allowing me to accept that even though this life wasn't my choice, it was okay to enjoy it. That was something I'd been searching for since I was five.

For the first time in my life, I didn't feel like I had to keep proving myself to everyone. Mitch knew me, and he loved me. The longer I thought about it, the more my perception of myself was shifting.

39

____

CROSSING CHAPTERS

THE ENGINE OF A BUS OR TRUCK APPROACHING FILLED THE MOUNTAINS, but I continued practicing tai chi with the boys. One stopped and tugged on my sleeve, pointing before he signed. *"They're here!"* his eyes full of excitement. Turning, he ran over to join the adults as they finished their practice, his brother chasing after. Following, I took my place amongst the others, Maria chuckling when the men gave me my space.

"Please remember this is a collaborative training exercise," Scott reminded us, his eyes intent on me. "Do not injure, maim, or kill members of the other chapter," Scott finished SimComing, and everyone else looked at me also.

Shrugging, I hooked my index finger and moved it down my cheek from my eye to level with my lips.

Scott huffed. *"Try hard."* He turned to watch the bus pull up in the car park and the door open. My lips twitched when Emily, head of the Hunter Chapter, disembarked. Three people behind Emily, Moses climbed down the steps. His eyes scanned across the eight adults before him until they found me and stopped. A smile split his face.

"Huh, a rude shock that guy is going to get," Neil quipped in French to Zane, having seen Moses's interest.

There were only seven Hunters other than Emily and only one other female. Close to thirty and attractive, she didn't seem to be attached to a male with them. That piqued the interest of our single men.

"Perhaps it's a bitch swap," Neil muttered. Some of the guys laughed.

"And you wonder why Lyza threw you out of the helicopter, Neil," Maria huffed. "She should have waited until you were at least a hundred meters up." The guys laughed while Neil grumbled about our attitudes.

Ignoring them, I kept my eyes on Moses, his smile growing as they came to line up before us, and I didn't even look at the other men.

"Everyone, this is Hunter Chapter. Their Mother, Emily, has agreed to a joint training exercise that will last for most of this week." Scott made sure he was in my line of sight so I could watch him sign. "Everyone is going to be partnered with a Hunter, and you are going to go on whatever job they have this week with them. You will shadow them, ask them questions about their procedures, take notes of their notes and the final report. It's important for all of you to truly understand what goes into those packages you receive, which ensures you the best chance of performing your jobs successfully and coming home afterward. Emily?"

"Would you mind signing? I haven't learned." Emily asked Scott politely as she smiled at me, bowing her head in recognition, to which I returned the greeting.

"Of course," Scott stayed by me, interested in how Emily knew me.

"My Hunters are more than just information seekers. They expertly perform the roles of three different chapters, liaising with other branches when needed. Their first role is in communications. When they are given a job, they use technology to try and locate the target. They are probably the most proficient hackers in the world. For this reason, I would highly suggest not letting them on your personal laptops.

"A Hunter then puts eyes on the target. Once this occurs, they stay in place until a Guardian or Scythe is sent in. In some instances, if the job is a high priority, a Hunter may take on the role of protector or assassin. We Hunters have the most multifunctional role in all of the chapters. We are Intelligence, Guardians, and Sythe in one. Your job files are as detailed as they are because of the work my Hunters do because they have been trained just like you, just like the Guardians, just like the Intelligence Chapters." Emily took a breath. "That is not to say that they are as good as you at your job."

Emily's eyes came to me briefly before continuing. "My Hunters are trained to pass level four combat. My understanding is that you Scythe reach a baseline of level five to be considered job-ready. You will find a lot of your training and skills are aligned with that of a Hunter, and you may wonder why you are a Scythe instead. I'm going to explain how a Hunter tests."

Putting her hand out to one of her people, Emily took a form I recognized well. The profiling test we all undertook at age fourteen.

"Psychological profiling is the first test. Hunters have profiles that match well with the analysis of complex data. They are problem solvers." Emily handed the test back. "In the physical, they will pass fighting, evasion, and covert activities. They may not be the best at fighting, but they will pass all three without necessarily excelling at any of them. The last test is intelligence gathering."

"I don't remember that," Zane murmured to Maria. She shook her head in agreement.

"Intelligence testing is only offered to a consistent pass who meets the psychological profile of an analyst and problem solver," Emily clarified for everyone. "Excelling in intelligence over all others will see you sent to the Intelligence Chapter. But passing it, along with tactical, will see you sent to be a Hunter. A good Hunter does not excel at any one skill but does well in them all."

Strolling casually, Emily moved towards me. "Out of all of you, only one had the psychological profile to do the intelligence test. The Guardians lost a great asset when she was disabled." Emily's eyes were curious as they looked me over. "Or maybe the Hunters did."

When Scott cleared his throat, Emily smiled and stepped away as Scott stepped back in. "When you are partnered up, your Hunter will live with you for the week. They will share your house and facilities until you leave here and when you return. I would prefer for partners to choose each other, but Emily and I will assign you a partner based on your skill if you can't. Would anyone like to volunteer to select a Hunter as their partner? Please remember, the Hunter can decline, but if you both agree, you will be stuck with each other for the rest of the week."

As I stepped forward, Scott blinked, surprised. Pointing to Moses, I then signed. *"I'll take Moses. I already know he can sign, so we will be able to communicate."*

Blinking once at me, Scott looked to Moses wide-eyed. Grinning, Moses hefted his pack to his shoulder and stepped forward. *"Lead the way,"* Moses signed without talking.

Exhaling, Scott nodded. "Head off and let your partner settle in," he directed. Smirking at the open mouths of nearly all my fellow Scythe, I turned, and Moses followed.

"Seriously?" Neil grumbled.

"I told you learning to sign was beneficial," Scott scolded.

"What was his problem?" Moses asked as we walked away.

Glancing over my shoulder to see the three guys I'd declined scowling after us, I held my left palm flat and flicked the tips of my right hand across it as if getting rid of a bug. *"Rejection burns the ego."*

Lifting a brow at my gesture, Moses chuckled. *"Is that what happened to his shoulder?"*

"He fell out of a helicopter."

Waiting for me to finish signing, Moses lifted a brow. *"Did you help him fall?"* When I shrugged, Moses laughed and put his arm around my waist as we walked away. He leaned in, glancing back over my shoulder, and dropped a kiss to my cheek. He started laughing as we turned the corner and took his arm away to sign. *"Even your Father wants you. I'm going to make them jealous this week."*

"Is your chapter based in New Mexico?"

"How did you guess?" Moses grinned.

"Good. If I'm pregnant after this week, they'll think it's yours and transfer me."

"What? Wait?" Moses stopped me from walking. *"Are you pregnant?"*

Putting my thumb side on to my lips, I stroked my nose twice quickly with my index finger.

"Possibly? Who is the father?" Moses signed angrily.

Lifting my eyes to his, I raised a brow and allowed him to see the plan forming in my head the moment I'd seen him step off the bus. Stepping back, Moses swept a hand through his hair. "Oh, Lyza," he breathed. "You're going to use me to go back to him."

Taking his hand, I walked him to my house. *"Come inside. You can tell me all about you and Stacey."*

Jaw falling open, Moses blinked, then he started laughing. *"You should have been a Hunter."*

Smiling at the compliment, I let him in. Once the door was shut, I showed him to the spare room and left him to settle in while I made us a coffee. Moses came back out, and I handed him a cup before we sat down to talk - well, sign.

"So, is your plan to claim the child is mine, marry me, and see Fairchild on the side?" Moses asked.

Frowning, I closed my index and middle finger down on my thumb.

"Can I ask what it is?"

"I'll inform Father I'm pregnant next week, if I am, and let them assume it happened this week."

"Which will get you transferred and us married," Moses huffed. *"But it won't be my kid."*

"I'm not going to suggest it is. They can jump to their own conclusions. If it allows me to be with Mitch, to be near him, for him to see his child, I'll do it."

Moses looked away. *"Mitch is going to be pissed if we marry."*

He cared that Mitch would be angry, I smirked. *"I can't marry you, so we can either let Chapter think we are, or they will have to suck-up us living together in sin."*

Watching my words, Moses considered me. *"So, you are suggesting we live together, raise your kids together, and carry on our relationships with others when it suits us?"* In response, I lifted and dropped one shoulder. *"Will we fuck?"* Moses asked, a wicked grin across his face. When I raised that shoulder again, Moses laughed and shook his head. *"Fairchild will kill me, but this could work. It's really no different to being swingers, I guess."*

"What are swingers?"

Bursting out laughing, Moses brushed his previous comment away. His face sobered. *"What if you're not pregnant? They'll test to be sure."*

At that news, I deflated. *"He gave me an ultimatum. I have two weeks to find a way to go home to him. I either go home with you pregnant, or I leave the arrow."*

"You know what would happen if you tried to leave," Moses warned.

"He's not giving me a choice anymore."

Watching my hands, Moses huffed as he stood up. *"Okay. Let's go fuck. If you're not pregnant yet, I'll make sure you are by the time I'm leaving."*

"Be serious!" I scolded.

Moses leaned forward. *"I am serious. Your way out is by getting knocked up. Whether to him or me, it doesn't matter. It's the only way you are leaving here alive."*

Sighing, I met his eyes. *"We're married. I'll be breaking my vows."*

Gritting his teeth, Moses looked away, seething. "Stupid ass, motherfucker!" he cursed out loud with his back to me. "Painted you into a fucking corner full of explosives." Lifting his head, Moses saw something out of the window and came back over to me. *"You want to deceive them, then it starts now."*

Yanking me from the chair, Moses pressed his mouth to mine. His kiss was consuming, his hands mapping my curves, groping my breast and squeezing it gently. When I heard the voices outside my door, I understood his play. Wrapping my arms around his neck, I slipped my bum up onto the table and wrapped my thighs over his hips. Moaning, Moses pulled me tighter against his front, letting me feel his bulge in the front of his pants.

"Knock, knock," Scott called as the door opened.

By the time Moses pulled back, and I was able to see, Scott and Emily were standing gaping at us. Moses and I chuckled as we made ourselves appropriate for the company. Creating a C with my thumb and index finger and shook it twice in front of my mouth.

"I'm guessing you two knew each other before now?" Scott gritted.

"Moses was the Hunter assigned to find Noel D'Avive," Emily gathered herself quickly. "He and Lyza became close when he located her and infiltrated Fairchild's company to gain access to her. Moses was assigned as Lyza's bodyguard by Fairchild."

"I thought she was sleeping with Fairchild?"

"I believe that was the case, but Moses did approach me requesting to marry Lyza as his breeding mate before the job finished. I didn't realize they had become intimate already."

Grinding his teeth, Scott took a deep breath. "I see. We will pass on the coffee, thank you," Scott signed as he talked. "I was just letting Emily know where to find her son."

While I bowed my head in acknowledgment, Moses signed a crude gesture about where they would have found him if given another five minutes. Pursing my lips, I didn't need to feign discomfort by his suggestion when Scott bit his cheek hard enough to bleed at the idea.

"Okay, we will keep moving. I'll be staying at Scott's if you need anything." Giving Moses a clear' be careful' stare, Emily stepped outside.

Keeping his eyes on me, Scott clenched his jaw as he signed. *"Remember what I told you?"*

He'd told me to take a lover, just don't get pregnant before marriage. Sadly, I had every intention of already being knocked up as I knocked the air in confirmation.

Unhappy but unable to do anything about it, Scott followed Emily out. Moses lifted his coffee to his mouth, his grin falling away. *"He wants you."*

Curling my fingers in, I touched my thumb to my temple in acknowledgment.

"I want you too."

Lifting my eyes to his, I repeated the gesture.

"Mitch is going to kill me," Moses huffed.

"Do you love Stacey?"

Closing his index and middle finger on his thumb like a duck's bill, Moses didn't even hesitate. *"Nope."*

"I love Mitch."

Eyes narrowing, Moses pressed his lips together as he assessed my confession. A moment later, he relaxed. *"Then divorcing him is going to hurt then, isn't it?"*

40

TRAINING RUN

'That's not going to happen.'
Moses leaned over me. 'If you want me to help you be with him, you need to give me something in return,' Moses demanded. 'I want you as my wife. I don't care if you fuck Mitch on the side, but I want you as mine.'

THE DOOR OPENED, AND I BLINKED BACK TO THE PRESENT. THE NUMBER of times I'd gone over that conversation the last few days. Walking in, Moses chucked a paper bag on the table next to me and placed down two coffees. Lifting the binoculars, he watched the target return to his hotel room. Opening the bag, I helped myself to a pastry.

Sighing, Moses put the binoculars down, opened his laptop, and tapped in a code. *"The tracker is working. That will make finding him easier for the protectors who take over."*

"So, we are done?" I signed, hoping we could head home.

"Not until the protector is on site. I'll get my full report written up in the meantime. Just chill. You done that pregnancy test yet?"

Standing up, I went to the bedside table and grabbed the test. Observing the line again, I didn't feel the disappointment I thought I would. Dropping it on the table next to Moses, I picked up the coffee he'd brought back.

"Not pregnant," Moses confirmed. He also didn't sound happy about it. *"I guess we need to have that conversation again."*

I closed my index and middle finger on my thumb.

"I could knock you up, right here, right now," Moses signed back, annoyed.

"We're on the job," I dismissed.

"We haven't even had sex. For all I know, we never will."

Huffing, I walked to the window. That's what it was about, really; he wanted to get laid. Standing there, watching out the window drinking the coffee, I considered I would have to leave the arrow. There was just over a week until I was due to meet Mitch in Geneva.

Coming to the window, Moses watched me. Tapping my shoulder, he waited until I was watching him to sign. *"You want to tell me why you are willing to give up so easily?"*

Closing my eyes a moment, I focused outside and put the coffee down so I had both hands. *"All those years with Noel, I never got pregnant. Maybe I can't."*

Moses considered me. *"Or it was him."*

"I was in the peak time of my cycle when I was with Mitch last week. I'm still not pregnant."

Sighing, Moses leaned against the window. *"Unless you go get tested, you can't know that's the case."*

Watching his hands, I nodded. *"Perhaps, I just need to accept that it isn't going to happen,"* I deflated.

Stepping forward, Moses started lowering his face to mine, but I put my hand to his chest, restraining him.

As if holding something in his flat palms, Moses offered it forward, then pointed to his chest before having his left bladed hand as if hiding something, jutting his pointed finger up behind it, and then in front of it asking for a chance.

Forming an L in front of my face, I flicked it back to the side of my face. *"I can't."*

Creating a hashtag with his fingers wide, he weighed it in front of him three times. *"Sex is sex; it's not going to hurt anyone."*

Shaking my head, I stepped back. *"Sex was sex until Mitch made it something better."*

Watching my hands, Moses inhaled deeply and closed his eyes, looking away, but I saw the slight lift of his lips in a smile. The phone rang. Shoving away from the window to answer it, Moses listened first. "But I'm not alone?" He waited a further minute. "Yes, Mother. We will be in place in five minutes." He put away his phone. *"Grab your stuff. We are to be on-site with the job until the Guardians arrive to move him to a safe location."*

"Is this normal?" I asked before grabbing my jacket and ensuring my bag was ready to go.

"It can be when the threat assessment comes back high. Chamber feels the target is in imminent danger, so we need to make sure it stays safe until the right people arrive." Grabbing up his bag, Moses opened the door. I followed.

Three minutes later, we knocked on the target's door. The man we had tracked and surveilled for over two days answered it. "Are you the protection?"

"If we weren't, you'd be dead," Moses answered, stepping in. "Your full team and transport are fifteen minutes out. Are you ready to go?"

"I am," the man answered, his eyes passing over me as I stepped in and shut the door closing the deadlock. "Who is she? Did you bring your girlfriend?"

"Not everyone uses their wife and kids as shields," Moses scowled.

The man went at Moses, trying to shove him against the wall. Dropping his stuff, Moses pushed the guy back. Moses was nearly a head taller and almost twice the breadth of the sexist pig. The guy straightened angrily. "Their lives would be nothing without me anyway," he declared.

Moses growled. "Well, your life will be nothing without this female. Trust me, if your enemy gets here first, your life will be highly dependent on both of us." Moses looked at me as I moved to the window to watch the street behind the hotel. Rarely did the enemy knock at the front door. Securing the rest of the room, Moses told the target to sit on the sofa, then came over to me. *"What do you think?"*

Bumping my pointed fingers together in front of me, I held my left index finger up in front of my right palm with fingers spread, then jumped my hand back to leave the left finger standing alone. Many people thought isolation was safer, but it could make a hit, especially an abduction, witness-free. *"We are better off in the lobby or restaurant downstairs."*

"Unless the enemy is happy to kill innocents to get to him," Moses offered. *"They already left his wife and kids locked in a closet. Had we not found them..."*

"He left them for dead to slow down the enemy while he sneaked away here."

Watching my sharp gestures of disgust, Moses smirked. *"I agree. Let's get him downstairs. The sooner we can hand him over, the better for us."* Turning from me, Moses addressed the job. *"Grab your stuff. We're leaving now."*

Going down the hall first, I called the elevator. Moses followed with the target once it chimed, and I held the door until they got there.

Same deal at the ground floor, I stepped out first, ensured the lobby was clear, and only held civilians. Just as Moses stepped out, his phone rang.

"Yes?" He answered, holding the elevator and not letting the target step out. "Perfect, we are in the lobby now. Pull up out front, and we'll bring him out." Putting his phone away, Moses signaled me to go ahead.

As I opened the front door, a grey sedan pulled up. It was unremarkable, so were the two men sitting in it. One hopped out and tilted his head to assess me, a smile blooming across his face. "Lyza," he signed hello.

Studying his face, I smiled. He'd been a member of the Australian Chapter as a kid. We'd met during my mother's affair with their Chapter Father. He must have tested for Guardian when he came of age, just like I had.

"You're the Hunter?"

Shaking my head, I indicated Moses as he stepped out with the target.

"Husband?"

"Cross-chapter collaboration," Moses answered once he had the job in the car. "He's all yours."

"Thanks. Stay safe. Word is his enemy tagged him about thirty minutes ago and were moving in, so we need to move. *Nice seeing you, Lyza,*" he farewelled. Dropping in the car, they left.

"Let's go," Moses signed.

We started walking towards the place we'd left our car. Reaching into his pocket, Moses stopped. "Crap!" He checked his other pockets, then his bag. Eventually, he met my eyes. *"Car keys are gone. I must have dropped them when that prick went at me. I'll go back to get them and meet you at the car."*

I moved my hand as if turning a lever with my thumb out. Nodding his head, Moses headed back the way we had come. Turning, I walked as if going to the car but then stepped into a doorway. When Moses reached the corner, he checked over his shoulder to ensure I was out of sight, then switched direction back toward the building we'd surveilled from. Pulling my jacket off, I grabbed the jumper from my bag and changed, pulling the hoodie over my head before following, crossing the road, so I wasn't directly behind him.

Stopping a few blocks over, Moses pulled a different phone from his bag. Making a call, he spoke for a second and then waited on the corner while he put the phone away. Stepping into the coffee shop across the road, I ordered two takeaway coffees and observed.

A familiar type of car pulled up, and I bit my lip as Mitch and Fred climbed out in their all-black tactical outfits. While I surveilled, Moses gave them what looked to be a tracking device. Watching their lips, I was only catching bits of the conversation because they turned their heads to keep watch around them. A ten-minute lead time, a registration number, something concerning a Henry Ryan. The conversation seemed almost over, but then Moses said something, and Mitch focused on him intently.

"Is she?" Mitch asked. Moses shook his head. Mitch's shoulders relaxed while Moses kept talking. "Did she agree?" Again, Moses shook his head. Whatever he said made Mitch happy.

"Your coffee," the girl behind the counter called. Smiling, I took them. Making my way out of the shop, I kept them in peripheral vision as I walked back up the street to the car. Once there, I changed back into my jacket and leaned against the car, considering what I had just seen.

Taking out my phone, I called Scott. He answered and took a second to line the camera so we could face time. Rubbing his thumb across his finger pads, Scott then pointed with his little finger and flipped his hand as he lifted his shoulders in question. *"Something wrong?"*

"Our job was hot. I'm wondering how the enemy found him so quickly. Can you call the Guardians and tell them to check him? I'm concerned he might have got tagged somehow. Tell them to keep moving."

Observing my gestures through the phone, Scott frowned. *"How hot?"*

"I suspect a team turned up just after we handed him off."

"I'll pass it on. We have a job when you get back," Scott informed and hung up.

Putting my phone away, I picked up my coffee and took a sip as Moses came back and removed the keys from his pocket. *"Who was that?"*

"Father. Just letting him know we handed off, and we're on our way back," I advised Moses. *"Any issues at the hotel?"*

Moses shook his head. *"Let's go."* He hit the button to unlock the car.

Handing him his coffee, I slipped into the car. Moses got the engine started and us moving. *"We could stop off for a night, try getting you knocked up?"*

"Father has a job for me. I need to get back."

The drive back to Geneva was reasonably quiet. On the helicopter back to Chapter, Moses studied me but kept unusually quiet. It made me tilt my head and appraise him, to which he raised a brow at me. Eventually, he leaned forward and lifted his hands to speak.

"Lyza, Scott wants to see you as soon as we land," Jonathan interrupted, tapping his index and middle fingers across the joints to their counterparts on the left, indicating Father to me.

Nodding, I watched Chapter come into view. Moses gritted his teeth. Glancing at me again, he sighed, scrubbing his hands against his thighs. *"I respect your choice, Lyza,"* he finally signed.

As soon as we landed, I led the way to Scott's house, where my Father was waiting at the door. "How'd it go?" Scott asked.

"Smoothly. Lyza is a good study."

"That, I already knew," Scott eyed Moses. "Your mother is by the lake waiting for you to report. I need to speak to Lyza about her next job."

Smirking, Moses kissed my cheek and walked away. Once we were seated, Scott started signing while talking. "The Guardians reported back. You were right about the tracking device. They got rid of it, but not soon enough. A team hit them while they reported back. Only one Guardian survived. He's in intensive care fighting for his life."

My stomach dropped. Picking up his drink, Scott observed me. I wanted to ask which Guardian survived because I wanted the one I knew to still be alive and have a fighting chance. I didn't want another person I knew to be dead. It was a strange feeling. It was odd to have feelings. "What are you thinking, Lyza?"

"I don't think I can do this job anymore. I'm starting to care when people die."

Assessing me, Scott turned his head and picked up a file, handing it to me. "Emily gave me this. I can't promise it will improve things for you, but it's an option."

It was a request to transfer me for the purpose of marriage to Moses. Eyeing the piece of paper, I felt my breath catch.

"You will need to marry here before leaving for this to be approved, but Emily has already filed it with Chamber. We should have an answer this afternoon. They wanted you married, so I can't see them refusing it."

Swallowing my concern, I considered that only Moses knew I couldn't legally marry. *"What grounds did she file this? Did Moses request it?"*

"Emily filed it under the rule of sexual relations," Scott educated me. *"The rule allows that if a chapter parent becomes aware of a sexual relationship between unmarried members, they should move to resolve a marriage as soon as possible."*

"I wasn't aware of that rule," I frowned.

Scott lifted a brow. "Moses was." That answer made my eyes jump from Scott's hands to his eyes before going back to his hands. "Which is probably why he ensured both Emily and I witnessed a physical exchange between you." Pressing my lips together, I cursed internally. "Have you had sex with him?"

Meeting his eyes, I exhaled as I shook my head. Taking another drink, Scott nodded. I think he suspected that was the case. "I can ask this to be rejected as false." He offered, taking the file back, but I shook my head again. Bigamy would have me moved closer to Mitch, at least.

There was a knock at the door. Pursing his lips, Scott got up to answer it. "I think you are right about someone in Chamber having it in for Lyza, and I think I know who," Emily's voice traveled. "The move was rejected. Debbie Fairchild used veto power to refuse the marriage despite the other members voting unanimously in favor."

"Why would she do that? She wanted Lyza married," Scott debated.

"Exactly, but she argued that the Hunter Chapter would put her in the vicinity of Lyza's civilian lover. She said she believed Lyza seduced Moses to enable this transfer and that it brings Lyza's loyalty into question again. Debbie is making an order that Lyza not be permitted to do a job solo and that her movements must be accounted for at all times."

"I haven't seen anything to question Lyza's loyalty," Scott argued. "I do believe she is suffering depression, though."

"As a result of her torture and imprisonment?"

"Yes. I think it is what enabled Fairchild to seduce her."

There was a moment of silence. "If Debbie is the one after Lyza, you won't be able to protect her much longer. Debbie will find a way to take her out."

"Did no one in Chamber disagree with Debbie's decision?" Scott queried.

"Two other chapters voiced opposition. Cyber voiced dissent, and the Guardian Grandfather openly accused Debbie of punishing the child for her father's choices. I think they are the chapters we need to cross-train with next. I'll contact Jobe when I get home."

"I'll call Claude," Scott concurred.

"What about Lyza?" Emily worried.

"I'll manage it personally."

"Scott, it was pretty obvious to everyone on that job that Fairchild really cared about her. If what we suspect is true, you need to be careful with her," Emily warned.

"Right now, I'm trying to stop the lookout looking appealing, Emy. From the moment her father brought her to Chapter, Lyza's had to fight to survive. That's nothing new for her. But whatever happened out there, it's made her unable to settle back in here, and I've been watching her chafe like a wild animal caged since she came back. So, right now, my primary concern is keeping one of our best from losing her way. I'll worry about Fairchild if and when he becomes a problem."

Swallowing, I closed my eyes. When I opened them, Scott was back in the room and sitting down opposite me. Waiting until I was watching, he opened the file, took out the transfer request, and tore it to shreds. A single tear fell down my cheek.

41

COLLISION

The snow was falling heavily. The ground was covered in knee height drifts as we made our way to our destination. Scott regularly checking over his shoulder to ensure I was still with him. The Hunter Chapter departed yesterday with all jobs complete. While our situation didn't end well, it wasn't seen as our failure, but the Guardians' team.

Before he left, I'd given Moses a copy of the job files that showed what information hadn't been passed down to me for him to keep safe. While I knew his loyalty wasn't to the Arrow now, I also believed he wouldn't do anything to hurt me. He hadn't propositioned me that last night together at my house. He'd acted like a friend, which made me think his attempts had been a test of my loyalty to Mitch.

Turning off the path into a stand of trees, we started hiking uphill. I had to admit, for his age, Scott had a nice ass and could navigate these conditions with ease. Right now, I focused on Scott's ass because it didn't hurt like it did to think about Mitch. It didn't confuse me like trying to puzzle out where all the pieces fit.

Mitch was on a job, a big job, one that at least once collided with Arrow interests. Moses was not only intimate with Stacey and still in contact with Mitch, but he planted that tracking device for him and enabled Mitch's team to track and kill a man that Chamber wanted protected. Was Moses a plant for the Arrow, or was he another member recruited to the shadow company, or did he trade loyalty after meeting Mitch? Where did it all connect?

And Debbie wanted me dead? Emily said she hated me for something my father did. That wasn't hard to fathom; he was an asshole. But what did he do to her that made her hate me? By the time my mother and father married, Debbie had already left Scythe and married Mitch's dad. Hell, Debbie was out raising Mitch by then, so how did her hatred transfer to me?

There was so much mess in my head. Chaos didn't lead to successful jobs, so I needed to clear my head and focus on the task ahead. To find and kill Henry Ryan. The man Mitch talked about to Moses, no doubt. But why?

Shaking my head, I refocused on Scott's ass. It was a good ass attached to strong thighs, supporting a muscular back. The backpack he carried wasn't light, yet he moved with ease. It told me he could have just as quickly piggybacked me up this snow-covered mountain.

My brain reminded me of how easily Mitch could lift me. How he could hold me unsupported in his arms, my legs wrapped around his waist as he took me. Mitch made me feel as light as a feather. I wondered if Scott was that strong. Shaking my head again, I forced the image of Mitch and me breaking that kitchen chair away. Still, the smile spread over my lips as I remembered that night in detail.

A hand grabbed my shoulder, jolting me from the memory to meet Scott's eyes. He studied me. Glancing around, I realized we were near the top of the mountain. The cabin we were seeking just over the ridge. Appraising the peak, I frowned, realizing there were men out and about in this weather too.

Without Scott having to explain, I fell to my knees and dropped my pack to the ground beside me. Removing my jacket, I checked my gun was loaded. Scott waited for me to hide my bag behind a tree and mark it before kicking some snow over it.

As I rose up, Scott caught my shoulder again and checked my eyes. He relaxed when he realized I was now intently focused on our surroundings. Releasing me, he let me take the lead. I moved through the trees like the breeze that blew up the mountain. Light and flowing.

As I reached the ridge, I moved carefully, ensuring I was covered. The first guard stood just on the other side of the ridgeline. Watching from the trees as a man stood in the clearing behind the chalet chopping wood. Turning, I marked him for Scott, then I moved further along the ridgeline to where another guard was squatting.

This one was watching a football game on his mobile device with the volume off. Moving in behind him, I slipped my blade free, then covered his mouth as I thrust into his throat, stopping him from calling out an alarm. He dropped his phone to go for his gun, but my knife pierced his eye and brain next.

Pulling his body behind a tree, I relieved him of his gun, jacket, and earpiece. It wasn't for me to hear as much as looking like one of them at first glance. They wore a uniform. That would be what they looked for before anything else. Having the earpiece again displaced their brain's concern for another moment. It would take a second longer for them to realize my face didn't belong.

Gazing across the ridgeline, I saw Scott doing the same with the first guard. He listened to the earpiece, then signaled me. I wasn't supposed to hear anything, so for him, my earpiece was purely for show. Shoving the dead guard back over the ridgeline, I watched his body roll and slide down the hill a little. Covering the blood over with snow, I picked up his phone and squatted in his place, pretending to watch the game.

The guard chopping wood stopped and looked up. He checked the guard stood where Scott did, that a guard was squatting where I was, then he wiped his brow and piled the wood into his arms and walked it over to the back deck. He piled it up, then rechecked our locations. The English team scored a goal; I reacted by mouthing a curse at the phone. The guard chuckled and returned to the chopping block to start his next load.

Standing up, I moved to the side and down the hill. The chopping was rhythmic. Nearly all his actions musically making noise. Any guard inside would be hearing it subconsciously and notice if the rhythm broke. So, I crept around to the cabin and peered inside. Turning to see Scott up the hill, I gestured three. Scott nodded.

Keeping below the windows, against the wall, I moved in behind the woodchopper. Signaling to Scott, I then pointed to the chopper. He nodded his head once again.

The chopping stopped. The guard lifted his head to check positions and faltered when no one was there. He was dead before he could draw breath. Removing my blade from his eye, I started dragging him back to the cabin and hiding his body beneath.

If I was Scott, Mitch, Moses, or any other man that could bench press me and not break a sweat, I could have broken their necks, and the whole thing could be less messy. But breaking necks takes a lot of force and strength. It also requires being in a higher position than your victim. Requirements that go against a female when she is up against well-built men who are already taller than her. Hell, the last one's neck was as thick as my thigh. Even Mitch would have struggled to break that.

Picking up the piles of wood, Scott walked them to the back porch. He piled them, then went back to the chopping block and started chopping, keeping the same rhythm as the previous guard.

Grabbing the window jam, I pulled my body up to look inside. Two more guards and our target, Henry Ryan. Lowering myself slowly, I was about to move when something on the body I'd just dragged across the ground caught my attention. Dropping to my knee where his shirt had ridden up at the hip, I reached out and slowly moved the jacket to see the rest of the sword tattoo. Like Wenda, this man had been in a chapter long enough to pass his first test at fourteen but then failed out before active duty at eighteen. Considering him for a second, I moved to where I could see Scott. When he turned to take the next load of wood to the house, I signed to him.

Pointing my hand like a gun, with middle and index finger as the barrel, I put it to my shoulder and squiggled the fingers down my left upper arm before pointing to my hip. Then I curled my fingers as if they were holding an epee sword and turned my wrist like I would to fence and jutted my wrist forward.

Scott hesitated, nodded, and piled the wood. Circling his hand, Scott walked up the porch steps while I ran around the front, pulling out my gun as I did. Clicking off the safety, I fired into the open air. The house came alive, and so did my earpiece.

As I fired a second round, Scott went through the back door then gunshots started inside. Running up the front porch, I kicked in the front door. A gun fired, and I ignored the burn through my side, shooting the guard, so he dropped, exposing his charge. Two shots later, my target was dead.

The guard looked at me with wide eyes as he held his bloody thigh. "Lyza?"

My eyes widened as Dustin looked up at me. Stepping back just as confused as he seemed, I put my hand over the burning sensation on my side. Dustin saw it. "You didn't know it was us?" I shook my head.

When Scott came through the door, Dustin lifted his arm. Stepping forward, I kicked the gun from his hand and then kicked him in the head. His head lolled to the side, unconscious. Scott went to shoot him, but I knocked his arm to the side, and stepped in his way.

"What are you doing?"

"We need to go," I signed. *"There is a second-team nearby. Throw that guy outside."* I pointed to Dustin.

"That's not protocol," Scott argued.

"Fuck protocol," I signed angrily, tears filling my eyes.

Watching me a moment, Scott took my hand and observed the blood on my palm. He exhaled. "You knew him?"

Bowing my head to the side, I bit my lip. I was going to start crying on a job, in front of the Chapter Father.

"How bad are you hurt?"

Holding up my left palm, I hooked my right index finger and flicked it from the outside palm to my left thumb. It was just a scratch, nothing serious.

"I'll meet you at the tree," Scott ordered. "Cover me in case the other team turns up."

Swallowing, I looked at Dustin apologetically and turned, walking out the back. Two gunshots sounded inside. Two tears escaped my eyes. Running up to the ridge and the tree I'd marked, I dug my backpack free. Dropping the jacket that I'd taken from the guard, I pulled my coat back on and took my pack up to the ridge.

Finding a good cover position, I pulled out the sniper rifle and set myself up. From the ridge, I watched Scott retrieve his pack from the trees and collect the hatchet to take it inside. The mountains' silence made the sounds of the ax hitting something with a wet thunk echo around us. I'd never beheaded someone, so I was glad someone more adept with such methods was attached to this job.

Adrenalin was surging through my body. I'd been on the kill high until I saw Dustin. Recognized, this wasn't the enemy's team, but Mitch's. Mitch had taken over Concealed, but what else had he taken on when he took over the Sword corporation? What had I gotten myself mixed up in?

My earpiece came alive. "Dust, we're about to arrive. Everything good up there?" Fred asked.

Exiting the back door, Scott shoved the canister with the target's head in it back in his backpack as the fire in the cabin blew out one of the windows.

"Dust?" Fred called again. "Jones? Marshall? Anyone?"

Getting his pack on his back, Scott ran up to the ridgeline just as a car came up the drive. Packing my gear up, I got my backpack on and raced down the hill diagonally to meet with Scott. Yelling was echoing up from the other side of the ridge. Taking the earpiece out, I threw it into the trees.

Weighed down with a head, Scott was only jogging through the snow, so I caught up with him quickly. Then we moved together to the path. We had to slow down here, gravity not helping our escape anymore and the snow trying to trap us. Stopping, Scott unstrapped the two snowboards from his pack and handed one to me. We changed out of our boots, got ourselves set, and boarded down the path.

Scott was a pro. Once he started, he was gone. Taking a few seconds to get my balance, I had a wobbly start, but once I stabilized, I was fine. Catching movement in the trees above, I rounded the first corner in the path. The decline became more significant, and I zipped down the rest of the mountain behind Scott.

My heart was beating rapidly in my chest, expecting any moment to see Mitch step out in front of me with a gun pointed to my head. Of course, he didn't. Once we reached our car, we dropped our gear in the boot casually, slipped into the car, and made our way out of there.

Scott didn't say a thing as we drove. He kept his thoughts to himself until we arrived at the prearranged drop, and he handed off the canister with the head to whoever was waiting for it. It was after dark now. Driving us another hour towards home, Scott pulled into a hotel. Again, he didn't say anything as he checked us in and got us a room.

Once the door shut, that changed. "How did you know him?"

Watching Scott's hands, I closed my eyes for a second, then spelled out Mitch's surname.

Nodding as he threw his jacket on a chair, Scott ordered room service. Conversation over, I removed my coat, my boots, and beanie. When I turned around, Scott stood right there in front of me.

"I won't ever cover for you again," he warned me, too close to sign, forcing me to read his lips despite his verbal expression. "Next time you see one of his men on the job, you do what you were trained to do. Leave your conscience at home."

Adrenaline was surging through me, fear mixed with the thrill of the escape. Scott cuffed the back of my neck in his steady hand. "Be sure that the only reason I'm covering for you now is that you still protected me up there. You took him out of commission when he would have shot me. It proved to me you are still an Arrow at heart, even if you doubt it."

My heart racing in my chest, I watched his lips. Scott squeezed my neck. "Look at me," he urged gently. When I lifted my eyes to meet his, he studied my face, his pupils dilating. "I don't want to see you hurt, Lyza. I'll protect you if you let me." Carefully, Scott lowered his lips to mine and kissed me.

I didn't fight it. Scott was the Chapter Father. If he wanted me, I was his as far as everyone was concerned. To disobey your chapter parent was an instant death sentence. A rule my real father had used to his benefit.

So, as Scott's hands unbuckled my belt, pulled my top off, shoved my pants to the ground, and his mouth and hands explored my cold skin, I stood there and did nothing but wince when he touched my wound.

I didn't help, but I didn't stop him either. I just vacated the vicinity of awareness, returning hours later to find myself still in my underwear.

Blinking, I rolled over to find Scott asleep in the bed beside me. Lifting the blanket, I could see his boxer shorts were on, and my wound was clean and bandaged.

Taking a deeper breath, Scott lifted his hands and started signing. "We didn't have sex. I recognized you had gone into shock and stopped. I patched you up, put you in bed, and warmed you up. Go back to sleep."

For a moment, I didn't know what to say. My real father had never touched me because I was his, but I'd never seen him show even an ounce of that much consideration for another person. Unsure what to feel, I moved closer to this man who respected boundaries and had tried numerous times to help me.

Opening his eyes, Scott watched as I placed a non-passionate kiss on his lips. Dropping my face, I kissed his chest, right over his heart, then I snuggled into the warmth of his body, closed my eyes, and rested. Scott was a good man. I knew that in my heart.

42

FORGOTTEN

"M ITCH, I'M SORRY. I DIDN'T KNOW THEY WERE YOUR MEN. I NEARLY got myself killed because I couldn't kill Dustin," I confessed to my empty bedroom the following day. Stroking over the rings on my ring finger, tears welled in my eyes. "If you found my blood, know I'm okay. Dustin shot me before he knew it was me too. He'd still be alive if it'd just been me. I'm sorry. I'm basically on house arrest now. The doctors are calling it recovery, but I'm being watched everywhere I go. I'll be at the hotel by twelve, though. I promise. I don't want to go through yesterday again."

Swiping the tears from my face, I cursed. I'd never been like this before. I was so emotional; it made no sense. When did I start caring?

"I can't wait to be with you permanently again. I've missed you so much."

My alarm sounded to wake me up. Turning it off, I rolled over. Sending up a prayer to whatever god may be there, I fidgeted with my rings another minute before I slipped them off and put them under my pillow. Then I went out to start my day as usual.

THE SNOW WASN'T LETTING up. I'd planned to go hiking three days ago, but Scott vetoed that. He may not have agreed with Debbie's behavior, but he kept a close eye on me. However, to meet Mitch's demand and keep my promise, I needed Scott to relinquish his hold on me for a few hours. Today was New Year's Eve, and I had three hours to get to the hotel and meet Mitch so he could take me away from here.

Someone joined me on the lookout, where I stood wondering if I could base jump to my freedom. Turning my head, I found Scott watching me. "Something on your mind, Lyza?"

Avoiding the intense observation of his eyes, I focused on his hands, then lifted mine. *"I booked into a hotel in Geneva to watch the fireworks tonight. I was going to spend the day in the spa, then watch the fireworks from the hotel."* Having answered his question and laid the seed, I turned my gaze back to the view.

Considering me in my peripheral vision, Scott tucked a strand of hair back in my beanie. The intimate action made me turn to look at him. Raising a brow, Scott touched my chin before he continued signing. "You have to give me a name by midnight, Lyza. Don't let them choose for you."

Taking a deep breath, I looked away. Refusing to be ignored, Scott stepped around into line of sight. *"Compromise?* You can spend the day at the spa, but you come back and watch the fireworks from here. Jonathan will pick you up at six to bring you home."

All going well, I'd be wheels up with Mitch by six. That was good enough for me. When I let the hope light up my face, Scott smiled. "Bring me back an answer, Lyza. If it's time you need, I'll fight for you, but you need to give me a reason why."

Launching at him, I gave him a big hug and kiss on the cheek, then I raced back to my house to get a bag to take with me. Glancing over my shoulder to give Scott another smile, I didn't take the way his smile dropped or the way he turned to stare back out over the mountains to heart. He was hoping I'd choose him, but he knew I loved Mitch, so I'm sure he was just worried about me choosing someone else. Not that there was much choice. Scott, Jonathan, and Kit were about the only decent ones here.

At my house, I started packing. I couldn't look to be going for anything but the day, so I chose the essentials and the phone Mitch gave me. When I got to the helipad, Maria was there. She was dressed to the nines, make-up all done.

Hesitating when I saw her, I forced a smile. Climbing aboard with her purse looking very happy, Maria turned to me as I closed the door and took the seat across from her. "Tate and I always spend New Year's Eve together," she informed me. She turned her eyes back to the window. "I miss him so much." She rubbed her tiny belly. She was only a month along but already showing on her petite frame. "At least I know he's safe as a trainer. It's better than him being out there and the fear of him never coming home."

I considered that it was the opposite for Tate, knowing Maria was still doing the job. It's probably why he kept getting her knocked up every chance he could. While she was pregnant, she was inactive from conception until the baby turned two. Still, she would be stuck with three kids to raise by herself, more if it was twins again.

Maria tilted her head. "I know. It's horrible being left behind. If he went to another chapter, I would have been allowed to go with him. But as he's a trainer, I get left behind. It's insane me, and the boys couldn't go with him. Live with him and for me to work from there." She frowned deep in thought and looked out the window again. "I know we aren't meant to fall in love, but I did. I love Tate, and I miss him every day."

When she smiled at me, I returned it, finally understanding exactly what she was talking about. Her eyes went to my hand and the wedding rings I was wearing. "Are you going to see him? The guy you miss?"

Holding my breath, I lifted a brow in question.

"It's so obvious. Not to those idiots," Maria dismissed the other men of our chapter. "But I've seen the way you stand at the lookout searching the distance for him. You never did that with Noel. I figured the guy who gave you those rings came after."

Looking down at the rings, I felt guilt creep across my chest. I'd still been married when Mitch put these rings on my finger, and I hadn't even thought twice about sleeping with Mitch. I hadn't considered it cheating. Yet, the idea of being with anyone since Mitch felt wrong.

"I think sometimes they have it wrong," Maria murmured. "Making us marry within, these strict ideas about how we raise our kids, that we shouldn't fall in love. Love doesn't weaken us; it strengthens us. I became a much better fighter when I had Tate to come home to after each job. I improved again when the boys were born. Love made me better because I want to come home to them. I think when you don't have that, it makes you more susceptible to failure."

Blinking away tears, I considered I'd never failed until Noel. Until I couldn't pull that trigger and kill him first go. My mind flashed back to last week with Dustin. Was it Dustin that stopped me from taking that shot, or was it the fear of walking in and having to shoot Mitch?

My eyes widened as I realized why I failed last week, but I kept my face down. Maria went back to looking out the window. Studying my rings, I ran my thumb over them. Fear was a powerful emotion. That's what had been crippling me slowly since my return to Chapter—the fear of losing Mitch.

Understanding that instantly made me more relaxed. Watching the helipad grow closer, I felt confident today would change everything for the better. Mitch and I would fight to be together. I didn't doubt we could make it work as long as we were together.

Collecting her phone from the locker, Maria walked off excited to see Tate. Smiling after her, I knew exactly how she felt at this moment. Standing at my locker, I didn't take my Scythe phone. There was no point. Instead, I checked my personal cabinet and found a gift inside a bag. Taking the bag, I went out to the waiting taxi.

Once inside, I turned on Mitch's burner phone and messaged I was on my way. Opening the gift, I found a set of sexy red underwear and a beautiful scarlet dress. The note was written in Mitch's hand.

For New Year's Eve. Our first date as real husband and wife.

Brimming with excitement, I put it back in the bag. Giddy with anticipation, I just wanted to be in his arms, to hold him, kiss him, and god, I wanted to make love to him. My sex itched with need just thinking about him being inside me. Checking the phone to see if Mitch messaged back yet, I exhaled but didn't let the silence detract from the joy I felt. Today, I was going home.

Arriving at the hotel, I went into the lobby and approached the desk. Smiling, I signed I was deaf. The receptionist called her manager over. He signed a greeting.

"I'm meeting my husband here. I'm not sure if he's checked in. His name is Mitchell Fairchild."

The manager nodded and went to the computer. I was so excited to see Mitch that it took me a moment to realize the manager didn't call upstairs to tell them I arrived.

"I'm sorry, Mrs. Fairchild. Your husband had a booking to arrive yesterday, but he never checked in. The booking was only one night, and check-out would have happened already, so I can't offer you the room. Did you wish to book another room?"

The first seed of doubt dropped into my stomach like aniseed. *"No, I might just wait in the lounge. He assured me he would be here by one. Are there any messages? I had no cell reception where I was."* My hands shook a little, the adrenalin of excitement giving way to that small poison of doubt that Mitch not being here caused.

"One moment," the manager stepped away to check the message box. When he came back with a sad face, the second toxic seed dropped and took root. *"I'm sorry. There are no messages."*

Touching my chin in thanks, I forced a smile. *"I'll be in the lounge should he arrive or call."* The manager smiled and nodded. Walking across the lobby, I pulled out Mitch's phone to recheck it, refusing to let those two seeds of doubt bloom.

I'm here. Waiting in the lounge for you.

Perhaps he got caught up. He promised he would come, and I trusted Mitch to keep his promise. Taking a seat overlooking the water, I pushed my anxiety aside and ordered some lunch.

By the time one o'clock came, I'd eaten and started to get antsy, so I ordered another drink. By two, I was tapping the table and checking the phone every five minutes.

Mitch, has something happened? I'm worried you're not here. I'm starting to freak out. Please tell me you're okay and just running late.

No response. Getting up, I checked again at the front desk. No messages. Maria and Tate were in the bar, laughing and schmoozing like the loved-up couple they were, only making my mood grow darker.

By three, I ordered my first alcoholic drink. Those seeds had taken root and were blooming into a big fucking tree of doubt and fear. By four, I was up to my third cocktail and feeling the effects as someone who rarely drank.

Mitch. Please! I need to know you are alright.

Never in my life had I pleaded for anything, and here I was doing it via text. Placing the phone on the table before me, I tried to mind-control it into answering. "Please text back," I whispered, hugging myself. "Please be coming for me. Please be alive."

Five o'clock came and went. The hotel was packed with people arriving for the New Year's Eve celebrations in the restaurant and waterfront. When the phone buzzed at five forty-three, I picked it up anxiously. The message was cold and angry. I was crying before I even finished reading.

I'm not coming. You fucked things up in Germany.

My heart plummeted. The tree of doubt bloomed flowers, grew fruit, and any hope I had left shriveled up, strangled by its roots.

I'm sorry.

Putting the phone down, I sat there frozen for a minute, tears pouring down my face.

Mitch replied immediately.

Me too. I'm sick of losing my friends because of you.

Sobbing to my chest, I squeezed the phone. Noel had said he went after Mitch to stop from losing me. Mitch lost many friends, including his best friend that night, then he lost Mark the next time Noel came for me. Even if it was said from anger, he was right.

Struggling to breathe through the pain, I looked out the window at the people gathering to celebrate the new year, and I hated every one of them. Taking a deep breath to stop my tears, I pulled myself together. Looking at the time, I stood up. Walking to the front desk, I requested to leave a message.

The receptionist handed me a pen and paper and an envelope to put it in.

Mitch,
I'm sorry that doing my job messed things up for us. You knew what I
was, but you lied to me about your role. Maybe, if you had told me
who you were, I could have stopped this or never fallen in love with
you. You are as much to blame for this as I am.
Goodbye.
Oh, I'll be needing that divorce.

Folding the note, I took off my rings and slid them into the folds, then turned off the phone and slid it into the envelope before sealing it. Writing Mitch's name and address on the front, I gestured the manager over.

Holding up my index finger on my left hand, I put my right pointer to it and swiped it away. *"I'll need this couriered,"* I informed the manager and handed him a hundred dollar note.

"I'll take care of it," he assured.

Walking out, I caught a taxi that was dropping someone off for the party. Handing him the card that I kept directing my drivers to the helipad, I sat back and used the car ride to clean myself up. We arrived at ten past six, but Jonathan was still there waiting. Scott stood in the waiting room watching me walk in, sniper rifle strapped across his back.

Placing his right palm in his left, he opened his arms out to the sides before making a small juggling gesture to his right to represent bubbling. *"How was the spa?"*

"Nowhere near as relaxing as I hoped," I signed. *"I'm sorry, I'm late. I'm ready to come home."*

As Scott assessed my eyes, I doubt he missed I'd been crying. "Then let's go. We can't be in the air when the fireworks start." Scott opened the door for me, and we boarded the helicopter.

The ride was quiet. Scott sat watching me while I tried to decide if I wanted to cry or kill something or throw myself from the helicopter. Scott's eyes kept flicking down to my left hand. I knew why. I'd never left Chapter without my rings, even for a job. Since I'd come back, I wore them out, and I wore them back in.

Wisely, Scott didn't say anything. Sitting back, he packed away the rifle. When the helicopter landed, he walked me back to my house.

Two fingers to his chest, Scott pushed them towards me, then wiped his thumb down his chest, sweeping it away as he lifted his shoulders. *"Are you okay?"*

"Have I ever been?"

Frowning at my hands, Scott bowed his head. Stepping inside, I shut the door. The tears started flowing the moment I was alone. Walking into my bedroom, I dumped my bag on the floor. Going to the window, I stood there looking out into the dark. Alone.

"You broke my heart," I spoke to myself. "Why?" The snow fell gently outside. "Just why?"

The night exploded in colors and lights. Glancing at the clock, I acknowledged it was the kids' fireworks. Turning away from the bright colors, I saw the gift Mitch had left me on the bed. Peering back out at the fireworks, I let my anger get the best of me. I wasn't going to waste the dress.

Showering, I changed, found a pair of heels to match, and pulled on my coat. Leaving my house, I walked to Scott's, knocking on the door. Scott opened it, clearly freshly showered himself. Wearing track pants, he was pulling on his shirt. "Lyza?" Opening his door, he let me in.

Stepping inside, I walked into his lounge room. Taking off the jacket, I turned around. Scott's eyes popped wide as he took in the dress. "Um, *drink?*" He gestured.

Touching my chin, I curled my fingers down in request.

Scott poured me a scotch and a double for himself. Taking the drink, I sculled it in one hit. Scott watched with his brows raised. Putting the glass aside, I faced him. Pointing to my chest, I made an L in front of my face flicking it away, gestured placing a ring on my finger, then pointed to Scott. *"I can't marry you. I can't marry anyone because I'm already married. To Mitchell Fairchild."*

Watching my hands, Scott took a really long drink and sat down on his sofa. *"Legally?"*

Forming an L with my thumb and index finger, I put it to the top of my left fingers then dropped it to the base of my palm.

"Shit, Lyza!" Scott drank the rest of his drink in one hit. Assessing me for a moment, Scott shifted forward and picked up his phone. "It's Scott. Lyza D'Avive needs to have her name updated. Lyza Fairchild. They managed to legally marry before she returned to Chapter. It means she can't be married." Scott waited to hear what the other person said. "Thank you." Scott hung up.

He stood up. "Chamber will discuss it in two days and determine how to proceed. In your favor, Mitch is the son of two elevated Arrows. He has proven himself a success. They may approve of this. Highly doubtful, but a lot of decisions coming out of Chamber of late have been unique. Most likely, since they can't kill your husband because Debbie protects him, you will be forced to divorce him."

Taking a deep breath, suspecting that may be Debbie's solution, I stood there watching Scott. After a moment, I took steps to close the distance, stopping within his personal space. Not missing my intention, Scott caressed my cheek. "Fucking me is only going to give you temporary relief from that anger and hurt."

Nodding, I stepped into him and pressed my lips to his. Scott kissed me back. We stood there making out for several minutes while I assured myself that I wanted this, no, needed this. Mitch was gone. He'd abandoned me and left me in a worse place than the one he'd found me. He was probably regretting ever taking me out of that hole in the ground right now as much as I was resenting him for coming for me in the first place. Still, he had, and now I had to find a way to move on with the existence I had.

Lifting Scott's shirt over his head, I traced the scars on his skin. Lifting his face to the ceiling, Scott cursed. Taking a breath, he threaded his hand in my hair and forced my mouth back to his. Heat suffused my body, adding to the warmth from all the alcohol I'd consumed.

Picking me up, Scott carried me easily upstairs to his bed. Raking my nails up his back, I loved how he moaned for me. I hadn't lied to Moses. Sex stopped being just sex with Mitch. What I did with Scott wasn't sex. After my life had fucked me over so often, it was my turn to be the one fucking.

IN THE EARLY MORNING, I left Scott's bed, dressed, and made my way out to the lookout. Tears fell down my cheeks as I approached the railing. I'd never come this far out on the deck before, scared the temptation would be too great. Today, there was no resisting.

Not that I was here to kill myself, I didn't believe in suicide. No, I came here to see the beauty of the world when it was so bleak within me. I didn't believe in god or sins or redemption. I didn't believe in heaven and hell. But, at times, I stood there, letting the silence surround me, and I found a moment of peace and forgiveness in my soul for the life I lived.

Today, the forgiveness wasn't there, and I didn't expect it to be either. My heart was broken. As I looked at the beauty of the rising sun burning off the fog, I knew the peace this place used to offer me would never happen again.

"Lyza," Scott called behind me. Wrapping his arms around me, Scott signed from behind, so I could see his words while he restrained me. *"You never chose the easy way out before. Don't do it now."* Holding me to him, he rubbed his nose behind my ear. *"Please, I promise I'll protect you, and this will all work out."*

Mitch had promised me the same thing; look where that had left me.

"Please?" Scott begged as he turned me to face him. "Don't make sex with me your breaking point. If it was that bad, we never have to do it again."

Meeting his eyes, I knew he was just saying that to make me laugh or feel bad, but I couldn't feel anything beyond the heartache. Pointing to his side first, I put the tip of my fingers to my heart then shook my hand, fingers still glued shut. *"It hurts. Every breath hurts."*

Scott's eyes changed from panic to sympathy. Pulling me into his arms, Scott held me while I stood there, accepting this pain in my chest as a permanent fixture. Turning his head to a noise, Scott lifted me into his arms and carried me away. Over his shoulder, I caught sight of Kit standing watching, his face full of sympathy too.

It was all around Chapter by lunch. I'd tried to jump, and Scott stopped me. No one seemed to know we slept together, but everyone knew that I'd finally admitted I was married. Lawfully married to someone suspected of being the enemy. Because, as it turns out, for the last three months, Scott had been investigating Mitch again. Now, they firmly believed that while Mitch wasn't connected to the shadow company, he was the go-to man for the shadow company when it needed to outsource.

It's incredible what you hear curled up in someone else's bed when everyone around you thinks you are deaf.

43

REVELATIONS

It was the helicopter that woke me mid-afternoon. It was different from the sound of Jonathan's copter. Lifting my head, the din of the chaos downstairs filled the room. Scott and two others were in the house talking in disgusted tones.

Moving to the window, I watched as Emily, Moses, and two other Hunters climbed out of a different helicopter. Saying something to Emily, Moses walked towards my house. Emily and the others rushed towards Scott's.

"The Hunters just arrived. We'll coordinate emergency responses with the other chapters and report on our status hourly," Scott explained to someone.

The door opened. "Scott, any more news?"

"It's still filtering in, but currently, all are presumed dead," Scott answered. "Kit and Zane are sorting through the images being sent in. It is believed the attack took place shortly after midnight."

"What has Chamber said?" Emily asked.

"It wasn't an expected move. We are waiting for the list of men registered as visiting the compound to find out if there was anyone they took or wanted dead specifically," Scott confided. "I'm wondering if it was personal."

"Because of yesterday?" Emily murmured. "We take his woman; he takes ours?" Emily considered.

"Where's Lyza," Moses stormed into the house.

There was a moment's silence. "Upstairs."

"Why is she in your house?" Moses growled.

"Suicide watch. She tried to jump from the lookout this morning."

"Jesus, let me talk to her," Moses cursed.

"Protocol doesn't allow for interfering if someone decides to check out," Emily chastised.

"Do you want to tell Mitchell Fairchild his wife topped herself because we forced his hand," Scott grumbled. "Jesus, go look at the images of what last night cost us already. Fairchild is on the warpath now. He needed Henry Ryan to make his play, but we took that away. He's going to find another way, and he's going to make us pay."

"You are reading too much into this," Emily worried. "This may not have been Fairchild. It could have been the shadow company."

"We have that list," Kit called.

There was a knock at the bedroom door before Moses came in. Shutting the door, Moses took three steps to cross the room and turned me to face him. *"We need to talk,"* he signed hurriedly. I just glared at him. *"They knew you were leaving. I didn't know a Hunter had been sent until two days ago. They knew you went to see him in Rome; they've known every time you've seen him since."*

Making a gun with my fingers, I put it to the bottom of my chin and flicked my index finger forward before turning back to the window. At this point, I had zero fucks to give.

Moses forced me to face him. *"I get that last night ripped you apart, but they knew you were leaving. I don't know how, but they knew you were going, and they were going to kill you if you tried. Mitch did what he did to save you."*

Gritting my teeth, I shoved Moses away. *"He didn't save me! He condemned me!"* I signed angrily. *"I've told them we are married. You know what they will do. I had to give them an answer by midnight or a reason why I couldn't take a new husband. So, I did."*

Watching my gestures, Moses stepped back as his face fell. "Jesus, Lyza. *What the hell did he say to you?"*

With fingers splayed, I crossed my hands and lifted them as I pulled them apart. *"Too much. Not enough."*

His forehead creasing, Moses studied me. *"Whatever it was, it's what he needed to say to get you to react how they needed you to,"* Moses tried to reassure. *"The Hunter was there in the lounge with you, watching and waiting. If you tried to leave with Mitch, he was ordered to kill you. If you tried to leave by yourself, he would have followed and killed you. The only way to keep you alive was to leave you, so that's what he did. It's not what he wanted."*

Meeting Moses's eyes, I glared at his persistence. Jabbing my finger into my chest, I put the gun to my chin and flicked it out harshly to punctuate my response clearly. *"I. Don't. Care."* Shoving Moses out of the way, I stormed out angry because I lied. I cared too much. That was the problem. I'd been raised not to, and I wasn't sure how to suppress this now that it was eating away at my insides. No one warned me those butterflies you feel falling in love turn into flesh-eating beetles when love breaks your heart.

Rushing down the stairs, I whimpered when Scott caught me and got in my way. "Where are you going?"

Holding my palm facing him, I lifted it as if driving it over the hill and down. My rage was going to tear me apart. I needed to go home and wash him from me, rinse away the night and scrub everything from my body.

"No. I'm caught up and can't keep an eye on you." Face softening, Scott caressed my cheek. *"Just stay here for now."*

"I need a shower and to change," I argued.

"I'll watch her," Moses jumped in from behind me. "I'll keep her breathing."

Gritting his teeth, Scott met my eyes. *"Come straight back,"* he ordered. Stepping out of my way, he stepped into Moses's. "Keep your hands off her. Don't take advantage of her vulnerable state."

"What, like you did? I saw the bed. I know what you did."

Scott didn't smile, didn't gloat. "You don't know shit. Do you think she'd be alive right now if I let her go home last night? Not everyone here looks at her and thinks with their dick. She was in pain; I gave her something to hurt."

"Next time, take her hunting," Moses growled. Shoving past Scott, he grabbed my hand and led the way outside.

Once we were down the stairs, I pulled free of his grasp and turned to face him. Rubbing my thumb across the slope of my breast, I pointed to Moses and then the ground as I lifted my shoulders in question.

Moses huffed. *"Work, sadly, but it worked well because Mitch wanted to know you were okay."*

Clenching my jaw, I shook my head, unable to believe Mitch gave a shit after those messages last night. *"Why are you so buddy-buddy with him? Why are you betraying the Arrow telling me I was a target? Why?"*

Watching my hands speeding through my questions, Moses pursed his lips and looked away. Shaking my head, I stormed back to my house. The pain was like a second heartbeat inside me. Energizing me, driving me forward. Following me, Moses caught my door before it could slam in his face. "Lyza," he grabbed my arm. Turning, I disengaged his grasp before punching him in the face. "Shit!" Moses fell away from the impact.

Advancing on Moses, I jabbed at his side as the raw hurt came out in my gestures. *"He left me there for hours worrying he was dead. He let me slowly fall apart, and if what you say is true, they watched the entire thing happen. Weakness and love, in a Scythe? They'll never accept that. Then he sent me those messages. You say he loves me; then why didn't he send someone to take them out? Why didn't he come for me?"*

Moses looked down at his toes. Slowly, he lifted his eyes. *"Are you loyal to the Arrow or Mitch?"*

Making a circle with my thumb and index, I swept it from my chest and out before putting my pincered thumb and finger to my lips and taking it away like I was pulling something from my lips. *"Don't ask me that!"* Dismissing his question, I walked into my bedroom, pulling out clothes.

The truth is, I wasn't sure where my loyalty lay since the moment Mitch took me from prison. I loved Mitch, and I wanted to be loyal to him, but then last night ripped that apart too. I was starting to doubt loyalty existed.

When I moved to go into the shower, Moses was in the way. *"Henry Ryan worked for the shadow company. He was the accountant. Mitch needed him for the names of those in Chamber who are corrupt. For those who tried to silence him five years ago. Noel was sent in by those same people to ensure Mitch couldn't exchange that information. Now, he has to go to more extreme levels to get what he needs, and he's doing it all for you. Mitch just wiped out an entire compound to get a name. Now, he's going after that name and will put them before Chamber as a witness. When he does that, they'll give you to him!"*

Frowning, I wasn't sure if I heard him right.

"Mitch knew at least two members of Chamber who were not corrupt," Moses revealed. *"He approached them months ago with a deal. He gives them the evidence they need to find their traitors, and they give him you and leave you alone. He's been doing this all for you."*

Shaking my head, I brushed my thumb down the top of my breast. *"Why didn't he tell me that?"*

Moses just met my eyes. Those flesh-eating bugs gnawed along my spine. Trust. Mitch wasn't sure he could trust me. Stepping forward, Moses took my shoulders in his hands. Sympathy smothering his features, but I didn't want it. Shrugging out of his grasp, I stepped back angrily.

"What's it like to be a traitor and still trusted by everyone?" I asked, my hands harsh and sharp. *"Because I have always been loyal and never been trusted."* Tripping him as I shoved forward, I forced a surprised Moses not only to fall but to do it out of my path. Storming into the shower, I slammed and locked the door.

Rage burned inside of me. Trust. It all came down to trust, and there was none. It took starting to wash myself a third time to realize the dirty feeling couldn't be fixed with soap and water. As soon as I let that thought hit me, it grew and bloomed into resentment. Not towards Mitch like I first suspected, but the Sword and Arrow. Towards Chamber for forcing me to come back. I was never going to fit back into this life after being out. They should have known that.

Squeaky clean physically, I dressed and stepped out to the lounge room. Moses sat there with an ice pack to the back of his head. Making myself something to eat, I made Moses something too, and we sat eating quietly together. Afterward, I cleaned up and checked his head—just a bump, nothing more.

"They're going to regret their next move," Moses murmured while I was behind him. "Selling him Noel's company gave him more men, already trained, and extra resources here in Europe with inside information about us. Giving him that company gave him leverage inside their home base. Debbie was a fool arranging that sale. She never gave Mitch credit for how smart he is and hoped it would deviate his interest from you."

Standing up, Moses turned to face me. *"The Sword Corporation isn't the shadow company everyone's been looking for. The shadow company was never an external thing, not until Mitch was paid very well by the Arrow for the information that he went to provide his father. Mitch started his company after he realized he'd been betrayed by that same prime shadow company."*

Biting my lip, I stared at Moses. *"When I saved him?"*

"He told me for the five years he looked for you, that he called you his angel of death," Moses agreed with a sigh. *"Up until Noel died, there were three shadow companies to the Arrow. Each with their own agenda, but only ever the first was damaging or threatening the Arrow. Then, they took you from the man who loves you. They sold him the second company making his reach further than the prime, and they targeted you. Mitch isn't taking down the Sword and Arrow, Lyza. He's taking down the prime shadow company. He's taking down his mother."*

44

GIRL TALK, GUY TALK

The coffee machine cut off, and I removed the cup and turned to put it on the table for Moses. Touching his chin and then moving his hand forward, Moses took it. Going to the lounge room, I watched out the window. Scott's place was a hive of activity. In the last hour, reps from the Intelligence and the Guardian Chapter had arrived. While I still didn't know what happened, I found I didn't care much either. A vibration sounded behind me, and in the reflection of the glass pane, Moses removed a phone from his pocket.

"Hey. I'm at Chapter, so they'll pick up this signal in under a minute." Moses took a deep breath. "She's not good. Whatever you said to her last night broke her. She tried to kill herself this morning." Moses shook his head. "No, she tried to throw herself off the lookout, so not physically hurt, just heartbroken. I told her, but I'm not sure it made a difference. I have to hang up." Moses waited another second. "I'll try, but she's on suicide watch, and they've activated threat status. We'll be holed up here until they action a plan." Hanging up the phone, Moses turned it off.

After washing up his coffee cup, Moses came over to me. *"We should see what's happening,"* he signed.

"You go. I'm not interested."

Watching my hands, Moses sighed. *"I'm not stupid enough to leave you alone,"* he huffed, taking my elbow. "Come on," he said as he tugged me forward. Knocking his hand off me, I stormed out. "Jesus. H. Christ!" Moses swore behind me. Picking up my pace, I jogged across the gardens to the running track.

"Hey, let her go," Maria warned behind me.

"She can't go off alone."

"She's going to run it off; it's how she's always coped," Maria argued. "It's run or kill. Everyone here knows that. Do you really think you can take her on, especially while her mortality means very little to her?"

Glancing over my shoulder as I hit the track, Maria stood defiantly in Moses' way. Facing forward, I focused on the snow-covered trail and started running. There would be no time limits, no set laps. I would run until I couldn't and work all this anger and hurt out.

For hours, I ran; until my legs gave out, and I fell in the snow. It was then that someone crunched across the ground to reach me, a hand coming in front of my face. Peering up to see Maria looking down at me with sympathy, I took her hand to stand. "I'll make you a coffee," she offered.

Following her back to her house, I could barely walk. The boys were playing in the gardens, practicing their fighting. When Maria held the door offering for me to come inside, I stepped in and took the chair at the kitchen table she indicated. She made us coffee and sat down opposite me.

"You've been good to my boys. You've taught them, and in doing so, you've taught me how to be a mother in this life. Thank you." Watching her lips, I gave a slight bow of my head. "I don't know what happened yesterday, why Scott let you leave, and why you returned with Scott like you did."

She looked out the window to the helicopter pad. "I see everyone come and go. I know, whatever happened yesterday was the end for you. I could see that in your eyes as you got off that helicopter." Maria shook her head. "If you broke the rules, they would have killed you, so I'm bewildered about what went down."

Sitting back, she rubbed her tummy. "It's not been easy, staying here, raising my children without their father. I'm angry that he's gone all the time. I'm angry that he comes back long enough for a roll in the sheets, and then he's gone again for another month. We are meant to be partners. That is what we are taught from the moment we lie in their beds. Whether we fall in love, we are partners till death, and I believed that. Then he reached level ten, and he left. I felt betrayed."

Sitting watching her, I sipped my coffee. Maria lifted her eyes to mine. "I couldn't imagine what it would be like, to be betrayed by him the way Noel betrayed you. To spend years in prison, tortured and," she looked away. She swallowed something hard.

"When you came back, and Scott explained to everyone that your first job had been to kill Noel, it triggered something inside of me. Everyone else was suspicious of you because you so obviously didn't want to be here, but I understood. This life is sheltered and protected. You can't take someone out of here for years, expose them to the elements, have them kill the one person they were taught would be their rock, and not expect them to chafe at coming home. They should have let you go."

Her head turned to the gardens and the twins running around. "I'm grateful you did come home, and I will owe you one favor for the better way of life you've given my boys." Maria returned to drinking her coffee for a few minutes. "We should spend some downtime together. Go shopping in town together, catch a movie, go to the spa. Do something normal women do as friends. Would you like that?"

"I've never had a friend."

Watching my hands, Maria looked confused. She grabbed a notepad and handed it to me. "I'm going to need to learn your language, I think," she decided. "I'll find a program and start learning tonight. I'm good at languages. I score better than you do in that, at least."

It made me smile. She winked. We finished our coffees, my short replies to her conversation on the notepad. I'd never had a friend other than Wenda, and we were more like soldiers who fought a war together than friendship. We'd protected each other, depended on each other, but we'd never been close personally. It sounded like an excellent idea to have a friend who understood me. It cleared a little of the darkness from my soul.

Maria was the more kick-ass version of Stacey in my mind. She'd never been mean to me; we'd just never really talked either. She was close to five years older than me, closer to Noel's age. As night came, Kit called and told Maria we were all needed in the hall. It was time to find out the action plan.

"We need three teams," Scott informed. "We have three possible targets. We need to find them and secure them."

"Secure?" Zane asked, surprised.

"Secure," Scott repeated. "They are members of the Arrow, being targeted by one of the shadow companies. We need to ensure they are safe. Two Scythes will be teamed with a Hunter and a Guardian. The Guardians will be in charge of protecting the targets, and the Hunter will liaise between teams and secure the area. We are there to deal with any threat."

Scott broke everyone up into pairs. The only two not given a target were Maria and me. The rest were told to check the job file on their computers, and Jonathan would take them all to Geneva in one hour. The other groups were conferring amongst themselves and getting ready to depart.

Scott waited until they all left, then came to Maria and me. "Maria, with your condition, you'll be staying here with your boys. I'll need you to take the point of contact from our people."

"Where will you be?" Maria frowned.

"There is a fourth target. Emily and I agreed that we didn't know who we can trust currently. Lyza and I are going to secure the fourth target. We should be back by morning. If you don't hear from me by sunrise, you'll take over here as Chapter Mother."

Maria looked shocked. "But I'm not the eldest."

"No, but you have filled in for me, and we've worked closely, so you'll have a better chance of picking it up after me," Scott decided. "Besides, it will keep you here, give your children security in knowing their mother will be there for them." Maria blinked, unsure what to think. "Go get yourself set up." He waited for her to leave, then turned to me and started signing. "Get your gear and meet me at my place. You'll need something elegant."

Nodding, I jogged back to my house. My legs were tired from the run, but I'd been trained to keep reserve energy. Grabbing my stuff together, I chose an elegant evening dress, jewelry, and other accessories. Once I had everything I needed, I walked over to Scott's.

"Luther Hancock is our target," Scott informed me when I was inside. "Do you remember him?" Luther had been a friend of my father's. "He is in London for a meeting with some political figures. You are going to walk into that gathering and convince Luther to leave with you. I will meet you in meeting room two, where I will advise him of the threat and ask him to accept Guardian protection."

Pointing to my chest, I lifted my shoulders and arms out to the side before touching just below my eye. *"I don't understand. Why are Scythes going in to hand him off to Guardians?"*

"Because I am sure this will be the target," Scott informed me.

"Why?"

"Because the order from Chamber was to delete if he can't be secured. That is why I have been sent instead of Guardians." Scott walked up to his room to keep packing. I followed him up the stairs, the bed still evidence of the night before. Guilt churned in my stomach when Scott stopped to remake it. "I'm taking you because Luther knows you. I remember you taught him sign language for a few months, so he could interact with some important official."

Luther was of the Guardian Chapter and needed to learn sign language for a job he would be sent to. Some of our Guardians did long-term jobs guarding essential world figures. They worked on a six-month roster. When Luther was tagged to defend a deaf Australian political leader, he'd spent four weeks straight with me learning Auslan, then one week a month for the next few months getting advanced lessons.

"Luther developed a soft spot for you during the training. He used to bring you presents and treats if I remember correctly. Your father worried he was a little too fond of you." When I cringed at the idea, Scott nodded. "So, I need you to bring Luther out to me because if he sees any other Scythe walk in to meet him, he'll disappear. The added bonus is that you both speak a language that no other at that event will likely speak."

Checking his watch, Scott went to his window to watch the other teams head to the helicopter. "Once everyone has departed, we'll head off."

When he turned back to face me, I asked the vital question. *"What if Mitch turns up?"*

Considering me for a moment, Scott looked at the bed and exhaled. A slight twist of the knife of guilt right there. "I'll trust you to protect your partner like you were trained. Whatever you need to do to get the job done. I won't judge you."

He was trusting me to do my job. If that meant pretending to be on Mitch's side to do it, he expected it and would permit it. "I'm not going to question your loyalty," Scott continued. "I think right now, it would be asking too much for you to have loyalty to anyone but your own survival. But if you make sure we both get out of there alive, I'll make sure you get out of here alive."

Stepping in his way, I lifted my index and middle fingers, pressed together palm facing him, and quickly touched the index to the side of my cheek before it bounced away, spreading all my fingers open. It looked like I was telling him the number five, but I asked him to clarify that statement.

"You shouldn't have been cleared to return to us," Scott explained. "You are good, but you don't belong here anymore. If we get through this, I will do my best to convince Chamber that you should be reassigned."

"Reassigned, how?" I refused to move. I wanted to know if that was basically a termination order.

"Some members who spend long periods out there struggle to return. It's rare, but if they are worth keeping, we reassign them to still work for us as assets."

Watching his hands, I tilted my head. *"Spies?"*

"Asset. You get to live a good life with occasional check-ins to pass on information that could be useful to us. It's the best offer you could get. Take it." Scott moved off to keep packing. Shocked, I stared at his bed. I'd be free of here, but would it be somewhere I'd want to be?

45

COLLISION 2

The party was well attended and equally well guarded, but slipping into these sorts of things had been a regular practice since I was sixteen. Scott and I just acted like we belonged, and no one even asked for our name. Once inside, Scott and I separated. He went to the bar to keep watch while I went to find Luther.

When Scott said Luther was a friend of my father's, he didn't mean they were buddies or in the sense of what a civilian would consider a friend. They'd grown up in the same chapter, and when they were fourteen, they both tested out to different branches. They'd kept a loose contact, that's all. Chamber had recommended Luther to me for training.

Spotting someone in a tux against the wall who looked familiar, I narrowed my eyes on his earpiece. Following his line of sight, I found Luther talking to some political figures. Scott explained Luther spent too long out on a job years ago and had become an asset for Arrow now. Embedded as a critical figure with a significant influence on political parties, Luther now lived a very good life.

Instead of approaching Luther, I grabbed a drink from a passing waiter and observed all the others in the room. Spotting Mitch across the other side, I cursed under my breath, the pain of his abandonment scorching my insides. Breathing through the hurt, I let it flame to anger as I took out my phone and messaged Scott.

Enemy already on site. If I approach the target directly, it could cause an issue. Will bring target to me instead.

Pressing send, I put my phone away and observed Scott at the bar. Reading the message, he lifted his eyes to me, nodded once, and then started scanning the room. Doing the same, I spotted Andre in the room. The Italian noticed me and lifted his glass at me. Smiling, I made my way towards him, taking me close to Luther.

Spying me, Luther hesitated, his eyes widening slightly. Acknowledging him with a gentle smile, I continued on to Andre, who was stepping away from the people he talked to. Luther followed my movement with his eyes. "Lyza," Andre greeted, pulling me in to kiss my cheeks. "Beautiful as ever. Are you here with your husband?"

Shaking my head, I held up my hand to show it was ring-free. Andre's eyes smiled. "Oh, I'm sorry to hear that." When I lifted a brow in doubt, Andre laughed. "Okay, maybe I'm not. Still, Fairchild is here tonight." Andre pointed out where Mitch was talking to someone.

Mitch's eyes came straight to mine. No surprise, just suspicion. It left me no doubt he'd either already seen me or been told by someone else I was present. Turning my smile back to Andre, I shrugged, not affected by Mitch's presence. Grinning, Andre stepped closer. "We could find a room?"

Raising a brow, I tried not to laugh. Rolling his eyes, Andre stepped back. "Okay, that was rude to not even ask you out to dinner first." He was just about to ask when Luther stepped in beside us.

"Excuse me," Luther waited until I made eye contact and smiled. "Lyza, you've grown up beautifully." He kissed both my cheeks. Stepping back, I handed off my drink to Andre, so I had both hands and closed my fists, leaving only my pinkie fingers out. With knuckles facing Luther, I tapped the sides of my pinkie fingers together.

"What did she say?" Andre frowned.

Luther's brows furrowed a little, but his smile didn't waver. "She greeted me as her uncle," he answered Andre. Calling him uncle informed him I was on the job. When I let my eyes drift to Andre with a smile, Luther smirked.

Turning my body to ensure Mitch couldn't see what I signed next, I kept my movements confined. *"There is an enemy team here to take you. A man has been sent by Chamber to escort you safely from the premises. I was asked to tell you he will be waiting for you in meeting room two. If you try to leave alone, you will be taken and most likely killed."*

Luther was well-practiced in keeping a smile when he was being told something bad. *"And this man, he's not a Scythe?"* Luther signed, giving a real laugh like I was telling him something funny.

"He is. He is my Father and loyal to the Arrow. He came here with me and will ensure you leave safely."

"Then, I look forward to meeting him."

"I've got something to do before I meet up with you two. Wait until I leave to go."

Luther gave me a great smile. Touching his index and middle fingers beneath his eyes, Luther moved them towards me. "Of course," he signed and talked, allowing for Andre's benefit. "My love to your mother, in case you see her before I do." I kept the smile, but I heard the threat. Luther's eyes roamed the room. *"There is a silent contract out with your name on it. If anyone encounters you while on a job, they are to take you out or call the relevant people to take you out. I made the call before I walked over here. I give you this warning as a favor returned."* He kissed my cheeks, then stepped back to watch my eyes.

"Chamber?" I signed, surprised they would allow that.

Raising a brow, Luther licked his lips. *"A select member issued it to select trusted associates. I grieve that it's come to this. I had hoped you would join us."* Looking truly disappointed, he moved off into the crowd, already finding a new person to talk to.

"You're related to Luther Hancock?" Andre asked. Nodding, I took my phone out and messaged Scott that Luther would meet him, and to be aware, this was a trap for me, and Luther was shadow company. "So, did you want to leave? Grab something to eat?" Andre moved a step closer.

Putting my phone away, I smiled, fluttering my lashes. "Not tonight, Andre," Mitch's voice cut in as his hand grabbed my elbow.

"Mitch, I heard you were divorced."

"Separated. Excuse me, I'd like a word with my wife." Before Andre or I could protest, Mitch moved me away from the main party and down the hall. "What are you doing here?"

Glancing around to make sure we were alone, I tried to barely use my lips. "My job."

Shoving a door open, Mitch hauled me inside. "Who's your job?"

"It doesn't matter! It was a trap for me," I huffed. "I'm not going to make it out of here alive."

Mitch frowned. "Did Hancock tell you that?" When I nodded, Mitch exhaled rough. "Well, he would know. Hancock is my mother's second in command. He makes the deals on the outside." Letting me go, Mitch pulled out his phone. "Fred, get Jones to check the perimeter. There is another team on site. It might be a sniper or several, so get men to check anywhere a sniper could make a good nest." Mitch waited, his eyes watching me as I leaned against a desk and steadied myself. Pulling my phone out, I messaged Scott, passing the info of who Hancock was. "No, they're here for Lyza. She's walked into a trap set for her."

The trap didn't bother me because I wasn't afraid to die; I just didn't want Debbie to win. Disconnecting the call, Mitch touched my cheek tenderly. "I'll make sure you get out alive," Mitch promised.

Gritting my teeth, I lifted my eyes to his. "You promised you would meet me. You didn't."

"They would have killed you."

"No, they wouldn't have. My Father came down the mountain with another to protect me," I revealed. "If I'd tried to leave, they would have taken out the assassin your mother sent but still stopped me going."

Mitch tilted his head in consideration. "The only way to stop you from leaving with me would have been to kill me." When I blinked up at him, Mitch laughed. "I see. Your Father was hoping to eliminate the competition. Did he tell you this before or after you slept with him?"

Meeting his eyes, I wasn't going to be shamed for what happened last night. "On the way here. I didn't give a shit about anything but you breaking your promise last night to care whether he was there to kill you or me. I was so excited about being there with you that it didn't even click the other female leaving with me was sent to keep an eye on me until the helicopter could go back for the others."

Gritting his teeth, Mitch took my face in his hands. "I would never have broken my promise if I knew I could keep it. It was a trap for both of us. There was a mole in my inner circle who leaked the plan. I spent the time I should have been meeting you, finding the mole."

Lifting my eyes to his, I smirked. "Stacey."

"How did you know?" Mitch blinked.

Tilting my head, I stepped away from him. "I didn't until it clicked why Moses was pursuing her long term. You had him seduce her. You've suspected she was a mole for months."

"Since my mother turned up at my place and took you away within minutes of you making it back. When you pulled up, Fred messaged Stacey and told her we were all safe. Mum showed up not long after that. So, I encouraged Moses to get to know her better."

"But Moses is a traitor. They would know."

Lifting his brows, Mitch looked at his shoes. "No, Moses' main job is to identify shadow company moles in the Arrow and eliminate them, one by one. We had a mutual enemy. We've joined forces for a short time to achieve the same goal. Which is why he made a play for you. None of them want you leaving the Arrow, Lyza."

My phone vibrated in my clutch. Frowning, I took it out to see that Scott was calling. Turning to face Mitch so that he couldn't see the screen, I answered, lifting it to be on camera. Pointing to me, Scott held his left palm like a clipboard and ticked his palm. "You're right; he's a traitor. We need to get out. There is a team on its way to take you out."

Watching his warning, I held my palm out to the side and shook it. *"Where is Luther?"*

"I still have him, but I've recorded a full confession from him. It's video, so it can't be refuted. I just need to figure out who to trust to give it to."

"Moses," I signed out the letters of his name. *"He's been tasked with that job specifically."*

Lifting a brow, Scott pressed a few buttons on the screen before continuing. "I've sent it. Is that why you two were always finding time alone?" When I didn't answer, Scott huffed. "Okay. We'll head to Chamber straight from here. Hurry it up. We need to go-" Scott was cut off as Fred and a team of men stepped into the room and pointed guns at him.

"Get down on your knees and throw the phone over here," Fred ordered. "Got them. Hancock is beaten but alive."

Lifting my eyes to Mitch, I found him observing me as he slipped his phone away. Gritting my teeth on him crossing me, I hung up. "Let my Father go."

"He would have killed me, Lyza," Mitch replied calmly. "He sees me as competition. I can't see him letting me walk out of here tonight with you. Can you?"

"He's the only one I trust in all of this mess. I need him alive, so I'll be leaving with him." Miffed as I already was at Mitch, I stormed towards the door.

Mitch blocked my way. "You're coming home with me." He made a grab for me, I countered, he hindered it and tried to grab me again. Blocking, I threw a punch, twisting into him, ducking beneath his reaching arm, and spinning up to face him as I lifted my knee to his crown jewels.

Mitch was a brilliant fighter. We were probably on par with each other, but groins were usually a line most guys wouldn't cross unless they got desperate. I was female. Balls were my starting point against a male of equal skill when I needed the fight over fast. Mitch cringed enough for me to get past him but recovered before I reached the door.

When he grabbed me from behind, I ducked and dodged before he could get a good grasp. Falling back into my training, I pretended it was testing time. I wasn't willing to do permanent harm to Mitch, so I needed my mind to see this as testing rather than survival. Mitch, for his part, didn't throw one punch. All his moves were to get a hold of me and restrain me.

We were dancing, but without me acceding the lead. We moved into and around each other, blocking, grabbing, countering, spinning, and turning as he tried to get a hold of me, and I constantly escaped. Whoever said fighting couldn't be graceful had never fought someone they loved who was their enemy.

We both had stamina, and we could be doing this all night at the rate we were going. The problem was, I was running out of time to escape the noose Debbie was tightening. The next time Mitch grabbed for me, I spun out, then back into him and threw both hands into his solar plexus with everything I had. Having gotten used to me avoiding trying to hurt him, it surprised Mitch, and that's all I needed.

As he stumbled back, I used a round house to put him down. "I'm sorry," I apologized as he crashed to the floor. "I can't leave with you now. I've realized we will never win this, and I can't keep hoping only to be let down by you again. I need to accept my life for what it is." Blinking away tears, I moved for the door.

"I'm sorry too," Mitch groaned. "I refuse to give you up." My left arm went numb, and ice-cold started creeping up my neck. Freezing on the spot, I whimpered, knowing what came next. A second later, Mitch was on me, shoving me up against the wall. "I meant every word of my wedding vows, Lyza. Till death, and I'll be damned if I let my mother take you from me again."

Yanking my arms behind my back, Mitch zip-tied them faster than I could comprehend what happened. I wasn't down, and my nerves weren't burning a forest fire through my neural pathways; I was conscious. "How? You gave me the antitoxin."

Mitch turned me to face him. "We took out the toxin; we never removed the Nanos. Admittedly, they have probably deteriorated without the toxin to protect them from your immune system, but they are still there."

My eyes wet with tears, I blinked at him. "Mitch, don't do this. I have to get Scott out of here alive."

Caressing my cheek, Mitch rubbed our noses together, lips mere millimeters from mine. "Sorry, Lyza. I'm protecting you and my own interests."

When Mitch's phone rang, he pulled it out, answering it. "All taken care of? Okay, I'll meet you there in a moment. Yeah, she took a bit of convincing, but she's coming with us." Mitch smirked. "Yes, I had to use zip ties." Hanging up, Mitch grabbed my elbow and opened the door, walking us out.

46

———————————

LOVING ENEMIES

WITH MY BICEP IN HIS CONTROL AS MITCH WALKED US OUT OF THE room, I turned left, but Mitch pulled me around to the right. "You know that way takes us out to the party, Lyza. Let's go the back way. Less likely to draw attention to us," Mitch tsked. "I guess that answers my question about whether you give up yet."

Gritting my teeth, I didn't answer. We were out in the open, so I wasn't risking anyone finding out I could hear or talk. Through the door into the fire stairs, we went up a level. Tracking our location via the blueprints I'd studied on the way here, I knew where we were in orientation to outside, and I was locating escape points as we went.

Coming to the meeting room Scott had secured to meet with Luther, I smiled. We already had an emergency escape plan for this room. Even if I couldn't make it out of here, I'd make sure Scott did. Mitch knocked out morse code on the door. Then the door opened from the inside. Men I didn't know, but some with faces I recognized, surrounded Scott and Luther with their guns.

Watching a video on Scott's phone, Fred turned to Mitch and handed it to him. "The assassin got a full confession about his role in the

387

shadow company and who his boss is," Fred explained. "Do we still need him?"

"Let's take him with us just in case," Mitch decided. "Send that to a burner and then forward it to your phone and mine as well as Moses'."

"I've already sent it to my brother," Scott announced in accented English. His eyes flicked to me. "If you want Lyza to live through the night, she needs to leave with me now."

"That's not going to happen. I'm taking my wife home with me. I have what Chamber asked of me. Once I hand it over, they'll let her leave."

"You are gullible if you believe for a second that they will let you walk off with her," Scott huffed. "If she meant so little to the Arrow, she'd be dead already. She would never have made it back to Chapter alive. Debbie knew if she killed Lyza herself, it would infuriate the other Chamber members; that's the only reason Lyza is still breathing as it is. You should never have let her get in that car with your mother."

"How was I to know Debbie would hate her so much?" Mitch debated. "Lyza told me she had to go back. Moses told me it would go worse for us if she didn't, they were pointing guns at the woman I loved, so I let her go. Now, I know better, and I'm taking my wife back."

Bowing his head as he shook it, Scott exhaled. He knew there was no point arguing with Mitch. "You'll get her killed." Sitting back on his ankles, Scott lifted his hand to scratch his left eyebrow as if he was disinterested.

"Why isn't he secured?" Mitch growled.

"We couldn't get near him long enough," Fred grumbled. "We decided just to shoot him if he moved again. How do you want to go about this?"

Scott turned his attention to me. "I'm sorry, Lyza. I tried to get you through this." He pronounced it slow so I could read his lips. Mitch was speaking low with Fred, making plans for getting out of here.

Bowing my head, I looked to the window as I did. My eyes came back to Scott, and I blinked five times. He folded his hands in his lap and closed his eyes.

Luther started laughing. "Jesus, Debbie did herself a disservice, not bringing this girl in." Shaking his head, Luther lifted his face to ensure I could see his lips. "I told her you were too good to waste. Her jealousy and hate for your father wouldn't let her see clearly. Make it quick, for the sake of the friendship we formed?"

When I gave him a short nod, Mitch turned to look at me. Suspicion in his eyes. Turning me, he checked the zip ties still held me. Satisfied my hands were secure, he turned back to Fred. "Let's get out of here. Have the cars come around to the staff entry."

Mitch's phone started ringing. Checking the identity, he started moving to the door. "Get it organized. I'll meet you in the car." Opening the door, Mitch answered the call as he stepped outside. "Is she taken care of?" The door closed.

Fred exhaled, taking me in. "She's going to be the difficult one. I'll need four of you on her going down." Focusing my eyes back on Scott, I exhaled dynamically and released the fists my hands were in. It instantly made the ties looser. I couldn't get out of them, but I could move them.

"But she's his wife," one of the guards argued.

"Yes, which means he is the only one here she won't kill. The rest of us are expendable if it means she gets her job done," Fred warned. "You four will take her. You two are on the double agent."

"What about the assassin?" Another asked.

"He's not coming with us," Fred answered evenly. "Shoot him."

The guard beside me clicked off his safety and pointed it at Scott. Shifting my weight, I shoulder barged him as he pulled the trigger. The shot went wide and cracked the window, weakening it. Pivoting into the guard, I head-butted him as I counted in my head. Swinging straight out as the guard recoiled, I bent over double. My arms went down behind my legs, my hands touched the floor, and I pushed my weight into them as I let my bum drop and fall to the floor. Bending my knees up to my chest as I landed at the guard's feet, I pulled my hands in front of me. Everyone was moving as I lifted my arms—the guard above me raising his gun to try and shoot Scott.

"No, Lyza," Fred called as he rushed forward. Grabbing the guard's wrist above me, I jolted his arm right as he pulled the trigger. The bullet went straight into Luther's left eye, and he fell back dead. I wasn't aiming for there, but it achieved the goal.

"Fuck!" Fred rushed in as I rolled back onto my shoulders, lifted into a shoulder stand, and kicked the guard in the face. Fred tackled my body to the floor before I could get the gun. A loud smash sounded, and everyone turned to see the window smashed, and Scott was gone. "Double fuck! Shoot him!"

Exhaling, I fought against Fred. He was trained but not near the capability of Mitch. In two moves, I had him on his back, my thighs straddling his waist, his gun in my hand as I trained it on the team member rushing towards the window. "Stand down!" Fred yelled.

The soldier heading to the window stopped and turned to see my finger twitching near the trigger. His eyes went wide as he backed up away from the window. Everyone in the room was still, eyes flicking over my shoulder and back to me. All their weapons were trained on me. Releasing the trigger, I clicked the safety on and slowly placed the gun down. Waiting until everyone else released the breaths they were holding, I rolled over my toes to press up into standing, then stepped aside, so I wasn't standing over Fred.

Getting up, Fred stepped directly in front of me. His eyes were angry, sad, a mixture of everything. "Are you done?" I nodded. "You will come quietly now?" I nodded again. Glancing at Luther's body, Fred shook his head. "Why? You could have been together."

"They will never truly let me go," I whispered. Sadness filled my chest, and a tear tracked down my cheek. "I've accepted that. I needed my Father on my side."

Caressing my face, Fred put his forehead to mine. "I warned you this would happen if you didn't get out." Watching his hand go into his jacket, I caught a glimpse of the stun gun, and then he tased me. Whimpering as the current cycled through my body, I dropped. Cutting my ties, Fred lifted me in a fireman hold. "Let's go. Clean this up," Fred ordered. Most of the team came with us as we headed out into the hall. Using the fire stairs, Fred carried me down to the waiting cars.

"What happened?" Mitch asked when we came out.

"Your wife can cause chaos with her hands tied behind her back. Her Father got away, and she took the target out. Once she knew the assassin was free, she surrendered," Fred explained. "I tasered her just to ensure no more issues before we got to the car."

"Damn it, Lyza! Get her in the car. Let's go. Moses took care of our problem at home for us. He got the confession and is going to meet us to take us to Chamber for the exchange. It won't work without Luther."

"Surely, the confession is enough?" Fred argued as I was placed in the car.

"I'll call Moses once we are at the airport and figure out what we can do," Mitch grumbled. "Tell the team to catch up once they've cleaned up." Sliding into the seat beside me, Mitch strapped the seat belt on. His thumb brushed my lips. "Why couldn't you trust me?"

"You promised you'd come," I whispered, still incapacitated from the shock. "You didn't."

Closing his eyes, Mitch bowed his head. "I was trying to keep you alive. Everything I have done has been about keeping you alive and bringing you home to me." His eyes opened and glared. "Why couldn't you work with me just this once?"

"You are the enemy. I can't be seen as cooperating with the man who has been hunting my brothers and sisters. Even if I love him." Licking my lips, I took a deep breath, feeling the effects of the electric shock wearing off. My muscles released, and I could move slowly. "I love you, but as far as the Arrow is concerned, we are at war. Life is unfair like that."

Mitch withdrew to his side of the car. "Well, you're with me now. Time to stop thinking of me as the enemy and start remembering I'm your husband."

A single tear fell down my cheek. Unlatching my seat belt, I cuddled into him, resting my ear against his heart. "I couldn't let you kill him. I'm sorry that messed with your plans." Arms wrapping around me, Mitch held me tight. Kissing the top of my head, Mitch exhaled hard.

"It's been a long six months. Trying to run my company, taking over the Sword Corporation, trying to get you back. I'm exhausted, Lyza. I miss you every day. Just say you'll come home. Stop fighting me. Trust me to protect you."

Lifting my face to his, I let him see the tears in my eyes. He wasn't the only one bone-weary by everything we'd been through. I wanted nothing more than to trust him, but it wasn't about trusting him. I wouldn't feel safe until the threat was dealt with, and I couldn't do that on the outside.

Caressing my neck, Mitch slowly moved our faces together. Our lips connected, my breath rushed out, my heart started beating frantically. Why couldn't it be simple? Why did we have to fight to be together?

As Mitch deepened the kiss, I lifted my leg over his thighs and straddled him. The driver muttered something, and Fred chuckled and told him to get used to it. It was all background noise to the beating of my heart as Mitch kissed and caressed me. His hands slid up my thighs, pushing my dress up with them. I gasped when his finger shifted the gusset of my knickers aside and slid between my slick lips. Worked up as I was, Mitch's hardness pressing against me told me he wanted me just as badly. Releasing his need from the confines of his pants, I lifted myself over him. Gazing out the back window, I noticed the car following in the distance had come closer. Closing my eyes, I lowered myself.

I bit my lip as Mitch stretched me open. His hands were on my hips, pressing me down until he was buried as deep as he could get. Our mouths worked each other with the same frenzy as my hips rocked over him. It only took a few minutes, pent up as we both were. Biting his shoulder as my body quaked with my feelings for him, I shattered myself upon his stubborn will. Groaning, Mitch thrust up one last time.

Coming down, I clung to him as we panted into each other's ears. The car behind us was nearly tailgating us now. Lifting my hips to release Mitch, I move my knickers back where they belong. Mitch tucked himself away while we kissed slowly, passionately.

"Do you think it's trouble?" the driver asked Fred about the car behind us. "I thought it was the team to start with, but they are still a few kilometers behind."

Fred looked around. "Could be. Be ready."

Pulling out of the kiss, I met Mitch's eyes. "I love you. I've never stopped loving you. I just need to do this my way."

The driver of the car behind lent out the window and pointed the gun. Mitch met my eyes, his full of worry. Giving him one last kiss, I cuddled into him, holding on tight. "I promise I'll find my way home to you."

Two loud bangs sounded in quick succession: the gun, then the tire. The car turned at a sharp angle and stopped abruptly when it hit something hard. Mitch's seatbelt kept him in his seat. My grip on him kept me there with him, but all of us were dazed by the impact. The car behind us braked hard further up, then reversed. Pushing open the door, I fell out onto the gravel shoulder of the road.

"Lyza," Mitch wheezed. The impact of our bodies together had winded us both.

Getting my feet under me as Scott threw the passenger door to his car open, I fell in, still struggling to breathe. The door closed with force when Scott hit the accelerator. Holding my chest, I tried to breathe through the pain of the impact, or was it the separation?

"Let's get to Chamber and save your life," Scott declared as we sped through the streets. "You, okay?"

"I'll live," I gritted my teeth on the pain as I signed. *"For now."*

47

CHAMBER

"YOU NEED MEDICAL ATTENTION," SCOTT GESTURED WITHOUT WORDS after we were airborne.

"It's just a rib. I'll make it to Chamber," I signed.

"Not if it pierces your lung, you won't. It will be a competition to see if you'll bleed out, or the pressurized cabin will suffocate you first."

Cringing, I tentatively touched the injury. It was the first rib and close to the sternum, my fingers feeling over the bump. Taping my right fist on top of my left, I had my hands explode open then pretended to snap something in front of me. Holding my fists facing each other, I pulled them apart a few inches then had them snap back together like magnets pulling them but connecting with the levels out of alignment. This didn't feel like a fracture, but it didn't feel like it was sitting where it should be either.

Moving my hands aside, Scott assessed the lump. "You might be right." Lowering his hands, he felt around my right side, causing me to wince. "And this one?"

Thumb to my chin with the first two fingers up and last two tucked, I snapped all of them into a fist as my hand moved to the left quickly, then shook my hand as if it had pins and needles in front of my right ribs. *"Fucking hurts, but not as much as when I cracked it."* Noticing the male steward looking our way, I lowered my hands to keep signing. My formal dress in business class had already garnered attention. *"It makes breathing a bitch, so maybe it's out as well."*

Noticing the steward's interest as well, Scott clenched his jaw as he signed. *"As soon as we get to Chamber, you see the doctor."*

"No, we go before the others together. Once Debbie is shackled and branded a traitor, then I will go to the medic."

Scott watched my hands with a scowl. *"Thank you for not making me drag you out of that car."*

Watching his hands, I kept mine firmly in my lap. Scott settled back in his seat. "Chamber won't give you up. Your bloodline is just part of it. You are one of the best they've ever had. They are fascinated by you. They won't sacrifice you either."

Arcing my finger as if indicating a group of people, I nicked the side of my neck with my finger and pointed to my chest, my hand gestures showing my annoyance.

Lifting his right hand, Scott closed index and middle fingers on his extended thumb like a duckbill as he shook his head. Taking a deep breath, he tucked his thumb and little finger to lay his three fingers across his left palm as he proceeded to sign Mitch's name.

My heart rate increased. Cupping my right hand over the palm of my left as if something precious was inside, I moved it back close to me, lifting my shoulders in question. Debbie protected Mitch.

Exhaling, Scott knocked his right hand twice in the air to affirm what I'd asked. Drawing a reverse C in the air, he gestured to me, placed his hands up in front of him as if creating an overlapping gate, and extended his right hand away from the left to indicate more. To finish,

Scott cuffed his right hand over his left palm and moved it back towards him.

Blinking at what he just revealed, I swallowed hard. Chamber wanted us both alive, and Debbie was protecting Mitch, but the rest of Chamber considered me more precious. They would kill Mitch if they were forced to choose. Unable to hold back my curiosity, I signed out the city name of Geneva. Scott had already told me he came down the mountain to protect me and kill Mitch if I tried to leave with him, but I didn't realize the order came from Chamber.

Pressing his lips together in consideration, Scott's hand came to my face, his thumb brushing across my mouth. "I know you love him, but no matter how this plays out, they will never let him take you from them," Scott enunciated, so I could read his lips. "Everything I've done was to protect you, Lyza. I've protected you from Debbie. I've protected your heart by making sure Fairchild was warned yesterday was a trap for you both, and I've protected you from yourself." Stroking his thumb down my throat, Scott frowned and sat back.

Biting my lip, I held my hands up in question, eyes itching, my brain and heart confused by his breaking protocol to save Mitch.

Taking the hand closest to him, Scott kissed my bruised knuckles before placing them back on my lap. "Because I was in love once, and your father took her from me." Laying his seat back, Scott closed his eyes. "That sort of heartache can break or make a Scythe. Get some rest."

Turning my head, I looked out at the darkness surrounding us. The hostesses hated the curtains open at night. I don't know why. The best thing about flying was this view of the never-ending darkness and the stars. Slowly, my eyelids drooped and closed, sleep stealing me to Mitch's arms.

CHAMBER WAS A HIVE OF ACTIVITY. Typically, the country estate not far from Oslo was relatively quiet. Today, cars were present to show occupation, and the helicopter just taking off told me the members had already flown in. As our car pulled up out the front, I spotted a few familiar faces waiting outside. Turning in my seat, I signed Mitch's name to Scott and jutted my head towards his men.

Ducking his head to observe the men who had been with Mitch in England, Scott nodded his head and opened the door, giving me his hand to help me out. Wincing from the pain in my chest, I declined the help.

Mitch's men watched us approach, and one typed on his phone as we passed. No doubt, he was letting his boss know we were here. Scott knocked, and the chief guard opened the door. He appraised us as he always had and opened the door, letting us in. Once the door shut behind us, Scott addressed him. "I gather Fairchild beat us here?"

"He's inside with his man and the Hunter Moses," the guard informed.

"Are all members present?" Scott checked.

"Debbie Fairchild has not arrived yet," the guard lowered his voice.

This made Scott frown. "She lives here."

"She took off late last night with her guard. I've received word she boarded her helicopter twenty minutes ago. She should be another thirty minutes, at least."

Turning his head, Scott assessed me. I was watching their mouths as they talked. "Lyza is injured and needs medical attention."

Stepping towards Scott, I shook my head. Jabbing my chest, I pointed at Scott and slid my hand forward and down to the ground.

"You'll go where I tell you to go," Scott gestured back. When I met his eyes defiantly, Scott didn't flinch or look away. After ten seconds, he quirked a brow. Exhaling, I looked at his lips. It was as close to submission as he was going to get from me today. Scott moved his attention to the guard. "I'll take Lyza in with me to start, so if the others have questions, they can ask them, then she will need the medic, so have him ready."

"I'll wake him up," the guard assured.

Taking my left elbow, Scott marched us down the hall to the meeting room. There was a guard at this door who looked us over before opening the door. Stepping into the grand dining room, the talk inside came to a stop. All eyes fell on us. Ignoring the four Chamber members present, my eyes found Mitch and Fred standing beside Moses at the petitioners' side of the table. There were chairs for them, but they weren't sitting. Mitch looked annoyed, but his eyes were full of relief as they watched me enter. Fred had a black eye, but they both seemed relatively unharmed from the car accident.

Automatically, I moved a step towards Mitch. Scott's hand caught my elbow, halting me, causing Mitch's eyes to drop immediately to Scott's grip on me. Using gentle pressure, Scott guided me away from Mitch and to the table to address the Chamber members.

"Father Scythe, Daughter Scythe, we've been expecting you," Marlyn Jones, the Grandfather of Scythe, greeted. He just so happened to be my grandfather by blood. My mother's father. Not that he ever acknowledged that relation; that's not how the Arrow worked.

"We apologize for our tardiness," Scott returned with a bow of his head. "Unlike some others, we don't have the benefit of a private jet to get us places faster. I trust the son of Hunter has shown you the confession I managed to extract from Luther Hancock?"

"He has," Anne Montrose, the Grandmother of Guardian, informed. "We were just discussing the video and whether that satisfies the agreement we made with Mr. Fairchild." Anne looked me over. "Lyza's breathing is shallow. Is she injured?"

"She is," Scott affirmed. "I thought it best she is here to answer your questions first before seeking medical attention."

"I have no concerns about the girl," Anne dismissed.

"Did she come with you willingly?" Marlyn queried.

"Yes. Lyza put her life at risk to help me escape. When I enabled her to do the same, she didn't hesitate to leave her husband to come with me."

"We don't need Lyza for this," Pierre Stoker, Grandfather of Cyber, announced in his thick French accent. "Let her see to her injuries."

"I have a question for her," Rupert Edda, Grandfather of Hunters and probably the scariest of all the Chamber members, declared. His eyes met mine, then he lifted his hands and started signing. He gestured to me, placed his hands on opposite shoulders, hugging himself, then pointed to Mitch.

Beside me, Scott tensed. Lifting my right hand, I knocked the air twice.

"You understand you betray all we've taught you by marrying a civilian?" Rupert signed.

"That doesn't make it wrong," I gestured as passionately as my ribs allowed. *"Mitch was born one of us. Marked or not, he is better than most of the other candidates available as a husband. He loves me. Look what he has done to ensure my return to him. Noel betrayed the Arrow and left me for dead. The man you chose for me betrayed all of us."*

All the members watched our exchange. Considering me a moment longer, Rupert then turned those studious eyes on Mitch. "She can go."

"Grandfather-" Moses stepped forward, ready to argue.

"To the medic," Rupert clarified while he signed for me to go see to my injuries. Bowing stiffly, I clutched my ribs where they ached and readied to leave, but Mitch held up his hand and told me to wait.

"We had an agreement. I've upheld my end of the bargain," Mitch declared, his annoyance like static in the room. "I want Lyza to leave with me now."

"You didn't gather the evidence; Father Scythe did," Marlyn dismissed.

"I would have brought Luther Hancock to you alive for questioning. Your people killed him, so I couldn't."

Rupert considered me, but his question was for Scott. "Why did you kill him when orders were to secure our assets?"

"My orders were to secure unless the enemy got to them first, in which case we must eliminate the asset," Scott defended.

The other four looked at each other surprised. "I remember signing no such order," Anne debated.

Pulling out his phone, Scott brought up screenshots of his job file. "We noticed anomalies in orders given and received a few months ago, even variations in what a parent receives and the agent. Brother Hunter can attest to this; he noticed the issue first in jobs sent to Lyza."

The grandparents looked to Moses. "What Father Scythe says is correct. I witnessed Lyza did not receive all the information needed for a job, endangering her mission and her life," Moses affirmed.

"Lyza and I then went over all her jobs since her return to Chapter and discovered most were missing vital information that had led to injuries," Scott continued. "The dossier sent to Lyza was not the same as the ones sent to me."

"I have a copy of all these varied dossiers that Lyza passed onto me for safekeeping," Moses confirmed.

"Why did she trust you with this information?" Anne queried.

"I am her friend. She trusts me. She was sure Chamber was trying to kill her and provided me with the evidence to pass onto my mother, which I did," Moses justified.

"I confirm that Mother Hunter raised this with me," Rupert revealed. "I discussed it with Pierre, and we decided it was best to sit on that information temporarily."

"Why?" Marlyn critiqued. "It was important."

"Because it indicated a Chamber member was involved, directly or indirectly," Pierre argued. "Until we had more proof as to the involvement, we couldn't take steps to deal with it."

The room was quiet as the grandparents pondered what they heard. I held no disillusionment that they were all thinking of the same name. Marlyn shook his head. "It changes nothing. Lyza stays with us."

Breaking away from the others, Mitch took three long strides to meet me by the door. Capturing my face in his hands, he kissed me intensely. Gripping his shoulders, my body held stiff, I kissed him back just as earnestly. Too soon, I had to pull away because I couldn't breathe. "This is your last chance. Leave with me, now. Defy them and walk out with me," Mitch whispered to the ear they couldn't see as he held me. "Please?"

My eyes stung with the pain of refusing his plea, but I hadn't forgotten my broken heart two nights ago, and now I couldn't leave until I'd finished this. My life, his life, would never be safe otherwise. Giving him one last kiss on the lips, I stepped back. Swallowing hard, Mitch watched me take another step. Pointing to my chest, I held up my index finger on my left hand and chopped the air in front of it with my right hand. I had always been loyal. I would remain so - to the Arrow and to my heart.

Sucking in a deep breath, Mitch dropped his face. "Don't. Don't do this."

With my spine straight, feet sure, and heart hoping I could make this work, I walked out the door.

The doors shut behind me with a thud. Blinking back the tears threatening to escape, I lifted my eyes to find the first guard Scott spoke to, watching me. "Sister. The doctor is waiting."

48

———————

TRAITOR

"BREATHE IN."

Looking through my eyebrows, I glared at the doctor and his stethoscope.

"I need to hear your lungs, Lyza," he justified.

Reading his lips, I gritted mine and inhaled. Pain lanced my side, causing me to exhale in a rush and crumple in on myself.

"Lungs are fine. I'll need an X-ray."

Making the duckbill sign, I quickly followed by putting my thumb to my chin, index, and middle fingers pointing straight up, then I promptly flicked my fingers to the left and made a fist.

The doctor frowned. "Don't give me attitude, Lyza. There are steps to an examination."

I gave him the finger, the middle one, to be exact.

The doctor's jaw clenched. "I'll get the X-ray ready. Change into a gown and come into the X-ray room." Taking my file, he walked out.

Easing myself off the examination table, I dropped my dress to the floor and slowly donned the medical gown, wrapping the ties around to tie it at the front. My body was well and truly stiff now, all the aches and pains of the night making me limp slightly. I walked straight over to the wall X-ray unit in the imaging room, having done this twice already this year.

"Is there any chance you could be pregnant?"

Holding my hand up, I swayed it back and forth. I had no doubt I wasn't, but I wasn't going to admit that to anyone here. The doctor decided to play it safe and wrapped a protective vest around my abdomen. Once the X-rays were done, I went back out to the examination room and lay down on the bed to rest.

As I was just on the verge of falling asleep, I heard the door get yanked open. My eyelids fell back, so I was staring at the ceiling. Shadows made me turn my head and observe Debbie Fairchild storming towards me, her assistant staying by the door.

With care, I sat up to face the oncoming squall of motherly anger. "Sign these," Debbie demanded, flinging a set of documents onto the bed next to me. "This farce is over. You will divorce my son and choose a fellow Scythe to be your breeding partner."

Frowning, I pick up the divorce papers. Already completely filled in, so that all I had to do is sign them. A pen appeared in front of my face. Taking it, I kept reading. Debbie started tapping her foot. Taking my time, I made her wait while I read the entire document, and then, I put the papers beside me, shaking my head once.

Debbie's eyes sharpen on me. "He doesn't love you, Lyza. You are sacrificing everything for him, but he's given nothing to be with you." Producing her phone, she presses play on the screen.

"The deal would enable you to be with Lyza D'Aviv," a male voice offered Mitch, who sat facing the camera. "You do the testing, you become an Arrow, and you can be together."

Putting my thumb to my ear lobe, I sweep my fingers to the top of my ear, then lift my shoulders in question.

Debbie glowers at me. "You don't need to hear. Read Mitchell's lips."

Returning my eyes to the screen, I watch the man I love reject me just like he told me he had. "No, I have no interest in being a slave. I'm a free man, and nothing you can offer me would be worth sacrificing my free will."

My eyes itching, I automatically take a deep breath to control my emotions but immediately regret that decision. Covering the right side of my ribs, I cringe.

Pocketing her phone, Debbie assessed my injury. "You were badly hurt tonight. Did you run into trouble on your mission?"

Watching her lips, I lifted my gaze to her eyes. The woman was a brilliant liar. I could almost have believed she didn't know anything about Luther calling in a team to take me out. Almost. There was just a little too much glee in her concerned features.

When I failed to answer, Debbie exhaled in annoyance. "Luther said you were too good to waste. Maybe we can come to an agreement." Picking up the forms, Debbie held them out to me again, waiting until my eyes returned to her lips. "Sign the forms, end your relationship with my son for good, and I'll transfer you to the Guardian Chapter."

It wasn't even tempting. Nothing that involved staying with the Arrow without Mitch in my life would be. Tilting my head to assess Debbie, I held my hands up in question. "Why do you hate me so much?"

Forehead creasing, Debbie grimaced as she watched my hands, utter confusion showing in her eyes. Snatching the documents from her hand, I flipped them over and wrote my question on the back.

When I held it up for her to read, Debbie scoffed. "I hated your father, I detested your mother, and you have shown enough of their character for me to feel much the same towards you."

Again, I held up my hands in question.

"Because unrequited love becomes bitter and resentful with time. Your father used me. He took me to bed with false promises when I was young and gullible and fell for his charm. Then he became Father, and he married me off to Lazar D'Avive. He walked me into the room, kissed me on the lips, and told Lazar I was his. I got no say in it, and Lazar hurt me. He forced me to his bed, forced his child inside of me, and I hated them all." Spittle hung from Debbie's bottom lip, her eyes fierce with indignation. Noel was the product of rape. That's why Debbie had left her one-year-old son to the mercy of the Scythe and never looked back.

Glaring through me, Debbie stepped closer. "I loathe your mother because she didn't fall for your father; she hated him, and he had to have her because of it. She hated him, so he married her, and you are just like her. You look like her, you are skilled like her, and you never loved your husband, just like her." Debbie's lips pulled back over her teeth as she seethed, exposing her gums, breathing her hate fire on me. "You can tell your pretty lies all you like. You killed one of my sons already, and I don't believe you are capable of love any more than your toxic parents were." She stepped back, eyes watching me, waiting for a reaction.

Taking a shallow breath, I turned the paper and started writing. Then I held it up for her.

Frowning, Debbie started reading aloud. "He did the same to me. Put me in a room with your son and waited outside, listening while Noel raped me. I am not the sadist my father was, and I'm not my mother either. I'm better than she ever was, which is why I am still here breathing despite your efforts to kill me. It's why I'm going to walk out of here tonight and return to the man I love while you are punished as the traitor everyone now knows you to be."

Pausing, Debbie lifted her eyes to me, assessing, scrutinizing me thoroughly, trying to determine if I was bluffing. Picking up my phone, I opened the message from Scott and pressed play. Debbie's eyes widened as the video confession from Luther played, her name clear, her role in the shadow company lucid, and how it could be proven unmistakably defined.

The color drained from Debbie's face, her eyes flitting around the room, looking for safety. Luther revealed Debbie not only killed her first husband Lazar but was the person to tell my father about the meeting with Mitch and that he should stop it from happening, effectively killing her second husband and both her sons.

Putting my phone back on the bed, I lifted a brow. Turning her watery eyes from me, Debbie walked to her assistant and started whispering to him. I couldn't tell if her sorrow was because she loved Mitchell's dad or that she was finally revealed for the callous traitor that she was.

Eyeing the doctor's cupboard beside the bed, I opened it quietly, removing one of the disposable scalpels he kept handy for emergency situations. Pursing my lips to prevent whimpering as the movement of straightening up stabbed my right side.

"Okay, Lyza, I have your results," the doctor walked back in as I palmed the scalpel and removed the blade protector with my thumb and index finger. "Debbie, what are you doing here?"

"Just checking on the patient, Jarod," Debbie excused, bringing her attention back to me. "Any major damage?"

"Two ribs not sitting where they should be; the rest is just bad bruising," the doctor explained, his face to me, so I could read his lips. "I'll help put those back, and then we'll do a blood test to check on that pregnancy."

With all the color draining from her face, Debbie became white as a ghost. "Pregnancy?"

"Yes, Lyza said there is a chance she could be pregnant. Don't look so surprised, Debbie. You're the one who wanted the implant removed." The doctor turned back to me. "When did you last have sex, Lyza?"

Resisting smiling, I wrote across the top of the divorce papers.

"I was with my husband only five hours ago in London," Jarod read aloud. "Well, then, it's definitely too soon to know. We'll do the test anyway." The phone rang. Glancing sideways, Jarod went to his desk to answer it.

Moving towards me, face pale, eyes dark and angry, Debbie peered at me through narrowed eyes, her hate for me like lasers burning into me.

"Yes, she's here," Jarod answered into the phone, then his eyes widened. Opening his desk drawer, he started to pull out a gun. A loud bang filled the room, and the doctor cried out as he fell to the floor. Debbie didn't bat an eyelid, her focus entirely on me while her assistant clicked the safety back on his gun and put it back in his jacket.

Stopping in front of me, Debbie revealed the gun she was hiding behind her back. "I was going to have others do this for me, but it seems my cover is blown, so there is no point trying to be subtle in dealing with you anymore." She started to raise the gun.

My leg snapped out to impact the inside of her knee, a loud pop filling the room before Debbie screamed. My hand had already grabbed the wrist of the hand that held the gun. Forcing it wide, my other hand drove the scalpel into her jugular. Debbie blinked.

Yanking the scalpel free, I stepped into her and turned us, my hand sliding forward on her wrist to grab the gun. I was quick, the assistant still pulling his weapon free as I squeezed the trigger, and his brains exploded out the back of his head. Stepping forward, I turned back to face my enemy. Her eyes were wide, pupils dilated in fear, hands clutching her neck, trying to prevent the blood from escaping, but it oozed through her fingers like red slime.

Putting the gun to her head, I pressed it against that point right between her eyes. "I warned you I was better than my parents," I declared verbally. Debbie's eyes widened impossibly further. "I survived my father torturing me, so you never stood a chance. I think that's why you hated my parents. You knew even as you gave yourself to him that you were never good enough. That's why you gave in."

"If you shoot me, they'll kill you for it," Debbie threatened.

"A quick death is for decent people." Dropping the gun away, I jabbed the scalpel into the other side of her neck. "You've never been decent."

Mouth and eyes opening wide, Debbie lifted her other hand to try and hold that wound. It didn't matter; she had minutes left. "You'll be dead not long after me," she choked. "You'll never have him." She crumpled to the floor, eyes blinking rapidly, breath gasping, blood leaking away her life.

Moving to the doctor's desk, I placed the gun and scalpel on top as I squatted down to check on him. He was alive but unconscious, the bullet going through his shoulder. Really, it wasn't even a deadly hit. It was the wound on his head that worried me; he'd knocked himself unconscious as he fell.

The door burst open, Chamber guards filling the room, guns pointed at me, and the corpses on the floor. Meeting the captain's eyes, I placed my fingers into the open palm of my left hand and moved it towards him as one.

"Get help," the captain ordered and came to my side to help the doctor. "Looks like none of us are getting any sleep tonight."

He was right. The doctor was rushed to the hospital, Debbie and her assistant were packed into body bags, and I was questioned repeatedly about everything that happened. Sunrise came and went; lunchtime passed by with no food or water. Sunset came, and so did Scott and the first bit of food I'd seen in thirty hours. I ate while he signed.

"*Chamber believe you*. The evidence supports your story. Coupled with Luther's confession, you won't be held accountable. Once you've eaten, get dressed, and you'll be taken to the airport and flown home. I'll stay behind and sit in on the discussion about your future in the Arrow." Scott squatted to be eye level with me. "*I'll do what I can to get you reclassified.*"

Pausing eating, I watched Scott, breath shallow. Reclassified could mean anything, something unknown or worse than a Scythe. Sighing, Scott caressed my cheek tenderly. "You've proven your loyalty, Lyza. I'll be your champion." Standing up, he placed my bag with my casual clothes on the table. "I'll see you back at Chapter and tell you the outcome." Pursing his lips, Scott walked out.

My gut told me to trust him. But four other people were calling the shots, and I wasn't sure I would trust any of them. After finishing my food, I followed Scott's orders. The captain drove me to the airport to catch my flight back to Geneva.

"Here," he handed me a note when the car stopped in the drop-off bay. "Your husband asked me to give you this. I read it. It didn't seem dangerous, so I figured I should give it to you."

While he watched, I unfolded the note.

> *I'm tired.*
> *When I didn't come to Geneva, I failed you. I realize that was your*
> *turning point. When I broke my promise, I lost your trust. But you*
> *stood there knowing everything I'd done to bring you back to me, and*
> *you chose them, so I won't go to war for you anymore.*
> *I'm letting you go.*
> *Know that I still love you, and I would change the day I let you leave*
> *if I could. You made me a promise that day. Just like you did in*
> *Geneva, I'll wait as long as I can for you to keep it.*

Be better than me. Don't break my heart.
Your husband, now and forever.
Mitch

Folding the note, eyes itching and filling, I looked away for a moment. When I got my emotions under control, I looked back at the captain.

"Was I wrong?" he asked.

Shaking my head, I sighed and lifted my hands to sign. *"Love shouldn't be this hard."*

The guard assessed me. "You've survived your father's brutal upbringing, being betrayed by your husband, left for dead, tortured, and imprisoned. You can endure this."

"Can I?"

Pressing his lips together, he shrugged one shoulder. Accepting that answer, I stepped out of the car. I would wait to hear what Chamber decided. Their decision would dictate how I moved from here. I was tired and sore, my ribs still out of place since the doctor was rushed away before he could fix it. So, for now, I focused on just getting home to my bed. The rest could wait.

49

A VIOLENT HOMECOMING

As I walked inside the heliport terminal, I couldn't stop yawning. On the flight to Geneva, I'd slept and then dozed in the taxi to the heliport. At the locker, I unloaded my phone from the mission. Closing the door, I locked it before my eyes and hands automatically traveled to my personal cabinet. On autopilot, I opened it without expectation. I froze when my other shoe, the one Mitch hadn't returned, stared back at me.

Hands trembling, I reached out and took the shoe in my hand. He'd told me he was keeping it to make sure I came back to him. Now, I had the pair. Was that a message in itself? Checking the shoe to see if it held any other written note, I closed my locker and walked over to the waiting area.

The shoe was clean. Nothing. As the helicopter landed, I stood up and went to the door to wait, stifling another yawn. Once I was home, I was having a bath, taking painkillers, and sleeping for two days straight.

The chopper earthed. Pushing open the door, I waved at Jonathan as I approached. Giving a quick acknowledgment, Jonathan picked up his phone to read the screen as I climbed aboard and shut the door. "Just received a message from Father. He's just landing now. I'll take you up and come straight back for him."

Watching his lips, I gave him a nod as I strapped in. The helicopter lifted into the air, and up we went while I kept looking at the shoe. Was it goodbye? I tapped the heel on my palm to the beat of my concern.

Glancing to the side, Jonathan reached out and adjusted a dial. With a frown, he turned his face to me. "Did you forget to drop your phone off?" Frowning, I shook my head. Johnathan considered his instrument panel. "I'm getting interference in my comms."

Setting the shoe aside, I opened my bag to check there was nothing in it that shouldn't be. After a thorough search, my gear was clean. Johnathan looked over; I held my hands out and shrugged. "It's okay, it stopped. Maybe I flew through something."

As I packed my gear up again, my eyes flicked to the shoe, but I didn't touch it immediately. Waiting until just before approach, I picked it up and studied the heel. There were no apparent signs of tampering, but that meant nothing. Mitch left Chamber a full day ahead of me. If he had my shoe on him, it would have taken him five minutes to bug it. Or maybe he just put a GPS locator on it.

The helicopter landed, and my thoughts about the shoe ended. "What the hell is going on here?" Johnathan vocalized without intent.

Opening the door, I saw two of the Scythe brawling on the path—the other men standing around watching, shoving Kit if he came within reach. Kit and Zane were fighting. While it didn't surprise me, their animosity towards each other had always been evident, infighting was frowned upon.

Disembarking the helicopter, I waved to Johnathan. Giving me a chin up, he shook his head at the guys. "I'll go get Father. He can sort them out."

Staying in a crouch as I ran to the stairs for the helipad, I eyed the fight. None of them paid any attention to the chopper as it lifted into the air and headed back to the helipad.

Making my way to the path, I kept my eyes intent on where Zane, Bruce, Stig, and Neil kept Kit from getting back to his feet. Turning to my place, I found Blake blocking my way. "Zane, the bitch is here," he called, ensuring I could read his lips.

"Forget him," Zane stepped back from Kit. "He's not our job." They all stepped away.

Kit was on all fours, bloodied and tired, but he wasn't out entirely. Raising himself up, Kit locked his eyes with mine. Placing his left hand parallel to the ground, palm down, he thrust his right index finger underneath to pass beneath his palm quickly. "Run!" He yelled as he lunged at Stig, renewing his fight.

Stepping back, my eyes took in the closing circle of men. As I dropped my bag to the ground, Zane raised a brow. "Lyzebel, you should have played along. Picked a husband and left the boss's son alone. Now, we have to take out the only chance we had at getting some regular ass."

Steadying myself as they came closer, I changed the grip I had on my stiletto shoe. I'd passed level ten, but my results were never revealed to the Chapter, so in their minds, I was a five. All of them varied between five and eight, but Zane was a level nine. To stand a chance, I needed to take him out fast and efficiently.

Stopping out of arms reach, Zane slithered his eyes over me. "We don't have to fight. You get on your knees and suck my dick, and I'll make the end quick. I promise." Zane's smile was growing as I stood there, watching them come closer.

No matter what, I wasn't getting out of here alive. That much, I could read in his eyes. My choice was quick and painless or getting beaten to death. Either way, I was pretty sure my night would end going over the railing of the lookout, and since Kit was a witness, he more than likely was going to join me.

With a shrug, I dropped to one knee. Zane's eyebrows lifted into his hairline. "Seriously?" He asked, astounded I'd take that option. Moving closer, he watched me acutely now. Keeping my face blank, I blinked slowly.

"She's fucking with you," Neil warned. Ignoring Neil, my eyes were all for Zane.

Smiling, Zane laughed. "Do I care? She'll be dead, and then I can skull fuck her if I want." He lowered his face towards me. "Open up, Lyza."

Smiling at his suggestion of orifices, I opened my mouth. Slowly. Zane stood fascinated with my lips as they slowly parted to reveal my tongue. Turning the heel in my hand, I cuffed the toe of the shoe with my fingers, getting a good grip. As my mouth opened, I licked my tongue around my lips, then punched my arm up hard and fast.

The shock registered on Zane's face as the stiletto of my heel went straight into his eyeball. Dropping back, Zane screamed, his buddies in shock as I pivoted on my knee and punched Neil in the gonads. While he crumpled, my body shifted into him, and my leg snapped out to hit Blake in the side of his knee cap.

My surroundings were men yelling as I turned to hit Bruce. He blocked and countered; I engaged, rolling over my toes to gain my feet as he came at me. Neil recovered and joined the fray, and then Blake and Stig were coming at me too. Keeping my eyes focused, I watched the shadows of moves rather than the people making them.

Blocking, I instantly fell into defensive as if it was our biannual training program. I flowed, spun, danced through the shadows, using their momentum to pull them in and by me, throwing them in the way of another, sliding around the perimeter of the penumbras. A dance of silhouettes in the darkness, the light of the helipad our sun, around which we gravitated.

The world narrowed to those shadows and the spaces of light in between—the safe places. Despite having my hearing, I'd spent six months without noise to protect me, and in that time, my father had ensured if I failed to block, I hurt. Sound became a nonexistent benefit, so light and shadows were my default programming when it was life and death. The murkiness was becoming sluggish, tiring of its assault, which was good because I was powered only by stubbornness, and even that was fading fast.

The shadows fell back, their panting heating the thin air. Hunching, I dragged as much of that air into my lungs as I could. I wouldn't give in. Between gasps, I heard it. A distant thumping of air broke through my focus—a helicopter. Father was coming, so I just had to hold them off long enough for backup. Driving forward, I pushed Bruce and Blake back as I tripped Neil into Stig, and I spun, moving towards Kit's injured form. He was conscious, nursing a busted knee which could bench him for some time, but Kit was conscious, and if I could take the fight to him, he'd pay these traitorous bastards with his rage.

When I was a mere meter from Kit, I blocked the others and turned my head a fraction to make sure I wouldn't trip on him. Bruce used that moment to do damage. Stepping into me, he swung his arms wide quickly. The present dissolved, Paris, twelve years ago, wrapped around me, constricted me in fear as my father swept his arms wide, cuffing the air before slapping his hands over my ears.

Air roared in my ears, pain exploding inside my ear-canals, vibrating through my skull, tears erupting from my eyes in an avalanche, a scream tearing from my throat. Agony tore me down, but before I could escape it, a balled hand impacted my throat just below my jaw. The cartilage collapsed, shutting off the scream, cutting off my air.

The ground rushed up to collide with me, the impact rolling me, the stars in the sky spinning. My father stepped over me, observing me. Shaking my head, I panicked that the monster was back, that he'd crawled out of the dark of my past to destroy me.

No! He can't be here.

My father's face and eyes being here collided with the memory of me shooting him. He couldn't be here because I killed the monster.

Paris dissolved, my present crushed back in as Bruce readied the final blow that would turn out the lights of my existence for good.

Mitch.

Moss green eyes swam through the shadows.

Mitch.

I'd made those eyes a promise, and no traitor was going to make me break it. Rolling to the side at the last minute, Bruce's fist impacted with the ground. Falling back in, I caught Bruce's arm and struck out, ears ringing loudly, all sound blocked by the loud buzzing alarm in my head. Moving into the periphery of the shadows, I struck hard— no more defense. No more waiting for help. Taking the hits, I breached the obscurity that surrounded me, and I made it bleed, ensured it felt my resilience, and I dominated that darkness of blinding rage suffocating me. I fought until it stopped.

The last shadow fell as I gripped his hair, yanked his head back, and thrust the heel of my palm into his nose. The nasal bone broke, shattered beneath my hand, and retreated into his brain. The body went limp. My insides were empty as Bruce slumped to the ground, eyes staring into the burning fires of hell.

A bright light blinded me. Falling back, I covered my eyes against the harsh spotlight of the helicopter, then pain embedded into the back of my neck. Knees hit the grass, my hands catching me hard. Tilting sideways, I rolled to my back, searching for that final danger. Zane stood, pointing a gun at me. A bloody cyclops of irrational hatred bearing down on me, a river cascading over my vision.

From beneath the ocean of pain bleeding out of my eyes, his lips moved. As he aimed the barrel of death between my eyes. A blood halo surrounded Zane's head, his body paralyzed, his one remaining eye contracting in surprise as his soul rushed free. The halo shattered, a fountain of blood and brains raining into the night.

Wheezing, breathing hard, and painfully, I turned my head. Maria stood pointing a gun where Zane was a moment ago. Our eyes met. Maria lowered her arm, tucking her weapon in the back of her pants. *"I told you I would owe you one,"* her lips revealed.

The pain burned through me, my lungs protested, I coughed, blood aspirating above me. Hands grabbed my shoulders. Scott yelling at me, then at Maria. Arms lifting me, Scott's mouth moving as he talked to someone, but I couldn't hear him or see his lips correctly as he placed me on the helicopter floor. Maria assisted Kit onto the bench seat at the back of the cabin. My eyelids dropped, shuttering off the world, sucking me into oblivion. There was chaos raining around me, but it didn't impact me. I was done, isolated from life and the consequences of this destruction.

There was a buzzer alarming in my skull; I wish someone would shut it off.

Mitch.

My eyelids opened, and bright light impaled me.

50

DÉJÀ VU

Light burned through my retinas. Water drowned my vision. When I squeezed my eyes shut, rivers cascaded over my cheeks. Silence. Absolute quiet. Déjà vu swept over me while misery, pain, and fear duked it out for pole position on my adrenaline response. When I tried to sit up, pain lanced my side, threw me back on the bed, and pinned me down.

Whimpering, my throat hurt enough to prevent me from trying to make any noise again. A second wave of déjà vu. I was fourteen waking up in the doctor's treatment room in Scythe Chapter, but I didn't remember my soul burning in agony like this before.

Gathering my strength, I dared to open my eyes again. A dam of pain opened, flooding my ears, pooling around my jaw. Pushing through, I blinked rapidly until the light wasn't painful. One torture down, the rest of my body to fix. Slowly, my pupils focused, though my vision swam and remained blurry around the edges.

Warmth encompassed my hand. The effort just to move my eyes almost depleting my reserves as I lifted them. Moss green eyes observed me, concern causing crow's feet to radiate out from the

420

sides. Mitch's usually smooth forehead buckled, the whites of his eyes were bloodshot, those kissable lips thin and grim in their set line.

When Mitch turned his head towards my feet, I moved only my eyes. A man stood holding my chart, talking. Soundless words falling. My vision was too unfocused for me to concentrate on the shapes his mouth and lips made. My pupils traveled around the hospital ward. All around me were curtained areas, nurses striding purposefully, and a machine beside me displaying lines and spikes in a steady rhythm.

All of it soundless. Someone took the volume of the world and pressed mute. Mitch's fingers were on my face wiping the cascade of pity away, turning my face slightly, so my eyes found him again. Lips moving, his eyes and posture determined. His words were too quick for me to catch, my brain not processing what I was seeing.

Raising my arm slowly because there were tubes attached to it and it ramped up the agony firing through my body like a constant electric current, I tapped my index and middle finger to my ear, then my lips. Mitch's brow furrowed, his pupils narrowing in deadly focus. Lifting his hand into the anarchy gesture, thumb out, Mitch tapped his index finger to his nose and folded it down, leaving just his thumb and pinkie out as he shrugged his shoulders.

Tears poured forward, the wave of emotion too much as I copied his gesture, then repeated mine. I was really deaf and mute all over again. Would it heal like it did twelve years ago? I couldn't be sure. I would know in a few days if it was even a possibility. Face falling, Mitch moved forward, careful when placing his hands around my face, his mouth moving towards mine. A breath between us, Mitch held back. He rubbed our noses, then lifted his lips to kiss my forehead.

Stepping back, Mitch moved his gaze to my neck, his Adam's apple bobbing. "I need… her with me…," he announced, ensuring I could see his lips move, but my brain only catching pieces. His head swung to the doctor; my eyes tracked to him.

The doctor was agitated, pointing to his neck, holding his thumb and index finger millimeters apart to indicate a small space or distance. The doctor shook his head and put my chart back on the bed as he kept talking to Mitch. Heaviness weighted my eyelids.

When I reopened them, Mitch was staring at the bottom of the bed. Following his gaze, the doctor was running something along the bottom of my bare foot. When I tensed, ready to be tickled, pain seared my nerves around my chest, but no tickle—nothing from my lower limbs. My eyes widened, realization clearing my brain, focusing my eyes. I tried to talk, nothing came out but pain and air. I knew that, but I couldn't be paralyzed; I had to feel my legs.

Placing his strong hands to my shoulders, holding me still, Mitch captured me in his gaze, moss green swimming in a sea of fear. He waited for me to calm, for my agony to encapsulate me, then Mitch removed his hands, picked up a button, and pressed it. A flood of relief shot through my system. Placing it aside, Mitch moved his hands to sign. *"It may not be permanent. The bullet to your neck caused swelling, but once it is healed, they will know more."* Mitch licked his lips. *"You need to be strong, but you need to rest and heal first."*

Raising my hand, I took his tentatively, squeezing it as I brought it to my mouth, and kissed his knuckle. Grimacing, I realized I'd busted my lip, and my jaw was swollen. Mitch gently stroked across my chin and removed his hand. His eyes were filling with pain by the second. *"You are still theirs."* Mitch exhaled hard. *"I came to take you home while they are distracted, and I thought..."* Mitch let it hang.

Mitch turned his face away, so my eyes went to the doctor. The doctor hung his head and politely ignored Mitch and me. When I squeezed Mitch's hand, he turned back, his emotions in check. *"If we move you, it could paralyze you permanently. You'll have to stay here. I'll come back as soon as it's safe and take you home. I'll know as soon as they let you move, and I will be here."*

Watching Mitch's hands, my stomach hollowed. When he finished, he took my left hand and kissed my knuckles. His head swung away as Fred rushed into the room, speaking urgently. My head became heavy, eyes unable to stay open. Shadows rushed to surround me, encasing me in darkness. I wept for the light. I cried for Mitch.

THE WINDOW'S view was of the countryside: the room, no longer the busy hospital, but a bedroom in the Chamber mansion. When I'd woken in the hospital next, it was to see Grandfather Marlyn, my real grandfather, standing over the doctor yelling. At the same time, an Arrow doctor disconnected me from the hospital equipment, changing me over to portable monitors. Two Arrows dressed as guards then proceeded to use a spinal board to move me onto a trolley and wheel me out of the hospital.

Mitch couldn't take me because he couldn't move me by road. The Arrow used an ambulance and transported me by road to the Chamber mansion in Norway. No one gave me an explanation. Marlyn Jones met my eyes for a moment, a flash of regret in the depths of his pupils, and then he'd walked out. My only contacts, the doctor and nurse who tended to me.

Within days, I'd lost track of time passing. Slipping in and out of consciousness and never knowing how long I'd been asleep for. To be honest, I lost interest. My world was pain, silence, and the view out of my window. No one tried to communicate with me, and no one came to see me. I was losing hope by the sunset. My mind kept turning to plans of how I could end myself, but then my thumb would brush over my ring finger and ease my soul. When I'd woken to find my wedding and engagement rings back on my finger, I had no doubt Mitch had put them there. That he was listening to everything said by the nurse and doctor by my bed.

Desperately, I wanted to talk to him, but my ability to communicate rested solely in my hands. After some time, when I could move my arm without exacerbating my injuries, I would tap out morse code on the bedhead.

I love you. I'll come home. I promise.

Rapped out at every sunset.

Eventually, they removed the tube draining blood from my lung due to a fractured rib that punctured my right lower lobe. I'd felt the pain that night, recognized my difficulty breathing, but been too focused on getting to see those moss green eyes again to let the pain stop me. A gunshot to the back of my neck eventually brought me down, but I'd fought tooth and nail to live. Or so the doctor told me when he finally listed my injuries and explained why I couldn't feel my feet.

The swelling around the bullet wound was putting pressure on the fractured vertebrae in my neck and compressing my spinal cord. He hoped the swelling would go down, and my ability to walk would return as the pressure released. He didn't look assured when he told me. My hearing or vocal cords weren't included in my injuries. The damage to my throat and airway was. In summary, it would be months of recovery.

Many more sunsets fell from my window before I tried sitting up, the torture of moving frustrating me, and I kicked my foot into the mattress. Stopping, I stared at my leg and disturbed bedsheets. Focusing on my foot, I wiggled my toes, a smile tugging at the side of my lips when the sheet moved. I could feel it.

While I wanted to lift my arms to the ceiling and scream my joy, the pain of my muscles tensing was enough to dissuade me from trying that. Focusing my mind, I tested the limits of my ability to use my legs. I could lift them a little and rotate my ankle, mind you, it was limited. My left hand went straight to the bedhead.

I can move my toes. I love you.

As soon as the nurse came in next, I pointed to my feet and showed her. Eyebrows high, she went to the phone, calling the doctor to come and see for himself. At this point, they started talking to me about physiotherapy. My brain was clear now; the IV of pain meds ceased, bringing everything back into sharp focus after another week. Everything started to come online.

Then, one morning I woke to white noise. No sound, but static was something. It was better than a buzzing alarm drilling through my skull. It was better than silence. It was hope. As the days went by, the white noise went from a whisper to a murmur, then to moderate volume over the next few weeks.

What I estimated to be six weeks after I first started counting days again, Scott came. He stepped into my room dressed in a suit and tie and waited by my door until I saw him, then made his way to the bed and took a seat by my feet. We looked at each other for a long moment, then Scott lifted his hands, signing without talking.

"Debbie sent the order before you killed her. We've just finished the investigation. Nearly every Scythe was on the shadow company's payroll. I wasn't permitted to come and see you until I had been cleared. Maria and Kit were also found innocent."

Scott took a deep breath. *"Kit tried to stop them, to warn you. Maria was busy on the phone hearing the report from Chamber about Debbie. By the time she hung up and realized what was happening, Zane was walking towards you with a gun. Maria opened my safe and came to help you. I got you to the hospital in Geneva and called Mitch. When Chamber found out he'd been there, they moved you here to stop him having a chance of taking you."*

Scott's eyes went to the wedding rings. His eyes dropped to his own hands, and he took a deep breath. *"I've been promoted to Chamber. Marlyn Jones is the new head of Chamber, I am the Grandfather of Scythe, and I'll be living here now. Maria is the Scythe Mother, but with only Kit remaining, Chamber has decided to change the situation."*

His shoulders straightening, Scott stood. *"It seems that Scythe was the heaviest involved in the shadow company out of all the chapters. While that makes sense, the Grandparents wonder if the isolation of our soldiers made them more susceptible. They are going to take time to deliberate. I will get to have a large say in how it moves forward."*

Stepping away, Scott stopped and turned back to face me. *"Your prognosis has been discussed. You will be retained. They will pay for the best to treat you and aid your recovery, and, once you are healthy and independent again, you will be assessed and redeployed."* Watching as I squeezed my eyes closed and tears escaped, Scott shuffled his feet. *"I'm here as your friend. No matter the hat I wear in that room, I am your friend first. I'll fight for you."*

Raising my flat hand to my face, I touched the tip of my fingers to my chin and offered it out in thanks. Scott nodded. *"Focus on your recovery. I'll come to see you whenever I'm free."* Spinning on his heel, he left.

Turning my gaze to the window, I thumbed the rings on my finger. Scott had signed without talking. I'd wait to see what decision was made before I updated Mitch on the changes. The sun lowered. I smiled, feeling a new hope rising in my chest. I was going to keep my promise. No matter what, I would find my way back to Mitch. First, I needed to get out of this bed.

Throwing back the sheet, I swung my feet to the ground. I'd fought to be alive too many times to quit now. If I was going to survive, I would fight to live on my own terms.

51

RECOVERY

Gazing up from beneath, the water rippling across the surface from the breeze. Pressing my lips tight, I looked down at my watch. Three minutes, thirty-seven seconds. Focusing my gaze on the surface again, my chest hurt, muscles tense, wanting to expel the air I was holding in my lungs.

Checking my watch, I grimaced in annoyance with myself and exhaled, bubbles rising to the surface. Shifting immediately, I swam across the bottom of the pool as far as I could, changing direction ninety degrees as soon as the last bubble left my nose. I needed distance before those bubbles breached the surface.

Bullets penetrated into the water, following the path the bubbles had given away. My hearing still wasn't back, but loud bangs broke through the white noise. It sounded like a silencer, despite the shooter not using one.

Making it to the wall, I waited another ten seconds, my lungs insisting I inhale. Rising to the surface, I ensured I broke through slowly to be quiet and didn't open my mouth because I would gasp if I did. Forcing my inhale to be slow, I controlled it through narrow lips, like I was sucking the air through a straw.

A straw! A great idea for next time. I had to remember to steal one from the kitchen before the next water ops test. With air back in my lungs, I checked the area of the pool. The obstacle course was set up to reflect a lagoon or river. Lifting myself slowly from the water, I stayed in a low crouch and made my way along the bank to where the gunshots had come from. The gunman stood there, monitoring the surface, searching the banks with his eyes.

Picking up a stone, I tossed it into the water two meters to his left. The gunman swung towards it, then instantly pivoted back towards me. He was dead before he came full circle, the knife I had jammed into the side of his neck, my hand covering his mouth. He froze, blinking his wide eyes at me, then I shoved him into the pool—a loud splash sounding in the enclosed arena. Lights came on, illuminating the obstacle course and the assessor sitting up high, watching.

"Fucking hell, Lyza!" Kit sputtered as he broke the surface again. "Did I have to take a swim?" Using both hands, I gestured to my fully clothed body. Kit glared. Though he tried to be menacing, the side of his mouth slowly tilted up. Lifting himself from the water, Kit stood looking down as water cascaded from his full combat gear.

When Kit shook his head at me, I winked. Glaring, Kit turned to look up at the assessor, one of the Chamber elite. "We good? Can we retire for the day?" Kit called, signing the discussion.

The assessor finished writing his notes. "Shower and change for the dojo. You are both training with my team this afternoon," Jason, the third in command, called back. Kit signed the reply for me. Jason left with no further discussion.

Turning back to me, Kit lifted an eyebrow and made a wanking gesture. Shoving Kit in the shoulder, I smiled quietly because he was right. Most elite guards wore their egos like medals of honor and acted like they had cocks that reached their knees. I'd seen most of them in the buff - the joys of unisex change rooms - they were all within the range of standard issue.

"Let's eat. They might not let us otherwise," Kit signed as we headed back to the barracks. My room was in the mansion still, but Kit was based with the elite guards.

Scythe was disbanded. Maria still lived at Chapter. The trainers who had always been of no fixed abode now residing there with their families. One of the suggested changes that came from the investigation findings. The men of the Arrow should be a part of their children's upbringing. A robust male influence might breed loyalty—the same with seeing parents together and loyal to each other.

Kit, Maria, and I were still considered Scythe operatives, but we were now the ones of no fixed abode. Maria, currently heavily pregnant, was on leave. Kit and I were now partners. Not a breeding pair. We just ran ops together. Well, we would, once I was cleared as fit for duty again.

The marriage situation hadn't been discussed further. No one demanded I divorce my husband, and no one discussed me being able to see him. Scott told me to put that to the back of my mind and focus on my recovery and proving myself. I'd followed his advice.

Entering the mess, Kit handed me a plate as we gathered up some food to eat. We ate quietly, Kit happy to sign in my presence. He liked to talk shit about the elite, knowing that while some knew sign language, they didn't always understand my dialect.

"What made you learn AUSLAN?" I asked.

Watching my hands, Kit smirked with a huff as he pointed to me. *"Before it came out that you were married."*

"You registered to date me?"

Kit shrugged. *"I put some effort into being eligible in case you decided not to go with Scott."* When I lifted a brow, Kit sighed. *"He connected with you quickly; I figured it was the sign language. I was running laps the morning you went to the bluff after we stopped you leaving with your husband. I saw which house you came from, so I know what happened between you two."*

"You didn't tell the others?"

"None of their business. Anyway, your husband destroyed Eden, and we went on alert. It stopped being important."

Signing out the name, I raised my shoulders.

Kit chewed his cheek. *"Females aren't told about Eden. It's for male Arrows only to visit."*

Studying Kit, the slight blush on his cheeks, I blinked as I sat straight. *"It's a brothel?"*

Kit's cheeks flamed. *"It was a place where women were housed and provided a living for taking care of male's frustrations. The ratio of females to males in the Sword and Arrow is one female to every ten males. They didn't want us running off to fall in love with civilians either, so they enabled our primal needs in a controlled environment."*

My chest tightened. Signing out my husband's name, I slashed my finger from the center of my throat back, and with my thumb out, brushed the top of my breast three times to indicate women.

Kit dropped his sandwich to the plate. *"One, but only the one who fought back. Otherwise, they killed all the men visiting the apartment complex at the time. They forced the women out and burnt the place to the ground. Those women, everything they owned was in that place. Some of them fought against losing that. One of them shot one of Fairchild's men, apparently, and he returned fire. The guy was a better shot than she was. Obviously."*

Sitting back in my chair, I didn't feel sorry for the women so much. Material possessions were better to lose than your life; still, we all had our attachments to some materialistic items. *"Go get changed. I'll meet you at the dojo."* Standing up, Kit walked away. With a silent sigh, I headed back to my room to change.

The elite were good fighters, but Kit and I were better. We never said it out loud, but Kit and I secretly enjoyed spending each afternoon kicking the elite's asses. For over two months, I attended daily physiotherapy and Pilates recovering from my injuries. Last month I'd been eased back into training. The doctor had argued I needed to wait longer, but I'd proven I could get back to it now. My bones were healed, my wounds merely scars.

After training, I returned to my room and soaked in a nice hot bath. While I may be healed, I still ached. During training, I guarded my right side too much, the muscles still tight, and my natural instinct to protect a weaker area of my body. Hot mineral baths and regular visits to the massage therapist were my way of getting through this. Chamber ensured I had everything I needed to recover, medically speaking.

After the bath, I dressed and went to the kitchen to find food. Only the Chamber members, and their assistants, lived in the mansion, and most of them were always away on business. When I finished cooking my dinner, I turned to plate it up. Scott stood watching me. He always wore a suit now, today, sans tie.

Pointing to his chest, Scott made a C in front of his nose and stroked his index down his nose to pinch it shut, then wafted something up to his nose before rubbing his tummy.

Smiling, I put a second dish out, serving him up some goulash. Adding a fresh roll of the dumpling to the side of his plate, I carried both to the kitchen table, taking a seat. Scott slipped his jacket off and left it on the back of the chair as he sat down. We ate in quiet. When our bowls were empty, Scott helped me clean up, then he walked me upstairs.

"Have you heard from your husband?" Scott signed as we walked. My brows lowered, and I shook my head. Scott waited another moment. *"He called today. How he keeps getting my phone number is*

worrying. That aside, he asked how you were and if you were fully recovered yet."

"Did you tell him the truth?"

Watching my hands, Scott then glanced up to my face. *"I told him you would be assessed for duty in the next week. Your future rests in your ability to pass a level five qualification again."*

Confident in my capability, I pointed to my chest and then ticked the top of my left index finger.

Smirking, Scott lifted his fist, thumb sticking out, and brushed it against his temple. *"I know."*

"Be my crystal ball," I tempted. *"What does my future hold?"* I turned to face him on the landing.

"I know what I want your future to be," Scott admitted, stepping closer. *"But I know I am not what you desire."*

"That's false. You are very desirable. Every time I come back worked up, the temptation to use you to vent is greater than I would like."

Scott blushed a little. *"Let me rephrase. I am not what your heart desires. I know you wouldn't choose this life if given a choice. When you pass your final assessment, I will argue for you to be based on the Hunter Chapter, that we use your connection with your husband to liaise with him, and for you to run your missions out of Albuquerque."*

Blinking at Scott, I stared, taking a second longer to close my mouth and get my hands to work. *"Will I be able to live with my husband?"*

Shoving his hands in his pockets, Scott rocked from heel to toe. His eyes watching me, ensuring my eyes were on his lips. "I'll make you no promises, Lyza. I am one man on the board. They hold my opinion of your capability and needs in high regard, but they will not throw open the gates and wave as you walk away from here. When they ask, you need to give them a tie to the Arrow, something they will believe you will honor."

"A tie?" I queried, unsure what that meant. *"What is your tie to the Arrow?"*

Smirking, Scott held his thumb and index finger on either side of his left eye, then moved them across his field of vision like he was scanning them, indicating laser focus. *"Ambition. I've been working my way towards being a Chamber member since I got my sword inked on my hip. I'm younger than I expected to become Grandfather. In fact, I'm the youngest in the history of the Arrow. My ambition is my tie. You need to work out what kept you loyal and tell them what it was. That will be your golden ticket."* Scott stepped back. "Night, Lyza."

Striding to his bedroom door, Scott closed it behind him. Thinking hard about what it was that kept me loyal to the Arrow, despite my upbringing and my father's treatment of me, I went to my room. Stripping out of my clothes, I pulled on an oversized shirt to sleep in. Turning off my lights, I went to the window and stared out at the darkness, contemplating why I chose to return.

Despite my protestations, I could have stayed with Mitch, relied on him to protect me, possibly gotten us both killed. Yet, I'd taken the gamble and come back to the Arrow. Was it fear or loyalty that made that choice? Or maybe it was both. Closing my eyes, I exhaled. Going back out into the hall, I walked down to Scott's bedroom door and knocked. Scott opened it with just boxers on. It was apparent he'd already climbed into bed. The tattoo of Scott's sword and arrow branding gullied between the definition of a V pack and the rise of his hip bone. When I lifted my eyes to Scott's, his brows raised, taking in my attire. "Lyza, *what's wrong?*"

Putting my fist to my chest, I then mimicked tying a knot before lifting my eyes to meet his again. *"Fear was my tie through my youth, and it's what brought me home. Fear of the Arrow killing the man I love is what brought me home. You are the reason I stayed. I still feared them hurting Mitch, but you proved to me that honor exists in the Arrow. You made a great Father. You are caring, and you treated us all like family. I came to depend on you, and I became loyal, not to the Arrow, but to you. Love, fear, and loyalty are my ties. My love for Mitch, my fear of the Arrow, and my loyalty to you."*

Standing there, Scott blinked at me, a beacon of amazement in his eyes. Carefully, I stepped towards him. *"I didn't sleep with you to hurt Mitch for breaking his promise. I wanted to have that physical connection with the one person I trusted who hadn't hurt me. I slept with you because I trust you to look out for me, to guide me, and to protect me."*

Breaking free of his surprise, Scott moved his focus from my hands to my eyes, then to my shirt. Grabbing his left pinky with his index finger, Scott dragged it down to his hip, spread his arms, and pinched his fingers together as he swept them into his center and then pointed to his chest. *"Stay with me—just tonight. I want to be with you because I've come to care for you more than I expected too. I know you'll go back to him, but give me one night before you do?"*

Biting my lip, I didn't hesitate to step into his room and let Scott shut the door. I'd been attracted to Scott for some time now. Realizing that attraction went further than physical needs meant something to me. Sex was a primal need. That's what we were raised to believe. That no emotional attachment was necessary. They were wrong. Sex was sex until I met Mitch. Now, it needed to be more.

As Scott lifted my shirt over my head and dropped his boxers to the floor, I understood why it was a primal need. Sex wasn't just about venting, mating, and breeding. It wasn't just getting off or love. Sex was a physical expression of attachment, a way of connecting with someone on a plane where only the two of you existed. It didn't need to be love. Love was only one of the basic human emotions in a toolbox. Connection to something, or someone, knowing they will be there for you and using physical intimacy to express your appreciation, vulnerability, and loyalty, was another.

As Scott lifted me into his arms and carried me to his bed, I knew that's what this was between us. When he found a condom and used it, he further demonstrated he wasn't using me for his gain. Scott felt our connection just as much as I did. It wasn't love. We'd both experienced love before, and that wasn't what bound us together. This was companionship, trust, and loyalty. Scott was the only man I was intimate with who hadn't betrayed me or broken his promise to me. Scott told me from the very beginning he would protect me, and he had.

The bond formed between Scott and me wasn't something I expected a civilian to understand. I wasn't even sure if Mitch would be able to comprehend what I had found with Scott, but I knew it felt right to me, and that's what mattered.

52

APPOINTMENT

Sunlight filtered across the bed. Scott's naked musculature adorned the sheets, pooling low over his hips. A bird started chirping in the distance. Smiling automatically, I then froze. Pushing up on my elbow, I stared at the window. A sparrow sat on the sill, singing its morning song. By Scott stirring, I knew it was loud, but to me, it sounded well into the distance. Still, the fact I was hearing anything above the white noise of my last three months was exciting for me. A hand caressed my face, and I looked down to see Scott watching me. *"Is it singing?"* I asked. *"I can see its throat moving."*

Scott's eyes closed and reopened, only a glimpse of pity. Knocking the air twice, Scott put his thumb in his ear with his index finger pointing up and then took it away from his head, telling me it was very loud. It was apparent the noisy bird had woken Scott up. The hand he used to cradle my face urged me down towards him. Running my hand down the torso of him, I smiled. Scott moaned, the vibrations of it felt by my palm on him, not heard by my ears. Still, the bird sang in the distance. I let its song fill me with the joy of knowing that I was healing.

"YOU'RE STILL GUARDING your right side," Kit stepped back, signing. *"You know they will go for it as soon as you protect it."*

"If I can take on the elite, I can beat level five."

Kit shook his head. *"Don't aim low on this one. You need to be better than you were before this all happened. You need to aim for ten."*

Grimacing, I shook my head. *"I never want to do ten again,"* I gestured.

Kit's eyebrows lifted. *"You made ten? Why weren't you taken as a trainer?"*

"Maybe my chi isn't right for Master Usagi to consider me."

Watching my hands, Kit chuckled. *"Do you have any chi?"* I stuck my tongue out at him. It made Kit laugh again, then he sighed. *"Okay, but you need to push the envelope, show that you want this. I heard Sherwin talking to Jason. You are being considered for asset placement. They don't approve that based on reaching a certain level; they grant it based on you fighting until you are dead. You have to be willing to do anything and everything to survive."*

Sherwin was the captain of the elite and Chamber guard. He had probably witnessed a lot of these assessments. If he said it, it was probably right. Kit stepped into the ready position. *"If you are going to guard your right side, I will strike it."*

Observing his hands, I nodded. We bowed and engaged in sparring. When I guarded my right side, Kit went for it repeatedly, but I fought back just as hard. Kit was still recovering from having his knee ligaments torn. As a result, he favored his left leg, so I focused my attack on taking that leg from him. Kit hit the mats again, his facial expression clearly broadcasting his cursing, even if I couldn't read his lips to know the expletives he just used.

Getting to his feet, Kit turned towards the door. When I turned around, Scott was standing there watching. "Lyza isn't the only one protecting a recent injury," Scott reminded Kit, his hands signing as he spoke. "The assessors have arrived. You are both going to be assessed today. You will fight independently, then you will fight together."

Frowning, Kit and I glanced at each other and then back to Scott. Never in our assessments had we been assessed on fighting with a partner.

"The Arrow is in the midst of change. Things will be done differently in some situations." Scott stepped closer. "While you are being assessed, the Chamber is going to be meeting. Once you finish your assessment, shower and come to the mansion. You'll wait until you are called before your grandparents." Scott's eyes lifted to mine. "You'll know by the end of the day what your future holds."

Kit and I nodded, and Scott left. Blowing out a breath, Kit turned his eyes to me. *"I'm guessing you two sleeping together is going to have an impact on the Chamber decision?"*

My brows lifted. *"How do you know?"*

Kit smirked. *"You are calmer. He's the only male here you give the time of day to other than me. It doesn't take a genius to work it out,"* Kit teased. *"That and the mansion corridors are full of security cameras. The guards have been speculating about it since you spent the first night in Scott's room."*

It's not that we were sneaking around these last few weeks, but I didn't want Chamber to base their decision on something which didn't change my end game. Blowing out a breath, I moved towards the door. I wanted this assessment over and done with. I wanted to know if I'd done enough. I needed to understand their plan before I could make my own.

The mansion dojo was customarily reserved for the grandparents. Master Usagi and his seven students already occupied the room. They watched us enter, eyes assessing even the way we walked into the space. Kit and I went to the mats and set ourselves down side-by-side, kneeling and sitting back on our ankles.

Kit's jaw clenched as he sat back on his ankles. The ligaments in his knee were still tight, and he needed to be careful kneeling like this. For my part, I made protecting my right side evident; I even hammed it up a little, rubbing over the scarring from the chest drain.

Flicking his eyes to my hand, Kit lowered his brows as he watched me. *"What are you doing?"* He signed quickly.

Waiting for Master Usagi to address his students, so their eyes no longer on us, I took a shallow breath. Moving my hands as if holding a present forward, I stealthily pointed toward the trainers and arced my finger to include them all and then put two fingers in the palm of my left hand and wobbled them like weak legs.

Peering at me through narrowed eyelids, Kit snapped his focus forward and up, and we both turned our attention to the Master.

"We will start with Kit," Master Usagi announced. "Lyzebel, you can watch it." He indicated the cushions to the side where he would sit.

Glancing at Kit, I pointed my index finger to touch my nose then moved it away, tucking the index finger and leaving my thumb up to wish him good luck. Kit bowed his head. Rolling over my toes, I went to the observation area.

Master Usagi instructed his team, then came to sit beside me. They started Kit at level three. He faced off against the one opponent, testing his basic sparring to pass level three before taking it up to intermediate for level four. Kit was trying hard to hide his dependency on his left leg because I could barely notice it at this stage.

While Kit fought, I studied the other trainers, the way they watched Kit, trying to pick any moves or patterns he depended on. Everyone did it when they attacked. They had a combination of punches that they favored. Moving my hand to my ribs, I massaged the scar tissue, kneading between my rib bones, loosening up the muscles, and releasing the tension.

Kit passed level five. While he rebalanced his stance, a second trainer came to join the assessment. Both attackers stepped in and followed the usual choreography for the first minute. Kit danced with them beautifully. They stepped back, nodded to each other, and attacked randomly.

Sitting forward a little, I was intrigued that they had broken from the traditional choreography. Their attacks were responsive to Kit's defense instead of testing set parameters. The assessment was now entirely based on being able to foresee his opponent's next two moves.

Master Usagi grunted beside me, the base notes of his body vibrating through the floor. The two trainers stepped away. A third joined, the fight started anew, Kit already breathing heavily from the last assault started favoring his left leg. I saw it, and so did the spotter. Leaning forward, the spotter whispered to the trainer in front of him.

Kit fought hard, defending and attacking, but he wasn't going to last much longer. At Chapter, Kit was taken down by four, and those four were nowhere near as skilled as these men. When Master Usagi's base notes trembled through the floor, the attack stopped.

Kit was struggling as the fourth opponent stepped in. As soon as they began attacking, the new trainer went straight for Kit's left leg. They took him down, but they didn't let up. Frowning, I kept waiting for them to step away, but they didn't. They aimed their hits to make an impact. While they were pulling their punches, they made sure Kit felt it first. As a result, Kit was getting pummeled.

My body tensed. I'd never seen this happen before, and it didn't seem right. Rising automatically, I found myself moving towards them, intent on bringing it to an end, of protecting Kit. As soon as I stepped on the mat, the remaining three swarmed towards me.

There was no rhythm, no dance to their attacks. They swarmed and attacked, reacting to my auto defense. They crowded, I danced. Every single one of them targeted my right side. Smiling, I countered and drove them back. This time, I didn't pull my punches. This wasn't a typical training scenario; I would treat it like a fight for my life situation.

A fourth joined the attack, leaving Kit to the other three. I'd shown them a weakness purposefully, and they were all focused on hitting that target. Just like the last time I fought these men, I deliberately misled them to see something that wasn't there. And while they were aiming at my right side, they were leaving my neck and left shoulder alone, which were the actual areas of hurt.

A heavy grunt vibrated along the floor when I took down the first one, then a second attacker, blood aspirating from a broken nose—a yelp issuing from a dislocated finger. The trainers fell away, the others left Kit to take their place. Stomping on an ankle as I tripped another, the trainer fell with a thud, his ankle at an odd angle. While I didn't feel it snap, I knew he wouldn't be standing on it immediately.

A hit to the side of my jaw, more to my kidneys and abdomen, but I took it and kept them away from Kit, circling the mat, giving him an opening. Understanding what I was doing, Kit crawled to the side and thumped the floor hard with his hand. Landing one last punch, I blocked the attacks as I backed away. Reaching the edge, I stepped one foot off the mat as I ducked another fist, then dropped to my knees and held my hands out in surrender.

The attack stopped immediately. While I knelt there gasping for air, the trainers bent over heaving. We all stayed there, catching our breath, checking our bodies to ensure the sore bits weren't more profound injuries. When the spotter caught his breath, he tapped his comrades on the shoulders and told them to line up.

A hand appeared in front of me. Looking up to meet Tate's eyes, a perfect mirror of Maria's twin boys, I took his hand and let him help me stand. He bowed, I returned the gesture, then he went to help assess the extent of the injuries I'd inflicted.

As I turned, Master Usagi stepped before me. He bowed, I returned it. He waited until my eyes were on him. "Do you understand?"

Watching his lips, I nodded. *"It was never Kit's assessment. Always my test to fail,"* I signed. Kit, who was still sitting on the floor, smiled and verbalized my response.

"Oh, it was his assessment too, but when he reached his failure point, your test took over." Master Usagi reached out and touched my left shoulder. He moved his fingers, and the tension between my shoulder and neck released. His fingers felt like heaven. The Master smiled. "Nice feint, Lyza. Go, rest."

Bowing my head in respect as he walked away, I blew out a breath. He knew I'd misdirected his students and picked up on my real pain. Helping Kit up, we limped our way out of the room. My neck feeling the best it had since it got shot.

An hour later, I was showered and dosed with paracetamol, waiting outside the meeting room with Kit as instructed. The front door opened, and we both looked up to watch Jonathan saunter towards us. "What are you doing here?" Kit asked, signing for my benefit.

"I don't know. Scott called and told me to pack my bags for permanent redeployment and flew me here," Jonathan took the seat across from me. "Is that why we are all here?" When I nodded, Jonathan's brows lifted. "Curiouser and curiouser." Sitting back, Jonathan crossed his arms to wait.

Sherwin, the captain, came out and gestured for us to all go in. We stood, Kit and Jonathan waiting for me to go through the door first. I wasn't sure if it was manners or using me as a shield. Limping into the dining room, I waited on this side of the table for the others to join me behind the chairs. With a gesture from Marlyn, we all took a seat.

"Grandfather Scythe, you'll sign for me, please?" my grandfather requested. Nodding, Scott raised his hands, ready. "Scythe Chapter is no more, but you are still Scythe. Therefore, all three of you are to be redeployed as a call-out team. Sons of Scythe, you will both report to the Hunter Chapter in Albuquerque, New Mexico. You will be provided lodgings within the chapter's base, but you will not be of the Hunter Chapter."

Stealing glances at each other, then to me, Kit and Jonathan frowned. Why wasn't I getting sent to Hunter?

"Daughter Scythe, you are also heading to Albuquerque. There, you will reunite with your legal husband," Marlyn paused, watching my reaction. Other than my hands clenching my thighs in hope, I kept my face stern. "You will be an asset to us. You may reveal to your husband that your duty remains to us. As far as anyone else is concerned, Kit will be your training partner when you are not on a mission. Jonathan will be your pilot and personal driver."

The room fell silent as Marlyn took a rest. Moving my eyes from Scott's hands to my grandfather's genetically similar features, I waited. "Lyza, if you notice anything that we should be aware of within your husband's business, you will communicate it to your handler immediately."

My brows lowered. Making loose binoculars with my hands, I lifted the eye holes in front of my cheeks, then dropped again as I raised my shoulders. I was getting a handler?

"Every asset has a grandparent as their handler," Marlyn continued to explain. "Your handler will be Grandfather Scythe. Since you already have an intimate working relationship, we wish you to continue in that capacity." Peering at my grandfather, I was not happy with his wording. "You will be given briefing reports to prepare you by tonight. You have the afternoon to pack and rest; your transport will leave at zero six-hundred tomorrow morning."

As Marlyn sat back, the entire room turned silent. We sat patiently while Marlyn studied us. "Sons of Scythe, you are dismissed to prepare for your departure."

Everyone waited while Kit and Jonathan stood. Squeezing my right shoulder gently, Kit followed Jonathan out of the room. As soon as they were gone, all the Chamber members got up and left, except two.

"Lyza, your Grandfather revealed why you returned to us," Anne, Grandmother of Guardian, began to talk while Scott continued signing for me. "Fear and love can be great motivators. While we would have preferred your loyalty, we understand why we don't have that. Your father destroyed your trust and ensured fear was your motivator." Opening a folder in front of her, Anne slid a piece of paper across the table to me.

Wary, I took the piece of paper and looked at it. A highlighted report drawing my eyes, my stomach dropping as I read it.

"You are the last descendant of our founder. You and your genes are important to us, Lyza. You achieve the best test results than any of your Scythe colleagues, and you have a one hundred percent success rate. Your skills are needed to be passed on to the next generation."

Dropping my eyes back to the paper before me for a moment, I then lifted my gaze to Scott's. He kept his features controlled. In my peripheral vision, Anne licked her lips. "We want you to appeal to your husband for you to use his training facilities to train individual candidates we send your way."

Confusion surrounded me for a moment. Indicating Ann, I then pointed to me and, with both thumbs untucked, circled my fists back towards me.

"You want me to be a trainer?" Scott translated for her.

Anne pressed her lips. "You are the only female we have that has successfully achieved level ten even once, let alone twice. While we would like to credit Master Usagi with that accomplishment, he assures us that your abilities only began with our structured training program. He feels that he is not master enough to teach a female of your caliber and credits your abilities not to his teachings but to your survival. We want to send female candidates to you for you to train as best you can."

"I was tortured by my father and my captors to become who I am," I signed aggressively. How could I teach someone that sort of torment?

"We have females who have endured a similar childhood outside of the Arrow. They have been recruited into the program from civilian life. We want you to train them." Anne waited for me to scan the report before me before I looked up again. "Would you be willing to try?"

"What Great Grandfather said about my continued intimacy with Grandfather Scythe? Was that an order?"

Swallowing, Ann glanced at Scott. Scott signed without talking. *"That is between us, and Chamber need not know if we merely talk or if I offer you physical comfort. As your handler, I will be there for you however you need. No expectations other than you do the job,"* Scott reassured.

"Do you think I should do this? Train these women?"

Inhaling, Scott watched my hands and continued to answer without talking. *"They are young girls rescued from orphanages or found held by those we are sent to dispatch. You made a difference in the way you trained the twins. As a trainer, you are also removed from active duty other than for training ops or when no one else has the skill set required. I would recommend you agree. This post would keep you where you want to be."*

"Only if Mitch agrees."

Watching me spell out my husband's name, Scott raised a brow. *"Why would he reject the deal that will deliver you to him for keeps?"*

Exhaling, my shoulders dropped, and I nodded. Anne exhaled, relieved. "A dossier will be in your room for you. Once you have offered the deal to your husband, you will contact your handler and organize the start date of your first candidate." Anne stood. "Do you have any questions?"

I held up the report, Anne nodded, and left. Left in the room alone, Scott watched me. *"That report is a week old. It was also the last bit of evidence I needed to convince them that you belong in Albuquerque."* Rising out of his chair, Scott sighed. *"I expect you will be busy tonight, preparing for your deployment. Call me when you are settled. I'll fly to the states to meet with you."*

Sitting back stunned, I remained in the room alone. Finally, I fingered the rings on my finger and smiled. I was keeping my promise.

53

FREEDOM WITH A CATCH

I WANTED TO SCREAM.

Invisible daggers were piercing my inner ear, my nails tore at the denim of my jeans as we came into land, gritting my teeth, head bowed, the pressure change forcing my inner ear to compress. Chewing the end of the pen in my mouth harder, I tried to use my jaw's movement to work the muscles around my ear canal.

Kit and Jonathan were across the other side of business class, and thankfully, nowhere near me. The pain became unbearable, I whimpered, adding more strain by trying to make noise. My nails dug deep enough to make me bleed through the denim. My ears were always sensitive to landing, but this was extreme.

My body jolted as the plane's wheels touched the tarmac, I bit clean through the pen, and my ears popped. A long, drawn-out squeal in my ears eradicating the white noise, making me cringe from the piercing scream in my head. After a second, it tapered to a hum and escaped the confines of my ear.

"Ladies and Gentlemen, welcome to New Mexico," the captain announced.

Freezing, I blinked as the sound came crashing in at full volume. My lips curved up, and I spat the pen out, lifting my face to the ceiling and sighing in absolute relief. There was a dribble down my ear lobe, which I used my hand to wipe away. My fingers revealed old blood. This happened the last time I got my hearing back. Grabbing a tissue, I quickly wiped my ear clean of the blood clot. By the time I was cleaned up, we were arriving at the terminal.

The arrival gate at the airport was busy as we walked through to the pickup point. The crowd walking in front of us parted to move around a man. He was built strong, my height, dark hair, tanned skin, and a five o'clock shadow. His dark eyes locked on mine as I approached. My lips twitched at the sight of him, despite the curdle of disappointment in my stomach.

Pointing to me, Moses put two fingers beneath his eye and moved them towards me. He clapped his hands together, palms at a ninety-degree angle to each other twice, then put a single finger beneath his eye and pointed to his chest as he smirked. His eyes assessed mine, weighing the depth of my soul, and his smile dropped. *"I take that back."* He still had the look of a priest to him. The all-black attire didn't help - black slacks, jumper, and the peak of a black shirt at the collar.

"I'm glad it's you bringing us in," I assured. *"I just hoped-"*

Watching my hands, Moses gritted his teeth. *"We haven't notified him you're coming. My collaboration with Fairchild ended the minute we could access Luther and Debbie's records. Now, I'm hunting down those that were smart enough to disappear when the news broke."*

"That should keep you busy. I'm surprised you're here." The list of shadow employees wasn't restricted to traitors in our own organization.

The side of Moses's mouth lifted. *"I made Mother promise me if you were redeployed to us, I got to bring you in."*

"We're not Hunters. Just using your chapter as our base now," Kit interrupted, signing as he spoke to let Moses know he followed our conversation. "I'm Kit, this is Jonathan. He doesn't know sign language."

Accepting Kit's subtle reminder that he was rude by excluding them, Moses nodded at both of them. "Sadly, we lost two Hunters to the purge, so your accommodations are only recently vacated."

"Traitors?" I asked, surprised. Scott didn't mention any Hunters that were identified.

Settling his heavy gaze on me, Moses shook his head as he closed his hand like a duck's bill. "No. They were hunting the traitors and died trying to bring them to justice." Moses lifted his eyes to my colleagues. "We know this isn't your doing, you've suffered a greater loss, but I'd warn you to be respectful of our recent losses. The Hunter Chapter is close-knit."

"We understand," Kit reassured.

Moses's eyes came back to me. "I know you are keen to see Fairchild, but Mother wants to see you first. I'll take you all to Chapter, then drive you to your husband." I didn't argue. Mitch must have heard I'd be flying in today. Marlyn had verbalized our fly-out time, so Mitch's absence might be its own statement. Moses took my bag from my hand. "Follow me."

The drive was short, with the Hunter Chapter location within easy distance of the airport. We drove by the private plane hangars to get there, and I felt a wave of regret wash over me - Noel's new face, blood everywhere, and the love he still held for me in his dying eyes.

"How is she really?" Moses asked as we drove.

"She doesn't talk to us," Kit dismissed. "I mean, she doesn't talk to anyone, but we're not her confidants. Chamber did a full workup on her over a week ago, psyche and physical. I didn't see the results, but she passed. That's good enough for me."

Moses turned to look at Kit. "No one goes through what she did and not be impacted psychologically."

Turning his head, Kit glared at Moses. "She wasn't the only one to get betrayed up that mountain and to barely crawl out of there. She's recovered physically. She's set her sights on getting back to her husband and about to achieve it. Let her be."

Moses lifted a brow. "You too, hey?"

Exhaling, Kit turned to look out the window. "She's my sister, and I'm protective of her. We all saw what her father put her through. Lyza copped it harder than anyone else growing up. We're killers, not monsters. We have some humanity."

"Can we discuss something of importance?" Jonathan asked, sitting forward to interrupt the growing tension. "What are women like around here? With Eden out of commission, dating civilians is going to be on the cards."

Moses smirked. "As a loyal Arrow who follows the rules, I have no idea what you mean. As a male with a pulse, you'll find something to suit every taste. There's a good club in the next suburb over. When I get back from the next hunt, I'll take you on a tour. You know, to make sure you are familiar with the area."

Glancing at the rings on my finger, for the first time since Mitch refused to answer my question about other women, I wondered. I wouldn't be upset if he did. We'd been apart long enough, and love didn't mean possession to me. You didn't need to love someone to have sex with them, and just because you had sex with someone else didn't mean you stopped loving someone else.

Sex didn't equate to love. It didn't even mean you were just horny and wanted to get off. There were so many different complex layers to physical intimacy. I'd learned over the last six months that equating love with sex or loyalty was superficial and an archaic expectation of male possessiveness.

Mitch loved me; I knew that. After everything we had been through, what we felt for each other transcended the civilian understanding of love and commitment. Thinking about seeing him again, I fidgeted with the rings adorning my finger. They were looser than they used to be, almost to the point of falling off. I guess the last ten months since I'd returned to Chapter had taken a toll on my health. When I looked up, we were pulling into a gated estate.

"The entire estate is ours. Hunter ranks are over double that of what Scythes used to be. Probably because we don't have the high fatality rate you guys do," Moses educated. "Of course, now we know some of your deaths can be associated with your own family."

"You're referring to Debbie killing both her husbands and putting the hit on her own son," Kit assessed.

Pulling up to the guard gate, Moses waved at the guard before the gate opened, and we drove in. "And the death of Miles and Pierre. It's believed that Zane was given alternative orders on the missions that those two lost their lives on." Glancing at Kit, Moses paused. "You don't look shocked?"

"Scott went to our Father after Miles died and told him once is unfortunate, twice is a coincidence, but did we want to find out if it was enemy action or should Zane only do solo jobs from now on."

"Scott suspected?" Moses assessed.

Kit looked over his shoulder to me, then turned his face forward. "Scott is very good at observing and learning. He has an excellent grasp on what drives people."

"Why did you look at Lyza?" Moses drove through the estate, a large lake and parkland set in the middle, spreading the houses apart from each other.

"Because while you were hunting Noel, Scott was hunting Lyza. He studied everything he could about her to try and get in her head and find her. He argued for years she didn't leave willingly; he was sure she was dead or taken by force."

"He was right," Moses decreed.

"Yeah. Scott was right about a lot of things."

Moses pulled the car up in front of a quaint house. The gardens were well-tended, and it looked to be the epitome of civilian life. As we unloaded from the car, Emily came outside to greet us. Moses introduced Kit and Jonathan, and they quickly discussed rules about living in the Hunter compound.

"Moses, why don't you take Kit and Jonathan to their houses and show them around the estate?" Emily suggested. "Lyza and I will have a drink while we wait." Indicating I follow her, Emily walked away.

Watching the men leave, I followed Emily to her front porch. She indicated a chair, so I sat and waited while she went inside. A few minutes later, Emily returned with a tray. It held a jug of milk, two tall glasses full of ice, and a plate of cookies. It made me smile.

After pouring us both a glass, Emily sat down, picked up a cookie, and sat back in her chair. It wasn't until I went to pick up my drink that I noticed a business card beside it. Frowning, I picked it up and looked at the details for a specialist. Brows furrowed, I lifted my eyes to Emily.

"Scott called ahead. He said you would need someone. I asked around to find someone who is highly recommended for what you need." Reaching over, Emily flipped the card to show the date and time on the back. I lifted my eyes again to read her lips. "I made an appointment for you."

Touching my fingers to my chin, I offered them out in thanks.

For a moment, Emily studied me. "Scott didn't tell Chamber about you being in his bed four months ago. He could have, and it would have changed everything." We assessed each other for several long minutes; eventually, Emily sighed. "He asked me not to reveal it either. I trust Scott to know what he's doing. He assures me this was the only option that would see you thrive. I believe he is right, once again."

Saying nothing more, Emily sat back and enjoyed her milk and cookie. Relaxing, I helped myself to another glass of milk. Moses eventually came back with Kit, at which point, I stood up to leave. Emily gave me a hug, which surprised me. When she stepped back, her eyes were smiling. "I'd like you to come to visit me weekly, Lyza. There aren't many females around here, and I always wanted a daughter. I think you could use a mother too."

Blinking, I was unsure of how to respond. My mother had been a bitch, but I knew the truth now. She never took me to Paris to give me to my father. She contacted Chamber to arrange my transfer to Guardian, as per the norm, but Debbie was the Guardian Mother at the time and used that opportunity to exact her revenge by telling my father where to find his wife and child.

Stepping off the porch, I went to Moses. *"Where's Jonathan?"*

Moses watched my hands. *"Settling in. I told him I'd do this one. Better to have someone your husband knows, or he might think Chamber wants him dead."* Dropping his hands, Moses opened the car door.

Settling into the backseat, I waved goodbye to Emily. Kit and Moses taking the front seats. The guys chatted about the weather and the climate here in New Mexico as we drove, nothing of interest to me. My eyes went to my rings. Did he know I was on my way? Would he be happy to see me?

The milk I drank was curdling in my stomach, anxiety-producing bile, and the stress of the unknown, making me nauseous. Taking the report Anne gave me from my pocket, I read the highlighted part again. There were so many unknowns.

Before I was ready, the car came to a stop out the front of Mitch's ranch. Looking up at the house, I was torn between racing up to the door and throwing myself into his arms or waiting to see if he would come out and welcome me home. Both visions of what awaited evaporated.

Mitch sat on the top stair with a beer in his hand. The scene was reminiscent of the day I left with his mother. The day I made a choice to fight for my right to love. The day I unequivocally made the worst choice of my life.

Pushing open the door with shaking hands, I stepped out of the car, Moses and Kit joining me. Moses went first, offering Mitch his hand. "You knew she was coming?"

"I always know when she is coming." Mitch looked over Moses' shoulder. "Who's this?"

"Kit is Lyza's Chamber-appointed training partner and bodyguard. If she's not at home, he's with her," Moses explained. "He's still active, so if he needs to go on a mission, another will fill in."

"I have an entire company full of bodyguards. Why should I accept one of yours?"

"You want her, then you need to accept their requirements. She has an appointed bodyguard and driver. Both will live at Chapter. She needs to check in weekly, and she has her own job to do. They gave you your wife, but she's still part of our family," Moses clarified.

Taking my time, I walked up the garden path to the bottom of the steps. Mitch watched me, no animosity in his eyes. Moss green irises focused entirely on my legs, and that I was walking. His shoulders dropped a little, relaxing as if his worst fears hadn't come true.

Moses looked back at me. "Do you mind if I give Kit the tour, show him the layout? Give you two time to talk."

"I'd prefer you left altogether. I haven't seen my wife in four months, and the last time I did, I thought she was paralyzed for life," Mitch complained.

"I'll do the tour while you talk. If everything is hunky-dory, and Lyza is happy to stay, we'll leave quietly. Come on, Kit. First stop is the fridge for a beer. Then I'll show you the back patio." Moses opened the front door, Kit followed. Chuckling as they let themselves into his home, Mitch didn't take his eyes off me.

Putting my hand beside my head, almost in a salute with my palm forward and fingers up, I moved them out to the side.

Mitch lifted a brow. *"Just hi?"* Standing up, he stepped down the steps to meet me at the bottom. *"How about I fucked up the day I left? Or, they haven't released me. I'm now their spy, oh, and I'm going to be spying on you? Or we could just try, I'm home, I love you, I missed you, and I promise to never leave again? Frankly, I think you should lead with that one."*

Pointing to my chest, I hugged my shoulders then jabbed Mitch in the chest. *"I love you! I missed you! I am never leaving this home unless you are with me again!"* Staring up into Mitch's eyes, I took a deep breath. *"I fucked up. I didn't realize I had an enemy within the Arrow. I never expected my battle to be with you to be more than a matter of location."* Chewing his cheek, Mitch watched me, and my shoulders dropped. *"I haven't been a faithful wife, but I've been loyal."*

Shuffling his feet, Mitch sighed. *"You were faithful until I broke my vow to you. I shouldn't have said what I did. I shouldn't have left you waiting and let you fall apart."* Mitch exhaled dynamically. *"I fucked up just as badly as you, Lyza. We are both to blame for where we ended up. My first mistake was the Nano. My second was using it as a weapon. You still forgave me and fell in love with me. You could have fucked half your chapter, and it still wouldn't equate to how I hurt you repeatedly. I guess I'm no better than my brother that way."*

His eyes were watery, hands shaking as I stepped closer and took his hand in mine. Giving it a gentle squeeze, I closed the distance, put my head to his chest, and wrapped my arms around him. Mitch's arms closed me in, holding me tight. A trail of wetness slithered over my scalp, and my eyes swelled with my emotions.

"Fuck, Lyza. I never want to see you in a hospital bed like that again. They said if you take a training role, you become inactive. If that's what I have to agree to, I'll do it," Mitch muttered to my head. Squeezing him tighter, the dam in my eyes broke apart. Mitch paused. Turning his cheek to my crown and his lips to my forehead, Mitch lowered his voice. "You can hear me?" I squeezed him again, unable to let him go. "Can you talk?"

Rubbing my face back and forth across his chest, I wiped my emotions away as I stepped back. Indicating my throat, I then squished my fist closed tight in front of it. From what the doctor said, the ligament damage was more severe than last time. It might heal again, but with the amount of pain I was in, I'd more than likely spend my life mute.

"You didn't meet me at the airport?"

Watching my eyes, Mitch lowered his head a moment. "I couldn't. I wanted it to be private when we saw each other again. Just in case."

My heart stuttered in my chest. *"Just in case of what?"*

"In case of this." He moved my hand to his groin, his jeans straining over the hardness of his cock. Eyebrows jumping into my hairline, my eyes flicked down. Yeah, he wouldn't have been able to hide that in public. His hands cupped my cheeks, his lips pressed heatedly to mine. Pure happiness radiated through me. My pores opening, muscles relaxing, stomach slowly unknotting. The kiss was entirely indecent for public consumption, but I didn't care. I was home.

Closing my eyes, I shook my head and freed my hands so I could talk. *"It wasn't just the once."*

Taking my hand, Mitch caressed my rings. "Moses told me once that you can't refuse a request or order from the Chapter Parent. That resisting them can lead to a punishment of death. He told me your father was known to use that rule to force the females in his chapter and that he wasn't the only Father or Mother suspected of doing so. I suspect a Chamber member would be harder to refuse."

While I didn't argue his reasoning because everything he said was right, it wasn't in this case. *"He didn't force me,"* I offered, for the sake of starting anew on a foundation of openness.

"I appreciate your honesty. But I humbly request, from now on, you leave your rings somewhere else. I don't want to listen to it again."

"Did you listen before?"

Watching my hands, Mitch smirked. "As much as it pained me, it was kind of hot at the same time. But I'd prefer the live show from here on out." His hands pulled me tight against him, his lips capturing mine. My toes curled, back arched, my pelvis grinding against the hardness of his desire for me. My nails clinging to his shoulders for dear life.

Mitch pulled back, a smile covering his features. "You kept your promise. That's all that matters."

54

A NEW CHAPTER

My back hit the wall of the hall, fingers deftly dealing with the buttons of Mitch's shirt. Though I had to stop when Mitch's hands lifted my shirt over my head, I finished the last button and immediately started his jeans. Mitch threw his shirt aside, and then his hands were at my waist, trying to get my pants out of the way.

"Why the fuck did you wear button fly jeans when you knew you were coming to see me?" Mitch complained. Shoving him away, in a quick twist of my hands, all the buttons were open. Mitch's lip twitched. "That was so hot!" His mouth found mine, his fingers delving into my scanties, finding my clit and pressing hard against it.

"Okay, time for us to go," Kit murmured to Moses.

"Shh, I was enjoying the show," Moses muttered with a chuckle.

Groaning, Mitch kissed me one more time then stepped away. Walking straight to the back patio door, Mitch started shutting the doors. "Go over the courtyard wall." Locking the door, Mitch pulled the blinds. When he turned to face me, I slowly lowered my jeans and stepped out of them.

Smirking, Mitch shoved his jeans over his hips, boxers, and all. The sight of him naked and hard made me lick my lips. Mitch walked towards me. I stepped to meet him, then I was in his arms, legs wrapped around his waist as he carried me to his bedroom. "Don't ever leave me again," Mitch cooed to my right ear.

Bouncing when he dropped me on the bed, a grin filled my face as he yanked my knickers down my legs. As his afternoon shadow scratched across my lower lips, I gasped, back arching and my hands threading into his hair, directing his hungry mouth exactly where I needed it.

Caressing his sizeable rough hand over my smooth rump, Mitch gave it a squeeze, which tilted my pelvis automatically. Continuing to traverse forward, Mitch placed the pad of a finger against my heat. He didn't push in, just covered my entrance and applied intermittent pressure. It took seconds until I was squirming, Mitch using his spare hand to pin my hip.

I'd forgotten how strong he was until he held me effortlessly in place. Moaning in my chest caused a slight tickle of pain, mostly discomfort in my throat. It reminded me of that night in Geneva, how he'd left my throat sore. Tears leaked out the side of my eyes; I doubt we'd be doing any deep throat action any time soon.

Raising up, Mitch looked down on me, his eyes filled with concern as they searched mine. "Hey, did I hurt you?" His thumb wiped away my tears as I shook my head. "Is there something I need to know, Lyza?"

Palming his face in my hands, I met his eyes. A tornado of butterflies rushed through my stomach, making me struggle to breathe. "Mmm-ch," I gasped painfully.

"Shh," Mitch soothed, caressing my throat, feeling over the damaged cartilage. "You don't need to say it. I see it every time you look at me." His mouth brushed mine, his arm encircling my waist, and then Mitch lifted as he turned and pulled me further onto the bed with him.

It was only spring, but it felt like the middle of summer in that room: kisses, tender caresses, sucks, nibbles, bites, and hands grasping at flesh. I couldn't stay still in his hold, itchy and needy for his touch.

Groaning, Mitch pinned me down as he settled his weight between my thighs. His tongue dominating my mouth before he pulled away and fed the smooth slick dome of his cock between the velvet folds of my sex. My nails gripped his biceps as Mitch pressed into me. He'd been sure not to penetrate me even with his tongue getting to this point, making sure his being inside me again was breathtaking for both of us.

From that moment, I was lost to our bodies moving together, the feel of Mitch's hard thrusts contradicting the way his lips held mine prisoner with tender kisses. Our bodies were slick with sweat, our chests heaving and gasping for breath between lip locks. It was just us in this room, and the world outside stopped existing. The Arrow didn't hold me, Mitch wasn't the enemy, and I wasn't a trained killer. Together in this room, we were lovers, and nothing outside could touch us.

Mitch's hands were the only binds that existed. His weight grinding me into the mattress was all that could hold me down. In Mitch's arms, I felt the most alive I ever had. Wrapping him in my thighs, I opened to him, bidding him to find the deepest part of me and claim it as his. Lifting my pelvis to meet his slow, torturous grind.

"Fuck, Lyza!" Mitch cursed, breaking for breath. Lifting his upper body, he grabbed hold of the bed head for leverage with one hand, his spare hand grabbing my ass and raising it as he thrust deep and hard.

My eyes opened wide, my breath rushed out, and with it, a long, tortured, and broken moan. I didn't care; my throat could hurt. Knowing I was staying with Mitch, that this was just the start of our lives together, made the pain barely noticeable. My entire being was encapsulated in making love to Mitch.

My body grew tighter with every press of his. My nerves were in sensory overload. Pleasure flooded my core, filling me up, and then it exploded outward, nerves firing, muscles tightening, air rushing from my lungs as I cried out soundlessly in relief.

Grunting, his eyes closing, face grimacing, Mitch put all his strength into finding his happiness within me. His eyes went wide, the bed creaked beneath his grasp, and the beating against the wall lost its rhythm. Mitch roared as he came, the bed echoed his release, and then Mitch fell. I fell. We fell together and landed with a loud thunk.

Eyes wide, Mitch and I looked at each other, and then we needed to take quick action to prevent sliding headfirst into the wall on the sudden incline of the bed. Arms above my head, I met Mitch's eyes, we blinked, and then his lips twitched. Pressing my lips together, I held back from laughing, but Mitch's amusement bounced around the room, the rich base of his voice vibrating his entire body, which just happened to still be in mine.

Gasping, I bit my lip at the fantastic tremors. After gently extracting himself, Mitch rolled to the side and safety, then he helped me up. Once Mitch hauled me to my feet, we both looked down on the collapsed bed and laughed again. Mitch externally, my humor restrained to prevent pain.

Cupping my neck in his hand, Mitch enfolded me in his arms, and his lips kissed me until I was relying on him to keep me from collapsing to the floor myself. "Okay, we need a shower, food, and then I'll look at the damage." Without waiting, Mitch hoisted me over his shoulder and smacked my rear. "I think I need to get sturdier furniture to future-proof this house."

Letting my body go limp, I bit the top of his bum. Mitch yelped, then reciprocated on the side of my cheek. As he placed me gently on the ground, I caught his face and kissed him gently. Grinning like the Cheshire cat in Wonderland, Mitch turned on the shower.

Ticking my thumb on my left index finger, I tapped my finger to my temple and brought it forward, leaving it hooked at the end. Pointing to myself, I crossed my arms, so I touched opposite shoulders, then indicated Mitch. Making rings with both thumbs and index fingers beside each other, I shifted them to swap to the other side. After slicing the jugular of my neck, I pointed to Mitch.

Moving closer to me, Mitch took my face in his hands, so my eyes met his. "I'm glad you decided to love me instead of killing me too." Lips on mine, Mitch pressed his body into me, so I could feel his hardening devotion. Lifting me into his arms, he stepped us into the shower, where we washed away our pasts and focused on our futures.

THE WARDROBE still held my clothes from before I left since I hadn't taken any of them with me to Chapter. Happy I still occupied half the space, I walked out to the hall and grabbed the shirt Mitch had been wearing when I arrived, my fingers nimbly buttoning it up as Mitch came out and found his pants.

His eyes smiled at me when he observed me in his shirt. Walking towards me as he zipped up, Mitch lifted his fist up in front of his chest and slid it to his midline before twisting his wrist to have the underside facing me as he swept it back the other way. *Still the hottest thing I've ever seen you in,* he signed.

Cheeks heating, I grabbed my jeans from the floor and tossed them over the back of the lounge while continuing to the kitchen to make a start on food.

"What's this?" Mitch asked. I turned in time to see him pick up the business card Emily had given me from the floor. "Dr. Ronstandt, an obstetrician specializing in IVF Medicine?" Mitch turned around to face me. "Lyza, are you pregnant?"

Holding both hands out with the middle finger pointing down, I bumped them twice like I was playing the piano.

"Not yet? Then why do you need to see an obstetrician?"

Exhaling, I walked back to the lounge, pulled out the folded report, and handed it to Mitch before starting to make us a light supper. Out of the corner of my eye, I observed Mitch scanning the results of my medical tests. I knew when he got to the highlighted section. His shoulders dropped, and his eyes closed. "You can't have kids."

Lifting my hand up, I waggled it back and forth in a maybe. *"The test indicates I don't produce the right hormones for the egg to bind, and so I would miscarry, likely without realizing it."* After finishing the food prep, I pushed a plate across the bench to him. *"Mother of Hunter has made an appointment for me to see a specialist and see what options I have."*

Mitch tilted his head. "That's why they let you come here because if you can't breed, you're no good to them."

Shaking my head, I closed out that idea with my hand into a duckbill. *"No, they let me return here because they were told the best chance I have is to be happy and to no longer be suffering major injuries."* That's what the doctor prescribed in the report. Right or wrong, his advice brought me home to the man I love.

Gritting his teeth, Mitch reread the report. "Will they expect our kids to work for them?" Meeting his eyes evenly, I knew the glare was a little angry before I looked away. Glancing at the business card again, Mitch tapped it against his finger. "Are kids important to you?"

"They weren't until you told me you wanted four."

"That was before I fell in love with you, Lyza, and the complication of your family." Mitch held up the report. "And speaking of family, this says your father isn't a genetic match. He wasn't your biological father."

Tapping beneath my eye, I then shook my thumb at Mitch. I'd read the report and saw that the monster of my teenage years wasn't even my real father.

"Do you think he knew your mother cheated on him, that you weren't his?"

Considering it, I shook my head. *"He would have raped me himself if he thought for a second that I wasn't his daughter."*

When I went to turn away, Mitch reached out and grabbed my hand before I could. "I'll come with you to see the specialist and hear what they say, but I think we should leave it up to nature. We are both fucked up enough that not breeding won't impact the world gravely. However, if we are blessed to become parents, you need to know, I won't let them take our kids." Mitch's eyes darkened, pupils focused, reinforcing how determined he was in his words.

Nodding my head, I decided to change subjects. *"Do you have a new personal assistant yet?"*

Letting go of my hand, Mitch dropped his shoulders. "You'll meet her Monday at the office. Fred is looking forward to seeing you again. I was going to have Dustin guard you, but since you have Kit, we'll have to bring him in and induct him."

My eyes opened wider, pupils dilating. *"Dustin's alive?"*

Mitch tilted his head. "You only shot him in the leg, Lyza. We were able to get him treatment in time. He took a few months to recover, but he's back at work."

Surprised that he was alive, I blinked. When I'd heard the gunshot, I was sure Scott ended the witness.

Mitch assessed me. "Scott didn't tell you it was Dustin's phone that he sent the messagefrom warning me coming for you was a trap." Pressure building in my tear ducts, I shook my head. "Well, Scott let Dustin live as a gesture of good faith that he was telling me the truth."

Standing up, Mitch pulled me into his arms. "What's done is done. We're starting anew as of now. On Monday, you will come to work with me not only as my wife but employed as one of my trainers."

Frowning up at Mitch, my forehead pinched in confusion. Mitch smoothed his thumb across my brow. "It will give you the cover for the training you will do for the Arrow. It will also better prepare my men for encountering a female who can kick their asses."

My lips lifted, a little bit of ego loving that idea. Mitch grinned broadly. "But, until Monday, we have the weekend to make up for that honeymoon we never had."

"I'd prefer a real honeymoon. I could use a few weeks of massages and you."

Watching my hands, Mitch's eyes lit up. "I'll see what I can arrange, Mrs. Fairchild." His lips nipped my neck. "Ready for round three?"

"Don't we need to fix the bed?"

Taking my hands in his, Mitch grinned. "It can wait. I'll just pull the mattress onto the floor for tonight." With a smirk, he led me to our bedroom and welcomed me home again.

EPILOGUE

Getting out of bed, I pulled on Mitch's jumper and went to sit on the cozy in the corner. Watching him sleep, I tried to map out my day head, but some unknowable's made that impossible. "What's wrong?" Cracking his eye, Mitch assessed me in the chair.

Knocking my fists together, I then tapped my index and middle finger of my right hand over the same fingers' knuckles on my left. *"Grandfather arrives today."*

Now both of Mitch's eyes were open. "You didn't tell me."

Tilting my head, I shook my head as I started signing to remind my wonderful husband of the rules. *"I'm not supposed to tell you. I found out last night, but I needed to think first."*

Sitting up, Mitch patted the bed beside him. Not hesitating, I crawled into his arms and cuddled into his warmth. "Why are you worried? Scott doesn't scare you like your not-father did."

Pointing to no one, I turned my hand to have my fingertips touching above my heart with the thumb up. *"He's a good man."*

Kissing the top of my head, Mitch tightened his hold on me. "You respect him." There was a moment's silence. "Do you love him?"

Hugging my shoulders, I lifted them in question. *"Love? No. It's not that."* Not love, but it was more than loyalty or friendship. From the time Mitch failed to come for me, Scott became the only person who had ever been there for me with no expectations. The night I went to his cabin, my intentions evident, Scott offered me the out and understood what brought me there. He broke protocol for me, and in the months I was at Chamber recovering, whatever it was that brewed between us, blossomed into a companionship I'd never felt with anyone else. Was I worried about how that would feel now that I was with the man I love? Yes.

"But having to go meet with him today worries you?"

"I have to go in clean, Mitch. I have no idea what might be discussed, how sensitive it may be. They have to know that they can trust me to be loyal to them even though they know I love you."

Sighing, Mitch watched my hands, then leaned his cheek on my head. "Scott was the one who told Moses to tell me what happened and where to find you. I think he hoped I'd steal you away before Chamber closed around you. My worry is, with my mother gone, and with it her protection, what happens if they send you after me?"

"Then I kill all of them." Turning in Mitch's arms, I looked up into his eyes. *"You are my husband. I will always choose you first."*

Drawing my mouth to his, Mitch rolled me beneath him, worshipping me for those words.

SLIPPING FROM THE BED, I collected my clothes and dressed. Expecting gnawing guilt, I inhaled sharply when it was only a slight niggle. Maybe that would grow with time. Perhaps the psychological conditioning I'd been raised with prevented the society norms from triggering the right emotions. Whatever the reason, as I scooped the file from the table, my mind and soul were clear.

The studio apartment Scott was staying in was the equivalent of a nice hotel room. It had a bed, bathroom, kitchen, lounge, and a desk. Flipping the file open, I looked over the information again. When I lifted my focus back to the bed, I twinkled my fingers against my mandible. *"When?"*

Sitting on the edge of the bed, Scott stood as he signed. *"She will arrive next week. She needs to go through the usual Chapter handover first, then Moses will bring her to you for training."*

Not ogling how hot he was - well, more than usual - I kept my focus on the new recruit and pointed to the floor with purpose as I shrugged. *"Wouldn't it be better for me to meet my trainee on Chapter soil?"*

"Not this one. She has authority issues and is a bit wild and unwieldy. Hence, why they are sending her to you. You are outside the system. You won't just be training her but also reforming her. You need to teach her loyalty and why compliance is better than death."

Shaking my head, I closed the file and put it on the table to use my hands. *"I can train her to kill without notice, but submission to the Arrow... How am I going to teach anyone that?"*

Pulling up his pants and zipping them, Scott stopped right in front of me and lifted a brow along with his hands. *"You never failed to follow orders, even when you didn't want to be there. You always followed through. Why?"*

Pointing to my chest, I put my hands out as if playing the piano, then flipped them to cup the air before tucking my thumb, ring, and pinkie fingers on both hands, then dropped them down, so the index and middle pointed forward like the refs do when a goal is tried. *"I don't fear death, but I'm not looking for it either."*

Tapping the file, Scott dropped his face to keep the connection. *"This one is just like you. You can show her there is a way to have a life and serve."*

"I only got this life because I nearly died, and there is little chance of getting me pregnant."

Taking a step back, Scott nodded. *"Speaking of which, how did the appointment with the specialist go?"*

Holding my thumb out, I turned my hand as if winding a jack in the box. All the tests suggested little chance of me conceiving without artificial means. Not that I was sure I wanted to have children. Bringing them into this life only to be forced into the Sword and Arrow just didn't appeal.

Sighing, Scott shook his head. *"You showed us a new way to raise kids, and it was far more successful in a shorter time with Maria's kids. Your children will be left for you and your husband to raise how you feel is right."*

Huffing, I resisted laughing as I scrawled my hand across the air as if writing. *"Get it in writing."*

Smirking, Scott collected his shirt. *"We are putting the cart before the horse. How does your husband feel about it?"*

Again, I turned the handle for the Jack-in-the-box. The truth was, Mitch wanted kids, but not yet. I think he worried as soon as I got knocked up, Chamber would take me away again. He wasn't the only one.

"Is he willing to shoot into a cup to get them?"

Lifting a shoulder, I put the file into my bag.

"Give me something positive to assure them you are still playing along."

Meeting Scott's eyes, I looked pointedly at the bed's messed sheets before looking at him again. Bowing his head, Scott nodded. *"Point taken. I'll be back in two weeks. You should be able to report on your first week with her."*

Nodding my head, I turned for the door. Grabbing my wrist, Scott waited until I was facing him to release me to sign. Pointing to me,

Scott created an upturned fist, and keeping his thumb and index tucked, he released his other fingers as if tossing a juggling ball. *"I'd rather you didn't have sex with me just to prove loyalty. I know you. I don't need you to spread your legs out of forced expectations. I care for you. If that's not two-way, I'd prefer we return to how things were before between us."*

Pointing to my chest, I touched the index knuckle of my fist to the side of my mouth and twisted my wrist forward. *"I wouldn't have sex with you if I didn't want to."* Leaving it at that, I stepped out the door. Making my way outside to the car where Johnathan and Kit were waiting, I slid into the back seat.

Coming here, I didn't plan to sleep with Scott. I knew it was a possibility, but if what we'd had at Chamber had fizzled since coming back to Mitch, I would have stepped back when Scott made a move on me. The hesitation when he kissed me told me Scott was just as unsure as I was, but once our lips were touching, there was no denying the bond we'd formed was still there.

Flipping open the file, I read deeper into the history of my first trainee. Orphaned, she was a late external recruit saved from a human trafficking ring. The abuse she suffered came out in her aggression, and she tested for death, but only within the scale of viable. A few more points higher, she would have been given the choice of joining the girls at Eden or put down as a danger to society.

When we got to Mitch's workplace, I went to the office Mitch provided for me and chucked the file on the table before turning to face Kit.

"How does the new girl look?"

Holding my fists forward together as if holding a stick, I broke it up and to the sides, then put my hands back behind my head, fingers splayed, and swept them forward as I swiveled my wrists before tilting one of my hands back and forth in front of me. *"Broken or deranged, it's a fine line."*

"Should be fun." Sitting down, Kit kicked his feet up on my desk. *"Go find Mitch and fuck him. He's not going to hate you."*

Bowing my head, I licked my lips as I signed. *"How can you be sure?"*

"He was raised one of us. Would you hold it against him if the shoes were reversed?" When I shook my head, Kit smiled and nodded towards the door.

Pushing the file towards him, I headed to the door. Snickering behind me, Kit picked up the folder. "Lucky bastard."

Going next door, I knocked, then pushed the door open. Through the glass door, I could see that Mitch was in his office alone, so I wasn't worried about interrupting him. Looking up at me, Mitch locked his computer and slid his chair back to study me. After a minute of me standing there, he inhaled sharply and patted his lap. Once I was comfortable, Mitch took my face in his hands. "We're, okay?"

Nodding, I gave him a smile. Dropping a kiss to my nose, Mitch nodded. "That's all I need to know." His mouth on mine was everything. As he lifted me to set my ass on the table, spreading my thighs for him, I knew there was never a chance anyone could make me stop loving Mitch. We could keep work separate and still be together because of how we were raised. Personal and professional had clear lines. Ours were a little blurrier than most in our fields since Mitch protected people for a living, and I killed them, but I'd defend Mitch with my life if it came to it. Hell, I already had.

As I lowered Mitch's fly, his eyes checked the glass wall and the walkway outside. Frankly, I didn't care if anyone watched us, and going on past experience in the car, Mitch didn't either. If it was that big an issue, Mitch was going to have to get blinds. Smirking, Mitch turned his focus solely on me, his eyes sparkling and happiness radiating out of every pore.

When we were done, Mitch stayed buried inside of me, holding me tight. "Did you get your first trainee?"

I nodded.

"When?"

Moving as if to tap a watch with an index finger, I had my wrist hit where the watch face would sit to indicate next week.

"Anything I should know?"

Nodding again, I pointed to his side, then twisted my fists in front of me like I was wringing a rag before lifting my hand to my mouth as if it held a lollipop and dragged it down.

"That could be problematic here. There are a lot of men."

Sighing, I smiled up at Mitch and waved it away. She would need to learn to deal with it. After all, half the time, her job would require her seducing men enough to lure them away. She signed her life away, knowing fully what it entailed. She chose Scythe over Eden or death. I'm hoping, as long as she wasn't expected to fuck men, she'd be able to cope around them. I guess we would find out soon enough.

The End

JOIN THE BEAUTIFUL AND DEADLY

Join Ebony's Mischief List

Sign up to Ebony's mailing list for the following perks:

- latest news on new releases
- heads up on upcoming promotions
- exclusive freebies like coupons to read Ebony's stories on Radish for free
- first chance at Giveaways
- get a free book

Go to https://ebonyolson.com for more information

RAIN
A DARK PAST ROMANCE

The more put together someone looks, the more they have to hide.

Rain has spent years trying to recover from the trauma of her youth. She's pulled her life together, got herself a career, and has even managed to try a relationship. Stuffing down her fight or flight response into a socially acceptable behavior has been hard work, but she's done it. Still, she feels too broken to ever find true happiness. Until she meets Jet.

The gorgeous brother of Rain's gay best friend, Jet is polar opposites to his brother. When Jet decides to pursue Rain, she's swept off her feet, but it is not a relationship about which either of their families are happy.

It turns out Jet and Rain both have traumas they need to get past.

Can two broken souls make a future together?

RAIN
CUM STAINS

Someone was snoring. Potentially it was me.

"Wake up, Cinderella," the sexy voice from my dreams whispered in my ear. Things tightened downstairs and I smiled.

The snoring kept going even after I became aware of being in bed and having woken up. Frowning, I forced my eyelids open. Nope, that wasn't working. They seemed to be glued together. Lifting my hand, I wiped the sleep from my eyes and finally managed to open them.

The bedside table wasn't mine. It held a glass of water with what I hoped was aspirin diffusing in it. Not one to look a gift horse in the mouth, I pushed up onto my elbows and started drinking. Turning my head, I froze at the body in the bed with me, still snoring. Looking down at my chest, I found my bra still in place but the dress I'd worn to the office Christmas party was absent. Oh, this was going to be awkward if naughty things happened. My eyes glanced at the clock, then I shoved my boss in the shoulder repeatedly until he stopped snoring and jolted awake.

"What?"

"You have to be on that teleconference in two minutes," I grumbled.

"Shit," Aubrey collected his phone from the bedside table and peered back at me obviously struggling to have his eyes open. "How's your head?"

"Holding its own heavy metal concert."

"Mine is in the snake pit. Think you can find me some aspirin?"

"I didn't find this one, it was waiting for me to wake up." Finishing the glass, I put it aside. "We didn't have sex, right?"

Aubrey laughed. "You have to ask?"

"Valid point. So, I'm half naked in your bed because?"

"Hold that thought," Aubrey held up his hand as the call connected.

With a huff, I stood up and looked around for my dress. Unable to find it, I grabbed one of Aubrey's shirts and put it on while I went to hunt for an aspirin. Searching his bathroom, I found more packs of condoms than the chemist stocks, and more variety, but nothing for headaches. My boss was a whore, but the committed kind. He always dated his sexual partners, just very few lasted the quarter mile.

"I'll fly into Auckland on Tuesday."

"Wednesday," I corrected as I passed back through the room, Aubrey's eyes tracking my legs.

"Sorry, Wednesday. I'll be at a conference all day, but I can meet you for dinner Wednesday evening."

Stepping out of the room, I walked towards the stairs. The smell of coffee captured me, so I followed my nose to the kitchen. Pushing through a door, I found two men standing in the kitchen drinking coffee. Both ridiculously handsome, one tall with pitch black hair, short and styled and looking all business in his tailored suit. The other was my height and blond, Chad, my boss's current beau. If he'd been straight, I still wouldn't have drooled because Chad's beauty really didn't penetrate his epidermis. Sadly, as my best friend's boyfriend, I had to be nice.

His eyes spotted me and glanced over my lack of clothes. "Rough night at the Christmas party, Rain?"

"Could have been worse," I shrugged.

"Really? How?" Chad moved forward all tease. "It gets worse than sleeping with your gay boss?"

"Hell, yes. I could have had sex with my gay boss."

The suit nearly spat coffee everywhere. His onyx eyes laughing as he looked me over. He looked familiar, but I couldn't place why.

"Are you sure you didn't?" Chad challenged, a tinge of jealousy showing through.

"If I had something that big inside me last night, I'd be walking rough this morning. I'm good." The suits mouth fell open.

Chad laughed. "You seriously have seen way more of your boss than I have of mine."

"Well, yes, but I'm so past walking in on him having sex in the office now, that I may as well take popcorn and watch the show," I announced as I went to the coffee machine and made myself and Aubrey a coffee. The suit spat coffee everywhere.

Chad blushed handing the suit a hand towel. "Again, I'm terribly sorry about that."

"Saying sorry after the fact doesn't undo you being bent over my drafts table yesterday morning. Aubrey has his own office you know."

"He was showing me the plans for the tactile museum you were working on. We got carried away."

"On said plans. Cum stains is a term for a reason you know." The suit gave up on his coffee at this point, forcing himself to swallow what was in his mouth. "Now, I'm hungover and going to spend the day redrawing the plans you defaced."

Chad sighed putting his cup on the sink. "You were just in bed with my boyfriend. Let's call it even?"

"Not a chance. I didn't leave cum stains all over him." The suit was trying really hard not to laugh.

Chad's mouth fell open. "You are so vulgar, Rain."

"Blow me."

Chad gave up. "I'll go say good morning to my boyfriend."

"Take him some water and an aspirin, will you?"

Chad turned to the other man. "Aspirin?"

Opening a cupboard, the suit popped two aspirin in a glass, filled it with water and handed it to Chad.

"Thanks, Jet."

Turning my back to them as I made coffee, I bit my lip realizing Jet was Aubrey's older brother. His very straight, ridiculously intelligent, workaholic lawyer brother. Not that the entire family wasn't the same, but Jet hadn't gone into the family architecture business. He'd applied and been accepted to study at Oxford in England. When he returned to Australia, he started his own law firm, and he was now one of the most highly sort divorce lawyers in Sydney.

"I don't think we've formally met," the sexy voice that woke me up teased over my ear.

Turning around, I discovered Jet standing right behind me, hand out in greeting. Hesitating only a moment, I took the hand. "Rain Noir, one of your brother's architects."

"Jet Landy, provider of aspirin to the hungover."

Taking my hand back, I picked up my coffee and took a sip. "Thank you for the aspirin. I think your brother needed it more, though."

"I'm sure he did, but you deserved it more." Jet stepped back to the meals table as he checked his watch and started placing a notepad and file into his briefcase. "You made sure he got home safely, even though it put you out."

That was nothing new, so I shrugged. "He was off his face and Benny from accounting was all up in his ass trying for promotion. I was drunk enough that Sleezy Dudley from marketing was trying to cop a handful. If that doesn't tell you to call it a night, you deserve to wake up next to a hairy stranger."

Lifting a sexy eyebrow, Jet turned to look at me. "Speaking from experience?"

"Not yet. My drunken regrets tend not to include hairy strangers. I'm kind of picky. Thankfully, being here meant Aubrey didn't miss the important call he's on."

Picking up his briefcase, Jet looked me over again. "Do you remember much of last night?"

"I remember the work party. The after party at Murphey's gets really blurry about the fifth round of shots your brother ordered, and it is gone completely after I got him in the cab. Did I miss much?"

Jet slipped one hand in his pocket. "Not much. I need to get to work."

"Oh, do you know where my clothes are?" I asked as he turned to leave.

"Shoes and bag are by the front door. Your dress is in the laundry after my brother threw up over the both of you as you helped him in the door."

Getting a flashback of the moment, I cringed. "Crap, sorry. Did we wake everyone?"

"Just me. Luckily, mum and dad are overseas."

"Sorry."

"Don't worry about it. By the time I came downstairs, you had stripped you both off and cleaned the floor."

Remembering Jet coming downstairs in his boxer shorts wondering what the hell was happening, I frowned. I may have drooled on the floor admiring him. "You accused me of taking advantage of your brother."

Jet blushed. "If it's any consolation, I was extremely impressed you managed to seduce him. My brother has been gay since he got his first erection. He was actually ogling you last night. I wanted to film it for blackmail."

"Wouldn't be the first time he's perved on me," I dismissed. Then his words hit me. "Wait, you didn't take video of me half naked right?" I stepped forward concerned.

Jet smiled. "No, Rain. I'm not a perv."

"Right. You do realise you've talked to my boobs this entire time, right?"

Jet's eyes flashed up to mine, dropped, lifted, and lowered. He shrugged one shoulder. "Well, they are quite nice, and I did get to see quite a lot of them last night. I have to go."

"Nice meeting you," I gave a singular wave as he moved through the door. With a sigh, I finished my coffee and went out to the front door to find my bag and shoes. Locating my phone, I called a taxi, then took Aubrey his coffee. Not thinking to knock, I opened the door like I would at the office.

"Crap!" Closing my eyes, I turned around quickly at the compromising position my boss was in with Chad. "Okay, coffee. I'm heading home to change but need some pants for the trip. Do you have a pair of sweatpants I could borrow?"

"Wardrobe," Aubrey laughed.

Placing the coffee down, I crab walked to the wardrobe and borrowed a pair of sweatpants while Aubrey and Chad went back to working his hangover off.

"Don't forget you have a team meeting at nine o'clock to give us the specs for the new job," I called as I left.

By the time the taxi dropped me home five minutes down the road, it was already eight. By the time I showered and dressed and caught the bus to work, it was nine.

"I'm surprised you're standing straight this morning," Barbara, the receptionist groaned.

"Aspirin and coffee," I smiled, saluting her with the super large coffee I picked up at the coffee shop on the corner. Putting mine down on the counter, I lifted a normal sized cup out of the tray I carried and put it on her desk. With a wink, I headed back to my office.

"Lifesaver," Barbara moaned.

Aubrey arrived five minutes later, sticking his head into my office on his way passed. "Morning, Rain." When I handed him his coffee, Aubrey sighed. "God, I love you."

"That's not what you were saying an hour ago."

Settling into the spare seat in my office, Aubrey smirked. "What time is our meeting this morning?"

"Five minutes ago. I called and told them you were delayed. Gave everyone else time to go get coffee. I think we are all a little hung over today."

"More than likely. After the meeting, I'm out for the day?"

"No, you will be in interviews for your new intern until five."

"Who scheduled interviews for the day following the Christmas party?"

"You did."

"Why didn't you talk me out of it?"

"Not my job, you have an assistant for that. Now, we need to get going."

"You're evil," Aubrey called after me. "You could have reminded me. A good friend would have."

"Pay back for puking on me."

"Oh, god. I didn't?"

"There was a reason my dress was missing this morning. I actually think I would have preferred you trying to have sex with me."

"You wish. Get your ass to that meeting." He started following me out.

"Have you got those specs ready?"

"Shit." Aubrey raced next door to his office.

Smiling to myself, I went ahead to the meeting room. The amount of groaning and heads on the table was hilarious and pathetic. It's not like any of them spent the night in the boss's bed with him snoring.

Flashes of last night passed through my head like a faded dream. Jesus, I told Aubrey I wanted to sleep with Jet instead of him. Closing my eyes in humiliation, I dropped my head to the table. I'd said it in front of Jet.

When I groaned, the others reciprocated.

Eight hours later, I was just finishing redrawing the plans for the tactile museum. "I'm heading off, Rain," Barbara called. "You're the last here so I'll lock the door."

"Have a good weekend," I answered and went back to work. I was showing these to the client on Monday, so they needed to be finished.

As I was grabbing my iPad to scan the plans, an expensive black suit stepped into my doorway. My heart raced as I stepped back. When I recognized the face, it didn't put me at ease. "Jet? How did you get in here?"

"Family business. I have a key. I quite often drop by to see Aubrey and Rae." Rae was their father and the owner of the firm.

"Oh," I frowned slightly unsettled and relaxed my stance. "Aubrey isn't here. He was leaving straight from his last meeting to have dinner with Chad."

"I'm not here to see him," Jet smiled slyly, his eyes staying pointedly on my eyes. "It's Friday night. Can I take you to dinner?"

My body charged with adrenaline, but I was practiced at pretending I was fine even when my flight system was activated. Moving back to my drafts table, I scanned the plan. "Thanks for the offer, but I still need to upload these plans before I can leave. Besides, after last night, I think a bath and bed are my only agenda items."

"I'm adding new business in the form of dinner with me," Jet informed me. "Besides, hair of the dog will help. I need a drink and I hate drinking alone."

"Don't you have friends for drinking with?"

"Yes, but they all have families to go home to. I got the impression you're single, like me."

"If you're looking to hook up, try your brother's assistant, that's kind of her thing, not mine."

Jet's lips twitched in humor. "Just dinner and a drink. I have an early morning, so I'm not up to spending hours servicing you."

Something about the comment put me at ease. Folding my arms under my bust, I noticed Jet's eyes going to them while I jutted my hip out. "Huh, well at least you know who it would be on their knees. Okay, dinner it is."

Going back to my desk, I airdropped the plans to the server, adding an item to Barbara's to-do list to have them printed first thing Monday morning.

Grinning, Jet moved to look at the plans. "Are these the plans Chad destroyed?"

"Yes," I grumbled. "They should have gone out for print this morning. Now, it will be a rush on Monday to have them ready for our eleven fifteen with the client."

"Strange, the plans don't do a thing for me."

"Good, I don't have to worry about you trashing them then." Grabbing the roll of parafilm, I pulled it out to cover the plan before laying it over and cutting it off. "Just in case." Winking at Jet, I turned to grab my bag.

"Waterproof I take it?" Jet ran his fingers over the protective layer on the plan.

"Yes. Now, changes are erasable without destroying the original. If the client likes this plan, the second draft onward is created digitally. These get archived and can always be referred back to."

"I've never seen my father do this."

"It's only a recent way to preserve our work."

Nodding as if that made sense, Jet turned his focus to me. "Are you ready?"

❖

ROMANCE SUSPENSE BY EBONY OLSON

Hotel Series

HOLLY CLAIRE TRILOGY

Henderson

Cassidy

Holmes

Holly's Trilogy: Books 1-3 Hotel Series (Compilation)

JESS BUTLER TRILOGY

Best Man

Best Layover (Coming Soon)

Standalones

Black Mark: The Complete Saga

Calypso

Rain: A Dark Past Romance

DARK FANTASY / PARANORMAL ROMANCE / FANTASY BY EBONY OLSON

STANDALONES

Of Shadow and Light

Boundary

Silver Rogue

Halos

HIERARCH SERIES

(Radish Fiction Exclusive)

Succumb

Numinous

Masked

Exodus (Coming 2020/21)

RAVEN'S WING TRILOGY

(Radish Fiction Exclusive)

Phased

ABOUT THE AUTHOR

Ebony lives in Sydney, Australia, with her husband, daughter, and six rescue cats. She loves to read fantasy, thrillers, and paranormal romance, spending most of her free time with her nose in a book or writing.

Having always possessed an over-active imagination Ebony spent her younger years regaling friends with fantastic stories, holding her audience captive with the passion and suspense of her characters plights. In adulthood, she shows no signs of stopping her imagination from spreading across as many pages as it can find.

Website: http://ebonyolson.com/
Ebony's Mischief & Mayhem Peeps

facebook.com/EbonyOlson.Author
twitter.com/Ebony_Olson
instagram.com/ebony_olson
amazon.com/author/ebonyolson
bookbub.com/authors/Ebony_Olson
goodreads.com/Ebony_Olson